# VITA AETERNA
# /
# OUTLIERS

JAY ALLAN STOREY

Non Sequitur Publishing
Vancouver, BC

Jay Allan Storey/Non Sequitur Publishing
190 – 1027 Davie Street
Vancouver, BC V6G 1C9
www.jayallanstorey.com

Publisher's Note: This is a work of fiction. Names, characters, places, and incidents are a product of the author's imagination. Locales and public names are sometimes used for atmospheric purposes. Any resemblance to actual people, living or dead, or to businesses, companies, events, institutions, or locales is completely coincidental.

Book Layout ©2013 BookDesignTemplates.com

- 1 -

Ordering Information:
Quantity sales. Special discounts are available on quantity purchases by corporations, associations, and others. For details, contact the "Special Sales Department" at the address above.

Vita Aeterna/Outliers Jay Allan Storey. -- 1st ed.
ISBN 978-1-7776236-6-1

Vita Aeterna/Outliers

# BOOKS BY JAY ALLAN STOREY

Eldorado (2014)

The Arx (2015)

The Black Heart of the Station (2017)

Vita Aeterna (2018)

Black Heart : Arrival (2020)

Black Heart : Origin (2020)

Vita Aeterna: Outliers (2022)

JAY ALLAN STOREY

# VITA AETERNA

JAY ALLAN STOREY

# VITA AETERNA

..............................................

BOOK ONE OF THE VITA
AETERNA SERIES

# ONE

........................................................

# CAM-SURFING

"Ten seconds, Alex," Richie's voice nearly blew out my eardrum. I put a foot out to stop my board, and turned down the volume on the earpiece.

"Do you have to yell?" I whispered into the mic of the controller on my wrist.

"Fifteen," he said, ignoring me, though his voice sounded a bit more normal this time. He always put on this stupid, serious tone like he was counting down a space launch or something.

I scanned the soot-stained walls and broken windows with one eye, and watched the blinking light in my HUD, the 'Heads Up Display' implanted in my head, with the other. The tiny glow that showed I was in the clear was still green. So far, so good.

The cameras were usually easy to spot. The government wanted them visible so everybody would know there were eyes watching them. But sometimes they'd get sneaky and toss in a hidden one. It could be anything: a part of a light fixture, a fake electrical insulator, even just a tiny hole in the wall.

But the cameras had a footprint, like the circle from a spotlight. There was a hack that showed the footprints like a bunch of intersecting ovals. Whatever was on the display of your HUD sort of floated half-transparent in the space in front of you. The trick was translating what you saw to the 3D space you were in. The footprints covered a lot, but not everything. With practice, you could visualize where they were and avoid them. There was usually big enough gaps between them to squeeze through.

"One minute," Richie said. "You're doin' great. Keep it up."

That's how the game was played. 'Cam-surfing', we called it — seeing how far you could go without being tracked by one of the government's monitoring cameras. A lot of the kids played it. It really pissed the authorities off, which I guess was kind of the point. The hack we used also showed when a camera detected your presence. An indicator in the upper right of the display changed from green to red. It wasn't easy; the cameras were everywhere. You couldn't walk a block without being in range of at least one.

Cam-surfing was lots of fun, and I was really good at it.

We called ourselves the 'Lost Souls'. The name didn't mean anything, we just thought it sounded cool. We weren't really a gang, not like the *Killer Dragons*, or *Death's Heads*. We didn't commit crimes for money like they did, and we weren't into violence like they were. We just liked to take chances, and have fun (which are more or less the same thing).

Usually it was Richie, Jake, Spiro, and me.

4

Most of the time we just played against the clock, seeing how long we could go without being spotted. That's what I was doing now.

"Two minutes," Richie said in my ear.

I coasted on my board through the narrow gap between two camera footprints and around a pile of garbage, standing up straight and pulling in my ass to clear them. Anything moving in the center of an alley or an intersection was toast — the cameras would pick it up right away. The most effective way to stay 'invisible' was to stick close to the walls. But you still had to look out for the wild card cameras. They pointed in weird-ass, random directions, and unless you spotted them they'd screw you every time.

Just to make things more interesting, sometimes we'd find a way to bypass security for a building or an office, sneak in, and steal something. It was never much: a badge, a coaster, or a pen with the company crest — anything that would make a good trophy, that would prove you got inside wherever you were going.

The trophies were usually pretty much worthless, but the status for getting them was huge, and the penalties for getting caught were pretty steep. A friend of ours, Robbie, disappeared during a break-in about a year ago. They said he was sent up to Juvenile Detention, but we never heard from him again.

So why did we do it? The excitement, the danger, the prestige, status, whatever. I guess it was kind of pointless, but hey, when you're sixteen years old in Tintown, the place where I live, and you've got nothing better to do...

Later tonight I was going to do something no kid had ever done before: I was going to break into a building owned by SecureCorp, the

Corp that the government hired to police the city. Since policing and security are SecureCorp's business, getting past their defenses was the ultimate challenge — and the ultimate risk.

"Four minutes," Richie said.

I jumped off my board and tried to look casual as a vehicle, a rare sight for Tintown, crawled up the street and passed me. It wasn't a RoboTaxi — it had a driver. He glanced over at me and sneered, like I was a cockroach waiting to be stepped on. There were no Corp markings, but who else would be driving something like that? Most Corp don't pay much attention to what we do anyway, but there was no point in taking any chances.

My Cam-surfing record, and as far as I know the all-time record, was ten kilometers, more than a hundred blocks, in thirty minutes — half an hour. There was another hack that confused the HUD's GPS locator, so for half an hour, the government didn't have a clue where I was. Half an hour being anonymous, invisible. That was probably longer than anybody in the city, even a Corp exec, ever had out of range of some kind of monitoring system.

Ads on HoloTV were always telling us that being monitored shouldn't matter if we weren't doing anything wrong. But it *did* matter. It was an incredible rush to know that for some interval nobody, not the government, not SecureCorp, not my dad — not even Richie — could say for sure where Alex Barret was. For a short stretch of time I had something rare and priceless: privacy.

I'd gone around seventy blocks in just over twenty minutes when it happened. It almost always went that way — a hidden camera that

I didn't spot until it was too late. A light on my HUD started flashing red.

"Shit!" I said.

"Busted!" Richie laughed into my earpiece.

I boarded back to the 'Center', the place we usually hooked up, in an abandoned warehouse on the outermost edge of Tintown. Richie and Jake were already there. I pushed aside the loose plank that blocks our secret entrance and squeezed through. As always, the place smelled like mold and rotting cardboard.

"Not bad," Richie said, standing near a beaten-up old couch in one corner and tapping the HUD controller on his wrist. He was a foot taller than me, and built like a wrestler. You'd never guess that he knew more about hacking the system than almost any other kid in the city. "Not your best," he said, "but still better than anybody else I know."

A cloud of dust poofed up from the couch as I flopped down beside him.

"Practice makes perfect," I said.

Jake lounged nearby, in an armchair with all the stuffing coming out. "It helps that you can squeeze through every rat-hole in Tintown," he laughed, with another dig about what a runt I was.

"Screw you," I said.

"You still feel up to going for the big one tonight?" Richie asked.

I shrugged. "You only live once, right?"

"You are one crazy dude," Jake said, shaking his head as he pushed himself to his feet and grabbed the board leaning against the chair arm. He stepped toward the exit opening. "Back here at nine?"

7

For a run as dangerous as the one I was planning, we had to wait. City security slackened off after nine PM.

Richie and I both nodded.

Jake smiled at me. "It's nuts, but hey, if you get away with it, you'll be a legend."

# T W O

..............................................

# AT HOME

I boarded home to our apartment, on the fifth floor of one of the thousands of dumpy, disintegrating high-rises that were standard issue for Tintown. The building loomed over my head as I climbed the outside steps. Twisted, dripping pipes dangled at intervals from walls stained with alternating splotches of bleached white and mildew black, like some giant had been wiping his feet on them for a few thousand years.

You could tell which places were occupied. The mostly broken windows were blocked off with makeshift security bars made from chunks of scrap metal, or had drying laundry flapping from them, and spiderwebs of wires spun out, gathering into bundles at the nearest standing power pole.

When I walked into the living room Dad was leaning forward in his chair watching HoloTV, like always — another stupid Safety Show. At least the electricity, off when I left in the morning, had come back on. Somebody must have climbed up again and re-jigged the rats-nest of cables that siphoned off power from the electrical grid in the Corp

Ring. There were brown-outs five or six times a day in Tintown, and complete black-outs at least once a day.

A lot of the old city was empty, which is why we were able to find our own apartment. It was tiny, and kind of a dump, but it had electricity (when it was working) and running water. The kitchen stove didn't work, but Dad managed to snag a working microwave, along with some furniture, in his job picking up garbage. Like everybody else, we paid tribute, usually some kind of barter, to a local tough who kept the bad guys away.

Dad's chair was only a meter away from the HoloTV pedestal. He didn't see so good, and he couldn't afford glasses. He didn't look up. On the pedestal display, some guy dressed in a clown suit bent down, grabbed a big heavy box with both hands, tried to stand up with it, and clutched his back in pain. A serious-sounding narrator warned: 'Remember — always lift with your legs'.

The HoloTV was blaring, as usual. Dad also needed a hearing enhancer for his HUD, but we couldn't afford that either.

"Dad," I yelled out to him. "I'm home."

He heard me, but didn't turn around. I went to the kitchen, grabbed a couple of government-issue FoodCorp packets from the cupboard, and tossed them in the microwave. Each packet was a thin plastic tray with an opaque film on top labeled 'Food' — we figured that was because it was never clear what the ingredients were. You didn't know what you were getting until you heated one up and opened it.

It didn't matter anyway. They almost always looked exactly the same — a dark brown mash. Nobody in Tintown could afford a pet, but my girlfriend Cindy was rich, and she had a cat. She showed me once what she fed it, and the stuff looked exactly like what we eat most of the time.

Once they were heated, I carried both packets to the living room, set one beside my dad, sat down on the couch, and opened my own. Yep, no surprises there. I attacked it anyway. Cam-surfing always made me hungry.

"Your dinner's there," I said to him.

He nodded and continued staring at the TV. That was his response to everything.

I guess I couldn't blame him. He'd gotten a raw deal on his Appraisal. His body was shriveled and bent, his skin mottled and wrinkled, and his wispy white hair almost gone from his head. He looked ancient, but in fact he was only forty-five years old. He'd 'negged out'. That is, the result of his Appraisal had been negative, less than one.

The way it was told to me at the co-op school, every species on earth's got an expiration date, like the food packet on my lap. Their metabolisms all run at different speeds, which means that some have a long lifespan, some not. The lifespan of a typical human is around eighty years. The lifespan of a dog is less than fifteen. I hear the lifespan of some trees can be more than one thousand.

About sixty years ago, long before I was born, scientists came up with this process, *Appraisal*, that 'resets' the metabolism of the person it's applied to. Appraisal can slow the aging process, so the affected person will live up to X number of years for every year of an 'average' human.

In Appraisal jargon, X is called the Life Extension Factor, or LEF. The LEF is a fraction, usually between one and two, based on an average age of 80. If you've got a LEF of 1.1, your life expectancy is 80 X 1.1 = 88 years. A LEF of 1.5 (I wish) would give you a life expectancy of 80 X 1.5 = 120.

But this is the bizarre part: people don't just live longer; their entire metabolism is affected. So, just like a fifteen-year-old human is way younger in real terms than a fifteen-year-old dog, a seventy-year-old with a high LEF is like a thirty-year-old with a low one. That's why on HoloTV you can watch seventy-year-olds playing squash, competing in Ironman races (and winning), and all kinds of other stuff that used to only be done by the young.

But, like most of the scientists' brilliant discoveries, Appraisal comes with some serious hitches. The effect is different for everyone it's applied to. Person A could have their lifespan doubled while Person B has almost no change. Even worse, in rare cases, like my dad, one in one hundred thousand they say, the LEF is less than one.

Not only did Appraisal not lengthen my dad's life, it actually shortened it. His LEF was 0.6, which gave him a life expectancy of 80 X 0.6 = 48. We call this 'negging out'.

Over the years I've heard of people with LEFs over two. They say that only happens for about one in a hundred thousand, like negging out. The highest I've ever heard of is two point five, but that might be bullshit.

And the killer is, Appraisal can only be done once. Doing it a second, third, or whatever time has no effect. The result is irreversible, and there's no way to predict what it will be. They say it's not dependent on genetics or any other known biological factor. No matter who you are or how much money you have, once it's done, Appraisal can't be undone; you've just got to live with the result. Even so, almost nobody ever refuses it.

Seems like the Barret family is cursed. My mother's Appraisal was negative too, though just barely. It didn't matter anyway, because she died of cancer eight years ago. You could have a LEF of two and still die early, from disease or an accident. I guess it's always been tragic when somebody dies before their time, but I think it's worse now, 'cause in most cases your 'time' can be so much longer.

Dad's depression about his Appraisal, and then my mom's death, turned him into some kind of zombie. I don't think he'd even bother feeding himself if I wasn't around. What made it so sad was that if he'd just chosen not to have the Appraisal in the first place, which he could have done, he probably would have lived to be something like eighty. But, like I said, there was no way to know ahead of time.

Travis, my teacher at the co-op school, says Appraisal has had a major impact on society. Knowing they're going to live longer, people are a lot more in tune with taking care of themselves. Nobody wants to get some chronic injury they're going to have to live with for the next hundred and twenty years.

I guess that's why the Safety Shows are so popular. People can't seem to get enough of hearing how to properly lift heavy objects, climb stairs, step off curbs, etc. Sound boring? You bet it is, but they're the most watched shows on HoloTV.

Even Dad watches them, which is a joke; there's no point unless you're going to live to a hundred or something. What does he care if he throws out his shoulder lifting a box the wrong way? He'll be gone in a couple of years. It's just something to do, I guess. He's got nothing else.

I made a vow a long time ago - that no matter what happened with my Appraisal, I would never wind up like him.

# THREE

........................................................

# TINTOWN

Tintown is a 'Quarter' — an area of about five hundred square blocks. It's one of thousands of tiny self-governing knots of humanity that make up *The Quarters* — part of a huge urban center. They say it used to be a great city, but now most of it's falling apart, and a lot of it's abandoned.

A long time ago, the ones who made it big in the world, the ones we call the Elite, moved to a gated community south of the city called the *First Circle*. I went to the edge of it once with Cindy. There's actually a massive wall around it to keep the riff-raff (like me) out.

Living in a sort of giant ring around the First Circle are the factories, offices, managers, and workers of the *Corps*, the giant corporations that produce all the goods and services the world needs. There's no wall around the *Corp Ring*, and nothing to stop us from going there, but if we hang around too long they find a way to get rid of us.

According to Travis, there used to be thousands of businesses, pumping out a huge variety of stuff, and almost everybody could afford at least some of it.

Now, there's only six, so besides SecureCorp there's five others.

**FoodCorp**, as I mentioned, handles all food production and processing, including the food packets we eat. **BuildCorp** designs and builds all large building projects. **InfoCorp** is responsible for all the stuff broadcast over our HUDs and on HoloTV, and for training and education. **TechCorp** designs, builds, and maintains all the high technology stuff.

And last, but definitely not least, **MediCorp** takes care of everything to do with medicine and health. Cindy says they're really good. Here in the Quarters our medical plan is we hope we don't get sick.

TechCorp and MediCorp are responsible for installing the HUDs. Everybody in the city, and the world, for all I know, has one. They're attached to your optic nerve and powered by your body heat. The HUD allows you to access the network from anywhere, automatically. My HUD is as much a part of me as my ears and eyes.

Scattered around the Corp Ring like fleas on a dog, there's the rest of us. We live where we can. Here in the Quarters, there's no services to look after us (who would pay for them?), so if we don't do something ourselves, it doesn't get done. A few lucky people have landed jobs in the Corp Ring, doing stuff the Corp workers don't want to do, and that can't be done by robots — things like sweeping floors, cleaning toilets, and working in the sewers. If it wasn't for the money those guys bring in, we'd probably all starve to death.

We can handle the crime, power outages, and garbage. What everybody lives in fear of is getting sick. If you get sick in the Quarters, you better hope your immune system will save you, 'cause nobody else will. And when you die, your body might lie around in the gutter for weeks until somebody gets tired of looking at it and dumps it somewhere.

Everything we've heard on our HUDs or on HoloTV points to over-regulation and government waste as the root of all the misery and poverty we deal with every day. But there *is* a sliver of hope - an organization called the CCE, the Council of Chief Executives, made up of the CEOs from all six Corps. They're kind of folk heroes for most of us. The CCE are constantly recommending ways to reduce red-tape and eliminate regulations, based on their years of experience efficiently running the Corps. That would free us to pursue our dreams and maybe someday even join the Elite, but the government never listens.

Charles Wickham, the CEO of SecureCorp, and one of the most famous people in the world, is the head of the CCE. If the CCE are folk heroes, then Wickham is their Robin Hood. He's the public face of the organization, and his picture is everywhere.

An election is coming up in a few months. The polls say the Freedom Party is more hated than any in living memory. All kinds of negative stuff has been coming out about them for the past year or so: party officials caught redirecting government money to themselves, accepting bribes, eliminating opposition.

It's not the backstabbing and dishonesty that's the problem — after all, like they're always pointing out in the media, if you can make money doing something, there's no rules — by definition. What infuriates people is that the Freedom Party were stupid enough to get caught.

The public are itching to vote so they can throw out President Foster and the Freedom Party and give the Enterprise Party a chance to clean things up. The Enterprisers also hint that they'll give more power to the CCE, something everybody wants, but that never seems to happen.

Let's face it — the CCE are the only ones you can believe, since they're not actually part of the government. They've worked their asses off trying to do something about government waste and inefficiency, but they've been blocked at every turn.

There's even a movement to ditch the government altogether and let the CCE run everything, with Wickham as leader, but whenever anybody mentions the idea, the CCE themselves shoot it down. They say it's important to preserve democracy and let whatever government we've elected rule. I've always respected that about them.

Anyway, for now, the city is a dangerous place. In the Lost Souls, we pretty much stick to The Quarters in general, and Tintown in particular. The other Quarters don't like strangers hanging around (neither do we). Once in a while we venture into the Corp Ring looking for trophies, but that's always dangerous. If SecureCorp grab you, you never know what they'll do.

The Quarters may be bad, but there's an even larger and more lawless ring outside all the others. Everybody calls it 'The Dregs'. It's almost completely abandoned; the only people that hang out there are the homeless and criminal gangs. When we were kids, our parents used to tell us scary stories about it to keep us out. The stories worked, and still do.

In all our dodgy adventures, we've never dared to go there.

I always found it depressing at home, so I usually got whatever I needed and got out of there as fast as possible. Tonight, I had an hour or so to kill so I hung around in my room. The muffled blare of the HoloTV filtered through the closed door.

I flopped down on my bed, laid back, shut my eyes and tried to relax, preparing for the run later, even though there really wasn't any way to prepare. You just did it and hoped you didn't get caught.

Always in the back of my mind was my own Appraisal, which was coming up fast. After what happened to both my parents it was tempting to refuse it, but I knew that wouldn't happen. I shoved all thoughts of it out of my mind, and finally fell asleep.

When I woke up it was almost time to leave. I got my stuff together and headed out. My dad was still sitting watching HoloTV. This time it was a government newsreel. Hap Happerston, the announcer that usually handles 'feel-good' stories, was gushing about some guy from the Quarters, Burt Harper, who'd made it big.

"Burt's Appraisal was nothing special," Hap beamed. "It was what he did with his life that counted."

Hap went on to explain how Burt, once an enforcer with the Death's Heads gang, had graduated to the bottom ranks at BuildCorp, risen quickly by systematically eliminating his rivals, and was now living the good life. A 3D image of a huge yacht appeared on the pedestal, with this bozo standing on the deck, grinning ear-to-ear, a bikini-clad babe under each arm.

Burt's rivals had never been heard from again. "We have no idea what happened to the poor guys," Hap said, laughing. "But wherever they are, nobody can pin it on Burt." Hap winked at the camera. "Hey, it's just business — nothing personal."

"I'm going out," I said to my dad.

He didn't acknowledge me, just stared at the TV. I headed off on my board to the Center to meet Richie and the others. On the way, I got a call on my HUD. It was Cindy.

*See you later tonight?* she texted.

*You sure you want to come?* I answered her. *It'll be boring for you.*

I didn't really want her there. I knew she'd be pissed at what I was planning to do.

*Don't you want me around?* she texted back. I smiled, imagining a cute pout sweeping across her face.

*Sure I do,* I answered, resigned. *I'll see you there. Ten o'clock.*

By that time, it would all be over.

# FOUR

........................................

# BREAKING IN

The others, Richie, Spiro, and Jake, were already at the Center by the time I got there.

"I was starting to think you were gonna jam out," Richie laughed as I squeezed through the opening.

I just sneered at him.

"You guys ready?" I said.

I scanned through the hacks listed in my HUD, double-checking that they were all there and ready to go.

Richie double-checked his own list. Finally, he smiled. "Okay — beat it."

I headed back out. "Good luck," he called after me.

Not wanting to take any chances, I boarded to within about ten blocks of the target, then strapped the board to my back and Cam-surfed on foot. On the way I passed one of the thousands of anti-crime posters that dotted Tintown. Superimposed on a backdrop of the city, the face of SecureCorp CEO Charles Wickham stared down at me, pointing his finger, as if to warn me off what I was about to do.

Twenty minutes later the target came into sight. I felt good. The intel from the web was that it was one of SecureCorp's less important locations. Looking at it seemed to confirm that. It was a crumbling brick building at the outer edge of the Corp Ring. Walking by, you'd never guess who it belonged to. We figured that, seeing as it wasn't an ultra-modern monolith like most Corp buildings, security wouldn't be as tight. At least that was the theory.

A crypted message had come in a few days ago about a flaw in the SecureCorp monitoring system. Richie and Spiro had rigged up a hack to utilize it. I volunteered to test it out. You never knew for sure whether these messages were some loser pretending they were clever, or maybe even deliberately trying to mess with the Cam-surfers. Some of the kids even claimed that SecureCorp themselves put some of the hacks out to catch us.

But this one came from a trusted source (if there was such a thing). Anyway, you only live once, right?

"I'm going for it," I whispered into my controller.

All I heard at the other end was an intake of breath. I flipped off the messaging functions in my HUD. There couldn't be any more communication until I said so. We all knew that if I got nailed I'd be on my own. I wouldn't expect, or even want, the others to help me.

The target door was in sight. It was some kind of delivery entrance, but it still had cameras focused on it, and a surveillance drone passed by every fifteen minutes. The hack the guys had come up with was awesome. Richie had set up my HUD's ID cast so it would

simultaneously freeze the outside camera images for ten minutes —
any longer and the video motion monitors would register a warning —
and crack the electronic lock on the door. They claimed that all this
would be undetectable by SecureCorp. Well, we'd see.

We'd cased the place enough times to work out the schedule of
the drone. All I had to do was wait until it had just passed, to give me
enough time to get inside, grab whatever I could, and get out again
before it returned. Piece of cake — in theory.

My HUD said nine-twenty-eight PM. The next drone run should be
at nine-thirty exactly. I positioned myself at a corner, in a camera gap
with a view of the door, and waited. The drones could detect the bat
of an eyelash for a radius of ten meters, so I had to stay perfectly still.
Part of my head was exposed as I peeked around the corner, but the
drones weren't as good at detecting and identifying shapes at a distance if the target wasn't moving.

Exactly two minutes later I heard the faint hum of the drone. My
spine stiffened as it shot around the corner of the SecureCorp building.
Its non-reflective black exoskeleton was almost invisible at night, but
we had another hack that edge-detected the outlines and enhanced
the image. It was still just a blur, but it was a blur you could follow, a
bright mesh of stitching against the night, outlining its insect-like
frame.

It stopped for a few seconds, scanning. I was sure I hadn't moved.
I fought against my fear and willed my body to stop shaking. The drone
headed toward the door. If it saw me, there'd be nothing to indicate
it. I'd find out when the SecureCorp soldiers surrounded me with their
guns drawn. All I could do was stand still and pray I was in the clear.

The drone hovered for a while, then took off. I waited for one minute after its last echoes had faded away. Then I exhaled, stepped out from around the corner, and took one last look. It was gone.

I studied the door. Assuming the hack worked, I could get inside without getting caught. Problem was, nobody knew what was on the other side. This was a SecureCorp building — anybody who'd seen the inside was either part of that organization or probably wasn't coming out again. That's why all I was planning to do was sneak in a little way, see if there was something I could grab, and run for my life. If I made it in and back out again I'd be a legend. If not, I'd be toast.

I scanned the connecting alleys in every direction, the blood thumping in my ears. There was nobody around. I held up the controller on my right wrist and made one last scan of the door, with detection on. The glow of a spotlight circled it like a halo. The cameras were there — two of them. I wouldn't know whether the hack worked until I was almost in front of them.

I lifted the bandanna tied around my neck to cover the bottom part of my face. If a camera caught me I'd be harder to identify. I swallowed hard and snuck toward the door. My HUD showed the proximity. With one more step I'd be in range. I was almost at the point of no return. I either had to activate the hack and pray that it worked, or walk away.

I pressed the button on my controller to turn on the hack. There was nothing, no alarm, no indication that anything had changed. After a couple of seconds, my HUD said the cameras were frozen. I was breathing hard as I rushed up to the door and tried the handle. The latch clicked open.

I had to hurry - the hack would expire in less than ten minutes. I pulled the door open. I was facing a long, dimly-lit hallway. Glowing arcs from the overhead lights bloomed on the yellowing walls. High on the right-hand wall about halfway down was another camera, but I was sure I could squeeze past it. I slid inside and closed the door behind me, my heart hammering against my ribcage.

The door thunking shut jolted me back to reality. *What the hell was I doing?* But I was in. I edged along the closest wall, out of range of the camera. The motion detectors that dotted the hallway appeared on the HUD as yellow dots. The hack was supposed to disable them as well. There were no boots pounding toward me and no screaming sirens, so it must have worked.

There was a door a few meters along the wall I had my back against. Light streamed out through a small window at head height. I made for it, holding my breath. When I got there, I put my ear against it. Silence. My body shook as I stood on tip-toes and peeked through the window. I was staring down another hallway, about twenty meters long, with another door halfway along it, on the right. That door was open, and light spilled out from it to the hallway floor. Beyond it, the hallway continued for a few meters then took a right. My HUD didn't show any alarm on the door in front of me, and it was out of range of the nearest camera.

I hesitated for a few seconds, then took a deep breath, turned the handle, and opened it. Nothing. I breathed out as I stepped inside, gently eased it shut and rushed down the hall.

I was so stressed out that at first I didn't notice the humming sound in the outer hallway behind me. When it finally registered, it was unmistakable — a drone, headed in my direction. It was almost at the door I'd just come through. I raced to the door ahead of me, and ducked inside just as I heard the first door click open.

I moved away from the opening, pressed my back against the inner wall, and held my breath. I glanced around. The room was large and antiseptic white. Workbenches with what looked like high-tech medical instruments ran along the walls, and above them were mounted glass-doored cupboards full of equipment.

There was a single examination table in the center. I looked closer and froze. There was a guy strapped to it. He looked impossibly ancient: wispy white hair and beard, and pale, mottled skin hanging from him like cords. At first I thought he was dead. Then he lifted his head. My heart just about stopped.

The drone hummed along the hallway outside. It paused at the open door beside me and hovered for a few seconds, while I stood just out of sight, shaking. Finally, it continued down the hall without coming inside. The old man was staring at me. In a few seconds, the drone hummed by going the other way. I heard the outer door open and close again, and the hum faded into the distance.

I was about to take off, then I remembered why I was here. With one eye on the old guy, I checked the bench beside the closest wall. Nothing. Finally, I noticed a card storage case in one corner. It had a keypad on top — protected by an electronic combination. I grabbed the top and pulled on it — it was locked. There's no way I was going to carry the whole thing around when I left, and anyway it was anchored somehow to the bench.

I glanced back. The old man's lips started moving.

"Help me," he whispered, in a voice like dried leaves.

I couldn't just abandon him. I approached the examination table. There was a strap across his chest, and another one across his ankles. Both straps were buckled down at the bottom of the table where the guy couldn't reach. I checked the reading on my HUD — less than seven minutes. In a panic, I undid the straps.

"Can you walk?" I whispered.

He tried to slide his feet toward the edge of the table, but they barely moved. He closed his eyes and his fists clenched.

"They drugged me," he said. "It's no use."

I felt like a jerk, but there was nothing I could do for him. I'd be lucky if I got out of there myself.

He lifted a shaking right arm and pointed. I followed his hand. He was pointing at a poster taped to the wall beside the card case. It showed a golden sun rising over a range of mountains. Below it was a caption: Celebrate Our World: 11-10-64.

"That's what you want," he said.

I glanced back at him. He was still pointing. Suddenly it hit me. I rushed to the card box and entered the numbers from the poster on the keypad of the storage case. A tiny light on the top turned green. I checked on the old man. He'd dropped his arm. I grabbed the lid of the unit and it opened.

Inside were a set of cards. Most of them didn't look that interesting. I didn't have much time. I grabbed one at the back that had the SecureCorp gold-shield logo in one corner. In the other corner was a line drawing of a butterfly. I scanned it with the HUD controller. No locator, or at least the locator wasn't enabled, so it would be safe to take it.

I stuffed the card in my pocket, and turned back to face the old man.

"It's alright," he said, with the saddest of smiles. "Save yourself. Get out while you can. They'll be back in a few minutes."

I took off. When I got to the hallway door I peeked through the little window. The main corridor was empty — there was no sign of the drone.

I checked the time and drew in a breath. I'd been inside for eight minutes. The hack was about to expire. If I didn't make it through the exit and out of camera range in two minutes I was dead.

I slunk along the hallway as fast as I could. I reached the door, and opened it a crack. A SecureCorp cycle was crawling by. The rider didn't look my way — just routine. I closed the door and waited. I checked the time — twenty seconds.

They ticked by: fifteen, ten. I opened the door again. The cycle was just disappearing around a corner. Seven seconds. I opened the door and slipped outside.

Three seconds. I took off like a bullet.

# FIVE

.................................................

# THE PRIZE

Back at the Center, my hands were still shaking as I pulled the 'trophy' card out of my pocket and stared at it. Richie leaned over my shoulder to see. It was kind of disappointing. Plain white on one side, with the SecureCorp logo and the butterfly drawing. The other side had two columns of numbers in the center. It wasn't that impressive. It didn't even really prove I'd been in the building.

"What do think the numbers are?" Richie asked, obviously not that impressed.

I shrugged, and shoved the card back in my pocket. "I'm not going back to find out, I can tell you that much."

While I'd been on my way back, Spiro and Jake had made a run to steal some beer. They picked up my girlfriend Cindy on the way. It was too dangerous for her to go anywhere near our side of town by herself.

I told them not to tell her what I was doing, so I was pissed when they showed up and she knew all about it.

"She asked why you weren't there to pick her up," Jake whispered to me. "I had to say something."

I explained to her what I'd done. It sounded stupid even as I said it. I showed her the card.

"So that's what you risked your life for?" she asked, nodding at the card. "Collecting souvenirs is one thing, but breaking into SecureCorp? Are you crazy?"

"Hey, I made it out," I answered, puffing out my chest. "Nobody's ever gotten inside a—"

"You're going to get yourself killed," she snapped, shaking her head. "For a stupid card. And it doesn't even do anything."

"It might," I said defensively.

"Nothing that would do *you* any good."

I stepped forward to hug her. She pushed me away. "If you're going to keep doing stuff like that, I don't want to see you anymore."

She moved away to a corner with her back to us.

I went over and put my arm around her shoulder. This time she didn't resist. "Hey, we're just fooling around," I said. "I promise I won't go near SecureCorp anymore. That scared the shit out of me anyway."

"I don't want to lose you," she turned and whispered into my ear.

"You won't," I whispered back. "Forgive me?"

Finally she smiled, and kissed me.

I took her hand and we joined the others. We proceeded to celebrate my run. We sat on the torn-up couches and armchairs, our beers in our hands. Cindy sat beside me. I showed Jake and Spiro my trophy. They said it was great, though I got the feeling they were underwhelmed. Their eyes were wide as I described breaking in, finding the card box in the examination room, and escaping. I didn't tell them about the old guy. It was so creepy, and I was still trying to figure out what was going on. I felt guilty about leaving him there, but what else could I do?

Anyway, I'd done something no other kid had ever dared to do — broken into a SecureCorp building. The mood was ecstatic, but something overshadowed all our laughter and back-slapping. It was like we all wanted to say something, but we were all afraid. We'd talked about it so many times before, but back then it had lurked in the distant future - it was something we could kick down the road and worry about later.

Now it *was* later. We were all about the same age, so we'd all be having our Appraisals sometime this year.

Richie brought it up first. It pissed me off. I didn't really want to talk about it.

"I'm not worried," he said. "Everybody in my family's done okay. I'll be in the high teens."

"It's got nothing to do with heredity," Spiro said. "They proved that a long time ago."

Richie sneered at him. "They're full of it. I'll do okay."

"I'll outlive all of you losers," Jake laughed, a bit nervously I thought. "You wait — I'll be a two."

"Good luck," Richie said shoving Jake's shoulder. "You'll be one of those white-haired forty-year-old guys sleeping in their chairs with the HoloTV on and..."

He blushed and glanced over at me. Nobody else spoke. "S...Sorry Alex," he finally said.

I just shrugged and looked at the ground.

"What about Spaz, here," Jake said. He nodded his head toward Spiro. "Bet he negs out big time."

Spiro's face turned red and he clenched his fists.

"You shut up!" he yelled at Jake. He stood up, ready for a fight.

"Settle down," Jake said. "I'm just joking."

Spiro stood shaking for a few seconds. "And don't call me Spaz," he mumbled as he finally sat back down.

"What about you, Cindy?" Richie said. "Your daddy's rich. He should be able to buy you a good one."

"I don't want to talk about it," she said. She looked scared. I took her hand.

"Screw you, Richie," I said. "Leave her alone. Anyway, you know it doesn't work like that."

"That's what they say," Jake said, "but who really knows."

"Shit, you guys are touchy," Richie said.

He looked at me. "Anyway, Alex, what about you?"

I was annoyed with the direction the conversation was going. "How the hell do I know?" I said. "Whatever happens, happens. Let's just shut up about it."

I'd just turned sixteen. I was the oldest, so I'd be going first.

My Appraisal was just one week away.

# SIX

......................................

# THE QUARTERS

Tintown is managed by sort of an ad-hoc council. If you're lucky, they'll pick you to do odd jobs around the Quarter, sometimes for money, but usually for barter, like food, or medicine.

A few years ago, they hired my dad to help pick up the garbage that the rats and stray dogs didn't get to. He gets enough barter to keep us going, but he constantly has to fight to keep his job. Like I said before, it's survival of the fittest — the way they're always telling us — the way it should be. But Dad's not as healthy as he used to be. He's slowing down.

The luckiest guys are the ones who work security. They take care of anybody that gets out of line, and defend our Quarter against attacks from outside. The job's dangerous, but you get lots of barter, and lots of respect. But jobs like that are hard to come by. They probably wouldn't want a runt like me, and even if I was lucky enough to snag one I would have had to fight like hell to keep it.

Since the Corps are all private and for profit, none of them lift a finger without getting paid, and the amount they do is directly proportional to how much they get. For instance, BuildCorp is responsible for collecting garbage. How much they collect, and how often, depends on how much they get paid. If they're not paid anything, they don't do anything. If the garbage piles up and rats and disease are everywhere, too bad.

Like all good private enterprises, the Corps would all like to swallow each other. Travis says they've reached a standoff — they jockey for position and dominance, but mostly they put up with the status quo.

In the Quarters there's always a few small backroom setups: corner stores, repair shops. But if they grow to any size the Corps either absorb them or drive them out of business. Then there's the black market, which the Corps are constantly trying to shut down. With all the stuff on HoloTV about free enterprise and competition, you'd think they'd approve. I guess when it doesn't bring in money for them, suddenly it's evil. But for us, buying from the Corps is just too expensive. For us, the underground market is all there is.

Life in the Quarters can be tough, but they say it used to be a lot worse. The newscasts talk about how in the past, every time you made a dollar you had to pay part of it to the government. They called it 'taxes'. Nowadays we're free from all that. Whatever we make, we keep — period.

Travis says that's a joke — that if what you make is pretty much zero, which it is for us, not having to pay any of it back isn't a big advantage. According to him, a lot of the stuff the Corps do now used to be done by the government and paid for by taxes. And since everybody paid a share, and they didn't have to make a profit, it ended up costing less.

Sounds like a stupid idea. Why pay for stuff that you might not even want or need? Nowadays, if we want something, we pay for it - if we can. If we don't want it, we don't. We're free — free to follow our dreams. We don't have to depend on anybody else's help. Anybody — even people like us from the Quarters, can make it big and join one of the Corps — even the Elite.

After my mother died, my dad never seemed to take much interest in what I did. He never asked me where I was going, who my friends were, even whether I was happy. Mind you, it wasn't just me — as far as I could tell, my dad didn't give a shit about anything or anybody.

That's why it was so weird — about school. I had to go. He was fanatical about it. He couldn't actually force me — he'd be out of breath just walking across the room. But he'd make my life miserable if I didn't go, hounding me and getting on my back. Since he cut down on his work schedule, that was pretty much the only reason he ever took time off from watching HoloTV. I kept offering to take over the garbage work for him, but he'd get mad and tell me to concentrate on finishing school. In the end, it was easier to go than listen to him. Anyway, as pathetic as my dad was, I still felt like I owed him something.

Of course, like everything, regular school cost. There was only one proper one in the Quarters, but even when Dad was working full time it would have been too expensive. When he got old and sick, there was no way.

Our only choice was the co-op school. It wasn't really even a school — just a couple of people from the neighbourhood who volunteered to teach the local kids. I didn't really mind going. I actually might have liked what they call higher education (that is, anything above about grade eight), if there was such a thing in the Quarters, and if we could afford it.

Travis was just the teacher that showed up most of the time. He was what you'd call eccentric, but I always got along with him. He seemed to take a special interest in me. He said I was one of the few of his students that had an 'inquisitive mind'. Teaching people as igno-rant as we were, you could say pretty much anything and they wouldn't know any better, but I'd been able to confirm enough of Travis' claims to at least think about what he said.

After all the time we'd spent together, I still didn't know his last name, or what he did when he wasn't teaching. He just showed up at the allotted time, like the rest of us (when I say 'the rest', I mean the three or four that could be bothered). I asked him once where he got all his education, but he wouldn't tell me. One of the other kids said he had a daughter about my age, but I'd never met her. Apparently, she went to the regular school — who knows how he could afford that.

Travis taught me to read and write, and some math and science. He tried to teach me what he called history, too, but it sounded like bullshit. Anyway, what was the point of hearing about stuff that hap-pened before you were even born? You hardly ever heard anything about it on the HUD or on HoloTV. If it was important you'd think they'd talk about it. Nobody cared about it — nobody except Travis, that is.

And he liked to talk about philosophy and politics. More lame subjects. He'd go on about democracy and freedom of choice and all that, which I didn't get. How could you be any more free than we already were?

Anyway, like I did twice a week, on Wednesday I boarded down to an abandoned office building a few blocks from us, where they'd set up the co-op school. More history. More philosophy. More politics. Boring.

At a break between classes I cornered Travis in the courtyard outside. Most of the time he managed to make classes pretty interesting, but today was a snoozefest.

"Maybe you find it boring," he said, "but it's stuff you need to know."

I laughed. "I need to know about politics?"

He gave me that look he had.

"What's the difference between the Freedom Party and the Enterprise Party?" he asked.

"How do I know?" I answered. "Anyway, who cares?"

"Well, they're the only two parties you can vote for. If they stand for the same thing, why vote?"

"You have to vote. It's the law."

He held out both his hands with the palms facing up, like he was balancing something in them. "Look, if I force you to choose between a red ball and another identical red ball, do you actually have a choice?"

"I don't want a red ball," I laughed.

He droned on and on. I got tired of listening to it.

"Shit, man," I finally said. "All you do is complain. What more could we want? We've got the vote — we *have* to vote. We've got free speech—"

It was his turn to laugh. "What good is free speech when there's nobody to hear you?"

"I can talk to you," I said, "and Richie, and my dad—"

"But you can never reach a large crowd. You could never broadcast on the net to people's HUDs. You could never talk on HoloTV. You could never change anything."

"Sure I could. I'd just have to make enough money."

"And how would you do that?"

I looked at my feet. I had to admit it was a pretty stupid idea.

"You'd have to join one of the Corps," he answered for me. "Even then it would be tough. And in the incredibly unlikely event that you managed to claw your way up the ranks to a position of power, your agenda would be the same as all the guys in the Corps now."

I was getting annoyed. "If things needed changing," I said, "I'd change them."

He stared at me, like he was studying me.

"You know," he said, "maybe you would."

He glanced over at the other kids kicking a ball around the court-yard, then turned back.

"Let me ask you this," he said. "Have the government and the Corps ever given you anything for free?"

I laughed again. "Why would they do that? If you want stuff you have to pay. Everybody knows that."

"But in fact, there's two exceptions to that rule," he said, smiling.

"Oh yeah?"

He nodded at the HUD controller on my wrist. "There's the HUD. Don't you think it's strange that everybody gets one?"

I shrugged. He was always coming up with stuff like this. I can just barely remember when I got my HUD. I think I was about seven or eight years old. Travis says they're a pretty recent thing, developed within the past fifty years. So I guess there was a time when nobody had them. I can't imagine what it would be like without one.

"Everybody — even bums living on the street — get the HUD," Travis said. "Why do you think that is?"

I shrugged again.

"The same reason they sell the HoloTVs for almost nothing," he said. "Control." He pointed at his own head. "The HUD feeds you information, but it's *their* information — the information *they* want you to believe. If you can access something on your HUD, it's because they *want* you to have it. If they choose not to show it to you, it might as well not exist."

For once I thought of a comeback. "What about the hacks?"

I figured I had him on that one. Hacks like the one that confuses the HUD's GPS locator, and the ones we use Cam-surfing, are pretty common. They've never done any real damage, which I guess is why the crackdown hasn't been harder.

At first Travis' eyes opened wider, like I'd reminded him of something. The look disappeared, and his brows came together. I smiled. I'd stumped him.

"That I can't answer for sure," he finally said. "Maybe the kids aren't coming up with this stuff on their own."

"What do you mean?"

"I mean maybe they're getting help. Maybe there's people in the Corps..." He stopped short, like he didn't want to say anymore.

I was starting to tune out, like I usually did when he got on one of his rants.

"You know there was a riot last night?" he said.

I looked up. "What?"

"A riot. People in the streets, throwing rocks and bottles. In ShakeTown, the next Quarter over. They're desperate. No jobs, no money, no future."

"You're so full of it," I laughed. "I would have seen it on my HUD."

"You think so? Like I said, if they don't choose to tell you about it, it's like it never happened."

"Well, if it's so secret, how do *you* know about it?"

He leaned in toward me and whispered. "I was there. The SecureCorp thugs opened fire. A bunch of people died."

I stared at him. "I don't believe you."

He shrugged. The riot thing was new, but I was getting a little bored with the conversation. I thought about changing the subject, but I couldn't think of anything. Then I remembered.

"So, what's the second thing?" I asked.

"Second thing?"

"You said there were two things they gave us for free — what's the second one?"

He smiled. "Appraisal — they pay for everybody to have it, even you. Why do you think that is?"

I stood there like a moron. I've got to admit the thought never occurred to me before.

"You're so smart," I finally said. "You tell me."

"Because they're looking for people," he said.

"People?"

"People who respond to Appraisal — in a certain way."

"What do they care?"

His expression turned dark. "For all they go on about freedom and democracy, it's the farthest thing from what they want."

"So, what *do* they want?"

"Everything," he said. "They want everything. And they've almost got it. The only stumbling block is Appraisal. They can't control it. They have to put up with the results the same as everybody else. They can't stand that.

"They've poured trillions into research, trying to find a way to change the outcome, but nothing's worked. That's why they give the Appraisal to everybody. They know that statistically a certain number will be worth studying."

"You can't know all this," I said.

"You're right," he said. "I don't know. I'm just guessing. But it's the only explanation."

"Who's this 'they' you keep going on about? The government? Everybody knows what bozos *they* are."

He smiled at me. "I don't think you're quite ready to hear about that yet."

# S E V E N

......................................................

# A P P R A I S A L

The week before my Appraisal appointment crawled by. I didn't feel like talking to anybody, not even Cindy. Then something happened that seemed like some kind of bad omen. One day I showed up at the co-op school and Travis wasn't there. I asked around. Nobody seemed to know what happened to him.

There were a couple of other teachers, but they weren't much more educated than I am, and I'd never connected with them like I did with Travis. As the days crept by he still hadn't shown up. I was already feeling uptight about the Appraisal. This just made it worse.

When the day finally arrived, I got up and got dressed, just like always, though I knew it would be like no other in my life.

"I'm going," I called to my dad from the front door. His body stiffened for a second, but he didn't move. He just sat staring at the Hol-oTV.

At the Appraisal clinic, I avoided eye contact with everybody in the waiting room. I knew they'd all be freaked out. Hey, I was freaked out myself — who wouldn't be? It didn't help that both my mother and father had gotten negative Appraisals. Everybody swears heredity's got nothing to do with it, but it's hard not to worry about it.

The clinic closest to us was in an older concrete building just inside the Corp Ring. In the waiting room, a bunch of kids, most about my age, sat fidgeting on the plastic chairs spaced along the walls. Some had their parents with them. Most, like me, were alone. Posters on the walls displayed slogans like: *Appraisal - Passport to More Money,* and *High Appraisal = Crush Your Competitors.*

I confirmed my appointment at the front desk, then found an empty chair in a far corner.

There was nothing left to do but wait. I stretched out my legs, laid back my head, and closed my eyes. I tried to focus on something pleasant.

I thought about how Cindy and I first met. It was about a year ago, when me and Richie were Cam-surfing. Usually we only did it at night, but we were bored and needed some excitement. We staked out the Museum of Democracy, deep in the Corp Ring. As usual, we got there by latching onto the backs of empty RoboTaxis and letting them tow us on our boards. Government buildings were always more of a challenge to get into, and we'd just gotten ahold of a hack that was supposed to unlock some of the museum doors.

The hack worked; we made it inside through a delivery entrance. The place was actually open, so technically we could have just walked in as visitors, but it cost and we had no money to pay, even if we wanted to, which we didn't. Anyway, they would have taken one look at us and told us to get lost. The hack was also supposed to give us access to some of the inner offices — much better for trophies.

That was when I saw her. She'd snuck away from the group on one of her school outings. Later she told me she'd lied to them and said she had to use the bathroom, but then she took off to explore.

She came around a corner and caught us just as we were breaking in. She was wearing a school uniform: plaid skirt, a blinding white blouse with a school tie. Her blond hair curled around the shoulders of her uniform jacket. Her reckless blue eyes bored into me. I thought she was the most beautiful girl I'd ever seen.

She took one look and knew what was going on. I figured for sure she'd scream or rat us out or something, but she didn't do anything.

"Looking for souvenirs?" she whispered.

At first we were both too shocked to say anything. Finally, I just nodded my head.

"I know where you can get some good ones," she said.

Richie and I looked at each other. It could be some kind of trick. She gestured to the right and started walking. I turned and followed her.

"Are you crazy, man?" Richie whispered, trailing after me. "She's gonna turn us in to security."

"I don't think so," I whispered back.

"My name's Cindy," she said when I caught up with her. I was in love.

She seemed to know where she was going. Once or twice we saw uniformed people, but we managed to hide before they spotted us. We eventually reached a door that said 'Storage #2'.

"Here," she said, nodding at it.

I tried the hack. We heard a click. Richie and I looked at each other. I shrugged and turned the handle. It opened. I half expected a squad of SecureCorp soldiers to jump out from behind it. The room was empty of people, but we stood for a few seconds with our mouths hanging open. It was the storage room for the entire souvenir shop. There were shelves and shelves of stuff — a trophy-hunter's paradise. Richie and I grabbed a couple of the best ones we could find.

"We better get out of here," Richie whispered.

"Thanks," I said to Cindy as we backed out the door. She smiled. It seemed ridiculous to even suggest it, but hey, you only live once. I said: "I want to see you again."

She didn't say anything. She punched something on her controller and her HUD address came up on my display. I gave her one last smile. I felt ten feet tall as we took off with our trophies.

After that me and Cindy were together all the time. Sometimes I felt like a loser with her; she had all this money and opportunity and this incredible education, while I had nothing, and could barely read and write. All I had was what I learned from the volunteer guys like Travis in the Quarters.

There were holes in my education you could drive a truck through, but she never laughed at me or said anything about it. Sometimes she'd correct me about something, but she always did it with love. Cindy...

Something bumped against my feet and I woke from my daydream. Some old lady was trying to get by. She gave me a nasty look.

*46*

I pulled in my legs and sat up straighter, but laid back and closed my eyes again after she passed.

My mind spun ahead double-time. I thought about the milestones in people's lives: birth, marriage, children, and of course, finally — death. All of them had been around in some form for as long as people existed. And none of them had changed all that much since then — except the last one. The newest milestone, Appraisal, had been around for less than a hundred years, but it was a doozy.

I heard muffled voices behind the door in front of me. I lifted up my head and opened my eyes. The door opened. A girl, about my age, stumbled out, crying into a handkerchief. A nurse in a white uniform had an arm around her shoulders, comforting her. The girl removed the handkerchief and blew her nose. For a second, she looked up and her eyes met mine. I cringed. This was exactly what I'd been trying to avoid.

I couldn't help studying her face. It did look a little wrinkled — nah, that had to be my imagination. There's no way you'd see anything this early. The girl staggered past and out the door. I laid back again. Thinking about it was a drag. I tried to blank out my mind and I must have fallen asleep.

I woke with a hand on my shoulder. I jumped and drew back. The same nurse, the one that was comforting the girl, was standing beside me.

"Mr. Barret?" she said. Her eyes were sad.

I nodded. *How can somebody handle a job like that?* I thought.

I followed her through the door the crying girl had come out of and down a hallway. By this time I was totally wired. She pointed to a small room on the right and I went in. She shut the door and I waited.

For my whole life I'd been able to put the whole issue of Appraisal out of my mind. Now the moment that every kid my age looked forward to with a mixture of anticipation and dread, was finally here. I thought about trying to go back to sleep, but now I was too strung out.

I figured I was probably screwed. Talk about bad genes. My mother, my dad. There was something screwy about my uncle's Appraisal too — my dad's brother. I'd never met my uncle Zack. I always assumed he was dead. Dad would never talk about him, or what happened to him, but it must have been something bad. Another negative Appraisal, I figured. Seemed like everybody else in my family had gotten screwed. Hey, why not me too?

I thought about how I'd react to the result. If it was bad, I'd accept it and be a man. There was no way I was going to end up like the girl I saw in the waiting room. Or like my dad...

If it was good, I'd be — what was the word — humble. I wouldn't flaunt it and look down on the unlucky bastards with low multiples like some of the older kids I'd seen. If it was mediocre, well — that's what most people's was anyway. Nothing wrong with that.

A different nurse knocked softly, opened the door, and led me to another room, with a raised bed and benches full of tools and instruments.

*This is it,* I thought.

In a few minutes a man in a lab coat came in, carrying an electronic notebook.

"Mr. Barret," he said, smiling. He reached out his free hand and shook mine. "I'm Doctor Ryman. I'm going to do your Appraisal today."

I swallowed hard, as the reality hit me.

"Just relax," he said. "It won't hurt a bit."

He swept a hand toward the bed, and I climbed up on it. The nurse held out a tray with an electronic hypo. It looked a lot smaller than I was expecting. Such a small gizmo producing such huge consequences. Dr. Ryman picked it up, checked the dosage reading, and pressed it against my upper arm. I felt a slight pinch, like Cindy did when she was teasing me. Dr. Ryman put the syringe back on the tray and the nurse carried it away.

They both took off for about ten minutes, left me lying on the bed, shaking. When they got back, Dr. Ryman took a blood sample. That was a more involved procedure than the actual Appraisal. I watched my red blood filling the test-tube. It looked normal enough.

*What an idiot,* I thought. *How would you expect it to look?*

Dr. Ryman stepped back and took off his gloves.

I was lying there like a dummy waiting for something else to happen, but the nurse just motioned for me to get down from the bed. She led me back to the room I'd been in before.

*'Anticlimactic' — yeah,* I thought. *That was the word.*

Funny, I didn't feel any different, even though I knew the injection could transform my life. Twenty minutes later Dr. Ryman walked in. He sat there for a few seconds, staring at me like I was some kind of freak.

*What's the deal?* I thought. *Is he trying to psych me out or something? Is this part of it?*

"Mr. Barret?" he said.

*Is that all anybody says around here?*

I nodded.

His face twisted into this weird expression. "I'm afraid there's been a bit of a glitch."

"What?" I said, like a moron. "They gotta do it again?"

He just sat there staring at me. I tried to figure out exactly what his expression was, and I felt a lump in my throat when it finally occurred to me — it was fear.

"Would you follow me, please?" he said.

We left the room and headed down the hall. At the very end was another room with a narrow, padded bench on one side and a chair against the far wall. It looked a lot like the one I'd just been in, but something was different.

"Please wait here," he said. He shut the door and I jumped when I heard the thunk of the latch outside. I tried the handle. I was right — it was locked.

"Hey," I pounded on the door. "What's going on? What the hell are you trying to pull!"

That was when I figured out the difference between this room and the one I was in before. My shouts faded into the walls and disappeared instantly. It was a hardened, sound-proof cell. I was a prisoner.

I pounded on the door for another twenty minutes before I finally gave up. I sat down and tried to figure out what was going on. I'd been preparing for all kinds of different Appraisal scenarios my whole life: high, low, even negging out. This wasn't like any of them. I'd talked to older kids about how their Appraisals had gone, and none of them had mentioned anything like this.

My hands were shaking. It was like all the pins that held my world together had been pulled out. Strung out and exhausted, I lay down on the bench. Maybe it was stress or something. Maybe it was the injection. Whatever it was, in a few minutes I fell asleep.

I woke up when I heard voices in the room. Two white-coated men were standing just inside the open door. I jumped up and rushed at them, hoping I could push them out of the way and get out of this place. They each grabbed one of my arms. Before I could even yell anything one of them pressed an injector against my shoulder, and everything went black.

# EIGHT

........................................................

# A PRISONER

When I woke up, it felt like bombs were exploding inside my skull. I tried to sit up, but the pain almost made me pass out. I closed my eyes again, lay back down, and waited for the pounding to subside.

A few minutes later I tried again and finally made it. The room was about twice the size of the one at the clinic. It looked like a hotel room. It had a proper bed, which is what I was sitting on, and a night table with a lamp. There was a couch in the farthest corner, and a coffee table and a single chair. There was a bathroom off to the right.

What it didn't have was a HoloTV, a phone, or any other way to receive or send information.

I had no idea how much time had passed. I looked for the clock reading in my HUD, and realized something even more freaky, something I hadn't experienced in living memory. My HUD wasn't working. I frantically pushed buttons on the controller, but nothing happened. It was like part of me was missing — like there was a gaping hole in my reality.

Now I really did feel sick.

I swung my legs over the side of the bed. The throbbing in my skull intensified, and I tasted bile in the back of my throat. I stumbled for the bathroom, collapsing to my knees, my head over the toilet, just in time to puke my guts out. Thank God there was a bottle of painkillers on the sink. I staggered to my feet, gulped down three, and headed back out to check the door of my room.

Surprise, surprise — it was locked.

*What the hell's going on?* I thought. *What did I do?*

I thought about my dad - at home, probably still glued to the Hol-oTV. I clamped my eyes shut. He couldn't help me - I was on my own. The news media were full of stories about how the CCE have worked to make people's lives better. If they knew what was happening, maybe they could do something - but I had no way to communicate.

I lay down, still in a daze, and eventually passed out. I woke up with a start. There were shuffling sounds outside my room. Just as I looked over, the handle of the door turned. I jumped out of bed and moved to a corner next to it, positioning myself so I could make a run at the opening, crouching down, ready to spring through the gap. As soon as the door opened, I flew towards it.

Unfortunately, the space was occupied by two burly guards: one in some kind of uniform, the other in a white tee-shirt. Both of them were a foot taller than me. I threw myself against them anyway. They grabbed my arms and forced me back into the room.

A third man walked through the now open door. He was smaller and more intelligent-looking, with slicked-back hair and black-framed glasses. Like Dr. Ryman, he wore a white smock and carried an electronic notepad. Unlike Ryman's, his smock had a small symbol, like a stylized butterfly, on the lapel. It looked familiar, but I couldn't figure out where I'd seen it before.

"What the hell am I doing here!" I yelled at them.

"Settle down, Alex," the man in the smock said, smiling. "Nobody's going to hurt you. Have a seat."

He closed the door and motioned to the chair next to the coffee table.

I struggled against the guards, but finally gave up. There was nothing else I could do. I sat down in the chair. The guards moved away but stood by the door. The white-smocked man took a seat on the couch.

"First, let me introduce myself," he said. "My name is Doctor Charles Knowles. You can call me Chuck."

"Well screw you, Chuck," I said. "What the hell's going on here?"

Chuck's smarmy grin gave me the creeps. Somewhere behind it was the same expression I'd seen on Dr. Ryman's face.

"Settle down," Chuck said. "We just need to do a few more tests — to make certain there are no side-effects."

"You drug me and kidnap me and lock me in this room, just so I can have some tests?" I said. "And what's with the goons?" I nodded at the two men by the door. The uniformed guy, a gorilla with a square, over-sized jaw, sneered at me.

"I apologize for that," Chuck said. "There was a bit of a mixup. It's important that we do these tests. We didn't want you running off before we got the chance."

"Some mixup," I said. My head was still throbbing. "So do the tests and let me out of here. And what's my Appraisal? That other doctor never even told me. Why doesn't my HUD work in here? And where am I anyway?"

"All in good time, Alex," Chuck said, putting a hand on my shoulder. He nodded to the guy in the tee shirt, who opened the door and took off. "Don't worry," Chuck said to me. "Everything's fine. We'll do our little tests and get you out of here before you know it."

I relaxed a little, but the whole thing still felt like bullshit. The door opened and the guard that had left reappeared with a bundle of clothes in his hand.

"Put this on please, Alex," Chuck said.

I stood up. My head exploded with pain. The throb that had been fading away rushed back like a tidal wave. I swayed sideways. Chuck reached up and held my arm to steady me. After a few seconds the pain finally subsided. I got undressed and put on their stupid hospital gown, one of the ones where your bare ass is sticking out the back.

Each of the guards took one of my arms. They opened the door and led me down a hallway. It opened into large, empty room with several examination tables, mobile instrument carts, and giant over-head lights. I shuddered - it looked a lot like the room where I'd seen the old man. I tried to pull away and the guards tightened their grips.

"Don't be so jumpy," Chuck smiled. "You'll be out of here in no time."

I was still groggy and confused, but one thing was becoming crystal clear: I needed to get out of this place — right now. I relaxed like I wasn't going to fight them anymore, waiting for a break.

Even if I got away from them — where would I go? I didn't even know where I was. I didn't care. I had to try. We reached one of the examination tables and Chuck swept his hand towards it. The guards let go of my arms so I could climb up. I put my hands on the table. There was still a guard on either side of me. I swung my legs up onto the table like I was going to lie down, but then I didn't stop, I just pushed myself off the other side. That put the table between me and the others.

I took off and started running. I could only see one exit. I had to run in a wide circle to stay out of the reach of the guards, and by the time I got to the door they'd caught up with me. One of them took a flying leap and tackled my legs. I fell forward. My head bounced off the floor and I was gone.

Days, then weeks, went by. Three times a day some orderly-type, always accompanied by at least one burly guard, would bring me a meal — the only bright spot about being here — it was actually real food rather than FoodCorp packets. Other than the guys who worked there, I never saw another soul.

The part about letting me go was bullshit, but the part about testing was true, at least so far. Chuck still hadn't said anything about what they were actually after. They hadn't done anything bad to me (though I had a sickening feeling they were going to). They'd taken blood samples, urine samples, hair samples, and done body scans. Everything they did was slow and deliberate, like they were worried about making a mistake.

The rest of the time I was trapped in my room. One night I had a dream — a memory - about my dad. It was just after my mother died. I was about eight years old. Already most of his hair was gone, and what was left was completely gray. He was apologizing.

"I was selfish," he said, his face already lined with defeat. "I knew I wouldn't be around to look after you, but we wanted a child. I always thought your mother would be there after…"

I woke up, the dream still fresh in my mind. I thought about my mother. The fact is, I don't remember much about her. Once in a while I'll have a flashback. It's never an actual image — I don't even remember what she looked like. When I try to visualize her, it always comes out like one of those interviews on HoloTV where they blur somebody's face to hide their identity.

I never remember her face, just the little details you'd think weren't that important: the warmth of her body as she tucked me into bed, the rhythm of her voice as she read me to sleep, even the smell of her hair as she bent down to kiss me good night. At least I tell myself I remember — it was a long time ago.

Travis said there's a cure for what she had, if we'd had the money. It's horrible to think that she didn't have to die, but like they're always saying on the newscasts, that's the natural order of things — survival of the fittest. It was our fault. Me and my dad. We should've made more money. We should've done whatever was necessary. If we had, she'd still be alive.

Living without her's not terrible. It's just — emptiness — like nothing's there. And I don't miss her. You don't miss what you never had, or at least don't remember having, I guess.

I wondered what my dad was doing right now. Would he be able to take care of himself if I wasn't there?

In all this time they still hadn't told me what my Appraisal was. At this point I wouldn't have believed anything they said anyway.

Every day the goon in the uniform, who I'd nicknamed 'Brickhead' because of his square, angular skull, would show up at my room. We'd march along a series of antiseptic white corridors and through a series of doors. Sometimes Chuck would be with him. Most of the time we'd be alone. Some of the doors were secured with biometric panels. Either Chuck or Brickhead would unlock them by pressing an index finger on the sensor.

There's dozens of labs in this place, but we almost always ended up at the same one. Twenty minutes later Chuck would show up. They'd force me down on the exam table, and the sessions would begin. By the third week I figured they must have done every test, probe, and scan it was possible to do.

They were preparing for something, and it was pretty clear I wasn't going to like whatever that thing was.

# NINE

..................................................

# WALTER

I hadn't been able to use the HUD since I got here. The building must be shielded somehow, and the staff either had theirs turned off or were using some frequency I couldn't read. It was like having one of my legs cut off or something, or like being deaf or blind. The world didn't seem normal anymore, like somebody had erased part of it.

That's why I nearly shit myself when Brickhead was taking me on my usual jaunt down the hallway toward the lab, and an image suddenly floated in front of me. It was a hologram, a standard projection like anybody would have in their living room, but produced by my HUD. Even more shocking was what I was looking at. It was the old guy I'd seen when I was Cam-surfing and broke in looking for a trophy.

It's hard to describe what he looked like. The closest I can come is that he looked dead. He wasn't dead, but he looked dead. Like the life had been sucked out of him. He looked like a corpse that was some-how reanimated and still walking around. I jumped when I saw him. I checked to make sure Brickhead hadn't noticed. When I glanced over, the goon gave me his usual sneer, like he'd like nothing better than to beat the living crap out of me. I had enough sense not to let him know what I was seeing.

"I mean you no harm," the image spoke in my earpiece. His voice was tired and weak, like every breath was an effort. "I'm your friend."

Maybe he was some kind of plant — put there to make me think there was somebody I could trust, though you'd think they'd use a guy who didn't look like he was about to drop dead to do it. Anyway, why should they care whether I trusted them or not? I hadn't figured that out yet.

"I can see and hear you," the image said.

I gave him the finger.

"Yes, I saw that," he said.

"Just testing," I said.

"What?" Brickhead turned and glared at me. Luckily, he hadn't seen my finger gesture.

"Nothin'," I answered. Brickhead gave me a shove just for good measure, and we continued.

"Sorry for contacting you now," the image said. "I only had a small window of opportunity when the monitors were down. My name is Walter. *They* can't know about this." He inclined his head toward the guard. "I'll contact you again."

My mind was racing as Chuck performed yet another barrage of tests. Who was this Walter guy? Was he for real, or were Chuck and the gang trying to mess with my head? And what was wrong with him? If he was as out of it as he seemed, how did he manage to contact me without them knowing?

Again, nothing much happened. More blood samples, urine samples, hair samples, body scans. When it was over they took me back. I was confused. I hadn't seen any more of Walter (or seen anything at all on the HUD). I started to think it was some kind of dream. When Brickhead shoved me back in my cell I was so stressed out I just collapsed on the bed.

I closed my eyes, hoping to get some sleep, but images kept swirling through my head: my dad, Richie, the Lost Souls, Cindy...

I thought back to a couple of months ago, when Cindy had snuck me into a HoloSurround chamber in the Corp Ring. She'd picked out the 'Rustic Farm' track, kind of a hokey, girl track, but I didn't mind. It was the first, and probably the last, time I'd ever experienced something like that. It was like a dream, but I remember every detail.


We entered the chamber, and the lights went down. When they came up again, it was mid-afternoon on a blazing summer day in the country. A breeze was shaking the branches of the trees surrounding the gigantic field where we stood. Little parasol-shaped dandelion seed pods wafted through the air, dragonflies buzzed overhead, crickets hummed in the tall grass. It was like the first summer of the world, like it must have been for Adam and Eve on their first day in paradise.

Cindy took off, and I chased after her. I flew across the field, and nearly lost my balance in the chase. Ahead, Cindy giggled and raced toward the old barn on the north side. She turned back and glanced at me, her face glowing with an inner light. For a fraction of a second, time stopped, like God had taken a snapshot and captured this one instant of joy and happiness — Cindy's backward glance frozen in place, her smile like the rays of the sun overhead. It was like I paused in midair, feet off the ground, lips parted, the laughter caught forever on my face.

I remember studying the frozen scene like I was some kind of ethereal being, floating above it all.

*I still can't believe it,* I thought. *I can't believe that she's in love with me.*

The moment passed and time started up again. My feet touched the ground and I caught up with Cindy near the barn. She giggled as I wrapped my arms around her and gently guided her down into the long grass.

She ran her fingers through my hair and gazed into my eyes, inviting me in. Without thinking, I leaned down and kissed her. It was like nothing I'd ever experienced before, like she was all that existed, like the world began and ended with her.

We lay for a long time without speaking.

Finally I said, "Let's make a pact."

"What?" she laughed.

I hesitated, petrified that she'd say no, or even laugh at me. "That we'll always be together."

"Really?" she answered.

"Do you love me?" I said, dreading her answer.

"More than anything," she gazed into my eyes and smiled.

"And I love you," I said. "So it's settled. We'll be together forever, no matter what."

She sat up and looked at me. "But what about my dad?"

An image rushed into my head of her father's bloated, red face glaring down at me in contempt.

"He'll come around," I said, trying to sound more confident than I felt.

"And Appraisal," she said. "What if we're not compatible?"

"You sound like you're trying to get out of it."

"No way," she said. She twirled a lock of her blonde hair around one finger. "If we really love each other, it doesn't matter. I don't care — do you?"

I felt better. "No, I don't care," I said.

She lay back down and put her head on my shoulder. "Yes, let's be in love and stay together forever, no matter what."

I wanted this moment to be frozen in time, like Cindy's backward glance.


A knocking sound snapped me out of my day-dream. At first I thought it was at the door, but then I realized it was in my head. I sat up on the bed and rubbed my eyes. My HUD fired up again and there he was.

He told me he was a prisoner, just like me.

"How can you see and hear me?" I whispered. I still didn't really believe anything he was saying, but it's not like I had anything better to do.

"The building is wired with microphones and cameras," he said. "They want to monitor what you're doing. I've devised a hack that diverts their feed for a short period."

"You're the guy I saw before," I said. "So, we're in the building I broke into? The SecureCorp building?"

He nodded.

"Sorry I didn't help you before," I said, looking at the floor.

He shrugged. "There was nothing you could have done..."

"How long have you been here?"

"More than twenty years," he answered. "When I arrived, I was the same age as you."

I cringed. "What! What multiple are you anyway — point five or something?"

"I don't know," he said. He looked down and shook his head sadly. "No one's ever told me. But I don't think my apparent age has anything to do with my Appraisal. They did experiments..." He swept his hands along either side of his body.

"*They* did that?" I swallowed hard. I still didn't really believe him. "So, what am I doing here? Who are they? Who do they work for?"

"I don't know," he said. "They've never told me anything. Every day they take me to a room, perform their tests, and bring me back. I've been able to hack into their control systems, but their information systems are heavily encrypted."

I shuddered, imagining the past three weeks stretching out for twenty years.

"One thing I have learned in my time here," Walter said, yanking me back to the present. "They'll do anything to get whatever it is they want. Kill, maim, cripple for life. Nowadays they only do the preliminary tests here. Soon they'll move you somewhere else — somewhere with much heavier security. You must escape."

64

"You're telling me," I said. "But I've been studying this place for weeks. There's no way out."

"There's one way," he said. "And I know what it is."

"If you know a way out, why haven't you escaped a yourself?"

"It takes two," he said.

"So nobody else has been here in twenty years?"

"There have been many."

"What happened to them?"

He smiled sadly. "This facility is being phased out, and some were transferred to the new one, as you will be. I'm so broken that it's probably not worth moving me. The experiments take a great toll. Some didn't survive. For some reason they have been more careful with me."

"They've hardly done anything to me so far..."

"Then you must be very special indeed."

# T E N

..................................................

# E S C A P E

Walter and I talked for a week or so, mostly at night, after all the poking and prodding was over. So far, my luck had held out. They still hadn't done more than a few minor tests. I asked him about getting word to the CCE. He said even with all his hacks, he'd never found a way to communicate to the outside. We never talked for very long. Walter figured we had about ten minutes at a time before Chuck and the rest figured out that something was going on.

"For twenty years I've studied them," Walter said one night. "It took years to modify my HUD controller and produce the first hack — that gave me access to their system.

"Luckily, I had lots of time," he gave another one of his sad smiles. "Sometimes their experiments made me sick. After one I almost died. Most times I felt well enough to work. I never gave up on the idea of getting out of here." His right hand clenched into a fist. "I have vowed that, one way or another, I will escape this place."

We went over his plan in detail. I still wasn't sure I trusted him, but I had nobody else.

He lifted a shaking hand to scratch his cheek.

"Are you sure you're in shape to get away?" I asked him.

His mouth formed a hard line. "Don't worry — I have enough strength to do what's necessary."

"They're going to shit themselves when they find us gone," I said, smiling. "You can stay at our place, until we figure out what to do."

He nodded and gave me a strange look. There were still some details he hadn't explained, but he told me I'd understand when it all went down — that I should just play along.

Finally the day came for the escape. Brickhead was herding me down the hallway, as usual. Walter said that the routine was that Brickhead would lead me to one examination room, and just after that, Chuck would lead Walter to another (they didn't need Brickhead or any other goon for Walter; he was too old and feeble to put up much of a fight). That way, Walter and I would never actually see each other.

This time, as Walter had instructed, I dragged my feet and stalled. Brickhead was getting pissed off, but I ignored him. It was a fine line, slowing as much as possible, but not so much that he'd figure out that something was up. He pointed to a closer hallway on the right instead of the regular one further away on the left.

"We got something special planned for you today," he smiled.

We'd be around the corner and out of sight in a few seconds if I didn't do something. I stopped and stood there. I couldn't think of anything else to do.

Brickhead kept walking. When he got a few meters ahead, he finally noticed I wasn't there and turned. "What's your problem?" he snarled back at me.

I didn't move. He returned to where I was standing. "Get moving," he said, shoving me forward.

I turned to face him with my fists raised.

"You looking for a beating?" he said, smiling. He put a hand on the club on his belt.

I stared at him for a few seconds, stalling, waiting as long as I dared. Finally I started walking again, as slowly as I could. Out of the corner of my eye I finally saw Chuck leading Walter into an examination room we'd passed already. I didn't dare look or I'd tip off Brickhead, but when he was turned the other way, I stole a glance. Since that time I first broke in, I'd never actually seen Walter in person. His expression was a weird mixture of fear, anger, and determination. The corner of his mouth curled up in a loopy smile, as he gave me a barely perceptible nod.

A few seconds later there was a loud shout and both Brickhead and I turned back to see what was happening. Walter was wrestling with Chuck. I saw a flash of light reflecting off a metal blade. Brickhead started running toward them. I ran after him. I got closer and saw a scalpel in Walter's hand. Chuck was trying to disarm him.

Walter broke away from his grip and slashed the side of Chuck's neck. Chuck screamed as blood spurted out. He forgot about Walter and tried to stop the flow. His hands were covered with blood. Brickhead was almost there. I was right behind him. I stuck out my foot and he went down hard. I jumped forward and landed on his hips, and something cracked. He screamed, flailing around like a dying fish.

I looked up and saw Walter grab a pair of cutters from the cart beside the examination table. Chuck was lying on the floor, blood still spraying from his neck. He was barely moving. Walter lifted Chuck's right hand, stuck Chuck's index finger in the jaws of the cutters, and snapped them shut. Chuck screamed again, for the last time.

Walter stood for a second holding the severed finger.

"Come on!" I yelled, gesturing at him.

He just shook his head and gave me another one of his sad smiles. He held up the finger, ready to throw it to me.

"No!" I screamed.

Brickhead staggered to his feet and there was something in his hand — a gun. He pointed it at Walter. Walter tossed the finger just as Brickhead fired. A patch of red bloomed on Walter's chest and he went down. I caught the finger and started running.

The finger was covered with blood. I wiped it off on my gown. Tears streamed down my cheeks as I ran. I could hear Brickhead's limping footsteps stumbling after me. I heard a gunshot, and a hole was blasted in the wall above my head. I got to a corner and flew around it, finally out of his sight. I reached the inner doors and fumbled to press the finger against the scanner. The access light went green and the latch clicked. I flung the door open and tore down the hallway. A siren started blaring.

Two more doors. I wasn't sure if they'd be disabled with the alarm. The first one opened. I got to the second. I pressed the finger against the scanner but nothing happened.

I willed myself to stop shaking, wiped it again on my gown, and tried again. It worked. The doors were still operational, but wouldn't be for long. I flew down the final hallway to another door. Suddenly my HUD was working. I must have passed through whatever was screening it. Another alarm kicked in.

I tried the finger on the final door. It didn't work. I tried three times. The place was in lock down. I was screwed.

I fought to stay calm. My restored HUD reminded me of the night I'd broken in to steal the trophy. I'd used the hack to fool the system into opening the door. My hand was shaking as I punched the controller buttons to set up the hack again. I prayed to God they hadn't changed anything.

Brickhead limped around the corner. He started firing as soon as he saw me. I screwed up one of the codes and had to enter it again. He was only a hundred meters away. His shots were getting closer. Finally the HUD light went green. I held my controller wrist up to the panel. The lock clicked open.

I smashed through the door into darkness. It slammed shut behind me. As my eyes adjusted I could see I was in a short hallway with a single door at the end. I pounded down it and glanced back just as three bullet holes punched through the door behind me. Pencil-thin beams of light from outside played on the floor. One last panel at the hallway door. Green! I pushed it open.

I was outside.

# ELEVEN

..................................................

# ON THE RUN

I flew around the nearest corner and down two or three alleys, hoping to lose Brickhead. It must have worked. I heard his lopsided footsteps thumping in the distance, but I never saw him again. A few of the cameras probably recorded me running away, but once I calmed down, my Cam-surfing experience paid off like I never would have thought. It was night. I checked my HUD. Thank God it was working again. It was eight-thirty PM.

I was still in the Corp Ring. There were cameras everywhere. I had to slink around walls and down alleys trying to stay out of their view. I was still wearing the hospital gown with my bare ass hanging out. I'd be screwed if anybody saw me. Luckily, it was late summer, so it was warm, and there was hardly anybody on the street. I crossed back into Tintown and made for home. I couldn't think of any place else to go. I wondered if Dad would even still be alive, without me there to help him.

When I finally got to the apartment, Dad was sitting in his chair, watching the HoloTV, like always. He didn't look up when I walked in.

"Dad," I called out to him.

"Where've you been?" he said, without turning around.

"I gotta talk to you," I said louder, to drown out the blaring audio.

He finally turned and scowled at me. "I just want to see this."

"It's important," I shouted. I walked over and turned the TV off.

He was pissed, but he didn't get up.

"I was watching that," was all he said.

"It's about my Appraisal," I said.

He cringed, but waved me off again and stared at the empty pedestal, like there was still a show on. I crouched down in front of him so he had to look at me. I hadn't been that close to him face to face for a long time. His hands were wrinkled like old parchment and speckled with age-spots, his face was lined and mottled, snow-white wisps of hair ringed the blotchy pink dome of his head.

He looked like he was about to nod off. I put my hands on his shoulders and shook him. His eyes opened. I looked into them and shuddered. There was a sadness I'd never noticed before, like staring down into a grave. For the first time in all the years we'd been together I felt like I understood what he'd been through.

He finally noticed my gown. "Why are you dressed like that?"

"Somebody's after me," I said. "They wouldn't tell me my Appraisal. They took me to some special hospital but I ran away."

His eyes opened wider and he stared at me.

He put a hand on each arm of his chair and pushed himself up to a standing position. I'd never seen him react so strongly. It was like he'd been asleep and had just woken up. I stood up, facing him. He stag-gered sideways and backed away from me.

"What?" I said.

"You," he whispered. "It can't be."

He was shaking, still backing away.

"What the hell's going on!" I yelled.

"Vita Aeterna," he whispered, his voice trembling with fear. "It's impossible."

It occurred to me that the look he was giving me was the same one I saw on the doctor's face after my Appraisal.

"Run," my dad finally said. He jerked his head towards the door, his eyes wide with terror. "Run and hide."

Sirens blared in the distance, getting closer.

"Run!" he shouted at me.

I jumped up and headed for the door.

"Find your Uncle Zack — Hurry!" he yelled.

I backtracked to my room, grabbed my pack, and threw in some clothes — and everything I could find that seemed important.

"Forget that!" my dad screamed. "Get out now!"

I'd boarded to my Appraisal, so my regular board was gone, but I had an older, even more beaten up one in my room. It would have to do. I grabbed it, rushed to the front door, flung it open and flew out into the hallway.

"Don't come back," my dad called after me.

I ran outside and tore down the street in a panic. The sirens were right around the corner. It was too late to get away. I flattened myself against the wall inside an alcove. A plain black van flew by me, siren wailing.

I took a chance and peeked around the wall. The van stopped at my building. Soldiers pounded out of it, up the stairs, and through the entrance. I waited a few minutes. I had to know what they were going to do. It was a hot night and our apartment window was open. Shadows flicked across the wall in the living room.

I heard them screaming at my dad, heard his voice mumbling back. A few minutes later the shadows converged at the living room window. There was a gunshot and a loud crash. I watched in horror as a body was jammed through the makeshift metal security bars and tossed five floors to the street below.

It was my dad.

Richie's apartment building looked at lot like mine, but the dark hid a lot of the dinginess and decay. I'd Cam-surfed there, after cowering in the shadows as the soldiers rushed out of our building and took off in the van, then changing into the clothes I'd brought. I had nowhere else to go.

I made my way to an abandoned parkade nearby that the Lost Souls had used a few times before, one that we could access out of sight of any cameras. Using our code name for the place, 'Dungeon', in case the anybody was listening, I texted Richie to meet me.

At first he didn't believe it was me. He finally agreed to come, and showed up at the meeting place. Half the parking stalls were occupied by rusting skeletons of cars, most stripped down to almost nothing by years of scavenging.

"You're s...supposed to be dead..." Richie stopped short when he saw me. His face was pale, like he'd seen a ghost. We hid behind the hulking frame of what was once a delivery van. "They told us at the co-op school," he said. "Some kind of scooter accident. We even had like — a special ceremony, you know?"

"I'm not dead," I said. The twinge that had been running up and down my spine for a while now tightened like an iron clamp.

"I can see that," Richie said. "What the hell's goin' on?"

"That's what I'm trying to figure out. How'd Cindy take it?"

"She hasn't been around either — for a while we thought maybe you two had run off or something. Then we heard..."

"What? About me being dead?"

"No, that was later. It was Cindy. We heard she negged out big time."

I stepped forward and grabbed him by the front of his shirt. "Screw you."

"I'm telling you, she negged out," Richie said.

It was hard to breathe. It was like somebody had nailed me with a baseball bat. For a few seconds I couldn't talk.

"What was her score?" I finally said. My brain was paralyzed.

"Bad. I think something like point five."

My gut twisted in knots. It wasn't possible.

"You better not be messin' with me," I said.

"Talk to her," he said. "Don't just take my word for it."

"Have *you* talked to her?"

75

"Nobody has. Like I said — nobody's seen her for weeks."

"Then how do you know?"

"It's in the grapevine, you know — everybody's talking about it."

"You're so full of it. There's no way she's got an Appraisal that low. That would give her a life expectancy of less than forty."

"Hey, don't take it out on me," Richie said. "I'm just telling you what's going around. It's not my fault."

"Well you shouldn't be repeating crap like that about Cindy," I said, letting go of his collar. "She's supposed to be your friend too."

"All I know is what I heard."

I told him about the kidnapping and escape.

"Wow, that's messed up," he said. I don't think he really believed me.

"Have you ever heard of anything like that happening?" I said. "It's got to be my Appraisal. Nobody would tell me what it is."

He shook his head. "Beats me. Maybe you're super-negative or something."

"What?"

"Well you know - after all, your mum and dad..." he looked at the floor.

"By the way," he said, looking up again. "I got a one point five. Not bad, eh?"

"That's great," I said.

He just stood there, like he was waiting for something. I think he was pissed because I wasn't cheering about his news, but I had more important things to think about.

"I need a place to hide," I broke the silence.

"What?"

"I told you — they're after me. After I escaped I went home. My dad told me to run away and find my Uncle Zack. They came to our apartment." I found myself choking back tears. "They killed him."

Richie stood with his mouth open. "K...Killed him?" he finally said.

"I need a place," I said. "Just for a few days — till I figure out what's going on."

"What are you talking about?" Richie stepped back, his eyes bugging out of his head.

I realized that in the space of one day I'd witnessed three people killed — one of them my own father. What *was* going on?

"I wouldn't ask," I said, "but I've got no place else to go."

Richie stared at his feet. "Look, man, if it was a regular thing..."

"Forget it," I said. "I'll find something."

I started to walk away.

"Hey, what if they came after me or something?" Richie yelled after me.

I waved him off without turning around.

# T W E L V E

..................................................

# C I N D Y

I headed for another hideout we'd come across cam-surfing, a tiny room in the basement of a building not far from the Dungeon. Its only window was broken, but it had bars so you couldn't get through. There was a long section that was out of sight from the street. You could jam something against the inside of the latch-less door to keep people out. Nobody ever came around anyway.

I sat on the floor and sifted through the trending news on my HUD. There was nothing about me (big surprise), and nothing about Chuck, or anything else that had happened, just the usual chatter about our freedom and everybody's potential for success.

I had to think. 'Find your Uncle Zack', my dad had said, which didn't make any sense. Uncle Zack was supposed to be dead. I'd never met him - he'd died before I was born. I'd only heard about him a couple of times growing up. I always figured he was like some black sheep of the family that nobody wanted to talk about. From the little I heard there was some problem with his Appraisal. Us Barrets and the

Appraisal — I swear we're cursed. I never really paid much attention, but now that I thought about it, things got kind of quiet whenever his name was mentioned.

I fished through my pack. I'd tried to grab everything that was important, but I'd only had a few seconds. I exhaled as my fingers touched the pouch where I kept my personal stuff. I couldn't remember whether I'd grabbed it or not. It took a few minutes to find what I was looking for. Our family info card was an old, cheap one, and didn't have any broadcast ability. I was grateful for that. I scanned it with my controller and the results materialized in my HUD.

There was hardly anything about Uncle Zack on the card — his birth record, a couple of old pictures of him, my dad, and my grandparents, some notes from the co-op school. But at one point all mention of him stopped, like he'd disappeared. I worked out how old he would have been at that point — sixteen — the same age I was now.

There was no mention of this Vita Aeterna, whatever that was. I was dying to look it up, but whoever I was up against would probably be on the lookout for anybody using that search term. I didn't even dare search for any information about my uncle, for the same reason. I rifled through the other stuff in the pouch. The card I'd stolen from the SecureCorp building was there. A lot of good that was going to do me. I almost tossed it, but then changed my mind. It might have some useful information. You never knew when something like that might come in handy.

I had no idea what was happening to me, or where I'd end up tomorrow, but there was one place I had to go, no matter how much of a risk I'd be taking.

Cindy's house was deep inside the Corp Ring, which was far more dangerous for me than Tintown, where nobody really gave a shit what you were doing. Maybe I was just paranoid, but it seemed like there were a lot more SecureCorp guys than usual everywhere I went. There were more cameras in the Corp Ring, and a lot fewer places to hide. Normally I would have been gawking at the gleaming sky-scrapers and mansions I was passing as I Cam-surfed through the streets, but now I had more important things to worry about.

I was careful, and made it to Cindy's without being seen. I'd been there a few times before, but I still pulled in a breath at the sight of it. It was like a palace, three stories high with vaulting roofs like a mountain range. I hid between a couple of bushes and cased the place. There were a few lights on in the lower level, but I couldn't see anybody inside. The light in Cindy's room upstairs was off.

I clenched my fists thinking about what Richie had said. I still didn't believe it. I had to see her and hear it from her in person. Her dad hated me, so I knew he wouldn't lift a finger, but I hoped maybe Cindy might find a way to help me.

I checked the grounds, and up and down the street. There was no sign of any SecureCorp, or anybody else for that matter. After about twenty minutes I worked up the guts to go and knock. Normally I would have thrown a pebble at her window or something, but I couldn't afford to stand out in the open for too long. Anyway, from what I'd heard she might not even be there.

Cindy's dad opened the door. His overflowing bulk filled the whole frame. When he saw who it was, for a second the contempt on his bloated face was the same as always. Then his jowls smoothed out as his lips tightened into a smile so broad it looked like it was hurting him.

"I want to talk to Cindy," I said. I tensed and stepped back, expecting him to grab me and rat me out to the authorities.

"Why don't you come in," he said instead, still smiling.

I was so stunned I just stood there like a moron. He'd never invited me into his house before. Usually if he even caught me on the grounds he'd threaten to call SecureCorp.

He stood aside and held the door open. I walked through it; I had to talk to Cindy. I'd never been inside before. It was like a dream. I craned my neck and gawked at the massive foyer, bigger than our whole apartment. Ahead of me, a curving marble staircase swept up to the next floor. A thousand points of light wheeled across the tiles beneath our feet. I tilted back my head and saw a gigantic crystal chandelier hanging ten meters above me. For a few seconds, I almost forgot where I was and who was standing in front of me.

I finally shut my gaping mouth and came back to reality.

"Mr. Edwards," I said.

"Call me Tom," he said.

Somehow his being nice to me creeped me out even more than when he hated my guts. I leaned my board against the wall. He sneered at it for a second, like it was going to contaminate the place, then, like he'd remembered something, he smiled again.

I followed him to another huge room off the foyer. The curved platform of a three-meter-wide HoloTV pedestal stood against one wall.

An oriental carpet the size of a city block covered the floor. Expensive looking antiques balanced on ornate wooden tables, and potted plants taller than me stood beside the wine-coloured plush leather furniture.

"Have a seat," he said, sweeping his arm toward one of the couches. "I'll get you a drink of water."

"I'm not thirsty," I said.

"Don't be silly," he said. "I insist."

He waddled off through a door to the kitchen. I sat down on the couch. I heard him turn on the tap and the water seemed to run for ages. I was about to get up and check on what he was doing in there when he stuck his face around the door frame.

"Be right with you," he smiled.

Something was wrong.

I heard a faint beep from his HUD controller. That's when I knew.

I got up and started for the door.

He was coming out of the kitchen. To my surprise he was actually carrying a glass of water. He dropped it when he saw me trying to run. I couldn't believe a guy with that much bulk could move so fast.

I got to the door first, but realized he'd locked it when I first came in. I started to twist the deadbolt knob. His massive ham-like fist reached out, grabbed my wrist and tore my hand away.

His face turned an even brighter shade of red, and the veins stood out on his neck as he stood there, still gripping my wrist like a vise. Beads of sweat stood out on his forehead. His mouth twisted with my wrist as he sneered at me.

"I've got you now, boy" he said, his hand trembling. "SecureCorp will be here any minute."

"I didn't do anything," I said.

"You little prick," he said. He twisted harder, driving me down to my knees. "All the decent, hard-working, successful people in the world that are condemned to early deaths, and you..."

He shook like he was going to explode.

"What *about* me?" I yelled up at him.

"It's impossible." He said — to himself. It was like he was in some kind of trance.

"What?" I said. I thought maybe he was losing it.

He wasn't even looking at me anymore. He was staring at the floor, or really his belly because I don't think he could see the floor.

"While my sweet little girl..." He hauled back on my wrist until I thought it would break.

"Where's Cindy!" I screamed, cringing with pain.

He snapped out of it. "Don't you defile her memory by saying her name," he said through half-clenched teeth. His words sprayed at me, like he was foaming at the mouth.

"What do you mean, *her memory*?" I said. "What happened to her!"

For a second it looked like he was going to faint. He relaxed his grip on my wrist. It was enough. I twisted it out of his hand, jumped back, and started running. He lumbered after me, cornering me in the living room. I grabbed a lamp on an end table. He smiled and pulled a gun out of his pocket.

I threw the lamp at his head. The gun went off, but missed. I jumped behind the couch I'd been sitting on. Two or three more shots went off and holes exploded through the leather back beside me. I crawled to the far end, followed by more exploding holes. There was a big glass sculpture on another end table, hidden behind the base of a potted plant. I reached up and grabbed it. I heard him stomping across the room, heading around the couch to get at me.

I was only going to get one chance. He couldn't see me right away because of the plant. I got up on my haunches and tensed, ready to jump. As soon as he appeared I sprang past him carrying my glass weapon. He fired, but he wasn't fast enough.

I landed, found my balance, and kicked at his gun hand. He screamed and the gun dropped to the floor. I lifted up the sculpture and brought it down on his head as hard as I could. He crumpled like a dynamited building and lay still. Blood gushed from his scalp, soaking into the plush weave of the carpet.

Sirens blared in the distance. I looked for the gun and realized he was lying on top of it. I couldn't move his huge bulk. I managed to jam my arm under his folds of fat, and groped for the gun, but couldn't find it. He was lying face down. I stared down at the bulge in his back pocket. I remembered I had no wallet — they still had it at the hospital. I worked the wallet out and opened it. Only a couple of dollars.

I checked through his cards. I was in a panic but I needed his fingers to deactivate the security on them. I found a MoneyAll card and pressed his thumb and forefinger against it, and it fired up, showing two thousand dollars in 'Unsecured Cash'. The blare of the sirens was getting closer.

The thought surfaced: *'It's impossible'* — *what was he talking about? And how did he know?*

I shuffled through the other cards and found one that was totally black. I pressed his thumb and finger on it and it. An image swirled into life — a logo — a butterfly, like the one on Chuck's smock. A lens appeared in the right-hand corner and a picture of my face appeared under it.

*Shit,* I thought. *A camera.*

I let go of his fingers, but the card stayed on, with my picture locked on it. I couldn't leave it here. I shoved it and the MoneyAll card in my bag, stuffed the wallet back in his pocket, and took off. By this time the sirens were right outside the house.

I ran to the front door and grabbed my board. Just as I got there a car screeched into the driveway. I ran for the back. I knew there was a back door, but it took a few precious seconds navigating through all the rooms for me to find it.

My hands shook as I fiddled with the lock. It finally clicked open. I flung the door open, flew down the back pathway and into the night.

# THIRTEEN

..................................................

# GETTING MONEY

My first priority was to get out of the Corp Ring. Back in the Quarters there was a lot less SecureCorp presence. I'd be dead if I stayed there. It was like some death-race version of Cam-surfing. Even just playing I'd managed to avoid the cameras for a half-hour at a time, and that was when my life wasn't on the line. I had a lot more incentive now.

Just as I crossed over into the Quarters, Richie's avatar came up on my HUD. I was confused. I figured SecureCorp could fake stuff like that.

Then some text came up. *The Stump Factory — 20 minutes.*

Since he mentioned the Stump Factory, I knew it had to be Richie. That was the Lost Souls' code for one of our meeting places, an old abandoned prosthetic warehouse not far from our apartment. I thought about my dad... then put it out of my mind. Only a handful of my friends knew about the place. Unless one of them had ratted on me...

I had to take a chance.

"Don't let them see you," I texted back.

"Tintown's crawling with SecureCorp," Richie said, when he showed up at our meeting place near the warehouse. "I'm not sure whether they're looking for you or they're here for some other reason."

"Sure you weren't followed?" I said.

"You know me better than that," he smiled. "I felt bad about not helping you before," he said, looking at his feet.

I told him what happened with Cindy's dad. I didn't mention that I might have killed the guy.

"What about Cindy?" he asked.

"I don't know," I lied.

We snuck past a couple of cameras and through a gap we'd set up ages ago. We headed for a space inside where the crew used to meet.

"A friend of my mother's negged out real bad," Richie said as we moved. "I think she was like a point six or something. Both her parents were one-point-fours. She ended up dying of old age before either of them did."

"I wish they'd never invented that shit," I said. "It's against God's laws or something."

"I'll put you up," Richie offered when we finally got there. "I'll hide you somewhere—"

"No," I said. "You were right the first time. Two people already died trying to help me. I don't want another one on my conscience."

"Then what—"

"I need a place to lay low for a while, someplace way off the grid."

Richie looked at the ground, thinking.

"We found a—"

"It can't be a place any of you guys know about," I interrupted him. "They might try to get to me through you. There's nothing you can do — don't worry — I'll find something. I gotta figure out what's going on. I need a crypted phone. You said once that you knew a guy—"

"I know a guy," Richie answered, "but he's an asshole."

I shrugged at him. "Not like I've got a choice."

"I can help you if you need money," Richie said. "I haven't got much, but you can take it — I'll go get it."

"Too dangerous. They'll know we hang out. If they're not watching you already they will be soon. Anyway, I've got a way to get money. Then I'll work something out with your guy."

"Don't call him my guy. He's no buddy of mine. You sure you want to deal with him?"

I nodded. He contacted the guy and arranged a meeting place.

"Thanks," I said. "I owe you."

"Keep me in the loop — somehow," he said.

It was rare to find a working streetlight in Tintown, but I guess the MoneyAll machines rated special treatment. The glow shone down like a halo on the machine I'd picked out for my attempt at getting some cash. Just finding one was hard enough. Nobody used cash anymore; just the act of trying to get some would probably raise a red flag somewhere. Hardly anybody in the Quarters even had a bank account. I hid in the recess between two buildings, checking it out.

The machine had two features that might allow me to use it without getting caught. First, it was in a location I knew really well — one I'd Cam-surfed lots of times and could escape from at top speed. Second, it was within running distance of a hiding place. One not so close that SecureCorp could set up a dragnet around it, but close enough that I could get there (or at least get out of sight) before they got to the machine.

The little square in front of me was deserted. There were cameras, but no more than usual. Of course, there'd be a camera on the machine itself, so they'd know it was me when I actually used it. There was no way I could avoid giving myself away. My only hope was that I could get the hell out of there before they could catch up.

Of course, the card would have a PIN number. Cindy had stolen it once or twice, without her dad knowing. I knew what the PIN was. All I could do was pray that her father hadn't changed it.

I didn't doubt that they could even stop the machine from giving me money — it all depended on how fast they figured out it was me at the machine, and that I had Cindy's dad's MoneyAll card. I'd been smart enough to put his wallet back, so it might take them a while to work it out. Anyway, the longer I waited the more likely it was that they'd block access.

I took a deep breath and took one last sweep around. Nothing. I snuck as close as I could, and tried to see where the camera (or cameras?) would be. I couldn't tell, but you could bet they'll make it next to impossible to use the machine without them seeing you.

I considered pulling the bandanna I had around my neck up around my face, but decided against it. As soon as they saw somebody trying to hide their appearance they'd have a swarm of drones dive-bombing me. At least without it the facial recognition software would take a few seconds, especially if I could angle my face to make it harder to recognize. I approached from the side, and mentally rehearsed what I was going to do when I got there. My plan was to jump in front of the machine, stick in the card, enter the PIN, extract the cash, and take off.

My heart was hammering in my chest as I leapt out with the card in my hand. I shoved it in the slot. I could imagine all the monitors in some SecureCorp bunker lighting up with my picture. My hands shook as I entered the PIN in a panic. Success! I went for the full amount: two thousand dollars cash. Lights started flashing around the top of the machine.

The display said: 'Four Hundred Dollar Limit'.

"Shit!" I said under my breath.

I confirmed the four hundred. I'd already been here too long. I stared at the slot waiting for the money. There was a whirring sound and a stack of twenty twenty-dollar bills seemed to take forever popping into the tray one by one. I waited for the card. Nothing. My hands were shaking. It was taking too long. They were screwing with me.

It finally popped out. I grabbed it and turned to run. As I reached the edge of the square I glanced back. A picture had come up on the screen. A guy in a SecureCorp uniform.

"Remain where you are," the guy in the picture said. "You cannot escape. A car will arrive shortly."

*Yeah, right,* I thought, as I made a bee-line for the nearest shadows. *I'll just wait here like a moron.*

"Remain where you are," the voice echoed off the walls of the alley, "you cannot escape."

I was so scared, at first I didn't even pay attention to the cameras. Then I calmed myself down and went into Cam-surfing mode.

I'd only gone a few blocks when a faint hum approached from the south. I checked the warning light in my HUD. It was still green — I hadn't triggered any cameras. Seconds later a swarm of drones screamed around the corner and started circling my head.

I batted at them and got a couple, but there must have been a hundred. I'd never seen that many in one place before. Sirens started blaring in the distance, getting closer. All the drones had cameras and GPS; I had to lose them or I was screwed.

I took off, with the swarm tearing after me. I didn't have time to get to the hiding place I'd planned on. As I ran, I hunted for a building with an open door. I finally spotted what looked like an old factory, now all boarded up. I headed for one of the doorways that had a couple of the boards torn off. As I reached it, a feathered dart embedded itself in a board beside me — a tranquilizer — some of these things were armed.

One board blocked me getting through. I yanked on it, the drones dive-bombing me and the sirens getting louder. The board finally came free. I used it to bash at some of the closest drones. I got five or ten, but there was still lots left.

I squeezed through the hole. A bunch of drones flew in after me before I could jam the board back in place. Some of the original boards were still lying around; I used them to plug every hole I could find. As I worked I could hear the swarm hammering against the outside walls like some kind of freaky hailstorm.

The ones inside were hovering around me. I found another loose board and smashed at them until they were all dead. Suddenly I thought about the MoneyAll card. I fished it out of my pack. A tiny red light blinked in one corner. A locator — no wonder they found me. It must have been triggered when I accessed the bank machine. I didn't want to destroy the card; I might still need it. And I couldn't disable the locator without the old man's finger.

From the gears, lengths of tubing, and chunks of metal strewn around the floor, the place must be an old appliance factory. I used our standard trick for disabling cards with locators. I found a scrap of thin metal sheeting, managed to break a piece off, and folded it around the card. It would be a pain to carry, but the metal would shield the signal until I could come up with something better.

I remembered the other card, the black one with the camera. It had turned black again, and I couldn't see any sign of a locator. I stuffed it, along with the one I stole from SecureCorp before, inside my makeshift shield just in case. I wasn't sure why I was keeping them. I guess I didn't want to toss anything I might be able to use later. I tied my bandanna around the shield so the cards wouldn't fall out.

Then I ran. Outside, in the distance, sirens rounded the building and gathered at the point where I'd escaped the drones. I headed for the corner farthest away and hunted for a way out. I heard the drones had some kind of smell sense like a dog, too, but so far no more seemed to have made it inside. I found a broken window, climbed out, and took off.

# FOURTEEN

..................................................

# THE CRYPTED PHONE

"No money, no gizmo," Richie's contact, a guy named 'Fatso', said.

He'd been showing me a crypted phone in an alcove in the darkest corner of another underground parkade on the outermost edge of the Quarters. The yellow light from the display on his comm-glasses danced over his forehead as he leaned against the rusted-out hulk of a vehicle. I didn't want to mention the four hundred dollars in my pack until I knew what to expect from him.

Fatso's appearance was totally at odds with his name. Skinny and emaciated, his withered, spider-like limbs were so thin that he wore a mechanical exoskeleton to hold himself up. It was a flashy one too, a carbon-filament job that must have cost a fortune. I'd seen his condition before. It was yet another of the wonderful side-effects of the Appraisal that happened one in every couple of million cases. Because of his condition his HUD didn't work properly — hence the comm-glasses. There was only one way somebody like him could get enough money to get their hands on gear like that — by screwing over people like me.

It occurred to me that I was going to be spending a lot of time with guys like Fatso, now that I was a fugitive. In the Lost Souls we knew a few tricks; these guys knew a lot more: how to get around without being seen, ways of encrypting and scrambling net accesses so that the broadcast's location couldn't be determined. They also knew a lot about helping themselves to stuff that belonged to other people.

But I needed the phone. To find out what was going on, I had to hook up to the deep net, and there was no legal way to do that without the connection being monitored and, eventually, my ID and location given away. But like everybody, Fatso was only interested in money.

"I've got a MoneyAll card," I said.

"Is it yours?"

I looked at the ground.

"If it's hot, it's worse than nothin'."

He stuffed the phone in the pocket of his coat and turned to leave.

"Wait," I finally said. "I've got cash."

He turned back. "How much?"

"Four hundred."

He stared at me, probably trying to decide whether he could jump me and take it. It looked like he decided against that.

Instead he just said: "Not enough."

"How much more do I need?"

"Four hundred might do for a down-payment," he laughed, as he turned away again.

"It's an emergency," I said to his back.

"Not for me," he said over his shoulder as he strolled toward the exit, the joints of his exoskeleton clicking faintly as he moved.

"Look, I'll sign an IOU or something," I called after him. "I gotta figure out what's going on. They're saying I'm dead."

Fatso stopped in mid-step. He turned back to face me.

"You're dead?" he said.

I nodded.

I took a step toward him. "I know we're not friends or nothin', but it took a lot for me to escape. Two people died trying to help me. I don't—"

"Hold it," Fatso said.

He reached up and pressed a button on his comm-glasses. His eyelids fluttered like he was having some kind of fit while he accessed the net.

"Wow, you *are* dead," he said.

"I told you..."

The eerie light from his glasses scuttled across his eyelids like a crawling caterpillar. A thin smile formed on his lips.

"What are you doing?" I said.

"Nothin'."

"You called somebody."

"Bullshit."

I turned to run. He tried to block me, skipping into my path like a spider and extending his arms like metal pincers. I jumped aside and managed to skirt around him. The tricked-out performance of his exoskeleton gave him a huge speed advantage. There was no way I could

96

hope to outrun him. Again, sirens wailed in the distance. He easily caught up with me.

I noticed that he was careful to never turn his back to me, and when I took a good look at his suit I figured out why. A thin bundle of wires, almost hidden but accessible if you approached from the right angle, ran from his hips to a single filament up his back. As he reached to grab me I jumped sideways, dove to the ground between his legs, and reached up under him.

He twisted around so fast I couldn't believe it, but not before I'd curled my right index finger around the exposed section of his wiring harness. I screamed, as searing pain shot through my finger, but something gave, and his legs started twitching grotesquely beneath him. He staggered in place, legs spasming, unable to move. I took off as fast as I could down the alley.

"Get back here," he screamed. "They're gonna get you anyway. Might as well let me make a buck off it."

I stopped. The sirens were getting closer. There wasn't much time. I needed the phone. I rushed back toward him.

"That's more like it," he laughed.

He lifted his pincer-like arms to grab me. I jumped out of the way. His legs were still convulsing and he couldn't keep up. I reached down into his coat pocket. He saw what I was doing.

"Get out of there!" he screamed.

I grabbed the phone and held on. He wrapped a vibrating arm around my head. Even with the damage he was incredibly strong. I stomped as hard as I could on his sandaled foot.

He screamed and let go. "You broke my foot you little shit!"

The sirens were around the next corner. I reached down with my free hand, grabbed his left ankle, and pulled as hard as I could. The foot lifted, and Fatso started to sway. I jumped out of the way as he crashed to the ground. I took off. He lay there, thrashing like he was having a seizure.

"Get back here!" he screamed. "Help me! I'm gonna get you, you bastard!"

I flew out of the parkade. A SecureCorp squad car passed me but I was hidden in the shadows.

In our old Cam-surfing game, nobody was actually looking for us. Cameras randomly picked up stuff all the time, but the crime detection algorithms weren't that accurate, and rumour was that normally not many of the camera feeds had anybody actually watching them.

Now, my gut told me there'd be an army of eyes scouring every camera. I couldn't afford to be seen. It was slow navigating through the camera footprints, but I've done it enough times. I felt safe on that score. When we played the game, there was always some kind of time element involved. Now I could take as much time as I wanted, so in theory I should be able to Cam-surf indefinitely. I traveled for about half an hour, to the deepest reaches of the Quarters, desperate for a place to hide.

I was exhausted, about to give up and just collapse in a corner somewhere, when I spotted an abandoned car factory. I prowled around for about ten minutes before I found a loose panel I could break open to get in. It was still night; this deep in the Quarters there were no streetlights — even outside you could barely see where you were going.

Inside, it was black as a cave, but after a few minutes my eyes adjusted well enough to navigate. I had to pick my way over the piles of debris on the floor, terrified of making any noise. I reached what looked like the factory floor. The skeletal remnants of the construction robots cut into the darkness. I couldn't be sure there was nobody there. The only sounds were the scurrying of rats up and down the hallways.

I could make out a room off to the east side, and I headed for it. It looked like it had once been some kind of office. The outside wall had a shattered plate-glass window. Inside was an overturned desk, half-demolished. Somebody had already scavenged it for sellable metal.

A couple of chairs lay in one corner. I grabbed a plastic one that would be less likely to be infested, stood it up, sat on it, and pulled out the phone.

The crypted phones foiled the SecureCorp location software by randomly switching between cell towers all over the city. They never stayed with any one station for more than a few microseconds, so there was no way for the software to triangulate a position. They also encrypted all messages so they couldn't be read from outside.

What they couldn't do was hide what information you were trying to access. Since any information SecureCorp was worried about was flagged and would send an alarm somewhere when anybody tried to access it, I still had to be careful about where I surfed. I was paranoid that doing a search on Vita Aeterna would light up a bunch of security indicators somewhere. It was probably a search term that almost no-body but me would use. I had a feeling I wouldn't come up with any-thing anyway.

In fact, I wondered what I *could* access without triggering some kind of response. In the end, I decided I had no choice but to trust that the phone was secure. Like I expected, there was nothing on Vita Aeterna. I did some research on my Uncle Zack. Officially, he died in an accident with a RoboTaxi. I'd been right before. He was sixteen, the same age I was supposed to have 'died'. I searched for Dr. Charles Knowles, got a slew of results, and sifted through some of them. Chuck was a mid-level drone at the Appraisal section of MediCorp.

I opened my eyes wide when I read one line in Chuck's list of roles: *Special Liaison to the CCE*.

It was insulting that an asshole like Chuck would have any connec-tion with the CCE. I searched for a picture of Chuck and found one. There he was — same smarmy, arrogant sneer on his face. I thought about Walter and wanted to reach in and wrap my fingers around Chuck's neck. He'd gotten his, anyway.

I poured through the web chatter for any news of Cindy. It was sketchy, but from what I could find, she'd OD'd on some kind of street pain-killer, during the time I'd been held prisoner at the clinic. They tried to say it was an accident, but I knew her better than that. I clamped my eyes shut. I hadn't been there to help her or comfort her. She'd died alone, not knowing where I was, probably thinking I was dead.

On top of all this I was still trying to deal with my Appraisal. All this had gone down right after I'd gotten it. It had to have something to do with that. But what did my dad mean? What did *he* know about it? The image of his body smashing through the window and onto the pavement resurfaced, and suddenly I was crying. It was like the tears just flowed out of me spontaneously.

Dad and I had never been close. In fact, I always thought he hated me, or at best didn't give a shit. Now he'd given his life for me — the second of two people to do that in the past few days. It was all too much.

I hung my head and cried until there were no more tears left. I didn't even care if anyone was around to hear. I cried for my dad, cried for Cindy, cried for Walter, cried for all the people who'd been screwed by the Appraisal. I cried and cried, then collapsed from exhaustion on the filthy concrete floor.

# FIFTEEN

........................................................

# INTO THE UNKNOWN

When I opened my eyes the next morning it took me a while to re-member where I was. I blinked my eyes and glanced around. I was still lying on the floor of the office where I'd passed out. For a few seconds I dared to imagine it was all a bad dream. Then reality came rushing back.

I sat up and rubbed my back and my eyes, and tried to piece to-gether all that had happened. My dad had been so panicked about Vita Aeterna. I guessed that it was some kind of organization. I figured the first thing I had to do was find out for sure. But even before that, I needed food and water, and I needed a safer place to hide.

I got ready to move. It was a pain carrying around the folded chunk of metal that shielded the cards. I decided to look for something bet-ter. Even in daylight the inside of this place was gloomy, but I could see well enough to have a look around. I'd been lucky so far; I hadn't seen another soul. Still I tried to step lightly through the dust and de-bris in the hallways.

In the southeast corner, I found a room that looked like some kind of electrical repair shop. Workbenches lined three of the walls, and smashed circuit-boards and pieces of broken equipment were lying around. I sifted through some of the junk and hit pay dirt — a conductive bag used for holding static sensitive parts. I'd seen them before in the computer shops in the Corp Ring.

It was just a little larger than the cards and flexible, like an ordinary plastic bag. I checked the bag for holes, brushed the dust off a nearby stool, sat down at one of the benches, and opened my metal shield just enough to get the bag in. There was no sign of a light on the MoneyAll card, so it wasn't getting to the outside.

I slid the bag over all three cards and folded the top over. Then I pulled the metal shield away, ready to put it back if the MoneyAll lit up. Nothing happened. I smiled. For the first time since my escape, something had gone right.

Holding up the transparent bag, I examined the black card I'd taken from Cindy's dad, and my heart just about stopped. It had turned a deep blue, almost ultra-violet. I didn't have the owner's finger to open it up, so I had no way of figuring out what it was. Part of me wished I'd pulled a 'Walter' and taken the finger with me, but I don't think I had the stomach for that — not yet, anyway.

Worse still, the ultra-violet card now seemed to be stuck to the SecureCorp card I stole Cam-surfing, which now had a line of moving light flashing up and down one side.

Shit! They were talking to each other. I had no idea what they were saying, but there was no way it was good. I kept the bag sealed, but worked the two cards around and gripped them, trying to pry them apart. No way — they'd somehow melded together. Travis talked about this 'nanotechnology' that made stuff like this possible, but I'd never seen it.

The joined cards were a bit thicker than a normal card, and I could still see a thin seam between them, but they were now a single unit. I guessed that by the time they finished whatever they were doing, the end result would look like a regular card. But — a card that did what?

I was about to toss them in a dumpster some place and get as far away as possible, but when I pressed on the black/ultraviolet one the same butterfly logo I'd seen at Cindy's place swirled into view. I hadn't noticed before, but at the angle I was now holding the card it was clear - the wings of the stylized butterfly actually formed two letters — VA. I'd seen the logo before — on the SecureCorp card, and Chuck's smock... Then I realized why the letters seemed familiar — VA — Vita Aeterna. I decided to keep them.

I found an elastic band and wrapped it around the bag, to make sure it couldn't fall open accidentally. Now I could tuck the cards, inside their protective bag, into my pack. I doubted if I could ever use the MoneyAll card again, but kept it, just in case. As if to remind me of the situation, I heard another siren in the distance, heading my way. It wasn't safe for me in the Quarters.

I found a regular plastic bag, stuffed the four hundred into it, then stuck it in my shoe. I switched off all the messaging functions of my HUD. From now on, the only way I'd communicate was with the crypted phone. I confirmed that the phone was still in my pack and headed out, boarding and Cam-surfing northeast.

There was only one place I might have a chance of escaping my pursuers. When I hit the farthest edge of Tintown, for the first time in my life, I kept going.

# SIXTEEN

......................................................

# BENNY

There's no distinct boundary between the Quarters and the Dregs. The garbage just gets deeper, the streets are more broken down, and the atmosphere is more desperate. My plan was to venture a little way in — far enough to be out of sight of SecureCorp, but close enough to dash back to the Quarters if things got too rough.

From what I'd heard, the Dregs was basically empty, so there were fewer cameras, and hardly any SecureCorp presence. It was probably as dangerous as everybody says, but it was also the place I was least likely to get caught.

I pushed on, still heading northeast. The buildings I passed were crumbling: shards of glass lining the window openings like broken teeth, walls black with mildew, moss, and even plants sprouting from every available crack. Most were ancient skyscrapers, so many that the streets were in shadow, even though it was still morning.

My HUD picked up the occasional camera, but they were so far apart that Cam-surfing was a breeze. Good thing, because I couldn't use my board. My footsteps crunched on a fist-thick layer of dust, garbage, chunks of cement, and broken glass.

I had no idea where I was going, or what I was looking for. Right now, I just wanted a hiding place — somewhere I could take a breath and think about what to do. I headed down one of the main streets, sticking to the shadows.

I'd walked for about twenty minutes when I saw an orange glow spilling from around the next corner. I snuck along the wall toward it. When I got closer I could hear voices — at least two — both male. I crept up to the corner of the wall, leaned out, and poked my head around.

Two guys in rags were sitting around a fire they'd built on the sidewalk next to a skyscraper. A couple of broken wooden chairs — their fuel — lay on the ground beside them. They were both holding sticks over the fire with some kind of meat skewered on them. The savoury smell wafting over reminded me how hungry I was. I thought about how I could get some. Maybe if I just introduced myself...

I jumped when a third guy appeared around the corner behind them. I jerked back, and a chunk of the brick I was gripping broke off and thudded to the ground. One of the seated men lifted his head, saw me, and pointed. As he turned, his stick moved closer to the flames, and I lost interest in sharing — what was skewered on it was a rat. The two seated guys jumped up and dropped their sticks, and all three ran toward me.

I took off. They followed for a while, but soon they were staggering, not running. After a few minutes they gave up and I was alone. I decided I had to get to someplace inside. I kept going, on edge, ready

*107*

to run and hide at the first sight of danger. I was surprised to see an entire family – mother, father, kids, scurry into a doorway and slam the door as I rounded one corner. I saw kids and old people alone. Once or twice they saw me, but we both kept our distance.

I walked for an hour or so, until there were no more people around. It started to rain, hard. Rivulets formed in the dust and debris on the street. I watched for some kind of shelter, and spotted a dilapidated building that looked like a good prospect.

Like all the others I'd come across here, it was worse than any in the Quarters — filthy and surrounded by piles of debris. I found an entrance that had once been boarded-up, but the boards had been torn away and lay in a pile just inside. The open door made the place easy to get into, but raised the question — who removed the boards in the first place?

I took a chance and stepped inside. The interior was dark, but there was enough light to make out a hallway with doors off either side running ahead of me for about fifty meters. I was about to start down it when a voice behind me said:

"Hey, where do you think you're going?"

I froze, and turned to locate the speaker. Half in the shadows of a graffiti-plastered pillar on my left stood a guy in his early twenties (I think — let's face it, it's hard to know). He towered over me - my head barely reached his shoulder. He had a few days' stubble on his face, and he looked like he hadn't washed in at least that long. His brown hair stuck out wildly from his head. There was an ugly scar ten centimeters long beside his right temple, and his right eye seemed to wander.

He was wearing what I guess was once a business suit, like what the big-wigs in the Corps like to wear, but it was torn, tattered and filthy. The top buttons of his shirt were gone; he'd fastened the collar together with a safety pin. What was left of a necktie was wrapped around the collar. It looked like he'd tried to tie it properly, like the big-wigs, but he must not have known how, 'cause it was tied with a regular square knot. The tie was all torn and filthy too, and the bottom part was missing, like it had been ripped off by a wild animal.

He was trying to act tough, but when I looked closer I could see he was shaking.

"Can't you read?" he said. He nodded at a torn piece of cardboard tacked to the wall where I'd come in. "Rent — $2.00" was scrawled on it in a shaky hand.

"Rent?" I said. His eyes were wild and distant. He didn't look dangerous, but I was ready to run.

He gestured around at the junk, dust, broken furniture, and collapsing walls. "To use the offices."

I started to laugh, but stifled it when I looked at his face. He was dead serious. Instead I said, "So — what — you own this place?"

He straightened up and puffed out his chest. "I own all these places — the whole block. I'm a entrepreneur."

"Well, I haven't got two dollars," I said. I wasn't going to tell him about the money in my shoe.

He scowled and took a step toward me. "Then you're in big trouble."

"Look," I said, stepping away, "I didn't know this was your place. Maybe I should just take off."

I started to turn back toward the door. He moved closer. I spun around and put up my fists in case he came at me. He jumped back, startled.

"I don't want any trouble," I said. I put a hand on the door jamb and lifted one of my feet to step out.

"Wait," he called. I stopped and turned back.

His expression softened. "I'm havin' a special right now — first week for free."

He stepped away and gestured for me to come in. I was pretty desperate. I was hungry and exhausted. It was still raining, and I needed a place to hide. I introduced myself.

"I'm Benny," he said, shaking my hand.

Benny led me to his 'office', a filthy, debris-strewn room with the remains of a desk in one corner. What must once have been a computer sat on the desk, surrounded by rotting stacks of used paper. Several other pieces of junked equipment were scattered around. I couldn't make out what any of them were.

"This is my command center," Benny said. "This is where it all happens."

"What all happens?"

He shot me a look of annoyance. "My corporate empire," he gestured around him.

A government poster tacked to the back wall was all but blotted out with graffiti written with a black marker. The words 'Fuck You' were scrawled over a photo of President Foster, and comments like 'bastards' and 'go to Hell' surrounded it.

Benny noticed me looking at it. "You're not with them, are you?" He staggered back in fear and disgust.

I laughed. "Do I look like I'm with the government?"

He relaxed a little. He leaned forward and whispered. "They've got spies everywhere."

On another wall was a picture of Charles Wickham. The head of the CCE stood confidently in front of some fancy building, with his arms folded across his chest, the light from above reflecting from his silver buzz-cut, a confident sneer on his craggy face. That poster was untouched by graffiti and, unlike most of the room, looked like it was cleaned regularly. Benny was obviously a lot more positive about him.

"Someday, we're gonna kick some government ass," he said, nodding at the CCE poster as if Wickham and him were buds. "Someday soon."

The walls of the room were plastered with pages ripped out of magazines. I glanced at a few — all were either anti-government or pro-CCE.

For the first time I noticed that there was no HUD controller on his wrist. I studied the scar on his head and froze. The silver HUD access connector on his right temple was missing. He was the first person over five years old I'd ever seen that didn't have a HUD.

"What happened?" I asked, pointing at his scar.

"Those government bastards tried to brainwash me with their evil bullshit," he rubbed the scar like he was remembering something painful.

"But it's hooked into your optic nerve," I said. "How'd you get it out?"

"It's like a poisonous plant," his hand shook as he rubbed the scar again and screwed up his eyes. "You just dig in and pull it out by the roots."

I cringed. "That must have hurt."

"Made me blind in one eye," he said, "but it was worth it." His voice dropped to a whisper. "What do think I'm doin' here, anyway?"

I shrugged.

"I'm underground, stupid," he sneered. "I'm gathering intelligence. I'm like a... 'field operative'."

In one corner was a huge stack of old food packets. He noticed me eyeing them and handed one to me.

"I'll put this on your tab," he said.

I checked the expiry date. It had expired a month ago. The packets were vacuum-sealed, and technically didn't have to be refrigerated, but that was getting pretty old. Anyway, it's not like I had much choice. I ripped it open and scooped out the brown mash with my fingers. I might not starve now, but I might die of food poisoning. He threw in some stale crackers, which tasted like cardboard. We left the office and he showed me the remains of an old kitchen where there was a supply of water.

"I'm glad I ran into you," I said, feeling better, but wondering what would happen when the rotten food hit my system.

Benny was out there. It was a long-shot, but I figured I might as well see what he knew. "I'm looking for information on some people. An org—"

"Don't say any more," he whispered, putting a hand on my shoulder. "They might by listening."

112

"So, you know who I'm talking about?" I asked.

He narrowed his eyes and nodded. He drew me closer.

"What do you want to know about them?"

"Who they are," I said. "What they're after."

He laughed and shook his head. "What they're after — yeah — what they're after. That's a good one."

He turned and stared at the wall for a long time and didn't say a word.

Finally, he turned back and put his lips next to my ear.

"You're CCE, aren't you," he said. "This is a test — I know. You want to see how much I found out."

I played along. "I can't fool you. So how much *did* you find out?"

"I can do better than tell you about them," he whispered. "I can take you."

*What the hell?* I thought. *I'm not sure I want to go anywhere with this guy. Maybe I better give up and get out of here before he loses it completely.*

Too late. He grabbed my arm and started dragging me out of the room.

"Hey, forget about it," I said, trying to pull free. He seemed to have flipped into some kind of hypnotic state. "Hey, asshole!" I yelled. "Let me go! I changed my mind. I don't give a shit who they are."

He wasn't listening. He dragged me across the entire building and through a hole blasted in the wall at the opposite end. We headed down a filthy alley. It had almost stopped raining. He wasn't even trying to avoid the cameras. I looked around and realized that this deep in the Dregs there were almost none anyway, and the few I saw looked broken. I checked my HUD and it wasn't registering anything.

"There's no cameras?" I said.

He finally spoke. "Smashed 'em all. Nobody came back to fix 'em. Nobody ever comes around here."

I finally gave up and went along. We traveled a few blocks, then entered another abandoned building. We climbed a half-demolished set of stairs for three floors, headed down a hall littered with garbage, and turned right into what had once been an office. A gigantic hole had been smashed out of the inside wall. The center of the building was open, and you could look through the hole right down to the bottom floor. There had once been an atrium with a garden. Most of the plants had died. Some of the hardier vines had spread around to cover the walls.

Benny sat down near the hole and closed his eyes.

"What now?" I asked.

"We wait," he answered.

I thought about trying to get out of there. The guy was obviously unstable, but so far he'd been harmless. There was a chance that he might actually know something, or at least might lead me to somebody that did.

He sat there like some kind of Buddha statue. He wasn't going to say anything else. I figured I might as well wait. I thought of filling the time checking the crypted phone, but wasn't sure what he'd do if he knew I had it. I cleared some of the debris from a section of the floor, laid my pack down for a pillow, stretched out, and went to sleep.

I woke up. Somebody had a hand over my mouth and was shaking me. I opened my eyes and looked up. It was Benny. He put a finger to his lips. I nodded and he removed his hand. I sat up and rubbed my eyes. There were voices in the space down below. Benny leaned in close to my ear.

"They're here," he whispered. He pointed down toward the voices.

I moved closer to the hole in the wall to look down.

"Careful," he whispered. "Don't let them see you."

I leaned out just enough to see a small group in the atrium area, sitting in a circle, talking. It wasn't much light, and they were about fifty meters away, but I could see them well enough to tell they were homeless and dressed in rags, like Benny. I didn't know much about Vita Aeterna, but I figured it was pretty unlikely these guys were them.

Unlike Benny, they all had HUD controllers on their wrists. They were passing a bottle around, talking and laughing.

"This is them?" I whispered to Benny. "They look like a bunch of drunks on a bender."

Benny scowled at me, annoyed. "That's their cover. Don't you know anything?"

"So what are they doing here?"

"Lookin' for me," Benny sat up straight and smiled. "But they'll never find me."

I heard a noise toward the door behind us. A voice said, "I thought we told you not to come back here."

We turned to look. A guy was standing in the doorway with a gun in his hand. He was young, tall and thin, with a scruffy dark beard.

"It's my building," Benny said. "I can..."

"Cut the bullshit," the guy said. "We don't want to hear about it." He nodded at me. "Who's your little friend?"

I got to my feet. "I can speak for myself." I probably should have been more careful. He had the gun, but his attitude pissed me off.

He raised the gun and pointed it at me. "Well I can blow your head off if I feel like it, and nobody — including this bozo —" he nodded at Benny, "will give a shit." He cocked the firing mechanism. "Now, what are you doing here?"

I stepped back. "Name's Alex," I said, losing the attitude. "I've been living on the street." There was no way I was gonna tell him the truth.

"For how long?"

I winged it. "A few months."

He scanned me up and down. I realized that my clothes, which weren't anything special, weren't rags either.

"How come we've never seen you before?" he said.

"What?" I said. "I gotta come and announce myself to you guys whenever I'm around?"

He stepped forward and pressed his gun barrel against my forehead. "This is our turf, and yeah, you *better* come and ask permission to be in it." He sneered. "If you were living on the street you'd know that." He waved the gun toward the door. "Let's go."

"No!" Benny yelled.

"I wasn't inviting you," the guy sneered at him. "You can get lost."

"If I come down, he comes with me," I said.

"You're not in a position to bargain," the guy with the gun said. "Anyway, you should pick a better class to be loyal to."

116

# SEVENTEEN

..................................................

# THE GANG

We left Benny and navigated down the garbage-littered stairs to the bottom. The group didn't look any better close up. There were four guys, including my captor, who introduced himself as 'Tory', and three women. I guess it was party time. They were passing a bottle of something around, laughing and shouting. They were all dressed in rags, and they all had this gaunt look like the life had been sucked out of them.

They took my pack and the board strapped to my back. Tory held a gun on me while one of the others frisked me. The guy was so pissed he didn't notice the cards, which I'd moved to an inner pocket of my pants, and didn't find the money in my shoe. One of them pulled the crypted phone out of my pack and held it up, smiling. I moved to grab it, but Tory cocked the gun and pointed it at me. I stepped back.

"Take care of it," Tory said to the guy.

I watched as he stumbled off, hoping to see where he put it, but he went around a corner and I lost sight of him. Tory shoved me forward and told me to sit down with the others. After the big deal he'd made about taking me down there, nobody really seemed to care whether I was there or not, but they still wouldn't let me leave.

At first they didn't want to share their booze (which was okay with me), but as they got more bombed, they changed their minds. I wanted to keep my head straight and maybe make a run for it once the rest of them passed out or something, but they got suspicious when I kept turning down drinks, so I gave up and joined them.

I told them about my Cam-surfing, and there was talk of me joining them — like that was some kind of honour. Anyway, they said the head-man, Cash — the guy who'd end up making that decision, was off negotiating with the leader of another group.

I asked Tory about their gang.

"We help each other stay alive," he explained as they passed the bottle around. "We sneak into the Quarters, even the Corp Ring some-times, and steal enough to survive, like everybody else. We stay to-gether for protection. If SecureCorp catches any of us, we're dead."

"Everybody else?" I said. "I thought the Dregs were practically empty."

Tory laughed. "Empty? Who've you been listening to?" he nodded at the HUD controller on my wrist. "That?"

The others joined in laughing. I felt my face turning red. "Well, how else are you supposed to know what's going on?"

They all laughed again.

I explained how Benny and I had met. I didn't mention anything about looking for Vita Aeterna or Uncle Zack, or what happened to me.

After what happened with Fatso, I figured I should keep my mouth shut. They seemed to buy that I was just a regular street kid.

"Where'd you get the money for a crypted phone?" Tory sneered.

I looked at the floor. "I didn't. I stole it."

I looked up. They were all staring at me.

My eyes locked with Tory's for a few seconds. Finally he shrugged. "Anyway, who gives a shit. Cash'll find out what's up with you when he gets back. Have another drink."

About an hour later the leader, Cash, finally showed up. He looked pretty much like the rest, in his twenties (I guess), ragged and unwashed, but with a little more intelligent glint in his eye. As soon as the others saw him they quieted down. The bottle was almost empty anyway, but they shoved it under a jacket — like he wouldn't notice.

Cash took Tory, who I guess was sort of his right-hand man, aside and talked to him away from the others. Tory pointed at me a couple of times. Cash looked over at me and smiled. It gave me the creeps.

Finally, Cash and Tory both came over. I stood to face them.

Cash stuck his face in mine. "Who the fuck are you?"

I felt my body shaking but I didn't move. "What's it to you? I was just minding my own business. It was you guys—"

"You're in our territory — your business is our business," he said. He shoved me back on my heels. "Tory says you're supposed to have been livin' on the street for a few months."

"Yeah," I said. "So?"

He sneered. "You haven't been out here for more than a few days." He stared at my clothes. "What the hell are you up to?" He smiled again. "You told Tory your name was Alex."

I cringed. *Why the hell did I tell them my real name?* I thought. *He's heard about me.*

Cash nodded at Tory, who left and returned with a couple of the other guys that were sitting around.

"I gotta take off for a while," Cash said. "I got some people to talk to — figure out what to do with you."

The others rushed forward and grabbed me. I tried to break free but they had me pinned.

Cash turned and walked away. They dragged me to a small room nearby, threw me inside, and locked the door. I pounded on it for a while and screamed, but they all ignored me. I could see a shadow moving occasionally through the crack under the door — they'd left a guard outside.

I sat down on the bare concrete floor with my head in my hands. After all that had happened — and Walter and my father giving their lives for me to get free...

I studied the room, hunting for a way out. There was nothing. Even if I could break through the wall somehow the guard would hear and I'd be put somewhere else. The room was around the corner from where the main group were sitting, but I could still hear the noise from the drinking party getting louder. They must have gotten another bottle from someplace.

❈

Twenty minutes later the party was in full swing — lots of shouting and laughing. I'd given up on escape for now. I slid down against the back wall, hoping to get some sleep, but images kept swirling through my head: my dad, Walter, Richie, the Lost Souls, Cindy...

I clamped my eyes shut and tried to drive the reality out of my mind. Cindy — I guess I always knew our relationship was doomed, even if all this hadn't happened, but I thought at least she would be out there somewhere — a little patch of beauty and love in a world that didn't have much of either. That alone would have made my life a little easier to take. But now...

I looked up when the guard outside the door made a funny noise. It was like he was about to yell but got cut short. There was a series of thumps on the other side of the door. The guard grunted and there was a snapping sound.

A few seconds later there was the tinkling of a set of keys. The door opened, and a figure filled the entire doorway.

It was Benny.

"We gotta get out of here," he said.

"You got that right," I agreed, smiling. "I've never been so happy to see somebody."

Benny stepped aside and I saw the crumpled body of the guard lying motionless on the floor beside the door, his neck broken.

*Mental note,* I thought. *Benny isn't so harmless after all.*

We snuck toward a door at the far corner of the atrium, away from the sound of the partiers.

We were almost there when a guy rounded the corner, unzipping his fly. He looked up and spotted us. Benny moved to run after him.

I grabbed his arm. "You'll never catch him in time — we better move."

The guy started yelling and we started running. I glanced back over my shoulder. Tory appeared, running after us with the gun in his hand. He raised it and fired. He was too far away to hit anything.

Benny and I tore through the doorway. He didn't even slow down as we switched direction into a corridor full of debris. I guess he knew this place inside-out. There was still yelling behind us, but it was farther away. After a half-dozen twists and turns we made it to a hallway that looked like it led outside. The yelling was moving away — our pursuers had taken a wrong turn.

We reached a door, but it was boarded up from the other side. Benny stepped back and kicked at it, and a couple of the boards broke, leaving an opening. We squeezed through and we were outside. We took off, trying to put as much distance as possible between us and the gang.

"Thanks a lot, man," I whispered when we finally stopped for a breather.

"You make sure you tell them about me," Benny said.

"What?"

He lowered his voice to a whisper. "The CCE — you'll tell them how I helped you."

I'd almost forgotten about that. "Yeah — yeah, sure I'll tell them. You did good."

I felt like a jerk playing him like that, but I wasn't sure what he'd do if I told him the truth. We walked for another twenty minutes. Finally he stopped and pulled a couple of stray pieces of junk away from the wall of an abandoned building. There was an opening behind them. He may be unhinged but he knows this place. We crawled in, then he reached through and pulled it all back in to cover the hole. We were in another hallway. We headed down it to another room full of debris, and sat down in a clear space on the floor.

"What did I tell you?" Benny said. "Those guys are a menace."

At first I wasn't clear what he meant. In all the confusion, I'd forgotten why we hooked up with them in the first place.

"Thanks for getting me away from them," I said, "but those aren't the guys I'm looking for."

Benny looked nervous. "So — who?"

I hesitated, not sure how he'd react.

"They're called 'Vita Aeterna'," I finally said. "Heard of them?"

His face was blank. He shook his head. He genuinely didn't seem to know anything about them. I pushed on.

"I'm also looking for my Uncle Zack," I said. "He disappeared a long time ago — before I was born."

He stared at me. "Disappeared?"

"I thought he was dead, but now I'm not so sure."

Benny's body stiffened. "Could be Dead Shift," he said. "What do you want with Dead Shift?"

"Dead Shift?" I said.

"I see them sometimes," he said. "They call them that because they're all supposed to be dead — whatever that means."

123

"Do you know where I can find them?"

He looked at the floor and wrung his hands together. "You don't want to find those guys."

I couldn't help thinking that somewhere buried within the tangled web of his mind he had the information I was looking for.

"Why not?" I asked.

He rubbed the scar on his right temple. "I don't want to talk about that." For a second I thought he was going to make a run for it. He was shaking. "Who are you, anyway?" he asked, rocking back and forth, suddenly suspicious.

"Relax," I said. "You can trust me. I'm just doing research."

He settled down a bit.

"You don't have to get involved," I said. "But do you know anybody that might know where I can find this Dead Shift?"

For a few seconds he was silent.

"You'd really be helping us out," I said, hinting that the CCE were behind it all.

He perked up at that, eager to help.

He leaned in close to me and whispered. "There's these guys called 'The Rebels'. They're trying to get rid of the government." He said the word 'government' like he was biting off something that tasted bad. "I tried to join them once..."

He looked down again at the floor. I figured it was best not to ask what happened.

"They might know," he continued. "I heard sometimes they talk to the Dead Shift."

"Can you take me to meet with these Rebels?"

He started fidgeting again. "Don't want to go there." He got up and paced back and forth in front of me.

"You don't have to come," I said. "Just tell me where I can find them."

He started whispering to himself, clenching and unclenching his fists: "No, I won't fail — I won't! I'll measure up!"

He turned to face me. "They move all over. There's a couple of places I've seen them before. I'll take you."

# EIGHTEEN

....................................................

# THE REBELS

There was no further sign of the gang. I was exhausted. Benny wasn't in any hurry to start our mission, so when I suggested we wait until morning, he agreed. There was a torn-up mattress on the floor beside us. Benny insisted that I take it. He slept on the floor, curled up like a dog at my feet.

In the early morning of the next day we headed out. Benny led me through yet another maze of alleys. It was daytime, but, surrounded by masses of skyscrapers, we were always in the shadows. Every one of them looked abandoned.

We walked for more than an hour, heading northwest. This was like another city I didn't even know existed. There was nothing here — no people, no vehicles, no cameras. Just crumbling ruins and piles of garbage. I thought we had it bad where I lived, but this was something else. I wondered at all the work that went into the buildings towering over us. Now they'd been left to rot.

We passed through a gigantic square with a pile of rubble that looked like it was once a fountain. Benny was starting to look nervous.

"Why don't you wait here," I said, trying to let him off the hook. "It's better if I go to meet them alone. Just give me the directions."

He ignored me and kept moving. A couple of hours later we reached another huge open square with an ancient-looking stone building in the center. I'd never seen anything like it. It had pointed spires that swept up from the roof, and what was left of a big round window with shards of coloured glass in some kind of pattern. There was a big cross at the front — a church. It looked ridiculously out of place in the midst of all the giant skyscrapers. Benny stopped. He was petrified.

"Is this the place?" I asked him. "This is where you last saw the Rebels?"

He nodded, staring at the building like it was going to fall on him.

"In there?" I asked, gesturing at the church.

He nodded again, faintly. I turned and headed for it.

I looked over my shoulder. Benny was still hanging back.

I stopped and called to him. "You coming?"

He finally stepped toward me. It was like he was dragging himself forward. I turned back and continued walking.

We reached the massive archway at the front. The wooden doors, which looked like they'd originally had some kind of picture carved into them, were in shreds. I walked inside. There were lots of holes in the walls, and even though there wasn't much light outside I could see well enough. I looked behind me. Benny was stuck at the front door, mumbling to himself — I guess trying to talk himself into coming in.

I turned back. I was standing in a gigantic open space. The floor was made of wooden boards. The ground underneath must have buckled, because the floor bulged up in the middle, like a huge pimple. A lot of it had been ripped up, probably for firewood. Here and there were scattered what was left of some benches. Ahead of me, at the far end of the building, was a maze of tubes of all different sizes, some round, some — the biggest ones — square.

I hiked over the bulge in the middle, avoiding the numerous holes in the floor, and reached the jumble of tubing. Stuffed into the center of the back wall, almost buried by the tubing and other junk, was what was left of a keyboard, like for a piano.

"A pipe organ," I whispered to myself. I'd heard of them, and seen pictures, but I'd never seen one for real.

I turned and looked back. Benny was standing on the highest point of the floor, like he was at the top of a hill. He was staring down at me. He took one step forward. I heard a board creak — but it didn't come from him — and it didn't come from me.

A voice came through my HUD, "Alex Barret, you need to come with us."

"Benny, you bastard!" I yelled up at him.

"What?" he said. He turned and looked back. "I didn't do anything, I swear," he yelled back.

A shot echoed through the building. Benny collapsed and slowly rolled down the incline of the floor in my direction. He came to a stop almost at my feet. A swarm of soldiers appeared on the floor/hill above us, their weapons drawn. From their ink-black business suits, like what the big-wigs wear only made out of bullet proof fabric, their black ties, and the blood-red stripe across each of their chests, it was clear who they were.

SecureCorp.

Benny started to push himself up.

"Stay down!" I whispered to him.

They rushed down the slope toward me. There was nothing I could do. When they reached me, a soldier moved to either side and gripped each of my arms.

The leader, a weathered, skinny guy with a pock-marked face, stood in front of me, staring. Beside him stood Cash, the leader of the gang who'd held me prisoner. A thin smile curled up on his lip.

"Didn't I tell you, Weber?" Cash turned to the pock-marked guy. "I told you I could get him back. Where else was he gonna go?"

"Help my friend," I said, nodding at Benny.

Cash sneered at me, then stepped over and kicked Benny in the head. Weber's expression didn't register anything. He and the others ignored Benny and led me out the way I'd come. I fought to get free but there were too many of them.

We marched out the front archway and into the relative light of the outdoors.

"I haven't done anything," I protested, struggling against the hands gripping me.

"Shut up," Weber said, without emotion.

The group turned and headed south, toward the Quarters, dragging me with them.

"Wait," Cash said, grabbing Weber's shoulder.

Weber turned his head and glared down at Cash's hand, like it had contaminated his uniform. He held up his own hand and everybody stopped.

Cash saw the look and removed the offending hand. "I found him," Cash said, "like I promised. Now let's have my reward."

Cash held his hand out.

Weber turned to face him. He didn't say a word. In one fluid movement, he hauled a gun from the holster at his belt and shot Cash point-blank in the chest. Shock registered on the gangster's face as he stared down at the gushing wound. Then he toppled over and was still.

"Let's get out of this shit-hole," Weber said.

He holstered his gun, waved his hand again, and we continued marching, like nothing had happened, leaving Cash's lifeless corpse in the street.

We marched through the rubble and shadows. I hung my head and trudged along, devastated. After all I'd been through — it was all over. And Benny had probably died trying to help me — another life on my head.

About ten minutes later, we'd just entered the junction of a cross-alley when there was the pop of a gunshot and the front man in our group went down. The SecureCorp soldiers rushed for cover as more shots took out several others near the front.

Weber motioned to the two guys holding me, then ran off directing the others as a gun battle went on. My captors dragged me behind what was left of a dumpster. All around us the firefight raged, shouts, screams, running boots, gunfire.

After a few minutes I heard grunts on either side of me and my two guards collapsed to the ground, blood pooling beneath them. I gazed around in panic, expecting to be next. Nothing happened. I was about to take off when a new pair of arms grabbed me and started dragging me backwards.

I finally got a look at my new captors. They were rough, like the gang I'd met before, but their clothes were clean and they had determined looks on their faces.

"Stay quiet," one of them whispered. "We're on your side."

The gunfire echoed into the distance as they led me down another series of alleys. We finally stopped, and one of my new captors talked to somebody on his HUD. He nodded to his partner.

"Who are you guys?" I said.

"You'll find out soon enough," one of them said. "For now, keep it down. We're not out of danger yet."

I could still hear gunfire, but it was sporadic. Then it stopped altogether. After about half an hour we stopped in front of a side door for one of the abandoned skyscrapers. The guy in front pulled out a key, unlocked it, and we went through. Inside was a massive open space. Far in the distance were a few doors to what looked like offices.

The guy holding me nodded to his right. We twisted and turned down a bunch of hallways until we finally reached another large empty space. All the debris had been cleared out, and there were cots positioned against the walls.

In one corner were several desks and chairs. We sat down on a couple of the chairs and waited.

After a few minutes, another group came into the room. I was shocked to see that two of them were holding up Benny, who was limping and looked pretty badly injured, but was alive. They led him to one of the cots and laid him down.

Before the guards could stop me, I rushed over. A woman was bending over him.

I grabbed her arm. "What are you doing!"

"I'm trying to save your friend's life," she answered over her shoulder.

They'd gone to the trouble of bringing him back here, so I assumed she was telling the truth. I stared down at Benny. He was unconscious. Blood from a wound in his side was soaking into the cot. The woman cut away Benny's shirt. The wound was nasty and still bleeding a lot.

"Is he going to live?" I asked.

"If I can stop the bleeding," the woman said. "You should leave me to it — there's nothing you can do. I'll come and let you know what happens."

"Don't worry," a familiar voice came from behind me. A hand was placed on my shoulder. "She'll take good care of your friend."

I jumped and turned. I couldn't believe what I was seeing.

# NINETEEN

..................................................

# REUNION

Standing beside me, like some ghost out of the past, was my old co-op school teacher, Travis. I stood there with my mouth open. He smiled, enjoying my confusion.

"Surprised?" he said.

"I figured you were dead or something," I said.

"Not yet," he laughed.

I was speechless, still trying to process what was happening.

"What are you–" I finally blurted out.

"Doing here?" he interrupted me.

He smiled. "My views were filtering up and starting to piss off some powerful people. I was already affiliated with this group part-time. It would have been full-time if it wasn't for Laura." I raised an eyebrow. "My daughter," he said, and I nodded. "The previous Rebel leader was killed during a raid." Travis closed his eyes for a second, remembering. "Meanwhile, I got wind that SecureCorp was planning to make me disappear. I beat them to it and went underground."

"You always were paranoid, man," I laughed. "Since when do they care what you say if you're not breaking the law? It's a free country."

He gave me this annoying sort of patronizing look. I told him all that had happened. He shook his head slowly as I described my Appraisal and the aftermath.

"We heard about you," he said when I was finished. "We've been keeping an eye out. Lucky we found you before they got you out of the Dregs. I'll tell you one thing. They really want you bad."

"But why?" I said. "What did I do?"

He motioned with one hand, and led me to a room with a few boxes and a large table in the middle.

"Let me guess," I said as we walked through the door. "You guys are planning to overthrow the government or something."

It was his turn to smile. "Not quite."

He nodded toward a couple of the boxes. We went over and sat down on them. We were alone. I was so glad I'd run into him. Maybe finally someone could tell me what was going on.

"What the hell's the deal with my Appraisal?" I asked. "Nobody's even told me what it is. There's something weird happening. According to my friend Richie, I'm supposed to be dead."

A light seemed to go on behind Travis's eyes, then it disappeared.

"Does that mean something to you?" I said.

Something changed in his expression. He shook his head. "I don't know exactly what they want with you," he said, "but I can guess. I told you at school how they were looking for people who respond to Appraisal in a certain way."

I nodded.

"My guess is that your Appraisal is unusually high," he said. "They want to study you. We've seen this scenario before, but judging by how desperate they are to get you back, you must be a special case."

"My dad said something about Vita Aeterna. I think it's some kind of organization. Have you heard of them?"

Travis' eyebrows came together. "Don't know them. I can make some inquiries..."

"My dad also told me I should find my Uncle Zack, but I don't understand what he was talking about. Uncle Zack died forty years ago."

Again, a flash of something crossed Travis' face.

"He died?" he asked. "How did that happen?"

"They say he fell hitching a ride on a RoboTaxi," I answered. I mentioned the Dead Shift, and there was another flash of recognition behind his eyes.

"What's going on?" I asked. "And who's this 'they' you keep talking about?"

The woman that had been taking care of Benny appeared at the door. She smiled over at me. "Your friend is going to be okay."

I relaxed a little — one less person dying on my account.

Travis gestured for her to join us. "This is Patricia Treadwell," he said. "She's our doctor-in-residence. She was one of the top doctors in the Corp Ring before she got fed up and joined our cause."

Treadwell offered her hand and I shook it.

She gestured with her head back to where she'd been treating Benny. "We've stitched him up — he's resting. I'd leave him for now — you should be able to talk to him later."

"G...Great, thanks," I said.

135

"We'll continue our talk later," Travis said to me. "First, we'll find you a place to sleep."

We got up and Travis took me in to meet the others.

"What do we want with him?" One of the men, a bearded, intense-looking guy named Rolf, complained after Travis had introduced me. "We're just drawing attention to ourselves for nothing. We don't know anything about him — he'll give us up."

I opened my mouth to say something, but Travis put a hand on my shoulder. He looked at me and shook his head.

"I know him," Travis said to Rolf. "And I don't want anything bad to happen to him. Yes, it's a risk, but if SecureCorp is so hot to get him, keeping him out of their hands is probably a good idea."

I tensed. Not all the Rebels were happy I was here.

"I feel a lot better," Benny said a few hours later, as I knelt beside the cot he was lying on. "I'm just kinda tired."

"You're a tough guy." I smiled at him. "It takes more than a SecureCorp bullet to take you out."

"But why are SecureCorp after you?" he asked. "It's some kind of test, right?"

I hesitated. I didn't know how to answer him. I wasn't really sure myself. "Yeah, something like that," I finally said.

"You'll tell them?" he said.

"What?"

He winced in pain as he leaned over and whispered. "You know, *them* — you'll tell them I took a bullet."

"Yeah." I patted his shoulder. "I'll tell them."

The run-in with Rolf had made me edgy. I leaned in and whispered. "What do you know about these guys? Can we trust them?"

"I don't know," he answered. "They hate the government, so they should be okay. But I heard them say something bad about..." He leaned closer and mouthed the words, 'Mister Wickham'.

"I know the leader, Travis," I said. "He's a good guy, but I didn't know about any of this..." I gestured around the room with my head. "Makes me wonder what else I don't know about. It's too bad. I had a crypted phone in my backpack that I could have used to do some research, but that asshole gang took it."

"I could..." Benny started to say. He put out his hands and tried to push himself up.

I stopped him. "You're not doing anything right now. Just get some rest."

Benny lay back down and closed his eyes. Dr. Treadwell was examining another patient in a far corner. She stood up and turned to leave. I caught up with her as she was going out the door. I asked her about Benny.

"He's lost a lot of blood," she said as we walked, "but the wound was pretty superficial. He should be okay once his stitches heal."

I stared at her. "Did you really quit working for the Corps to be here?"

She smiled. "I'm not the only one. It happens more often than you might think."

137

"What do you mean?"

She nodded toward the main work area. "You don't know about Travis?"

I shook my head.

"Travis was once a senior programmer at InfoCorp. He gave it all up, to join our cause."

"What!" I turned and stared where she'd been looking. "No way — nobody would do that."

Dr. Treadwell smiled. "You'd be surprised at what people will sacrifice for what they believe in."

She turned and walked away. My head was spinning. I thought about it — the things Travis knew about, the mystery of where he'd come from. It seemed impossible but...

I couldn't help thinking about Travis differently after what she'd said. I realized that I was exhausted. I headed for the cot he'd arranged for me, not far from Benny. As soon as I lay down I passed out.

I woke with a hand shaking me. "Alex," a voice said. "Alex, wake up." I sat bolt upright and stared around in confusion. Then I remembered where I was. Light was pouring through a nearby window — it was morning. I looked over. The voice belonged to Travis. His hand was on my shoulder.

"Your friend," he said, his expression grave. "He's disappeared."

# TWENTY

..........................................................

# REAPPEARANCE

It didn't seem possible that Benny could sneak away from this place. I didn't think he could even walk.

"Somehow he got past the guards," Travis said. "It would be impossible for anybody to break in unnoticed, but they're not watching as closely for people leaving. His wound was pretty severe. We all thought he was too injured to go anywhere. Obviously that's not true."

"Benny might be a bit slow," I said, "but I can't believe how well he knows these streets. If he's gone, we'll never find him."

"He's put all of our lives in danger," Travis said. "We're going to have to move. They're packing the stuff up as we speak."

"What?" I said. "Because of Benny? He'd never tell."

"We can't afford to take a chance."

"I'm sorry," I said, hanging my head.

"It was my decision to rescue him," Travis said. "It's me that's responsible. Anyway, moving's not that big a deal. We've done it so often we've got it down to a science."

Travis didn't seem like the same easy-going eccentric who'd taught me at the co-op school. Now he had an angry edge, something I'd never seen before. I had a fleeting thought that the Rebels might have gotten rid of Benny, then made up the story about him leaving. But then why save him in the first place? And why move if he wasn't a threat? I put the idea out of my head. Anyway, I had no way of finding him. If he'd wanted me to know where he was going he would have told me.

After a wash and a quick breakfast of some kind of mashed grain, I followed Travis over to a group that was packing up the sleeping area. They were folding up the cots, which were made from thick canvas strung across hinged tubular frames, and piling them on a wheeled cart.

"You can give them a hand," Travis said, gesturing at the group.

I nodded and joined them, collapsing the nearest cot and carrying it over. Nearby was a young girl, probably about my age. She had light brown skin and dark, curly hair tied back in a ponytail. Something about her was familiar. She looked up, caught me eyeing her and smiled. I felt my cheeks flush. I looked away and concentrated on cot folding.

Fifteen minutes later all the cots were ready. A couple of guys tied them down on the carts and wheeled them away. The guy in charge directed us to another room, to start packing up the cooking utensils. I tensed when the girl moved up to walk beside me.

"You're Alex, aren't you," she said.

I looked up, shocked. "Do I know you?"

She laughed and her face lit up. "Sort of. I came to a few of your classes at the co-op school."

I thought back. I couldn't remember. Finally it came to me — a skinny kid that showed up for class a couple of times. But she didn't look like this...

Suddenly I realized who she was. "You're Travis' daughter."

She nodded. "I'm Laura," she said, holding out her hand.

I shook it. Travis had never mentioned to anyone in class that she was his daughter, and I guess nobody asked. She'd only come a couple of times.

She had shining, dark eyes and a smile that overflowed with life. She was really cute, but I felt a stab of guilt even looking at another girl so soon after what happened to Cindy... Suddenly it all came rushing back and my throat tightened. I felt tears welling in my eyes. I looked away.

"Are you okay?" I heard Laura's voice, and snapped out of it.

"Yeah, I'm fine," I said, pulling myself together.

We headed for a door at the far end of the room.

"It must have been rough to go on the run like this," I said, fighting to take my mind off things.

She shrugged. "Yeah. I'm still sort of getting used to it. It's a hard life, but we've got no choice now."

I imagined what her life must have been like before, if what Dr. Treadwell had said was true. If she'd really gone from the luxury of the

Corp Ring to living in squalor and on the run, she didn't show any bitterness about it.

We split up again as the guy in charge directed us to different tasks.
I didn't see her again that day. I tried to focus on what was happening
with Travis and the rest of the Rebels. I asked Travis about trying to
find out if Uncle Zack was still alive.

"I'll get some of the tech-savvy guys to check into it," he said.
"While we're waiting, maybe you can help us out. We can always use
another man."

The move went pretty smoothly. Like Travis said, they had the process
down to a science. Our new digs were several hours away, in a monster building with a row of steps running up to a wide terrace, with big
stone pillars at the entrance. I guess they'd scouted out lots of potential hideouts ahead of time and picked one far enough away from the
one we'd been at. The building had running water, which was pretty
awesome.

Even with all the Rebels' experience, it had taken half a day to pack,
and another full day to complete the move. I felt like I was responsible
for it and all the disruption it had caused. I had no control over Benny,
but he'd been taken in along with me. Some of the Rebels were already down on me. This wouldn't help. I still felt guilty when I found
myself keeping an eye out for Laura, but anyway I hadn't seen her
since that first time.

A few days later we were settled in. I helped around the place, doing odd jobs. One day we were hauling some equipment up the front steps, which was pretty tiring work. During a break I stepped to one side to get my breath, and caught a movement out of the corner of my eye. I scanned the area. At first there was nothing. Then I saw it again, beside a building to the north. I glanced over at the guards on either side of the steps. They hadn't seen anything. I kept an eye out, careful not to let the guards see me. I didn't want to alert them until I knew what was going on.

Finally I saw it. Benny. He peeked out from the corner and waved. He was in a position where only I could see him. I took a chance and looked in his direction, nodding to let him know he'd gotten my attention.

*Tonight,* he mouthed the words, pointing at the north side of our new hideout. I nodded again, though I wasn't sure how I was going to swing it.

I'd been assigned a cot in a large room with a bunch of other guys. It was nothing fancy, but it beat sleeping in some alley waiting to get my head bashed in. But it made it hard to slip away. I wondered what Benny was up to. He was probably wise not to show his face back here after running off like that, but why did he leave in the first place? And now why was he back?

I decided there was no point in sneaking around. Late that night I just got up headed for the front door. A guard with a rifle was posted just outside of it.

I moved to push past him. He shoved his rifle out and blocked me.

"I'm going for a walk," I said.

143

"I can't allow that," the guard said.

I stepped back. "What do you mean? Am I a prisoner here or something?"

The guard hesitated. "It's a safety thing," he said. "It's dangerous out there."

I stared at him. I knew he was right. It was dangerous, but was that the only reason?

"I need to stretch my legs and get some fresh air," I said. "I won't go far."

He stood for a few seconds in the moonlight, studying me. "You can walk along the side of the building," he finally said, "but stay in sight."

I gave him one last look. At some point I was going to have to test whether I was free to leave, but not right now.

"Okay," I nodded, and started walking.

The guard moved out past the northeast corner so that he could watch me. I had nowhere to go anyway. I just headed down the wall, like he'd instructed. I wasn't sure how I was supposed to find Benny. I assumed he'd contact me somehow.

I walked right to the end, to the farthest corner, and turned to look back at the guard. He was still standing there, where I'd left him, nervously, with his rifle at the ready.

I stared into the blackness ahead of me, waiting. I respected Travis and the Rebels, but there was something else going on. I'd see some of them whispering to each other and stealing glances at me when they thought I wasn't looking. I kept bugging Travis about trying to find out more about Uncle Zack. He always claimed that they were working on it, but they didn't seem to be working very hard.

I glanced around, looking for Benny, trying not to be too obvious. There was the sound of a cough to my right. I froze. The space behind the building was in shadow even in the daytime, and now it was late at night — all was blackness.

"Hi," a voice whispered. A large shape stepped into a nearby patch of moonlight, behind the building, out of view of the guard.

It was Benny.

"Where have you been?" I whispered back. I made sure my back was to the guard so he wouldn't see my lips moving.

"Around," he said.

"Keep it down," I whispered. "They're watching me."

He reached into his inner jacket pocket. I couldn't see very well, but his shirt was torn open and it looked like he'd pulled out Dr. Treadwell's stitches and crudely sewn the wound back up himself.

"You're going to get an infection," I said, nodding at the wound. "You shouldn't be walking around like that."

"It's nothin'," he said. His hand emerged gripping a small rectangular shape.

"You said you wanted this," he said, holding up the object. It was my crypted phone.

"What!" I had to fight to keep my voice down.

He held the phone under the brightest part of the light beam. "It still works," he whispered. "I tried it."

"How the hell did you get it back?" I said.

"You'll tell them?" he said. "How I got it for you?"

He held it out. I stepped around the corner to take it. There were blotches of what looked like blood on it.

"That's great, Benny," I said. "But you shouldn't have done that. It's too dangerous." I gestured with my head back the way I'd come. "Come on, let's go in. I'll smooth things over with Travis and we'll get the doctor to look at you."

He drew back. "Don't like those guys."

"What's wrong with them?" I wasn't sure what they'd done that put him off. "They're trying to get rid of the government — that's good, isn't it?"

He hesitated.

"What's going on there?" the voice of the guard called out behind me. "Get back here. Are you talking to somebody? Who's there?"

I stuffed the phone under my shirt and stepped back around the corner where the guard could see me. He was walking in my direction.

"It's nothing," I called back, and tried to wave him off. He kept coming.

I turned my back on him again to talk to Benny. "Come back with me and I'll get Dr. Treadwell to sew you up again properly," I whispered. I glanced over, but he was gone.

# TWENTY-ONE

..................................................

# A DILEMMA

It was tough finding a hiding place for the phone. There was no 'private' space for anybody at the hideout. Travis might be okay, but I didn't trust some of the guys around him. I didn't want to tell them about the phone, and if I kept it on me someone would notice it sooner or later. I hid it behind a broken electrical panel in one of the storerooms. It wasn't that secure, but it was the only place I could think of.

The next morning there was another big meeting. I wasn't a fullfledged Rebel member, so I wasn't invited. The hideout was almost empty. I rescued the phone from its hiding place, found a deserted room, and checked it out. The battery was three-quarters drained. The phone had a solar panel, so it could be charged in sunlight, but I'd have to leave it out somewhere for at least a couple of hours.

I was about to check for messages when the phone vibrated in my hand. The ringer was muted but it was clear what was happening — I was getting a new message.

I tensed as I checked the display. Could it be one of Fatso's cronies? Or even Fatso himself? A disturbing thought surfaced in my head. The phone wasn't supposed to be traceable by SecureCorp, but what if Fatso had his own special way of tracing it? He was a crook, after all. Worse still, what if he'd contacted SecureCorp and was working with them to recapture me?

The screen showed a new entry. My hand shook as I pressed the button to display it.

*I talked to Richie,* it said.

My fingers whitened around the phone. Did another person get killed trying to help me?

*Who are you?* I typed.

*A friend,* the display returned.

*What did you do to him?* I typed.

*First, I need to be sure who you are,* the text returned. *Tell me — what's AMP mean to the Lost Souls?*

Everybody in the Lost Souls knew the place the message was referring to. AMP stood for 'Alternate Meeting Place' — an old furniture factory not far from the Center in Tintown. I wasn't sure whether to answer him. In the end, I couldn't see what harm it would do. If he knew about the AMP I wasn't giving anything away.

*Richie's fine,* came the reply after I'd answered. *Don't worry. We're going to help you.*

I considered turning the phone off. Maybe SecureCorp had caught Richie and extracted the stuff about the AMP from him. Maybe they were trying to trace the call.

More text came up. *I'll be at the AMP every day at four PM, for the next week — I'll wait for one hour. Come alone.*

The message was scary enough, but what really freaked me was when I looked in the bottom corner at the sign off.

It said: *Uncle Zack.*

I dropped the phone like it was red hot and stood there staring at it. It couldn't be Fatso. There was no way he would know about Uncle Zack. The phone couldn't be traceable; if they could find me they would have taken me already. I tried to check the calling number but it was obfuscated.

But how could it be Uncle Zack? In spite of what my dad said, Zack was supposed to be dead.

Then I remembered — I was dead. At least in the eyes of the world.

Whoever it was must really have talked to Richie, or one of the others. We were the only ones that knew about the phone. I swallowed hard. Was Richie really okay?

Uncle Zack.

Could he still be alive? Or was it just somebody who knew about him?

That afternoon Travis said if I was going to stay (I still wasn't sure if I was even allowed to leave) I should be assigned a regular set of duties. I was placed on kitchen detail. I wasn't really clear on what kitchen detail was. Other than zapping hot drinks and reheating packets from FoodCorp, I'd never actually prepared a meal.

To my surprise, and mixed feelings of joy, guilt, confusion, and sadness, Laura was there too. I was assigned to help her. When I showed up, she was washing these rough, brown, oblong objects in the kitchen sink. She handed one to me, gave me this gizmo with a blade, and told me to peel it.

I stared at it in my hand. "People actually eat these things?"

"It's a potato," she laughed. "It comes from the root of a plant. You've never seen one before? You've probably eaten them yourself thousands of times, you just didn't recognize what it was."

She demonstrated how to peel it, and gave it back to me. I turned the half-peeled potato over in my hands. "I always wondered what went into the slop FoodCorp makes."

"We don't get fresh food here very often either," she said. "Usually they just hijack a delivery truck and take the food packets. This time they just happened to get one that had fresh vegetables. I think it was headed for the First Circle."

I finished peeling the potato and dropped it in a bucket. Several others who'd also been assigned to the kitchen were chopping up vegetables Laura called carrots and beets across the room.

"You don't remember me, do you?" Laura said, smiling.

"Sure I remember," I said defensively. "But...well, you looked a lot different back then."

She laughed, and again I felt a twinge of guilt, as I felt myself drawn to her. She handed me another potato and I started peeling.

She blushed as she smiled and said: "You didn't notice me following you around at co-op school like a little puppy dog?"

It was my turn to blush. "I guess I wasn't too observant—"

"You've changed too," she said. "Older, more mature. It's so courageous of you to risk everything to come and fight for our cause."

I cringed. She had no idea why I was here. It occurred to me that that was probably a good thing.

"It's important," I went along, though at this point I still wasn't really sure what their cause was.

"Did your dad really work for InfoCorp?" I asked, changing the subject.

She nodded, sadly. "My mom, too. She was a reporter. Dad said most people in the Corps are in denial about the political situation. Mom wanted to change that. She wrote a piece about some stuff she'd uncovered, but InfoCorp refused to run it. Dad warned her to leave it alone, but she kept pushing and digging. She was supposed to meet with an informant one night alone. Dad forbade her to go. He said it was too dangerous. She left a note and snuck off anyway. We never heard from her again."

She was choking back tears.

"I'm sorry," I said. I thought about taking her hand, but I wasn't sure how she'd react.

She continued. "Dad spent months trying to find out what happened to her, but he kept hitting a brick wall. He would have kept going, but he was worried about me, so we gave up and moved to the Quarters. A friend of ours managed to sneak me into a school in the Corp Ring. Once in a while a bigwig would tour the place, so I'd have to make myself scarce."

"That's when you showed up at the co-op school," I guessed.

"And that's when I first saw you," she smiled. "When the Rebel leader was killed, it left kind of a vacuum. Dad had no choice. We came out here. He was originally planning to wait until I turned sixteen — after I got my Appraisal."

"When does that happen?" I asked.

"Next month," she said cheerfully.

After all that had happened, it seemed crazy that somebody could be so casual about it, but I didn't say anything. I dropped my peeled potato in the bucket with the others.

I thought about my own Appraisal. I still didn't know what it was, but from what Walter and Travis had told me...

"You can still get one — even out here?" I said.

She shrugged. "It's not that hard to do. It's just an injection. Dr. Treadwell's going to do it."

"You're not worried?"

"About what?" she said.

I stiffened. I should never have gotten into this conversation.

"Nothing," I said, smiling. "I'm sure it'll be fine."

# TWENTY-TWO

........................................

# REVELATIONS

I had a problem. I was almost certain that the Rebels wouldn't let me leave. Even if they didn't care about losing me (and I was pretty sure they *did* care), they wouldn't want me out there like Benny giving away their location. At the moment, there always seemed to be somebody paying attention to where I was, but I was free to go where I wanted. If I made it obvious I was trying to escape, that might change, and I'd never get away.

I thought about the night I'd met up with Benny. The guard had let me walk all the way to the end of the building before he tried to come after me. I'd come back willingly, so he'd probably let me do it again. I could walk to the spot where I'd met Benny, then just take off into the night. He wouldn't be able to stop me.

Then again, he might have talked to somebody about how far I should be allowed to go. I might not get away with that again. Anyway, did I really want to get away? Was it worth cutting my ties with Travis

*153*

(and Laura) and the Rebels just to contact some guy I'd never met, who might be setting a trap for me?

I had a week to think about it. For now, I'd leave things the way they were. Maybe Travis would come through with more on Uncle Zack...

I had trouble sleeping that night, my mind ticking over about Travis, his lieutenants, and the Rebels in general. When he was my teacher Travis had some outlandish views, but I felt like he'd always been straight with me.

Now it seemed like he was hiding something, but before I even considered going to see Uncle Zack, I wanted to give him the chance to explain. I decided to have it out with him. I found him outside on the front steps of the building, talking to a couple of his lieutenants. As I approached, they nodded to him and took off somewhere.

"Have you heard anything?" I asked, ready for a fight if I got the runaround again. He must have sensed my frustration. He gestured toward the entrance and started walking. I followed him inside to a room they'd set up for meetings. There was a large table with chairs around it. We sat down on a couple of them.

"Okay..." he said. He sat facing me, one arm resting on the table. "I was reluctant to tell you, because I was worried what you'd do. Yeah, we know about the Dead Shift. And their leader is a guy named Zack. How old was your uncle?"

154

I shrugged. "He was my dad's older brother. He'd be in his fifties, I guess."

"Zack seems pretty young to be him, but you never know with those guys."

He hesitated, like he was trying to decide how to tell me something.

"We see them once in a while," he finally said. "They're really secretive. It's different for them. SecureCorp doesn't really consider us a threat. They'll attack if we happen to cross paths — otherwise they leave us alone. But they're actively hunting the Dead Shift. Our groups have the same agenda, but for the Rebels it's political, for the Dead Shift, it's a matter of life and death."

Nothing was making sense. "You've got the same agenda?" I asked. "What agenda is that?"

"There's stuff you don't know."

I laughed. "Well, duh... yeah I don't know, because nobody will tell me."

His expression darkened as he leaned toward me. "You joked before about us trying to overthrow the government. You're actually close to being right. We *are* out to change the status quo."

"You're crazy man," I said. "We're about to have an election to get rid of them. Haven't you heard? The Enterprise party are going to eliminate more red tape and streamline the economy. They're even planning to give the CCE more say in government decisions—"

He smiled. "You haven't figured it out yet?"

"Figured what out?"

His smile disappeared. "There *is* no government."

"What are you talking about? What about President Foster?"

He snorted. "Foster's an actor."

"What about the cabinet — the parties — the opposition?"

"Actors, actors, actors." He shook his head sadly.

"Come on — so if there's no government, who's running things?"

"What's there to run?" he laughed. "Think about it. The two biggest functions of government are to enact and enforce laws, and to deliver services to the people being governed. Except for the one forcing everybody to vote, there's only one law — survival of the wealthiest.

"As for the services, the government used to provide roads, sewers, electricity, garbage collection, education, and health care for the people they governed. All that stuff is now done by the Corps. What's left for the government to do?"

I swallowed hard. I'd never thought of it before. What exactly *did* the government do? I just sat there with my mouth open. My mind had gone blank.

"A better question to ask," he continued, "is — who's in control? And that's an easy one to answer. Our true masters are on half the posters you see on the street, every other HoloTV show, and especially here—" he pointed to the HUD contact on his temple.

I was confused. I scrunched up my nose. "The CCE?"

He raised an eyebrow in confirmation.

"Bullshit," I said.

"They've been in control for decades," he said, "since long before you were born."

I laughed, shaking my head. "And how's that supposed to have happened?"

Travis shrugged and leaned back. "It was easy. The Corps are ultimately controlled by the Elite. From the beginning, Elite business interests had a massive influence on the government. Originally, they preferred to lurk behind the scenes, using their wealth and connections to get what they wanted, and letting the government take the blame if the result was unpopular.

"But eventually that wasn't enough. They got tired of just influencing, they wanted to be in charge. By pouring bucket loads of money into successive elections, they were able to place a core of their own people in key positions. Once they'd reached a critical mass, they just picked off the stragglers and eliminated the government altogether.

"Of course, they didn't tell the public any of this. As far as the average person knew, nothing had changed. The result is what you see." He gestured with his hand around us. "And it's not just this city. We're the biggest, but the same scenario is playing out everywhere."

I felt like I'd entered some backwards world where the rules I knew about didn't apply anymore. "So what happens when there's an election?"

"You ever played the slots at the big casino in the Corp Ring?"

I nodded. "Cindy took me once, and gave me some money to play."

"It's kind of addicting isn't it? That's because it's designed to take advantage of human psychology. You keep playing, looking for the high when you win. If you lost every time, eventually you'd get fed up and quit playing, right?"

"Is there some point to this?"

157

He smiled. "The slot designers know exactly how long you're will-ing to lose before you give up. Just at the point where you're about to walk away, guess what?"

"They set you up to win," I said.

He nodded. "You win a little, and that gives you hope — you think your luck has changed and you keep playing. But your luck hasn't changed. You're being played for a sucker just like before."

"Yeah, so?"

"That's exactly how the Elites' 'government' scam works — the changes in government give the public just enough hope to keep them from getting fed up and revolting."

I still thought he was full of it, but somewhere in the back of my mind his words had a ring of truth.

"But everybody's always going on about how much better things would be if the CCE ran the world," I argued. "You're telling me that they actually *do* run the world? What would be the point? Why set up this big elaborate scheme and make people hate the government and pretend you're trying to fix things? Why not just tell everybody the truth?"

"People need something to fixate on," Travis answered. "To hate. It distracts them from all their other problems, like not having enough to eat or not having proper medical care. It works especially well if an identifiable group can be blamed for everything that's wrong with people's lives, then punished, replaced, and forgotten about — until next time."

His hand on the table clenched into a fist. "Through their HUDs and HoloTV, the public are manipulated into believing that all their problems are the fault of the current government. Sophisticated software and armies of computer analysts track the public mood. When their analysis indicates that the level of dissatisfaction has reached a critical point, guess what? It's time for a new party to 'govern'." He held up two fingers of each hand like quotation marks.

His mouth twisted into a bitter smile. "It's just like with the slot machines — everybody thinks their luck has changed, that they're due for a win, but they're being played for suckers like always."

"But what about the vote?"

"The vote?" he smirked. "The ballot is tossed in the garbage as soon as you cast it. It's just for show. When people think they have a choice, they feel empowered, like they're doing something to improve their lives. Fact is, nothing at all changes. Exactly the same masters are in charge."

I was still trying to wrap my head around it all. "Anyway," I said, "if the CCE are this all-powerful force behind everything, what can you guys do?"

"There's no way we can hope to get rid of the CCE," he answered, "at least at the moment. There's too much power behind them, and the public aren't on our side — yet. But there is a flaw in their setup. Two flaws, actually."

"They better be big ones," I joked. I still wasn't sure I bought what he was saying, but it was clear there were things going on I didn't understand.

"Weaknesses as old as humanity itself," he said. "Arrogance and greed. You've got to understand about these people. They already have *almost* all the riches it's possible to possess. They could be

159

satisfied doing without the minuscule amount that's left, continue to live more extravagantly than the wealthiest sovereigns in history, and never be in danger of a revolt. But giving up something — even the tiniest scrap — isn't in their DNA."

He stared down at me. "They want everything. That's the way they're put together. They've got egos the size of these skyscrapers." He gestured out the window at the buildings around us. "The joke is, they don't even need what they already have, but that doesn't matter. They can only be satisfied by taking it all.

"That could be their downfall. If conditions get bad enough, the public will have no choice but to fight back. The Elite are incredibly wealthy, but they're a tiny minority. Their biggest fear is that the masses in the Quarters will get pissed off and revolt, and that a significant number in the Corps might sympathize with their cause and join them. That *should* limit how far they're willing to go, but their greed is tempting them to push the envelope."

"You haven't changed from school," I laughed, though I felt like I was just trying to convince myself.

He shrugged. "You can believe it or not. One way or another you're going to find out for yourself. Our hope is that we can get the truth out, or at least raise some doubt. Then maybe the public will wake up and support us. What we need is some kind of catalyst. Some event or revelation that will trigger the people to act."

"Where do I fit into all this?" I asked, by now dreading the answer.

"I think you're right that they're after you because of your Appraisal," he said. "But exactly what's so special about it, I don't know."

I closed my eyes. I'd been so happy when I met up with Travis again. I thought I'd finally find out what was going on. Now I had the feeling he wasn't telling me everything he knew.

I opened them again and looked up at him. "So — what about my uncle?"

His brows came together. "Look — there's something creepy going on with those Dead Shift guys — especially Zack. I didn't want to tell you about them because I don't completely trust them."

"What do you mean?"

"We have contact with the Dead Shift every once in a while. About a year ago Peter Barnes, the former leader of this group, arranged a meeting. He said it was stupid that both our groups were after more or less the same thing, but weren't working together.

"The meeting went well, and we agreed to meet again to map out a combined strategy. But a couple of days later, out of the blue, SecureCorp attacked our compound." Travis looked away. His hands clenched into fists, and his voice shook as he continued.

"Of the one hundred-twenty Rebels that were there, only seventy got out alive. That's when Peter Barnes himself was killed."

He hung his head and shook it slowly.

"We couldn't figure out how SecureCorp knew we were there," he said, looking up. "Nobody but us knew about the place. Later, one of our people admitted that he'd said something to Zack that hinted at our location. He'd been afraid to mention it, and figured it wasn't a problem, since the Dead Shift were supposed to be on our side.

"We met up with Zack later. It took everything I had not to kill him on the spot. I was sure he'd given us up. I don't know why. He claimed that he had nothing to do with it — that SecureCorp must have found us some other way. I didn't believe him."

"Maybe he was telling the truth," I said.

Travis shook his head. "I can't prove anything, but I'll give you some advice — even if we find him, don't trust that guy — there's something fishy about him."

"But he's my uncle."

"You don't know that. And, from what I've seen of him, I doubt it."

# TWENTY-THREE

..............................................

# A RUN

After the story he'd told me about the Dead Shift, I wasn't sure I believed Travis' claim that he was doing his best to locate Uncle Zack. I had nobody else to turn to, and I figured I was safer with the Rebels than being alone, so I stuck around. But once or twice I caught a couple of the other leaders eyeing me, especially Rolf, Travis' second in command. I still had a few days to decide whether to meet with Zack, but the deadline was coming up fast.

One day, Travis announced that we were going to conduct a raid the next morning on a SecureCorp outpost on the very edge of the Quarters, one of the closest to the Dregs. He'd gotten reports that a lot of the soldiers had been called away on a prolonged mission to deal with riots nearby (a Rebel diversion?), and that the place was only thinly defended. The Rebels were looking for weapons. I was bored, so I said I wanted to go. Travis said it was too dangerous, and insisted that I stay behind.

That night I heard him arguing with some of the other leaders in one of the offices. I tried to sneak closer to hear what they were saying, but there was a guard posted outside the door. The argument was pretty intense. There were lots of shouts and what sounded like fists pounding on tables. I managed to get close enough to see who came out when the meeting was over. There was Travis, Rolf, and a couple of the other guys who'd been glaring at me. None of them looked very happy.

Early the next morning Travis changed his mind and said I could come with them. I snuck away, grabbed the crypted phone, and stuffed it in my pocket, just in case something happened and I couldn't make it back. I was waiting in one of the empty rooms for the group to get organized, when Laura came to see me.

Every nerve in my body lit up as she took my hand. Again I was swamped with a confusing mix of guilt and excitement.

"Don't go," she said.

"It's just a raid," I answered, smiling, trying to sound braver than I felt. "It's no big deal. I'll be back this afternoon."

She looked up at me. "I've got a bad feeling about it. Something's going to happen—"

"I gotta pull my weight around here," I said. "I already said I'd go. I'm not going to back out now. Don't worry. Everything will be fine."

She removed a small brass medallion hanging on a string around her neck.

"At least take this," she said. "It'll bring you luck."

She reached up and hung the charm around my own neck. Then she grabbed it, pulled me close, and kissed me, full on the lips. I thought I was going to explode.

We heard footsteps approaching, and she broke away.

"Be careful," she said.

One of the fighters came through the door. He nodded at me. "Time to go."

I was gawking back at Laura, still stunned by her kiss, as the guy led me away. There was a thin, sad smile on her face as she stood and watched me go.

We gathered on the front terrace. I looked around, and was relieved when I couldn't see Rolf anywhere. We were about to start walking when he suddenly showed up.

Travis was pissed. "I thought you weren't coming," he said to Rolf.

"Changed my mind," Rolf shrugged. "Jimbo said he'd look after things."

Travis stood and glared at Rolf for a few seconds. Finally he turned and we headed out. I'd been scared shitless during my 'rescue' from SecureCorp, so I was stressed out about the prospect of another battle as we slunk through the darkened alleyways toward the outpost.

Half an hour later we reached an area I recognized, where I'd been held prisoner by Cash and his gang. As we entered an open square, Travis held up a hand for us to stop. I followed his line of sight and saw the reason. A half-dozen crows were feeding on something in the center of the square. The crows exploded into the sky as we approached, and a dozen or so rats scurried away.

As we got closer, I could see what was left of several bodies scattered on the ground. We approached cautiously. I guess you never know when it might be some kind of trap. At close range there was no doubt. All of them had been dead for a while.

My gut tightened when I recognized who they were. There were three of them — the guys that had captured me before. The women weren't there — they must have taken off once the party was over. We walked around the corpses, looking for anything worth taking. One thing I knew for sure they *didn't* have: the crypted phone. I fought the urge to be sick as I stood over the body of Tory, his head twisted into an impossible position, his eyes and entrails picked apart by the animals.

Travis stood scratching his head, wondering who'd killed them.

"Can't be SecureCorp," he said. "They would've just shot them." He pointed at the body closest to him. "This guy was beaten to death with something..." He wandered over to the next closest one. "Looks like this one had his neck broken."

The hair on the back of my own neck stood up. I thought about the snapping sound I'd heard outside the room where I was being held just before Benny rescued me. The bodies had nothing that interested us, so we left them alone and continued on.

A couple of hours later Travis motioned again for us to stop. This time it looked like we'd reached our destination, an open space in front of a collapsing low-rise building. He ordered Rolf, and a couple of other guys who'd been at the meeting, to scout the target outpost. Rolf didn't look too happy. He glanced at me, then back at Travis, like he was trying to decide something. Finally, he turned and went off, following orders.

When they were gone, Travis brought a guy over, one of the ones who'd originally rescued me and Benny from SecureCorp.

"I don't think you've been formally introduced," Travis smiled. For a split second he was the friendly, easy-going schoolteacher I remembered. "This is Bailey," he said.

Bailey smiled and stuck out his hand. He looked in his thirties, stocky with curly brown hair. He had a nasty scar on the right side of his face. I didn't ask how it got there. I shook his hand and said hi.

"Bailey's going to look out for you during the run," Travis said. His smile disappeared and he glared at me. "Do whatever he says."

Bailey and Travis seemed pretty tight — on better terms than the others, anyway. Fifteen minutes later Rolf and the other scouts came back. They stared again at me, then Bailey, as they went off somewhere with Travis. Bailey and I were standing beside a low cement wall. He motioned for me to sit down on it, then sat himself.

"You're just here as an observer," he said. He pulled a small gun out of his belt. "Ever use one of these?"

I shook my head.

He smiled. "There's a first time for everything."

He gave me a short lesson on holding and firing it, then handed it to me. "Don't use it unless you have to."

I took the gun and stuffed it in my own belt.

"When the fighting starts," he said, "stay right behind me. Don't ever let us get separated by more than an arm's length. Don't listen to anybody else — nobody — just me. Got it?"

I nodded.

He leaned in and lowered his voice. "Travis didn't want me to tell you this, but I think you need to understand. There's sort of a price on your head."

After all that had happened, I shouldn't have been surprised. He lifted his head and studied the group around us. I realized what he was saying. I'd been right — it wasn't just SecureCorp I had to worry about — anybody here might decide to make their fortune by giving me up.

Travis, Rolf, and the others returned from their meeting.

"It's a go," Travis said. I swallowed hard.

There were fifteen of us, including me. We were still in the Dregs, so cameras shouldn't be a problem, though we all monitored our HUDs just in case. After about ten minutes we reached the end of an alley that fed into a wide square.

Travis pointed to the right. "The outpost is just on the other side. The cameras start here, and they get pretty thick as we get closer, so be careful."

Bailey leaned down to me and whispered, "Stay exactly behind me."

I was annoyed. I was probably better at Cam-surfing than him, or any of them, but I kept my mouth shut.

Rolf took the lead, navigating slowly along one of the inside walls. I noticed that he not only avoided the cameras, but kept out of sight of any of the viewpoints around the square as well. I had to admit, he was good — but still not as good as me.

Rolf and another guy snuck away, while the bulk of us hid in a nearby alley. A few minutes later Travis got some kind of signal on his

HUD. He motioned for us to move forward. As Bailey had ordered, I hung right behind him. A few minutes later our objective was in sight, the side door of a solid-looking concrete building. It was open, and the bodies of two guards in SecureCorp uniforms lay just inside. We had to step over them to get past.

We crept through a network of hallways, looking for the armoury. There were doors at regular intervals along them. Bailey and I were at the rear. So far we hadn't seen another soul.

We entered a hallway that formed a 'T' intersection with another running at ninety degrees. The front of the group turned left down the new one, momentarily leaving Bailey and me alone. A guard emerged from a door right beside Bailey. He jumped at the sight of us, and went for his gun. Bailey was faster. He took out the guard, but the guy managed to get off a shot. Bailey collapsed to the floor, blood gushing from his left side.

The others rushed back to the junction, but a group of guards appeared, coming the opposite way. There was a firefight. That left me and Bailey stranded in the first hallway.

I knelt down to where he was crouched on the floor. "Can you walk?"

He managed to haul himself upright, but he could barely stand. He put his arm around my shoulder and I helped him stagger back the way we'd come. We emerged from the building, and had just reached some cover when he finally collapsed, unconscious. I tried to drag him to a better spot, but he was too heavy.

I stood up, trying to decide whether to go back inside. The firefight was still going on. I could still go and help the others. I was turning to leave when someone grabbed my shoulder from behind.

I jumped and turned. It was Rolf. His gun was drawn.

"He'll be okay," he said, nodding at Bailey. He eyed the gun in my belt. "You won't need the gun. Just come with me."

He had the same look I'd seen at the hideout.

"What about the others?" I asked him.

"They'll catch up in a few minutes."

I didn't move. There was still gunfire in the background. "It sounds like they're still fighting," I gestured with my head. "Shouldn't we help them? How did you get out here?"

"Travis said if Bailey got taken out, I should look after you," he said. He motioned with the gun down a nearby alley. "Follow me."

I stepped back. "You're full of it."

Rolf moved toward me, his gun pointing at my head. "There's no time to argue."

I turned to run. Rolf grabbed me by the arm.

"Let me go!" I yelled.

"You got any idea what your ransom would do for the revolution?" he said, finally showing his hand.

"Screw you!" I yelled, trying to pull away.

There was a blast from behind me, and a patch of red expanded on Rolf's chest. He let go of my arm and collapsed to the ground. I whipped around. Bailey was lying there with a smoking gun in his hand.

"Get away from here," he whispered.

"What about you?" I said. "I can't just leave you."

"I'm in no shape to go anywhere," he answered. "If the others get out they'll help me. Go — now!"

I wasn't going to leave him lying there. I got him to his feet and managed to walk him back to our original gathering point. I hoped the others would come back there.

I laid him down by the wall we'd sat on, and opened his shirt. There was a big gash in his side that was still oozing blood. I tore off part of my own shirt and wrapped it around him, hoping to stop the bleeding.

Then I ran back to the outpost to find the others. I peeked around the corner where we'd hidden before. Two SecureCorp guys were standing at the side entrance. One of them spotted me and pointed.

The closest one raised his weapon and fired at me. I took off.

# TWENTY-FOUR

......................................................

# AT THE AMP

It was too dangerous to go back to the Rebels. Rolf was dead, but there were others like him. Bailey was either dead or seriously injured, and I wasn't sure whether Travis would still be there to protect me.

The way I saw it, I had no choice but to meet with whoever had called me. It might be a trap, but I'd just have to take my chances. It took three hours, crossing into the Quarters, sneaking through back alleys and skulking along walls to avoid the cameras. I finally made it to the furniture factory — the place we in the Lost Souls called the AMP.

By now it was three in the afternoon; I had an hour to kill. I spent half of that time casing the place, suspecting some kind of trap, but there was nobody there. Like a lot of the buildings, the factory was basically gutted; it was nothing but a big open space, the floor a carpet of dust, glass, and wood chips. I climbed what was left of a broken staircase and found a hiding place with a view of the entire floor below.

I sat down and waited. I thought about Travis' story. He obviously believed Uncle Zack had betrayed him, but I didn't see why it couldn't have gone down the way Zack had said. Zack was my blood relative — or at least, he might be. I had to believe he was a good guy.

Just before four PM there was a scraping sound on the north side of the building. I had to shift to see what it was. Five men were sneaking along a clear space by the north-east wall, too far away to make out who they were. They were searching for something.

I leaned out from the corner I'd been hiding behind to get a better look. I finally saw them clearly and my heart almost stopped. SecureCorp. They were following a swarm of drones.

*Shit!* I thought. *Travis was right!*

I scoured the building for a way out. I was so preoccupied that I didn't hear the footsteps behind me until it was too late. An arm wrapped around my chest with an iron grip, and a hand clamped over my mouth. I tried to scream but nothing came out.

"Shhh," a voice above me whispered.

I tried to turn to turn my head but I was held too tight.

"Shut up and hold still," the voice said.

My captor slowly shifted backwards, dragging me with him, so that we were deeper in the shadows. I could still just barely make out the line of soldiers, their guns drawn now, scanning around them. They passed by our position and continued to the south.

As soon as they were out of sight, the voice whispered again: "I'm here to help you. I'm going to take my hand off your mouth. Scream and I'll be gone and SecureCorp will get you."

I nodded.

The hand was removed, and the arm loosened. I turned. A man stood facing me, his features blotted in the shadow.

He leaned over and whispered in my ear: "Stay exactly behind me and don't make a sound."

We picked our way, crawling carefully along a solid section of the floor. Far in the distance now I could hear the voices of the searchers. I froze when a faint hum approached us from the north. My companion heard it too. We turned and looked. A dark cloud of drones was moving toward us, their edge-detected outlines crowding together like stitches in the shadows.

My companion pulled some kind of device out of his pocket and pressed a button. The cloud stopped instantly and dropped from the air, producing a barely audible rain of clicks on the floor below. The SecureCorp guys started shouting and running back and forth looking for us. They knew we were around, but without drones they had no idea where.

My companion motioned to me and we kept crawling. After a few minutes I saw an opening in the wall ahead. We made for it and the footsteps of our pursuers faded as we passed through and outside.

We climbed down a ladder-like tangle of broken framework outside the building. I thought I was the master at getting around SecureCorp's surveillance cameras and drones, but these guys were at a whole other level. A stealth-equipped car was waiting beside the building, and a cloaking device hid us while we rushed for it. Whoever they were, they must be loaded to be able to afford gear like this.

The rear door of the vehicle slid open. My companion pushed me inside and slid in after me. The door closed with a thunk. Inside it was black as a tomb.

"We're going to cover your eyes," my companion said. "It's just a precaution."

A black bag was pulled over my head. I struggled.

"Settle down," my companion said. "It's only until we get where we're going."

We were both hunkered down in the back seat. We drove, crawling forward, for almost an hour. Nobody said a word. The only sounds were my own laboured breath, the faint hum of the vehicle engine, and the crunch of the tires on debris-ridden road below.

From the twists and turns and the rough ride, I figured we ended up somewhere deep in the Dregs. We finally stopped. I heard a deep rumble ahead of us, and the vehicle drove ahead a few meters. The driver knocked twice on the dashboard.

My companion put his hand under my elbow, motioning for me to get up. I sat up, and the bag was removed from my head. I was finally able to get a good look at him. The light filtering back from the vehicle's dash was dim, but I'd seen his picture enough to know.

It was my Uncle Zack.

# TWENTY-FIVE

....................................................

# THE DEAD SHIFT

"This is it," Uncle Zack said.

I could see his face in the dim light. From pictures I would have sworn he was my uncle, but he didn't look over twenty-five. Was it possible that this was my dad's *older* brother?

"Pretty fancy tech," I said to him, nodding at the vehicle.

"Some of us have been around a long time," he answered. "We've been able to accumulate some resources."

The lights of the vehicle switched off and we were in total blackness. It wasn't natural. It should be twilight, not night. I could barely make out the shadowy shape of the driver up in the front. We must be somewhere indoors.

The driver opened his door, got out, and opened mine.

"You can come out," he said.

I climbed out, holding onto the door frame like a blind man, and stood by the car. Uncle Zack climbed out the other side, walked around the vehicle, and joined us. We felt our way to the right, using

*176*

a wall to guide us. I was still almost blind. A door opened ahead and a dim light spilled out. I followed Uncle Zack and the driver inside.

There wasn't much more light in the space we were in now, but as soon as the door closed somebody switched one on. It was so bright I had to cover my eyes until they'd adjusted. When I opened them, we were standing in some kind of storage room, with boxes and miscellaneous junk piled around the walls. But the place was clean; it looked like they'd been set up here for a while. A table, surrounded by four folding chairs, stood in the middle.

There were three of us: me, Uncle Zack (I guess — it was still hard to believe), and the driver, a guy who looked a little older than me, with blond hair and a thin mustache.

Uncle Zack turned to me.

"Welcome," he smiled.

There he was: the curly dark hair, the penetrating black eyes under expressive brows. Somewhere in his expression I could see my dad — as he must have been... It was like traveling back in time, coming face-to-face with the grainy images from the family info card. Uncle Zack seemed to be enjoying my confusion.

"Have a seat," he said. He motioned toward one of the chairs.

I put my hand on the chair back. Maybe this was just part of some kind of twisted SecureCorp scheme to recapture me. I kept my eyes on both of them as I sat down. The driver took a seat to my left, Uncle Zack sat across from me.

"Well, Alex," Uncle Zack said. "It's great to finally meet you. You're the spitting image of your father. Do you recognize me?"

"I know who you look like," I said, "but it's impossible."

"You of all people should know it's not," he said, with a patronizing smile.

"Me — of all people?" I said. So far Uncle Zack was a bit too cute for my taste.

"Well," he said, leaning back, "if you're referring to me being dead, you've probably heard that in the eyes of the world you're dead too. If you're referring to the fact that I don't look much older than you... We'll get to that."

Uncle Zack nodded at the driver. "This is Connor," he said. Connor smiled and held out his hand, which I reached over and shook, still suspicious.

"What were those SecureCorp guys doing in the warehouse?" I asked. "It scared the shit out of me. I figured you'd screwed me over."

"Just bad luck," Uncle Zack answered. "They periodically send teams through the old buildings, hunting for 'enemies of the state'. They've stepped up the searches big time in the past few weeks."

"How come?" I asked.

"Looking for you," he smiled again.

He asked me about my father. I told him about my mother, what my father's life had been like, and how he'd finally given it up for me.

Uncle Zack looked at the floor and shook his head. "We both got screwed, in our own way."

*Only he's dead and you're still a twenty-year old,* I thought.

"How much do you know about what's happening?" he asked.

I shrugged. "After my Appraisal they kidnapped me, kept me prisoner in some hospital, and did a bunch of tests. A guy died helping me escape. Now everybody in the world's after me. My dad just said I should find you. He said something about some outfit called 'Vita Aeterna'."

Uncle Zack raised an eyebrow. He glanced over at Connor, like he was asking what he should do. Connor just shrugged. Uncle Zack described how he'd been held prisoner after his Appraisal and experimented on, like I was, for three months. When they drugged him for transport to a different facility, he'd woken up prematurely, in the back of a moving ambulance.

"I just opened the doors, jumped out, and took off," he said. "I went on the run. I dropped by home first, just to say goodbye." He smiled. "Your dad wanted to come with me, but of course I refused. He was just a little kid, anyway.

"But why?" I asked. "What are they after?"

"There's a lot you don't know," Uncle Zack said, "but we've got time." He stood up and paced back and forth. "You gotta understand about these guys — the Elite. They're used to getting everything they want. They want your house? They've got it. They want your wife, your girlfriend, your dog? Presto. They want you dead, you're dead. They want your life ruined, it happens."

He turned, and stared down at me. "There's only one thing they can't control: Appraisal. Nobody, not even them, can change how it alters someone's lifespan. That drives them batty. They can't stand the arbitrariness, the democracy, of it. It flies in the face of their belief in their own superiority — their divine right to lay ownership to anything they want by virtue of their power and wealth.

"They're enraged that the treatment can double the lifespan of some pathetic street bum while shortening that of one of their number." He started pacing again. "Over the years, armies of scientists, with a massive war-chest of funding, have toiled away in pursuit of one goal: controlling life extension.

"Their masters wanted Appraisal to be governed in the same way as everything else in the world: the more money you have, the longer you get to live. They wanted to be able to buy immortality the same way they buy everything else.

"But even with the trillions of dollars and tens of thousands of man-hours poured into the project, the scientists weren't able to change the treatment one iota.

"The guys paying for it all started to think the scientists were deliberately stalling — that they wanted the process to fail because of some twisted resentment of their masters' wealth, or some socialist vision of a world that didn't play favourites.

"One of the problems was that a lot of the scientists, Corp workers, and even some of the Elite themselves, were burdened by the remnants of morality."

I thought about Travis — and what Dr. Treadwell had said about him.

"They refused to perform certain types of experiments," Zack continued, "experiments that inflicted what amounted to torture on human test subjects to get the answers they wanted."

Uncle Zack stopped again and turned to face me. "So a group of the richest and most powerful of the Elite took matters into their own hands." He stuck out his chin and raised his fist. "This was the giving of life itself. Cheating death, or at least delaying it for a while, was the dream of the ages. If a few insignificant lives needed to be ruined, or even snuffed out, in pursuit of that goal, then so be it."

He turned back to me. "The group formed a secret society called Vita Aeterna — Eternal Life. Its goal was to carry the research work a step further, unbridled by the sentimental morality of the 'public' work.

"Vita Aeterna aren't constrained by any ethical considerations. Their only interest is to control the Appraisal process — at any cost. They recruited a cadre of scientists willing to do their bidding without question. Their work focuses on subjects with exceptionally high Appraisals. Such people don't show up very often. When they do, the organization is informed. They kidnap the high scorers and conduct experiments on them. They believe they can discover the secret of long life by studying people who have it.

"Over the years, some of those test subjects managed to escape, like we all did." He gestured with his head around the table. "We found each other and formed an underground resistance movement. We're all supposed to be dead, so we call ourselves the Dead Shift."

"So how do I fit in?" I asked, a feeling of dread creeping over me.

Uncle Zack sat back down and leaned toward me. "Do you know what *your* Appraisal is?"

I shook my head. "That's how this all started. Nobody would tell me, and then they're all after me."

"*I* know what it is," he said.

I tensed. The way everybody seemed to be acting about it, I wasn't sure I wanted to know. He sat staring at me. His expression reminded me of the one I saw on Chuck and the first doctor.

"Well?" I said.

He snapped up his right hand, with all the fingers spread apart. Again I was confused.

"What?" I said. I stared at his hand. Finally it hit me. "Five?"

He nodded.

"Five?" I said. "Bullshit."

He shook his head. "What it is, is the highest Appraisal anybody's ever scored. And it's yours."

It hit me like a sledgehammer. I was too stunned to say anything.

"Do the math," Uncle Zack said. "With an Appraisal of five, every fifty years you'll have aged ten. Fifty years from now your effective age will be twenty-six. In a hundred, it'll be thirty-six."

I was in shock. I was hardly conscious of what he was saying.

"In fact," he continued, "you put us all to shame. Connor, here," he nodded at the driver, "has an Appraisal of two point three. Mine's two point five. Still, if we ever have children, and those children have Appraisals as high as ours, they'll grow up, live their lives, and die of old age, and you'll still be going."

For a few seconds I was ecstatic, like I'd won the jackpot at the casino or something. Then the reality hit me, and a jolt went up my spine. Everybody — everybody I ever knew, everybody I cared about for the next hundred years, would be dead long before I'd even reached middle age...

"You're messing with me," I said. "It's not funny."

He shook his head. I looked over at Connor. He wasn't laughing.

*182*

I felt like I was going to be sick. My eyes were wet with tears. Suddenly I was sobbing. What was I going to do? I put my hands in front of my face.

Uncle Zack put a hand on my shoulder.

"What kind of fucked-up lonely-ass existence am I in for?" I said through my tears.

For the first time since it all started I truly wished I'd never heard of Appraisal, and that had nothing to do with being imprisoned or experimented on, or having those bastards chasing me all over the city.

"Don't worry, Alex," he said. "We'll look after you. We'll make it right."

"Nobody can make it right," I sobbed. "I'm screwed, and there's nothing you or anybody else can do about it."

Uncle Zack patted my shoulder.

"We'll leave you alone for a while to think about it," he said. He and Connor left the room, left me sitting there, staring into an empty future with nobody beside me - enduring the ultimate in loneliness. Appraisal had reprogrammed me to live for four hundred years, but right now all I wanted was to die.

# TWENTY-SIX

........................................................

# UNCLE ZACK

I lost track of the time, so I wasn't sure how long they were gone. Finally, Uncle Zack came through the door alone and sat down again across from me. I didn't really feel any better, but I'd come to a conclusion: this was the hand I'd been dealt. All I could do was accept it and go on. Anyway, I still had the immediate problem of a crack army of highly-trained soldiers trying to hunt me down. I'd have to think about the rest of my life later.

"By the way," he said, smiling, "under the circumstances you can dispense with the 'Uncle' bit. Just call me Zack." He leaned forward. "Now, let's get down to business. Statistically speaking, you're the holy grail. You could outlive everyone on the planet, even babies that won't be born for generations. They want you bad."

"So I'm screwed?" I asked. "I just keep on running until they catch up with me and rip me apart like a lab animal?"

"No," Zack said. "We fight back. That's the purpose of our little group here. The only chance we have of surviving and returning to society is to get rid of Vita Aeterna. As long as they're around we'll be living in fear and on the run. We want to destroy them, and make sure that they never come back."

"But what hope have we got of doing that?" I asked.

"It's a long shot," Zack said. "Our best chance is to eliminate the guy who's the big mover behind all this."

"And who's that?"

He turned and stared at a poster on the wall, the same one Benny had stuck up as a shrine in his office, the one he'd kept so pristine and new.

It was like Zack had shot me with a poison dart. "Charles Wickham?" I said. "The head of the CCE?"

Zack nodded.

I swallowed, thinking back on what Travis had said about them. "Then we *are* screwed. Us against him, the CCE, and all of SecureCorp?"

Zack shook his head. "We know we can't hope to win against SecureCorp. That's the difference between us and that ridiculous Rebel group you were hanging out with."

I looked up at him, shocked.

"Why so surprised?" he said. "We know all about what goes on around here. How do you think we knew about the phone?" He nodded at the bulge in my shirt.

"How *did* you know?"

"We ran into your friend Fatso." He smiled.

My spine stiffened. "He's no friend of mine."

"Then you'll be pleased to know that you won't have to worry about him anymore," Zack said without emotion. "We know where you've been. We don't know exactly where the Rebels are at any given moment, but we've got a good idea what they're doing. They've got this fantasy that they can wake the general public and engineer some kind of popular uprising. We know that's not going to happen."

"Why not?"

Zack sneered and shot me a look. He was my uncle, but I wasn't so sure I really liked him.

"The public are sheep," he said. "The thought has never even crossed their minds that anything can be changed, or even *should* be changed. They've bought into the idea that if they work like dogs and are willing to screw their neighbour, someday they'll be up there with the Elite."

He shook his head contemptuously.

I felt my cheeks flush. Up until a few days ago I'd been one of those people. I still wasn't sure I believed him.

"But if they knew the truth…" I said.

Zack scowled at me. "And how's that going to happen, nephew? Are *you* going to tell them?"

I glanced at my hands, then looked back up at him. "Well, if you can't change the public's mind, what *do* you plan to do?"

He shrugged. "There's only one option. It might not change anything, but at least it's got some slim chance of succeeding."

"What's that?"

His eyes locked on mine, and a thin smile curled up on his lip. "We're going to kill Charles Wickham."

We sat there staring at each other for almost a minute. I swallowed. If that was our best chance...

Zack finally spoke. "If we can get to Wickham, the organization will be crippled, maybe beyond repair. If we can couple that with getting out the word about them, in a way that they can't discredit, we might have a chance. InfoCorp controls the media, so if they say we're dead, there's not much we can do about it. We have to find a way to change that."

I still didn't say anything. I felt like I was already dead — I just hadn't fallen down yet.

"You could be a real asset," Zack continued.

"Me?" I said, snapping out of it. "What have I got to do with it?"

"Vita Aeterna wouldn't have a problem killing most of us — there's more where we came from. We're already on record as being dead, so if we make too much trouble for them, all they've got to do is get rid of us for real.

"You, on the other hand, are an anomaly — one of a kind. They'll want you kept alive so they can study you. We might be able to use that to our advantage. While they're tripping over themselves trying to get you, maybe they'll make a mistake."

I still wasn't convinced. And something about my uncle didn't seem right.

"You can bet your buddy Travis knows all about your Appraisal," Zack said out of the blue.

"No way," I said. "If he knew, why wouldn't he tell me?"

"He's afraid of us," Zack answered. "He told you some bullshit story about me, didn't he - about how I betrayed them - about how you shouldn't trust me?"

I stared at my hands on the table.

"He's not your friend," Zack continued, "no matter what you think. He's out to get us — all of us."

"But you and them have almost the same agenda," I said, looking up.

He laughed. "Only *our* plan actually has a chance of succeeding." He stared at the wall behind me, like he was mulling something over.

I heard the door open. I turned to see Connor poke his head in. He nodded at Zack, who pushed himself up and headed toward him.

"I've got some business to take care of," Zack said, reaching the door, opening it and stepping out. "Connor will look after you, and set you up with a place to sleep."

Connor came over and sat across from me. So far the only people I'd seen were him and Zack. The thought occurred to me that maybe there was actually only the two of them.

"How many people are there in the Dead Shift?" I asked.

"Right now?" he answered. He looked a little embarrassed. "Only twelve. Remember, it's made up of people who've escaped from SecureCorp. You know from experience how hard that is."

"I'm surprised there's that many," I said.

"Escapes only happen every few years," he said, "but we've been around for decades."

"So where are the others?"

He smiled. "You'll meet them soon enough. We have to be pretty careful about these things."

Connor talked for a while about how he got to be part of the Dead Shift. His story sounded a lot like mine. I guess all of them probably went through something similar. I got a positive vibe from him — a better one than I got from my uncle. He helped me program a contact for the Dead Shift into the crypted phone, in case I was ever in trouble or got lost.

Finally, he rose from his chair. "You must be tired."

I followed him out of the room, into the area we'd felt our way through when I first arrived. Now, the lights were on. I'd been right earlier; we'd actually driven inside a building. I was facing a wide-open space that looked like it was probably once a warehouse. Unlike most of the places I'd been lately, there was no garbage or debris lying around. The floor was spotless and all the lights worked — they must have been here for a while.

The stealth vehicle I'd ridden in was parked in one corner, just inside a sliding steel garage door. There was also a couple of motorcycles, and a large cabinet with shelves full of equipment. These guys were way more organized than the Rebels.

"Not all our setups are this sophisticated," Connor smiled, noticing me staring. "This is a special one. That's why you were kept in the dark on the way here. No one can know about this place."

There were doors around the perimeter. Connor led me to one of them in a distant corner. Behind it was a small room with a bed, a chair, and even a tiny desk, a step up from sleeping in the dorm-like arrangement at the Rebel hideout.

*189*

"Get some rest," Connor said, standing by the open door. "You're safe here. Somebody will contact you in a few hours."

Connor took off and I lay down on the bed. At first I couldn't sleep. So much had happened so fast. It was like some kind of accelerated nightmare. I thought back on my Appraisal. I'd been looking forward to it since I was old enough to know what it was. Everybody did. You basically put your life on hold until you got it, because everything you did after that would depend on how long you were going to live. I had all these dreams of somehow snagging a Corp job, having a career, getting past Cindy's dad and marrying her, having a family. If I had a good Appraisal I'd have lots of time to make enough money to enjoy my life...

I had to laugh. Now, in some twisted, cruel version of my dreams, I had the ultimate Appraisal. And here I was, running for my life. Cindy was dead, I might have killed her father, I'd broken out of a SecureCorp prison, and the whole world was after me. Two people, one of them my own father, had died trying to help me. I was destined to spend my life alone, outliving everybody on the planet. And I didn't know what to do. I couldn't dodge the cameras forever. Eventually I'd make a mistake and they'd catch up with me.

Finally, exhausted, I fell asleep. I woke to a knock at the door. I got up and opened it.

It was Zack.

He walked in and sat on the end of the bed.

"I've been thinking about what you said earlier," he said. "You know, about us and the Rebels being after the same thing. You might have a point there." He smiled. "What if I was to set up a meeting with

Travis? Maybe if the Rebels and the Dead Shift were to join forces we could actually accomplish something."

I was confused. Zack would reconsider working with the Rebels just because I suggested it? It didn't make sense.

"Travis would never go for that," I said. "Anyway, why now? You've had years to get together with them."

He put a hand on my shoulder. "You've added a whole new dimension to the equation. You've got a relationship with Travis *and* me. You can act as sort a liaison, the 'glue' that holds us together."

His eyes went wide, as if he'd had an idea. "You came here from the Rebel stronghold, right? You could take me to see them."

The hair rose at the back of my neck. I didn't like where the conversation was headed. Travis wouldn't want me leading anybody, even an ally, to their location. As far as that went, they'd probably moved by now. And Travis had made it clear how he felt about Zack.

"No way," I said.

"I don't suppose I blame you for not trusting me," Zack said. "It'll take longer, but we have ways of contacting them. If I set up a meeting with Travis, will you come?"

I studied him. He was my flesh and blood — my father's brother. I hadn't heard much about him growing up, but what I had heard had always been positive. His request made sense.

"I guess," I said.

The barest hint of a smile formed on Zack's lips. He got up and stood with his back to me for a few seconds.

Finally he turned again to face me. "We'll talk about it again soon. Meanwhile, let's keep this between us. Don't tell Connor or any of the others about it."

"Why not?"

"Some of them don't trust the Rebels. They don't want to have anything to do with them. If they found out we were trying to contact them, it might be a problem."

It sounded logical, especially after the way Travis had talked about Zack and the Dead Shift.

So why did my gut seem to have a problem with it?

# TWENTY-SEVEN

..............................................

# THE MEETING

After a couple of days, Connor took me in the stealth vehicle to another hideout. He never said why. Like the Rebels, the Dead Shift seemed to have an endless supply of them. Once again, I had to wear the bag over my head. His claim that the first one was special appeared to be true. This new one looked more like the Rebel hideouts I was used to.

It took a few days for Zack to make contact with the Rebels. I think he was pissed with me, knowing that I could tell him where they were, but wouldn't. I didn't care. If he wanted to contact them, he'd have to find them himself.

In the meantime, I was relieved when I finally met a couple of other Dead Shift people. A guy named Rick, and a woman named Monica. I talked to them both and they seemed great — we had a lot in common. I felt a little better about being there.

I followed Zack's instructions and didn't tell any of them about the planned meeting with Travis, even though I wasn't sure I bought Zack's

*193*

explanation of why that was necessary. One morning Zack came and told me he'd contacted the Rebels, and set up a meeting for the afternoon of the next day.

I slept badly that night. I had doubts about Travis and the other Rebels, especially after what Rolf had done, and what Zack had said about them. But at least I knew Travis. I'd spent enough time with him to be convinced he was a good guy.

Zack *was* my uncle; I had no doubt. But I'd just met him. Our family had never been that close, but I'd always been raised to believe that family ties were important. But there was something off about him, something that made me nervous.

A gut instinct told me something was wrong. I was surprised that Travis had agreed to the meeting. He'd seemed pretty down on Zack when I talked to him. One thing was crystal clear: either Zack or Travis was lying to me. The question was — which one? Or was it both? And if they were lying, what did it mean?

The next day, early in the afternoon, Zack came and told me it was time. We snuck out of the Dead Shift hideout, and walked for an hour to what I assumed was the meeting place, a small square in the middle of nowhere. We waited about twenty minutes, hiding in an alcove of an abandoned building.

Finally, we heard movement. Zack gestured for me to be quiet, and peeked around the corner. A few seconds later, he turned back to me, smiling.

"It's Travis," he whispered. "Stay where you are."

I didn't understand what he was up to, but I went along.

He stepped out from the corner with his hands up. But when his jacket shifted I saw that he had a gun stuffed in the back of his pants.

"You were supposed to be alone," I heard Zack's voice say.

"You can understand why I still don't completely trust you," Travis' voice answered. "Bailey's only here for insurance. If you're being straight with me, you've got nothing to worry about."

I felt relieved at hearing Travis' voice, and I was surprised and pleased to hear that Bailey had made it back and was okay. Maybe this get together could actually come off.

"Where's Alex?" Travis asked.

"He's right here," Zack answered.

He turned his head and motioned to me, and I came out to join him. Travis was standing about ten meters away. Bailey was standing to his left. He had a bandage around his stomach, but otherwise he looked okay.

I thought they'd be glad to see me, but as soon as I showed myself they tensed up and raised their rifles.

"I thought you said he was injured," Travis said.

Before I knew what was happening, Zack had wrapped an arm around my neck and held me like a shield in front of him. He pulled out the gun and held it against my head. I couldn't believe what was happening.

"A little white lie," Zack said. "Otherwise you wouldn't have come."

I struggled against Zack, but he was a lot bigger and stronger. I couldn't breathe.

"If you want the kid to live," Zack said, pressing the barrel of his gun against my temple, "You better come with me. I have some friends who want to talk to you."

"Friends in SecureCorp?" Travis said. "You know I can't do that."

I couldn't believe what I was hearing.

"You think I'm bluffing?" Zack yelled, and cocked the trigger, ready to fire.

Travis shook his head. "The movement is more important than any one person's life — even his. I'm sorry, Alex." He stood with his rifle trained on us, his expression a blend of horror and determination.

"That's what I thought you'd say," Zack said.

I felt the gun barrel move away from my head. Before the others could react, Zack turned the gun and shot Travis in the chest.

"No!" I screamed.

Bailey hesitated. I guess he was worried about hitting me. Zack fired another shot and Bailey went down. Zack grabbed me by the arm and started dragging me off.

I glanced back. Travis and Bailey were lying on the pavement. Two other Rebels came running from the shadows. One knelt over their bodies. The other ran after us, firing now, not even caring whether he hit me. Zack dragged me behind the corner of a building. He locked my head in the crook of his left arm while he fired at our pursuer with his right. After a few minutes I heard a grunt and the Rebel's firing stopped.

Zack let go of my neck and jammed his gun between my shoulder blades.

"Move it!" he said.

196

We ran through a network of alleyways. There was no sign of the Rebels. Zack didn't say a word. Tears welled in my eyes. What the hell was going on? Was Travis dead? What had I done? Twenty minutes later we stopped at a door in one of the buildings. Something smashed against my skull and everything went black.

# TWENTY-EIGHT

·····················

# THE HAND OFF

When I woke up, I was in a room I'd never seen before, sitting in a chair with my hands tied behind me and my feet bound. It felt like a pile driver was slamming against the inside of my skull. It took a few seconds for my eyes to focus. When they finally did, Zack was standing in front of me.

"You fucking bastard!" I screamed. The sound and exertion made my head explode. I closed my eyes and clenched my fists against the pain. I thought again of Travis and what I'd led him into, and felt tears running down my cheeks. "Do you know what you've done?"

"Sorry, nephew," he grinned, in a way that made me want to smash his face in.

"Why?" I said, still choked with tears.

"The deal was you and Travis," he said. "They would have preferred him alive, but they'd accept him dead, and that was easier anyway. I don't think they really care that much about the Rebels. You're my ace in the hole. I want to keep *you* to myself until I'm sure they're going to fulfill their end of the bargain."

"Who's they?"

"Guess."

"So Travis was right about you," I said. "You led SecureCorp to the Rebel hideout."

"That was a dry run," he said. "To convince them I was serious. Turned out the Rebels weren't important enough for them to give me what I wanted. Then you came along, like a gift from heaven. I decided a long time ago that I was going to get out of this. I'm going to need a lot of money to live on once that happens. After all," he smiled, "I'm planning to live another hundred and fifty years."

"You've made some kind of deal with the Vita Aeterna?"

"I'd been thinking about it since we first hooked up," Zack said, "but couldn't decide whether to go through with it."

He paced along the wall beside me.

"But now you've accepted that you're a complete asshole," I said, "so you're okay with it."

He stopped and sneered down at me. "You're still a stupid kid. You haven't got a clue." He smashed his fist against the wall. "Don't you get it? We're going to lose. Look what we're up against."

"So you're just going to give me up? Your own flesh and blood?"

"You know how old I am?" he asked.

I twisted at the ropes binding my hands. "My only interest in your age is that you don't get the chance to get any older."

"I'm fifty-six," he said. "You hate what you've been going through for the past couple of months? Well I've been dealing with it since I was your age, forty years ago."

I shuddered, considering what might be in store for me. It was hard to imagine. I'd barely been able to cope for the few weeks I'd been on the run. Forty years? Fifty? One Hundred? But nothing excused what Zack was doing.

I struggled, trying to free my hands. "I'm your brother's only son," I said, my voice breaking. "I'm the only family you've got in the world."

He shrugged. "I'll get over it. You'll be better off anyway. You said so yourself. What kind of life would you have — outliving everybody you ever knew or loved."

"I won't miss *you*."

He snorted and turned away. He started pacing again.

"Years ago," he said, "many years ago now, there was enough of everything to go around. Even back then the majority of the population were poor. The wealth wasn't distributed equally, but in theory it could have been.

"That option ended forty years ago, about the time I went on the run. Now, there's resources for about one percent of Humanity to live in luxury. The rest are screwed. In order for somebody to join that one percent, somebody already in it has to leave voluntarily."

Zack stopped pacing and stared down at me. "What do you think the chances are of that happening?"

Again I thought of Travis, whose death I probably caused. Again tears welled in my eyes.

Zack continued. "Since then, the Elite and the Corps have taken every opportunity to eliminate people they don't think are of any use to society — which basically means the rest of us."

I stared up at him.

"Why do you think there's so many abandoned buildings?" he sneered. "Didn't you wonder where everybody went?" He shook his head. "Natural death from squalid living conditions and lack of heath care, elimination of anyone they've determined won't be missed, and regular sweeps of death-squads through the Dregs have helped. But the process has been too slow for their taste. I have it on good authority that there's a 'Final Solution' in the works — a plan to 'cull' huge numbers of the population."

I swallowed hard.

"Robots do almost all the factory work," he continued. "The ruling class need a certain number of human drones around to do what's left — and a minimum gene pool as test subjects until they learn to control the Appraisal. The rest are a liability. Every body removed means one less draw on resources, one less HUD to be installed, and one less potential threat to deal with. The only question is how? How to do it without causing a revolution. Maybe a plague — but then there's a chance everybody, even the Elite, could get it."

"They're monsters," I said.

Zack shrugged. "They'll come up with something, don't worry. Probably some kind of poison. It'll look natural. They'll spin something out on people's HUDs — nobody will question it."

He moved in front of me and stopped. "They said if I got rid of Travis and delivered you, they'd move me out of the danger zone and leave me in peace. I've got a chance to finally have a life. I'm gonna take it. Can you blame me?"

I glared up at him. "And what kind of life is that gonna be — Uncle?"

"Shut up!" he screamed. He backhanded my face.

"We're not gonna lose," I said, breathing hard, my right cheek burning with pain.

"What makes you so sure?" he laughed.

"'Cause if we lost I wouldn't want to live anymore, and I'm planning to be around for another three hundred and eighty-four years."

Zack grabbed a roll of tape from the bench and tore off a piece. I moved my head back and forth trying to stop him, but he finally managed to stretch it across my mouth. I closed my eyes. It was over.

The worst part was what Laura would think of me after what happened. It was like I'd been standing on a platform and the pillars supporting it were kicked out from under me. Maybe the Dead Shift were some kind of bullshit con set up by SecureCorp to reel me in. And I'd walked right into it. It was like a black well opening up beneath my feet.

Zack left the room and I passed out. When I woke I couldn't check with my hands tied, but I figured I'd been out for half an hour. Zack was talking to someone over my crypted phone in the other corner of the room. I couldn't hear what they were saying. I tugged again at the ropes, but they weren't going anywhere.

Zack stopped talking and headed for the door. He didn't look at me. For that much I couldn't blame him.

A half hour later Zack came back. He avoided making eye contact. Big surprise. He untied my feet, hauled me up and dragged me out the door and down an alley. I had trouble breathing with the exertion and the tape across my mouth. He finally removed it.

"Are the rest of the Dead Shift in on this?" I asked him as we moved.

"Shut up," he said.

We stopped in an open space at the convergence of several alleys. He shoved me through the open door of an abandoned building and prodded me up a narrow flight of stairs. We entered what looked like it was once a hotel room, with a commanding view of the space below.

He pointed to a single chair in the middle of the room. "Sit," he said. "And don't try anything." He patted the gun in his belt.

"What, you're gonna shoot your precious bargaining chip?" I said.

"Shut up, or I'll tape your mouth again."

Ten minutes later Zack talked again to somebody on the crypted phone. He crouched down and peered over the window sill, waiting. In a few minutes I heard movement in the street below. A voice below called out something. I couldn't make out what it was. Zack spent a few minutes scanning the area, checking for a trap, I guess.

Finally satisfied, he grabbed me by the collar and dragged me back down the stairs to the door.

He let go and leaned in toward me, whispering, "If you know what's good for you you'll keep your mouth shut until I come and get you."

As bad as things were, I figured I was still better off with Zack than whoever he was trying to sell me to. I stayed where I was.

I guess Zack still wasn't convinced we were safe; he peeked around the corner of the wall for another few minutes before he finally stepped out.

"You said you'd come alone," he said to somebody.

"We call the shots here," a voice said. It sounded familiar.

"Let's see the money," Zack said, "and the letter."

"First, the boy," the other voice answered.

There was a pause. Zack came back, grabbed me, and hauled me out from behind the corner. A few meters away stood Weber, the SecureCorp guy who'd wasted the gangster leader, Cash. Beside him were a couple of his goons.

Zack held a gun to my head. "You better not be trying to screw me," he said to Weber.

Weber's mouth turned up in sort a sneering smile. "We'll take care of you, don't worry."

Weber reached into his jacket. The hand holding the gun against my head was shaking.

Weber pulled out a paper folder. "Come and get it," he said to Zack.

"Show me," Zack said.

Weber held the folder open to display a fist-thick bundle of bills, a fancy-looking MoneyAll card, an ID card, and some papers with an of-ficial-looking seal at the top.

"Throw it down here," Zack nodded at the pavement in front of us.

Weber shrugged. He raised his hand to toss the package, but instead of throwing it at the ground, he threw it at Zack's head. Zack flinched for a second, lifted the gun from my head, and stepped back. A rifle cracked. He grunted and staggered sideways. He was hit. A second shot missed its mark. Zack recovered and dragged me back behind the corner as another shot blasted a chip out of the wall beside us.

"Get them," shouted Weber.

We ran back the way we'd first come. Pounding feet echoed behind us. We headed down an alley, seconds ahead of the pursuers. Zack pushed on what looked like a solid section of wall and it swung open. A hidden door. Now I saw why he'd picked this building. He shoved me through, stumbled in after me and closed it behind him. Seconds later the footsteps ran by without stopping.

He turned to me. There was a patch of red spreading across his gut. He put one hand over it and shoved me forward with the other. The pounding feet and shouting voices faded into the distance. We traveled down a long hallway, made a few turns, and finally reached a door. Zack held a finger to his lips, and pushed it open a crack. It led to the outside.

"The bastards!" he said half under his breath. "It was all a setup."

"Big surprise," I laughed. He delivered a weak punch to my gut and grimaced. I think it hurt him more than me.

He pushed me out the door and we stumbled down yet another alley. "I know a place," he said. "It's not far."

# TWENTY-NINE

..............................................

# A MISSION

We walked for another five or six blocks. Minute by minute Zack was getting weaker. He was losing a lot of blood.

"You better do something about that," I said.

"Shut up," he said, and drove me forward.

I guessed that he was headed for another Dead Shift hideout. He probably would have arranged to make the hand-off somewhere close to one. But if it was more than a few blocks away, he wasn't going to make it.

We emerged from an alley into a huge wide-open space with a gigantic warehouse-looking building in the middle of it. He hesitated for a few seconds. I think he wanted to run straight across. It would be safer, but slower, to stay close to the edges.

Finally he decided, and rushed into the open. We'd gone about fifty meters when there was a gunshot behind us. On the far side of the square, a half dozen SecureCorp soldiers were charging across the broken pavement toward us. The guys we'd escaped from had found us again.

"Shit," Zack said, under his breath.

There was no time to run anywhere. Zack dragged me toward the warehouse. We reached it and he shoved me toward the front door. The door was intact but the lock was broken. We rushed inside and Zack slammed it shut.

"Get over there," he said, motioning toward a broken pile of crates. The place must once have been a storehouse for toys. Arms, legs, and torsos of broken dolls, along with toy cars and trucks, and gaming pieces, littered the floor.

Zack staggered toward a couple of intact crates and pushed, trying to slide them against the outside doors. He was weak, he was still bleeding, and he still had the gun in one hand. It was pathetic.

"Untie my hands," I called to him, "and I'll help you."

He stopped and stared at me for a second.

"I don't want them to get to us any more than you do," I said.

The shouts from our pursuers were getting closer. He came over and untied me. Together we slid the crates forward to barricade the entrance.

We stumbled across a debris-strewn floor to an inner section with another door, which we quickly barricaded as well. Zack glanced around the area, hunting for another exit. The entire southeast corner of the building, where there might have been another door, was piled several meters high with garbage and debris. There was no way we'd dig through it all before our pursuers caught up.

We made our way to a storeroom at the back of the building. I wasn't sure why; it was only a matter of time until they broke in and got to us. We had nowhere to go.

We sat barricaded in the storeroom. The explosive thuds of the soldiers hammering on the outside doors echoed through the building. There was an even louder crash as they must have broken through.

Zack's wound was bothering him. Blood was still seeping into his shirt and dripping onto the floor. He nodded off for a second, then jerked himself awake. He noticed me glancing at the gun in his belt and smiled as he rested his hand on it.

"What did you think was gonna happen?" I asked him. "You say you're so old and experienced. Didn't you figure they'd double-cross you?"

He stared at me. "Yeah, sure. Sure I figured that. What you don't get is that I had no choice. There's nothing left for me."

He grimaced, closed his eyes and grabbed his side. The SecureCorp guys were battering on the second door. I had to do something. I jumped up and rushed at him, to grab his gun. He heard me, opened his eyes, and jumped to his feet. He was a foot taller than me. He caught me with a kick in the stomach that knocked the breath out of me. I fell to the floor, gasping.

"You poor little shit," he said. He pulled the gun from his belt and pointed it at my head. "You've been nothing but a pain in the ass. And now you're worth nothing to me."

He cocked the mechanism. I lay there helpless, frozen in terror.

He hesitated, his face contorted in pain. He closed his eyes. He opened them again and smiled. "But then, after all, you *are* my nephew." He turned the gun, drew his arm back, and pressed the barrel against his own temple.

"No!" I screamed.

"Bye now," he said, as he pulled the trigger.

I sat for a few seconds, stunned. Finally I snapped out of it and twisted the gun from his dead hand. His body was blocking the door. I dragged it away, and rushed out to check on the inner door. A crack in it was expanding as the SecureCorp guys pounded on it. They'd be through it in minutes. I thought about the crypted phone. I rushed back and grabbed it out of Zack's pocket. Zack had accepted that the situation was hopeless, but I wasn't going to give up without a fight. I had another quick look around. There was only one door, and the goons were about to bash their way through it.

Right beside it was a large crate, about a meter square and about two meters high. I rushed back to the storeroom and wedged Zack's body into a sitting position in the doorway, with his shoulder and left arm visible, and his head wound turned away. Returning to the door they were pounding on, I slid a smaller crate up beside the large one, climbed up, and lay in the shadows with my gun drawn.

A few seconds later the door burst open and the SecureCorp goons crowded in. They scanned the area quickly but didn't notice me. One of them pointed to Zack's torso. The main body of the group edged toward it, while a few others fanned out to check the rest of the warehouse. My plan was desperate, but it was all I had. I crept out to the edge of the crate and looked down. I could just make out the toes of a pair of boots outside the door. They'd posted at least one guard.

The main group all had their backs to me and by now were at least twenty meters away. I climbed back down to the floor, hid behind the smaller crate, and peeked around. They were occupied with Zack's body and the debris at the back, and still hadn't noticed me. They were about to reach the storeroom door.

It was time to go. I formed a mental image of where the outside guard was standing, then tore around the crate and through the open door, gun firing. I hit the surprised guard and he collapsed.

I took off across the warehouse floor, heading for the main doors. Shouts and pounding feet echoed from inside and the soldiers soon emerged. I reached the outer door and ran for my life across the square. In seconds the others were outside and running after me. At the edge of the square, I tore down the nearest alley, and flew around a corner into a cross alley.

The SecureCorp guys were right behind me, but right now they weren't in sight. I hunted desperately for some kind of opening to crawl into, but there was nothing. I glanced back. A couple of soldiers rounded the corner. They were gaining on me. I hit another cross alley and raced down it. I wasn't going to last long like this. I needed a hiding place, or a way to open some distance between me and them.

I scanned the surrounding walls as I ran, crazy with fear. Down another alley I saw a patch of blood — this was the way I'd come with Zack. I retraced our route back, and breathed a huge sigh when I finally saw it — the wall with the secret door Zack had used to escape from the others.

I wished I'd paid more attention to how he'd actually opened it — my heart thumped in my ears as I groped frantically for the release mechanism. Nothing. Frustrated, I punched a spot near my head, and the door popped open. I rushed inside, jammed it shut, and lay against it shaking as my pursuers pounded by seconds later, yelling at each other.

I waited for a long time after their shouts and footsteps had faded away. Finally, stressed out and exhausted, I fell asleep. When I woke up, my HUD said I'd been out for about an hour. I listened at the door for ten minutes, but couldn't hear a sound. I opened it a crack. Nothing.

I took off and ran deeper into the Dregs. The level of decay and destruction, which had been bad enough before, got even worse. The ground was littered with debris and garbage. Some of the buildings had even collapsed, and were now giant piles of rubble that completely blocked the street. I just ran — away from the death, the terror, the betrayal, away from everything life had dealt me since I was born. I ran until I couldn't run anymore. I found an alcove hidden in the shadows, and sat gasping with my head in my hands.

Almost everybody I cared about was dead. Two of them died trying to save me. Lifelong attachments were over for me — for the rest of my incredibly long existence, stretching into the hundreds of years, I'd be alone. SecureCorp, and a remorseless secret society with bankloads of money, led by the most powerful man in the world, were turning the city upside down to find me.

The Rebels, the one group that could have provided me some kind of safety, now probably hated me and thought I was a traitor. The

Dead Shift, or at least my Uncle Zack, my only remaining relative, had betrayed me, and now Zack was dead.

Zack's gun was still stuffed in my belt. The image arose of Zack pressing it against his temple, just before... I hauled the gun out and stared at it. It was still slimy with Zack's blood. I lifted it toward my own head, ready to follow his example. I set it back down. I wasn't ready - at least not yet. At that moment, the phone in my pocket vibrated. I dreaded looking at it, but finally broke down and took it out. I had a message.

It was Connor. *Where are you guys?* it said. *We haven't been able to contact Zack for four hours.*

I sat for a few seconds staring at the phone. I didn't believe him. As far as I was concerned, the Dead Shift had screwed me once already — why not again?

I texted Connor: *Zack's dead, and good riddance. He murdered Travis. Fuck you guys.*

After a few seconds of hesitation, Connor texted back: *We knew nothing about it. Come and meet us.*

He described how to get to a meeting place in an area I was familiar with. I ignored it, turned the phone off, stuffed it in my pocket, and leaned back against the wall with my eyes closed. Now that everything was quiet I realized that the cards, which I had in my other pocket, seemed to be getting warm.

I pulled out the bag holding them. The two morphing ones had completed the process. The result was a single card, deep violet in colour, and still with the stylized butterfly in one corner. It now had a single red flashing number — thirty thousand — near the top, and a map, with some kind of route overlaid in green. Beside it were the words: 'Aug. 3rd, 1900 hrs'.

I'd seen that kind of thing before. It was a beacon. It indicated a location, probably for some kind of meeting. A glow that intensified as it approached the outer edge of the card indicated the direction. The number was the approximate number of meters to the target destination: thirty thousand — thirty kilometers. As you got closer, the number would decrease, sort of like the card saying: 'you're getting warmer' as you moved around.

When it hit zero, you'd arrived. But where was it directing me to? Wherever it was, I didn't see how it could be good. The beacon wouldn't work inside the bag, because it couldn't communicate through the conductive mesh. The number and direction must be measured from where I first got the cards, before I put them in the bag.

Again I studied Zack's gun. Before the raid with the Rebels, I'd never even held one in my hands let alone fired it at anybody. I fought to keep from puking as I wiped the worst of the blood off, held the gun up, sighted down the barrel, and shuddered. I shoved it in my belt.

The card was still warm. It was still working on something. Part of me wanted to toss it in the gutter and run as far away as possible. But based on the logo and where I'd gotten the original ones, the meeting was probably linked to Vita Aeterna. If that was true, I'd be needing the card.

Especially now.

I'd come to a decision. I realized the truth of everything Travis had been telling me - that millions had suffered and died because of the lies perpetrated by Wickham and the CCE. Zack had turned out to be a traitor, but he was right about the Rebels. They didn't stand a chance against the CCE. And he was right about Vita Aeterna. They would never give up — they'd chase me to the ends of the earth. As long as they were around, I'd be running like a hunted animal for the rest of my long life, or until I got fed up like Zack and took the final way out.

There was only one solution. It crystallized in my mind as I turned the glowing violet card over in my hands. I was going to carry out the mission Zack had talked about.

I was going to kill Charles Wickham.

Even if all of this went away, even if SecureCorp left me alone and Vita Aeterna disappeared, I'd still be a freak, outliving everybody on the planet. But at least Wickham's death might give my life some purpose.

If Wickham was taken out, Vita Aeterna would be crippled, and the CCE would be thrown into confusion — at least temporarily. Maybe his death would give what was left of the Rebels, and the Dead Shift, if they really were for real, the catalyst they needed to make an impact. Maybe the millions condemned to a life of poverty and sickness in the Quarters and the Dregs would finally be given a chance.

I guessed that the beacon would take me somewhere close to Wickham, maybe even directly to him. The card with the VA logo had belonged to Cindy's father, who must have been involved with Vita Aeterna. Maybe the beacon was his 'invitation'. If the meeting concerned that secret society, its leader would probably be there. But I couldn't use the map at this distance. It didn't show any detail, and there was no way to enlarge it. I could bring up maps on the HUD, but they only covered the Corp Ring — the Quarters and the Dregs didn't count, I guess.

Wherever I was going was in the Corp Ring. To start with I could make my way there. Once I got close enough I'd take the card out of the bag periodically, long enough for it to update, and check the direction indicator. That would probably allow SecureCorp to figure out where I was, so as soon as the beacon was updated, I'd have to cover it up again and run to a new hiding place. And I'd have to keep that process up until I got to the meeting location.

To accomplish my mission, I'd need to be mobile. I set off for the spot we'd seen Tory and the other dead gangsters. It wouldn't be much use in the Dregs, but back in Tintown I could cover a lot more ground if I had my board. I fought to keep my stomach contents down as I gave the bodies a wide berth and searched the area. There was no sign of my pack, but I found the board lying in a pile of other booty they'd locked in a nearby room.

Before I started, there was one connection I had to make. I'd had it with the Dead Shift, and I still wasn't sure about the Rebels, but somehow I had to contact Laura and explain what happened. Somehow I had to convince her that I wasn't a traitor.

I made my way back to the last place the Rebels had been. Of course, they'd moved. Alone, I'd probably never be able to find them. I was still new to the Dregs; I wouldn't even know where to start. But it occurred to me that I knew somebody who was an expert.

# THIRTY

..........................................

# LAURA

It took a whole day to find my way back to the building where I'd first met Benny — his 'headquarters'. My plan was just to hang around and hope I'd run into him, assuming he was still alive. The last time I saw him his wound looked pretty gruesome.

When I reached his 'office', there was no sign of him, but judging from the patches of blood on the chair where he usually sat, he must have been there recently. It didn't look like his wound had gotten any better. I realized that I was exhausted. I lay down on the floor and went to sleep.

A noise startled me awake. I looked up. Benny was standing in the doorway. I wasn't sure how he'd react when he saw me. I was relieved when he smiled.

"You came back," he said.

I checked out the wound in his side. His crude stitches had partially pulled loose and it was festering yellow and purple, oozing a mixture of blood and pus.

"You need to get that looked at," I said, cringing at the sight of the wound.

He got anxious and stepped back. "No way."

"You're going to die if you don't—"

"They're not gonna touch me," he said, his voice shaking. "I'm getting better."

"Okay, okay," I said. "Settle down."

I got up and stood in front of him.

"I need your help," I said.

"For the CCE?" he whispered.

I hesitated. "Yeah, that's right."

I gestured for him to come closer. He came and leaned down toward me. I lowered my voice. "I'm going to meet Mr. Wickham."

He stood up straight and stared at me in awe. Technically it was true, but I didn't tell him why. I felt like a shit lying to him, but I needed his help and it was the only way.

"First I need to connect with the Rebels," I said. "But I've got no idea how to find them. Will you help me?"

His face fell.

"It's important," I said. "Everything depends on it."

He stood motionless, staring at the floor for almost a minute, wrestling some inner demon.

Finally he looked up. "Wait here," he said. "I'll be back."

He took off without another word.

Benny was gone for two days. Luckily, the expired food packets were still lying around, along with the stale crackers and biscuits. I stuck to the most recent date-stamps, and they didn't make me sick, so I kept eating them. I found a secluded spot outside where there was enough sunlight to charge the crypted phone. Then I just hung around and waited.

Finally, early in the morning on the third day, he returned.

He led me through a maze of garbage and rubble strewn back alleys for five hours. We stopped in a part of the Dregs I'd never seen before, climbed to the fourth floor of an abandoned building, and peered through a window opening.

"There," Benny whispered, pointing down at what might have once been some kind of bus station.

"You've seen them?" I whispered back.

He nodded.

We hung around for a couple more hours, watching. He was right. I saw a few guys I recognized. I didn't see Laura. I was hoping against hope I'd see Bailey, or even Travis, but neither of them showed. The next problem was going to be how to contact Laura without alerting the others. A guard was patrolling the front of the building. I wasn't sure how the Rebels would react to me after what happened.

I went back downstairs and hid behind a corner near the hideout. When the guard was at the farthest extent of his patrol, I snuck to the opposite end of the building. I removed Laura's medallion from around my neck, threw it on the pavement in plain sight, and took off. Back at the hiding place I watched the guard return to the corner where I'd been. He picked up the medallion and looked at it, then looked up. I ducked away from the window as he surveyed the surrounding buildings. Eventually he wandered to the door, and called to somebody inside.

A couple of guys came out and searched the immediate area. We were ready to run if they expanded their search, but I don't think they had the manpower. They gave up and went back in. My only hope was that Laura would hear about the medallion and get the message.

Later in the afternoon, my heart jumped when she appeared at the entrance and stood talking with the guard. They argued for a few minutes, probably about how unsafe it was for her to be walking around alone. Finally, the guard waved his arm around, indicating something like: 'stick around this area'.

She wandered straight ahead for a few minutes. I got ready to move. When she'd gotten about fifty meters away, she ducked behind a corner and took off. The guard reacted, and started to chase after her, then realized he didn't dare leave his post, and came back.

I rushed downstairs and outside to intercept her. After a few minutes I heard her whispering for me. I headed toward her voice and found her standing in a cramped square, in the shadows. When she saw me, her face took on this look of something like loathing. I felt sick to my stomach.

"How can you show your face around here after what you did," she said. She nodded her head toward the hideout. "If they catch you they'll probably kill you — and you'd deserve it. I won't give you away, because part of me still cares for you, but you'd better leave."

She explained what she'd heard from Hank, the Rebel fighter I'd seen bending over Travis and Bailey before Zack dragged me away. He'd reported that Zack and I were working together. His partner had died in the firefight with Zack. Both had been waiting as 'insurance' some distance away, in case things went off the rails.

"My father's dead," Laura said, her eyes welling up and her lower lip quivering.

My own eyes filled with tears, my worst fears confirmed. "I'm sorry," I said. I stepped forward to comfort her.

She jumped back and pushed out her hands. "Don't come near me. This is all because of you. You and Zack."

"Zack's dead."

Her eyes went wide for a second. "I don't believe you." She shook her head slowly. "After all my father did for you…"

She said Bailey was alive, but moving in and out of consciousness. Hank had contacted the Rebels, who'd brought Travis, Bailey, and the dead fighter back to the hideout. Of course, they'd all had to move again.

"It's not like you think," I pleaded. "I didn't—"

"I don't want to hear any more from you," she said.

She was shaking, and the tears started to come. Instinctively I reached out to her. She backed away.

"Please leave," she sobbed. "And don't come back."

She turned to walk away.

"Wait," I called after her.

She stopped without turning.

"Benny's up there waiting for me," I said. "His wound is really bad. He needs a doctor."

She turned and stared at me for a second, like she thought maybe I was lying.

"He had nothing to do with any of this," I said.

"I'll keep an eye out for him," she finally said. "If he shows up, I'll make sure they don't hurt him, and maybe Dr. Treadwell can look at him. That's all I can do."

"Thanks," I said. "Laura—"

She shot me one last contemptuous look. "Come back here again and I'll give you up — or kill you myself."

She turned and walked away.

I felt like part of me had died as I watched her disappear into the shadows. I couldn't leave things like this — but I had to. Maybe someday she'd understand. For now, there was nothing I could do.

It seemed like I didn't have a chance in this world. It made me even more determined to complete my mission. Back at our hiding place, I tried to convince Benny to see Dr. Treadwell, but he didn't want to go anywhere near the Rebel hideout.

I appreciated him helping me find Laura, but I couldn't take him where I was going. I'd have to have to ditch him at some point, but I wasn't sure how to do that. I wished I hadn't told him about Wickham — now he was all hot to go with me, for the chance of meeting his hero. He wouldn't be so happy with me if he knew what I was planning.

For now, it was good to have him around. He knew how to navigate the Dregs to avoid the thieves and gangs, and if we did get into trouble, he was there to help me. I didn't want to think about what would happen when he figured out my real mission. For now, his excitement at the prospect of meeting Wickham was overriding his fear of leaving the Dregs. I hoped that once we got close to the borderline, his fear would win out and he'd give up on following me.

I left him for a few minutes and slipped the card out of its protective bag. The beacon light started flashing green. I mapped out what direction I should go, and checked the distance — thirty-two kilometers. I'd actually been closer the last time the card was updated, when I'd first entered the Dregs.

The meeting would probably be packed with assholes like Chuck — all the people that were after me. It would be like stepping into a swarm of killer drones. Zack had said that the main goal should be to kill Wickham. Zack wasn't around anymore to accomplish that task, if he ever intended to do it in the first place.

But I might be holding a free pass for a ringside seat to Zack's target.

# THIRTY-ONE

...................................................

# A VISITOR

Benny lightened up when I said we were finished with the Rebels. It was late in the afternoon, and we didn't want to travel at night, so we found a hiding place in an abandoned building not far from the Rebel hideout.

The next morning we took off, headed in the direction I'd figured out from the card. The first day went without a hitch. We reached the edge of the Quarters. As I'd expected, Benny started getting jumpy and anxious, torn between his fear of leaving the Dregs and his desire to meet Wickham. His fear seemed to be winning, which was fine with me. Tomorrow we'd be in my territory. I knew well enough how to get around there. We stopped just outside the border and found a hiding place for the night.

I couldn't sleep. Benny was snoring beside me as we lay on an upper floor of yet another abandoned building. I kept thinking about Laura. The look of loathing she'd given me at the hideout was etched into my brain. I knew she was wrong, but that didn't matter. A new goal was taking shape in my psyche like a gathering storm cloud. If I caught up with Wickham, not only could I take out my rage on somebody, I could end this nightmare once and for all, with Zack's ultimate escape.

I heard voices in the alley below, two male, one female. Then I heard a woman scream. I sat up, stuck my head out the window, and peered down. Lit by a pale patch of moonlight, two guys were dragging a girl toward the building across the street. It was obvious what they had in mind. The girl was screaming and fighting them. They moved closer to the light and I jumped up — it was Laura.

I leaned down and shook Benny's shoulder. "Benny, wake up!"

He sat bolt upright and grabbed me by the throat. "It's me," I barely managed to croak. He loosened his grip.

"It's Laura," I whispered, nodding toward the window. "She's down there. A couple of creeps have got her. We've got to help her."

He got up and leaned out the window. Laura was still screaming. We raced down the stairs, and got outside just in time to see the guys drag Laura into the building's smashed front door. We crossed the street and ducked behind the open doorway.

There was almost no light inside, but I could hear scuffling, and the sound of tearing clothing. Laura was screaming and her attackers were laughing. I had the gun, but didn't want to risk hitting Laura. As my eyes adjusted to the dim light, I looked for some kind of weapon. I spotted a length of two-by-four, but it was out in the center of the floor. I'd be in plain sight of the rapists if I went for it.

I was trying to decide what to do when Benny made my decision for me, running full-speed at the guys. I ran after him, picking up the two-by-four on the way.

Benny grabbed the closest one by the shoulder and tore him away from Laura. Before the guy even had a chance to scream Benny had snapped his neck. The other one turned to see what was going on. I could just make out a gun in his belt. He pulled it out and aimed it at Benny. I took a flying leap and brought the two-by-four down on his skull. The gun went off, but the bullet ricocheted off the floor. The guy went down, blood spewing from his head.

I grabbed his gun and held it on him, still breathing hard. He didn't move. Laura was on the ground. She staggered to her feet and swayed, like she was going to fall. I rushed over to hold her up.

"Can you walk?" I asked her.

She nodded. I took her hand as the three of us rushed out of the building. Outside, in the moonlight, we stopped and I checked her out. She was still shaking. Her shirt was ripped open, and her right eye would be black tomorrow, but otherwise she looked okay.

"We better get out of here," I said to Benny, stuffing the gun in my belt. "The gunshot will attract people."

We took off, putting as much distance as possible between us and the rapists. Benny found us another good hiding place and we hunkered down for the night.

"What the hell are you doing out here by yourself?" I asked Laura once we were settled. Moonlight streaming through the numerous window openings bathed her features in an eerie pale blue. Benny lay in a corner, snoring again like nothing happened. Laura and I sat on the floor, with the wall as a backrest.

Tears welled in her eyes. "Bailey finally regained consciousness and I talked to him," she said. "He told us Zack had a gun to your head. And our sources confirmed what you said about Zack being dead. I couldn't live with myself, the way I treated you. I had to find you and apologize."

I felt like a ten-tonne weight had been lifted from my shoulders. I turned and took her in my arms. Suddenly she kissed me, full on the lips. Again, I felt a stab of guilt about Cindy. But part of me thought back on what I was doing here and how my quest was likely to end. Would Cindy blame me for finding a tiny interval of love within the horror my life had become?

Then I was lost in Laura's kiss — lost in the warmth of her, in her innocence, her love. For a few seconds there was nothing else.

I leaned back, still holding her. "Thank God we were there to help you," I said, sobbing myself now.

I told her how her father had died, how I was kidnapped by Zack, and all that had happened after that. I didn't mention anything about my 'mission', or even where I was going. I knew she'd try to stop me. Anyway, there was no way I was going to say anything while Benny was around.

I closed my eyes and pulled her close. For a brief moment I felt safe and at peace. I could forget about the nightmare unfolding around me and lose myself in her warmth and love. For the first time since all this started, I was happy.

She finally broke away. We sat back in each other's arms.

"Who's in charge now?" I asked. "Now that..."

Her eyes went moist, but she got control of herself. "Bailey's taken over," she said. "He'd lost a lot of blood, but his wound wasn't that bad. He's been taking it easy — he's healing incredibly fast. It's tough for everybody, but we've been through it before. We all knew what life was going to be like when we got involved in the movement."

She wiped away a tear, and smiled. "I've got some good news..."

Her smile was infectious. I put my hands around her waist and smiled back. "I could use some of that."

"I got my Appraisal," she said

My throat tightened. "What was it?"

"Guess," she said.

"How should I know?" I blurted out. I cringed when I realized there was anger in my voice. She didn't seem to notice.

"One point four," she said, beaming.

She still didn't know. For a second I closed my eyes.

"What's wrong?" she said.

I opened them again, and forced a smile. "Nothing," I said. "That's great news."

"You've never told me what yours is," she said, teasing.

My gut clenched. I hesitated.

Her smile disappeared. "Oh God, is it bad?"

I smiled. "I guess great minds think alike — it's the same as yours."

She leaned forward and hugged me. "That's so wonderful. See, we're compatible in so many ways."

Benny was still snoring in the corner. I hated to spoil Laura's moment of happiness, but we had to talk. I held my finger to my lips and led her into another room.

"You can't come with me," I whispered when we were out of Benny's hearing.

The expression of joy still lighting her face collapsed. "Why not?"

I looked at the floor.

"What are you going to do?" she said.

I looked up. She was trembling.

"I can't tell you," I said. "But it's going to be dangerous."

"I don't care."

"Don't argue," I raised my voice. "You have to go back."

I heard Benny move in the other room. I snuck back to check on him. He'd just rolled over.

"Benny can take you," I whispered, nodding in his direction. "Neither of you can follow where I'm going. Maybe you can convince him to get Dr. Treadwell to look at his wound…"

She started to cry. I took her in my arms. "Look, if what I'm planning works out, I'll come back, I promise."

"And if it doesn't?" she said, her voice choked with tears.

I looked away.

"I don't want to talk about it anymore," she said. "If you don't want me around, say so. Otherwise, wherever it is you're going, I'm coming with you."

# THIRTY-TWO

..............................................

# CUTTING THE CORD

The next day, the three of us continued toward the border of the Dregs and Tintown. I gave the gun I'd taken from the rapist to Laura, for protection. Benny let it slip that we were going to meet Wickham. When Laura heard, she gave me this suspicious look, but she didn't say anything.

Laura and I talked as we walked. As always, I was torn between Cindy's memory and the feelings that were building inside me. I kept reminding myself about Laura's Appraisal, that we could never have a life together, but part of me refused to believe it. Maybe the doctors had been mistaken — maybe there was some way to fix it after all. They kept saying there was no way to lengthen your Appraisal, but had anybody ever tried to shorten it...?

Benny got more and more jumpy as we approached the border of the Dregs. I prayed that his fear would win out. There was no way I could take either him or Laura where I was going.

I started seeing stuff that was familiar. Late in the afternoon we crossed the fuzzy transition between the Dregs and Tintown. There were more people, who looked at us suspiciously. Once or twice a passerby gawked at the scar on Benny's right temple, where his HUD should be, at the absence of a controller on his wrist, and at the oozing wound in his side.

Every time we passed someone Benny would get more anxious and slow down, like he was being held back by some invisible force. I had to Cam-surf all the time now. Benny's eyes would go wide as he stared up at the cameras we were passing.

Late in the afternoon he started hanging back. He'd stand talking to himself, like he was trying to convince himself to keep going. I was stressing out too, as we got close to my old apartment. The image of my dad's face when I told him about my Appraisal, the sound of the SecureCorp guys interrogating him, and his body smashing to the pavement, rushed through my brain.

Benny started lagging farther and farther behind. Finally, he disappeared altogether. I probably could have gone back and tracked him down, but he couldn't be part of what I was planning, so I let him go. Anyway, I had a feeling he'd show up again before this was all over.

Now I had the problem of getting away from Laura. I'd been hoping that Benny could take her back to the Rebel hideout, but that option was gone now. As we got further into Tintown I felt more at home. Finally we were only a few blocks from where I was headed — the Center, our old meeting place. There was a danger that SecureCorp might know about it, but for what I wanted to do, it was necessary.

When we got there, I left Laura in one of our hiding spots nearby and staked the place out. It looked the same as always. I went back and got her. We pushed through the secret entrance, and settled in for the night. Again I told her to wait, and took off for a while. I had to make a phone call.

*Sorry about your uncle,* Richie texted over the crypted phone when I got through. I'd told him about Zack's betrayal, and how he finally died.

*You said you were looking for him,* Richie continued. *He had proof who he was...*

*It's not your fault,* I texted back. *Neither of us knew how things would turn out.*

He told me about the other guys in the Lost Souls. Jake had an Appraisal of 1.1. Not great, but acceptable. I envied him. Richie hadn't heard from Spiro since my 'death'. That couldn't be good...

Zack had told Richie my Appraisal score, but Richie hadn't believed him. I confirmed it. After almost a minute of silence, Richie finally texted back:

*No wonder they're after you.*

I worried that SecureCorp could somehow trace me through the crypted phone. Richie and some of his buddies are a lot more tech-savvy than I am. He convinced me that the phone really was safe — that even SecureCorp couldn't hack into the signal.

*I need a favour,* I texted. *It's totally fine if you don't want to get involved.*

*You're dead, remember?* he texted back. *You need all the help you can get.*

I described my plan to him, and he agreed.

Back at the Center, I talked to Laura. "A friend of mine's coming to meet us tomorrow morning."

"Why?" she said.

"He's going to help us get to the Corp Ring without getting caught," I lied. The lie didn't really make that much sense, and anyway I hadn't told her why I wanted to go to the Corp Ring, or what I wanted with Wickham, but she seemed to buy it.

I smiled. "So, if you see a big lug with curly blond hair coming at you in the dark, don't freak out and shoot him — it's just Richie."

Her eyebrows came together. "What do you mean? You'll be there too, won't you?"

"Yeah, sure," I said. "I was just joking."

She looked at me funny. We were both exhausted. I brushed the dust off the old mattress we used to sit on when we hung out here, and we both lay down on it. I put my arms around her. She didn't resist.

"You know how I felt about my girlfriend, Cindy," I whispered to her. She nodded. "I really like you," I said, "but I'm still trying to work all that stuff out."

"Sure, I understand," she said.

I held her more tightly. "No matter what happens, know that I'll always care for you."

Her body stiffened, but she didn't say anything. A few minutes later we were both asleep.

232

I woke up, the HUD alarm beacon I'd set earlier flashing. I was still wrapped around Laura. She was asleep, breathing heavily. I carefully worked my arm out from under her and moved away. She twitched a couple of times, but didn't wake up. I took one last look at the dark wavy hair flowing over her shoulder. She was so beautiful I had the urge to bend down and kiss her, but I didn't dare.

I couldn't just run off and leave her. I'd contacted Bailey and arranged for somebody from the Rebels to come and get her, and Richie had promised me that he'd look after her until they showed up. I knew I could trust him, but I had to be sure he'd even make it here. SecureCorp knew he was my best friend — they'd be watching him.

I climbed up high into the rafters of the building, where I'd be out of sight. I could still see Laura lying there, her knees drawn up and her hands together like she was praying, a childlike form on a torn-up mattress in a crumbling building in a dying city.

I must have nodded off for a while, because I was jerked awake by voices below. In the shadows, Richie was moving toward Laura with his hands raised. She was cringing behind a pillar with her gun drawn, and glancing desperately around, looking for something — someone — me.

I wished I'd found a spot that was closer. I couldn't hear what they were saying. Richie got within an arm's-length. He said something to her. She lowered the gun, but started yelling at him. I still couldn't hear what she was saying. Richie was shrugging and trying to calm her down. She glanced around one last time. Finally, she just seemed to collapse inside. She hung her head and started to cry. Richie put a hand on her shoulder and she batted it away.

I felt tears running down my own cheeks. I wanted to go down there — to jump up from where I was crouching in the dark like a coward and tell her I was sorry — to make it all go away. But I stayed where I was.

Richie gestured for Laura to follow him. She resisted at first, and yelled something else at him. In the end, she stuffed the gun in her belt and followed. She didn't have any choice. As soon as they were out of sight I made my way down.

I checked my pockets: the crypted phone in one, the bag of cards in the other. Once I was far enough away I'd check the melded card again to see what direction I should go.

I told myself I'd done Laura a favour, and I knew it was true. I couldn't form any attachments; not ever, but especially now. Nothing could stand in the way of me completing my mission.

# THIRTY-THREE

..................................................

# TRAIN HOPPING

Now that I was back in the Quarters it was slow going. If I used the beacon too often I was bound to get caught. I only felt safe checking it once a day. Each time, I'd have to make a note of the number indicator to make sure I was actually getting closer. Once or twice I drifted in the wrong direction and the next time I looked I was actually farther away. The location the card was guiding me to was far to the west. I traveled west in the Quarters for as long as possible before turning south and crossing into the Corp Ring.

Something else had been scratching at the back of my brain since the beacon appeared. Apps like this always came with some kind of security. You didn't want some creep who stole your card to end up at one of your private meetings. But there was no hint of that with this one. I'd unlocked it at Cindy's, but shouldn't there be additional security for directions to a meeting of a secret society? Was the card leading me into some kind of trap? After all, it was the melding of cards for Vita Aeterna and SecureCorp. For now, I shoved the idea into the

*235*

background. Chances were that I wouldn't live long enough to get that far. If I did, I'd deal with the consequences when I got to wherever it was taking me.

In the afternoon, two days after I'd snuck away from Laura, I contacted Richie and he confirmed that somebody from the Rebels had shown up and taken her back home. He said she'd been upset, but in the end, had accepted it. She should be back at the Rebel hideout by now. I hadn't seen any sign of Benny. Had he gone back to the Dregs and forgotten about me, or would he overcome his fear and try to follow me to Wickham?

On the third day I finally made it to the edge of the Corp Ring. Now I had another problem. The distances I'd been traveling up to now had been small enough that I could make good time on my board. But according to the card display, there was another twenty kilometers to go inside the Corp Ring. Not only was that a long way to board, but there were far more cameras here. For every one of those kilometers I'd be under tight surveillance.

I decided to try a trick the kids used sometimes in the Corp Ring — train-hopping. It was a good way to travel long distances without being seen (or paying anything), but it was also incredibly dangerous. Hardly anybody I knew was wacko enough to do it on a regular basis, and a lot of kids had died trying.

The idea was to find a hidden spot, usually some kind of overpass, that spanned a transit line. First, you climbed up underneath the structure to a position directly over the line (which was dangerous enough — I knew kids that had died just doing that). The spot you chose had to be on a hill or a curve, someplace that the train would slow down (to at least give you a fighting chance of surviving what followed).

Then, when the train passed under you, you fought to keep from shitting yourself and jumped, and hung onto the roof by your fingernails until either you got bounced off and died, or got where you were going. The train made regular stops, so you could get off pretty easily (though doing it without getting caught was another issue).

I'd only ever done it once, and I had no desire to ever do it again. I like danger, and I like taking risks, but there's a difference between taking risks and committing suicide. The line between the two was really thin for train-hopping.

The joke was, I still had the four hundred dollars in my shoe. For the first time in my life I could actually afford to pay for a ticket, but I couldn't take the chance that I'd be recognized.

The spot I'd jumped from that one time wasn't far from my current position, just inside the Corp Ring. I swallowed hard as I approached it — a truck overpass with a latticework of supports that spanned a line running in the right direction. Images flew through my head of the time I'd nearly died doing it before.

There were cameras on all the access points, but the crazies who were into train-hopping usually broke them as soon as they were installed. I gaped up at the angular web of steel above my head, and was grateful to see they'd kept up that tradition. I was lucky; right now there was nobody else around. With my board slung over my back, I climbed up the supports and made my way to a location directly above the tracks.

When I got to the jumping point, I was ten meters in the air. I held on tight. There were trains every few minutes. Whenever one passed below, my perch vibrated like an earthquake hit it. If I was to fall, and if by some miracle the fall didn't kill me, I'd probably get run over by the train.

I let a couple of trains go by, mentally rehearsing what I would do when the time came, and working up the nerve. Finally, I couldn't stall any longer. I was facing away from the oncoming train, but I could hear it rumbling behind me. In seconds, it was directly under my position. The vibration almost knocked me off as I straightened up, getting ready to leap to my doom.

I waited for the lead car to pass, then leaned out and tensed my legs. I could see my distorted reflection in the stainless-steel roof of the car flying below: squat and ugly, like the toad I was about to imitate. I said a prayer, and jumped. I landed okay, but the shaking bounced me toward the edge of the slippery-smooth roof. There was nothing to hang onto. I was an arm's length from being tossed over the side and cut to pieces by the wheels. I scanned the roof in a panic. A finger-sized knob, an antenna or something, stuck out a couple of meters away. I kicked at the slick metal and got enough traction to propel myself at it. If I missed, I was dead.

As I jumped, the car jerked sideways and knocked me on my back. I saw the knob go by, but I was bouncing sideways. It was all over. I rolled off the rounded edge.

I was waiting for the end, but stopped with a jerk in mid-air. I twisted my head around and looked up. The strap of my board had caught on the knob. I was hanging from it, with buildings and streets flying by at eighty kilometers an hour, the steel wheels grating on the rails below. I turned my head and looked in the window. Inside the car, a middle-aged woman stared at me in horror.

The strap was old and frayed. It wasn't going to hold for long. I twisted my body enough to grab it, and hooked my right toe onto the gutter of the window beside me. My muscles screamed with pain as I hauled myself back up. After what seemed like an eternity, I worked my way onto the roof and held on.

So far we hadn't made a stop, and I knew we still had a long way to go. I wondered whether the woman who'd seen me would say anything, but when we made the first stop, nothing happened. If you were pressed flat on the roof, you weren't visible from the platform, so if she kept her mouth shut, I'd be safe — until I tried to get off.

I hung on, vibrating and bouncing around like a marble in a slot machine, for five more stops. The blur of buildings flying by gradually grew in size and got fancier, as we approached one of the wealthiest sections of the Corp Ring. Before I made the jump I'd worked out which stop was closest to where I wanted to go, so as we approached the almost empty station ahead, I knew it was time to get off.

Somehow I had to do that without running into SecureCorp.

The train slowed as it approached the platform, with me still lying in plain sight on the roof. There were hardly any SecureCorp people watching. That was unusual. It occurred to me that a lot of them might have been siphoned off to look for me in the Quarters.

I heard the stations had algorithms that analyzed the camera scans of the train and picked out anybody riding on top. It was dangerous, but I decided to get into position while the train was still moving. There was a spot at the very front of the car I was on, near the exit doors but away from any windows. My plan was to slide down onto the platform at the exact moment the train stopped. Then I could merge with the crowd pouring out of the exit.

It was easier than I was expecting. Once the train slowed, there was almost no vibration. The few guards I could see were looking the other way. I crawled along the roof and got into position. A female voice echoed through the sound system announcing our arrival. The train finally shuddered to a stop, and the bell dinged to say the doors were opening. I slid down and jumped to the platform just as a mass of humanity started pouring out. An alarm went off — the cameras had seen me. A couple of SecureCorp guys rushed over, but I was lost in the crowd.

I smiled. Something had finally gone right. I was alive *and* free. We were almost at the main exit.

That's when I heard it — a woman's voice shouting: 'that's him there'. I glanced around. The woman who'd seen me hanging outside her window had ratted me out after all. She was standing with two SecureCorp soldiers and pointing at me.

"Shit," I said, and took off.

"Stop!" yelled a voice behind me.

The exit turnstiles were straight ahead. There was a soldier to one side. I flew toward the opposite side and took a flying leap over them.

"It's him!" I heard a voice yell.

I had a big head start, but I had no idea where I was going, and I was in too much of a panic to Cam-surf. I turned down the nearest corner, then down another one. The excited voices behind me faded, but I heard cars starting, sirens wailing, and a chopper approaching in the distance. This wasn't like the Quarters — there were almost no abandoned buildings to sneak into.

They'd be monitoring the camera feeds and rushing to this spot. I willed myself to relax, Cam-surfed down the alley to a larger street, and spotted something that could be my salvation. A RoboTaxi, coming right toward me, and slow enough to hitch a ride.

I'd have to wait until the front fender passed. I ducked behind the corner of the alley and unslung my board. There was a humming noise behind me. My spine stiffened as I recognized it. I turned to look. A swarm of twenty or thirty drones was hurtling my way from the other end of the alley. It was too early to jump. The swarm was half way along now, their high-pitched whine growing constantly louder. They'd be on me in seconds. Finally the taxi's fender appeared. As it passed I ran, jumped on my board, grabbed ahold of the back bumper, crouched down to avoid the cameras, and hitched a ride.

The swarm was right behind me. They couldn't keep up to a vehicle going full speed, but we were still on a side-street, where the taxis were programmed to go slower. The drones were catching up. One fired a tranquilizing dart that clanked off the metal trunk I was holding on to. I was about to let go and run for it, when the taxi turned right onto a main street and sped up.

We pulled away from the drones. But now I had a new problem. Normally I would have let go by now — it was almost impossible to board behind a vehicle going at full speed. But this time I had no choice. I just hung on for dear life. The wheels of my board were rattling on the pavement. If we kept this up, they'd soon start breaking off.

We rounded a curve and the drones were out of sight. But I still couldn't let go — we were going too fast. After ten minutes of expecting to die, we finally turned onto a side street, and slowed down. I let go, coasted to a stop, and stood there for a couple of seconds, hunched over, hyperventilating.

I could still hear the choppers and sirens in the distance, but they were now far away. I relaxed a bit. I got control of myself and started Cam-surfing. The blood pounded in my ears as I tried to put as much distance as possible between me and the last spot where I'd been visible.

# THIRTY-FOUR

..............................................

# STAKEOUT

For some reason, I'd pictured the meeting place as some big, flashy celebrity hangout, like the ones they used in their Safety Award shows, but it wasn't like that at all.

In fact, staring down at the beaten-up brick building that must have been built a hundred years ago, at first I thought I'd gotten the location wrong. But that couldn't be. It was the right address, and the number on the melded card read less than fifty.

I was hiding out on the roof of a building across the street, deep in the Corp Ring. When I'd finally been able to stop long enough to catch my breath after train-hopping, I checked the card, and found that I was only a kilometer or so from my destination. I Cam-surfed the rest of the way without any problems.

My hideout was some low-level BuildCorp warehouse, so security was pretty slack. There were no guards at the doors, even the main ones, and all the cameras were visible. I just waited until somebody went in the side door, snuck in behind them before it closed, and found my way to the roof.

It was night now, the night before the date now flashing green on the melded card — the date of the meeting. It was a crazy scheme, but I was desperate; I'd never get another chance at Wickham. The truth was I hadn't really thought any of it through. Right now, my only idea was to keep watch on the building and hope the right opportunity came along for me to sneak in. What was the right opportunity? I guessed I'd know it if I saw it.

Now that I'd made it here, and had some time to think about it, it hit home that after all the effort I'd put into getting this far, I had no idea what the meeting was about (or even that there *was* a meeting — maybe it was all a trap), and whether Wickham would actually be there. Anyway, I couldn't get to Wickham if I couldn't make it inside, and I'd never do that alone. If I was to have any hope of accomplishing my mission, I'd need some kind of help.

*I need another favour,* I texted Richie over the crypted phone. It's going to be tough, and probably really dangerous.

*Hey, I'm getting used to all that by now,* he texted back.

He didn't respond for a few seconds after I described what I needed from him and his hacker friends. At first he thought I was kidding — hacking a high-level Corp meeting?

Once he'd gotten over the shock he told me he needed half an hour to contact his friends and talk over whether it was remotely possible.

Now that I knew where the meeting was I didn't need to unblock the melded card again, which meant SecureCorp could no longer track me. Of course, they'd probably been monitoring the beacon all along, which meant they didn't need to track me, since they knew where I was headed. They'd be waiting. Thus the need for the mother of all hacks I was asking for. The only way I had any chance of a shot at Wickham was to fool their system somehow.

It was more than an hour before Richie finally got back to me. *No way we can hack the doors open,* he texted. *Whatever's happening at this place, it must be big. It's got security up the ying-yang.*

*So I'm screwed,* I texted back.

*Not necessarily,* he answered. *We can't hack the doors open. But maybe we can do something else. Security for the entrances and exits are tight, but there's other systems they haven't paid much attention to — like the lighting, heat, sound.*

*How does that help?* I texted.

He texted back. *We can create a diversion.*

By the next night I was as ready as I was ever going to be. It was too dangerous to move around. I slept at my rooftop hiding place, and spent the day lying low and keeping my head down.

Now I was relieved to have the comfort of darkness again to hide in. The card was ticking down, now reading less than two hours before the meeting time. I peeked over the edge of the roof. The main entrance of the target building was still as dark as a tomb. It didn't look like there was anything going on. But then, Vita Aeterna was a secret society — it wasn't going to broadcast its meetings to the public.

The plan was that if conditions were right, I'd text Richie from the crypted phone, and he and his hacker friends would stomp on all the building's systems they could access. If there was enough confusion, maybe a door would be left open when nobody was watching.

I headed down, snuck around the place, and found a tiny entrance at the back, with a single dim light above it. I expected that it would be less secure, but even that one had a guard. That was a good indicator that I had the right place — something big was going on.

I hid in a camera-less shadow behind a corner of a building across the street, where I still had a partial view of the main entrance. I waited, and twenty minutes later a big black limo slid up to the curb at the entrance, and a light at the front blinked on. A guy got out. It was too dark to make out who it was. He stopped in front for a few seconds, I guess to pass through security or something, then went in.

Over the next half-hour about twenty vehicles pulled up. Their owners all went through the same routine as the first guy. So far I hadn't seen any way inside. The guard on the side door didn't look like he was going anywhere, and even if he left, the door he was guarding would be locked and alarmed.

Ten minutes later, a TechCorp van pulled up by the little door I was nearest to. A workman got out and strolled over to talk to the guard.

The guard contacted somebody over his HUD, then nodded at the workman. The workman went back to the van, opened the hatch, and unloaded a trolley with what looked like media equipment: speakers, floodlights, video projectors.

Finally it looked like I might have caught a break. I got ready with the phone. The media guy locked up again and wheeled the trolley to the side door. The guard frisked him, then sifted through the stuff on his cart. They talked again for a few seconds, and bingo! The guard reached over and opened the door.

I typed 'Go' and held my finger poised above the phone. The guard stood aside and held the door open, and the media guy wheeled the trolley towards it. As soon as the trolley was blocking the door, I hit the 'send' button.

All hell broke loose. Alarms sounded, lights flashed, and I could hear shouting inside the building. The guard talked to somebody on his HUD, then rushed toward the main entrance. The trolley and the media guy were left still blocking the door.

I jumped up with the gun in my hand and ran toward him, taking a route I'd already picked out to avoid the cameras. The media guy was standing there, stunned. I pointed the gun at him and shouted, "Get lost!"

He put a hand on the trolley.

"Leave it!" I yelled.

He put his hands up and ran towards his van.

I shoved the gun in my belt, pushed the trolley out of the way, and rushed through the door.

I tore down the hallway, avoiding the cameras. Alarms blared from several locations in the building, and both the emergency and the regular building lights were flashing.

"Good job, Richie," I said under my breath.

I wondered what the media guy would do. I hoped he was scared enough to take off and not say anything, but I had to assume that the security people knew about me. At least I was inside.

There was nobody around. I guess they were all dealing with what they assumed was some kind of emergency. A sign ahead said 'Conference Room One'. I found the door. Big surprise — it was locked. It had a small window in it. I stood on tip-toes and peered inside. It was a small theater. There were rows of chairs and a stage at the front with a lectern. I guessed that the meeting they were planning would probably happen here.

I looked up. A balcony wrapped around the room at the next level. There were stairs leading up to it. I was debating whether to sneak up there when the alarm suddenly stopped, and the lights quit flashing.

Without the alarms it was eerily quiet. I felt like the whole of SecureCorp were going to descend on me at any second. I was too exposed down here. I took the stairs to the next floor. A hallway running parallel with the back of the meeting room had two doors spaced evenly along it. I rushed to the first one and tried the handle. It was locked, but it had a window like the other one. I looked inside. It was an entrance to the balcony.

248

So far nobody else had showed up. I gave up on the balcony and ran down the hall looking for another place to hide. I turned a corner into another corridor. On the left wall was a door marked 'Maintenance'. No window in this one, but light was pulsing off and on through the crack underneath it.

A card scanner with a red light was mounted beside the locking mechanism. I put my hand on the cards in my pocket. They were warm. I thought about the melded card. If it was partly a Vita Aeterna card... But the beacon would tell them where I was. I took out the protective bag still holding the cards, held the open end around the detector, and passed the melded card over the surface.

The card was changing — the surface swimming in colours that seemed to be coalescing into some kind of image. I didn't have time to worry about what was happening. I looked over at the detector. Its light turned green and there was a click inside the lock.

I tried the handle. It turned. I opened the door.

There were footsteps and shouts heading toward me. I stepped inside and shut the door. The room was jammed with electrical panels, communications boards, and heating equipment — a maintenance room. Two or three large ducts ran up to the ceiling. Suddenly the lights stopped blinking. I heard the click of the auto-lock on the door and stared down at the open bag still in my hand. A few seconds later footsteps of several people ran past. Someone tried the door handle. I held my breath. It was now locked. More footsteps rushed away and I exhaled deeply.

But why had it unlocked it for me — and who locked it again behind me?

There was still shouting and the pounding of feet in the distance. I figured I was dead if I stepped outside the door, but that was the only way out. Then I noticed a grate in the ceiling for the ventilation system. I stacked a couple of boxes on top of each other, climbed up, and pushed on it. It lifted easily. I wasn't high enough to see inside. I stacked another box and poked my head up through the hole. Air ducts, big enough for me to squeeze into, branched off in several directions.

There was nothing else here, so the ducts looked like my only choice. All my life I hated being such a little runt. For once I was glad. I hoisted myself into the duct opening and pulled the grate back into place. After taking a few seconds to visualize the position of the theater I'd passed earlier, I moved in that direction. Occasionally I'd pass other grates in the ceilings of different rooms.

The running and shouting had died away now. All was silent. I peered down through a ceiling grate above the balcony I'd passed earlier. There was another one just ahead — one that I guessed would give me a clear shot at the stage.

# THIRTY-FIVE

..............................................

# VITA AETERNA

A door opened somewhere below, in the direction of the outside hall-way. I pressed my back against the duct. People started shuffling into the theater, and mumbling voices filled the space below. For ten minutes I lay there, frozen. Soon they'd all be seated and the room would be quiet.

*Shit!* I thought, as it occurred to me that I should have been head-ing for the closer grate while there was still noise to cover the sound. I started moving now. I'd hardly gone anywhere when the shuffling and talking died down and the room went silent. Now I was stuck about a quarter of the way from the balcony grate and the one nearer the stage. The light pouring up through the theater grating dimmed, and there was polite applause.

A male voice started speaking. I couldn't hear what he was saying, but it sounded like some kind of introduction. In a few minutes who-ever it was finished talking, and there was a thundering applause. I took advantage of the noise and slid closer to the grate near the stage.

By the time the applause died down I was about two-thirds of the way there. The new arrival at the podium started speaking. I could catch snippets of what he was saying.

I heard. "...slip through our fingers."

I took a chance and edged slowly toward the grate. In a few minutes, I was close enough to see the stage and the speaker at the lectern. The hair at the back of my neck rose, as I recognized him from countless appearances on HoloTV, and on posters everywhere I went.

It was Charles Wickham — the CEO of SecureCorp, the head of the CCE, and the force behind Vita Aeterna — the man I was here to kill.

Several other men and women were lined up on the stage behind him. I recognized the uniforms some of them were wearing: SecureCorp, TechCorp, MediCorp.

Where Chuck's face was smarmy and devious, Wickham looked downright evil. His eyes were like bullet holes, black and empty. At one point, he stopped talking and lifted his head. He seemed to be staring right at me. I froze. I was sure nobody could see me from down there, but...

He lowered his head again. I relaxed a little.

"This is an unprecedented opportunity," he continued. "Never before has such a multiple been available for our study."

I shivered. I had a bad feeling I knew who he was talking about.

Wickham finally shut up and went to sit in an empty chair, as one by one the others on stage got up and talked. They sounded like scientists or doctors or something. They went on for about an hour. I couldn't catch all they were saying, but the overall gist seemed to be that whatever they were trying to do wasn't going very well. With each speaker Wickham's expression got angrier.

I heard the final guy say: "It's as if an insurmountable barrier has been placed in our way, a barrier that we cannot cross — as if God has drawn a line in the sand and said 'this far and no further'."

This really seemed to piss Wickham off. His face turned red. He stood up and grabbed the back of the chair beside him, and for a minute I thought he was going to lift it up and throw it at the guy.

Wickham finally got ahold of himself, and said: "That is completely unacceptable. *We* control our fate. *Nothing* is insurmountable. That's just a pathetic excuse for failure."

The scientist looked scared. "We've been working like slaves—"

"Well work harder!" Wickham shouted him down. He pounded his fist on the back of the chair. "And find the boy! He's the key! Our sources tell us he's headed this way. How can one pissy little low-life shit evade the whole of SecureCorp?"

A couple of the people on stage bowed their heads. The SecureCorp guys tried to avoid his gaze.

Wickham strode up to the lectern, pushed the scientist guy away, and spoke again. "Some of you are lucky enough to have Appraisals that could allow you to live productive lives for well over one hundred years…" He cast his gaze around the room. "Don't jeopardize that gift by continuing to fail me!"

As Wickham was shouting I edged my way the final distance to the grate. I was now looking straight down onto the stage. He was no more than ten meters away. He paused, and there was silence around the room. Somebody at one of the tables cleared their throat. It looked like Wickham was wrapping up. He'd be leaving the stage within a few minutes.

I worked the gun out of my belt, released the safety, and gripped it in my hand. He was right in front of me. I was worried that the mesh of the grate would deflect the bullet. From the one I'd climbed through at first, I knew the grates were held in place by a set of clips. If I pushed hard enough on the one below me it would fall out and I'd have a perfect line of sight. But as soon as the grate fell everybody would know I was there.

When I was convinced that Laura hated me, I was willing, even eager, to die trying to complete my mission. When she came back, I convinced myself that somehow I could take out Wickham and still escape. Now it was obvious. There was no way I'd get out of here if I took the shot. I had to choose, and I didn't have much time.

Then I remembered why I was here. This was bigger than just me. I stared at the gun, shaking in my hand. If I could take out Wickham, at least I'd give future generations a chance at a life.

I looked up. Wickham had finished talking, and was turning to leave the stage.

I slammed my fist down on the grate. It bent open but didn't fall. There wasn't enough room in the cramped duct to get a good punch at it. Shouts went up from below. I hit it again and it finally dropped to the floor. Wickham was startled and rushed from the stage, surrounded by bodyguards. I held up the gun and fired. One of the guards went down. Wickham was running now. I fired again, but didn't hit anything.

*254*

One of the guards turned to shoot me, but Wickham's voice yelled, "No, it's him! I want him alive!" It was over. I'd failed. I couldn't turn around in the duct so I crawled forward. My only hope was to find a grate in another room, climb down, and run for it.

The duct I was in ran straight ahead for about twenty meters. That's the direction they'd expect me to go. But a couple of meters ahead was another duct angling off to the right. I took it instead, and followed it into another duct running at ninety degrees. There was another grate about five meters ahead. I crawled to it and looked down. Below was an empty room.

I stuffed the gun in my belt, punched out the grate, and dove through it to a desk underneath. I landed unhurt, but realized that the gun had fallen and was still up in the duct. There was no time to go back for it. I jumped from the desk, rushed to the door, and opened it a crack. An army of feet were pounding down the hallway, headed in my direction. They sounded like they were about to turn the corner to my left. I took off in the other direction and flew around a corner myself, buying a little time.

The alarms started sounding again. I had no idea whether it was Richie and his hackers or the security guys controlling them. I spotted a door to the outside. Was it possible I could get away after all? I crashed into it and to my surprise it opened. I took the steps to the street two at a time, reached the ground, and tore up an alleyway. I ran until I thought my lungs would burst.

I had to stop and get my breath. I spotted a dumpster and squeezed in behind it, gasping for air.

Shouts, car engines, and running feet echoed in the distance. As soon as I had the strength I raised myself up and got ready to take off again.

I froze when I heard a muffled voice coming from the pocket of my pants. I reached in, like I was expecting a trap to snap shut on my fingers, and pulled out the packet of cards.

The MoneyAll was missing. I fished around in the pocket and found it. The elastic holding the bag had fallen off. The bag had opened, and the MoneyAll had fallen out. I turned it over. Its surface was filled with the video of a face — the face of Charles Wickham.

"You can't run, boy," Wickham said, a sneer curling up on his lips. "We've had you all along."

I felt sick. "You're lying," I yelled at his picture.

I tossed the MoneyAll in the dumpster, with Wickham's face still frozen on it. I looked at the bag. The melded card was now glowing. I considered tossing it too, but it had helped me find Wickham and get access to the maintenance room; it might still be good for something else. I wrapped the elastic securely around it, took off my shoe, shoved the bag and card into it along with the money, and put it back on.

I took one last deep breath and stepped out from behind the dumpster. A line of SecureCorp soldiers stood facing me, their guns drawn. I turned to run. I heard a sound behind me. Before I could turn around, a muscular arm wrapped around my neck and squeezed. After a few seconds I blacked out.

When I regained consciousness, there was a face hovering just above mine. My eyes weren't focusing properly yet, but I didn't need them to recognize who it was. I'd know the stench of his breath anywhere.

Brickhead.

He reached down and clamped a hand around my throat.

"Lucky for you Wickham wants you alive," he snarled.

He pushed down, compressing my windpipe until I almost passed out again. He finally let go, probably worried that he'd kill me. I gasped for breath. He dragged me to my feet.

The line of soldiers had moved closer.

Brickhead shoved me toward the leader. "Take him to headquarters," he said.

Two of the soldiers dragged me toward a SecureCorp vehicle parked nearby. One of them frisked me. He dumped the crypted phone, the money, and the card, which was now pulsing on and off, into a big envelope, and tossed the envelope onto the seat of the driver's compartment. His partner slid open the side door. They handcuffed me and dragged me inside. The back was empty, except for a bench on each side. They sat me down on the far one, strapped me in, and slid the door shut. A few minutes later we started moving.

It took a few minutes of twisting and stretching, but I managed to unbuckle the strap holding me in. I thought back on Zack's story about his escape. Crouching to stay below the window of the cab, I made my way to the side and rear doors of the vehicle and pushed on the handles with my bound hands. Both were locked; I wasn't getting out that way.

I returned to the bench and peered through the side windows at the buildings flying by. They got bigger and fancier with every block — mirrored glass, concrete polished as white as a cloud. And we kept going, deeper into the Corp Ring than I'd ever gone before.

Finally I sat back on the bench and closed my eyes, exhausted, powerless, and defeated. My mission, the one act that would have given my life purpose, had failed.

That's when it happened. A deep blue glow appeared on my HUD, and a shape coalesced in front of it — the head and shoulders of a human being.

But it wasn't human. It was like a 3D representation, an avatar. Eyes, a nose, and finally a mouth, gradually formed. When the mouth was finished forming it started to speak.

"Hello, Alex," it said.

# THIRTY-SIX

..............................................

# A FRIEND

I sat up straight. The glow had faded but now it was pulsing on and off. For a second I thought I was hallucinating. I shook my head and blinked my eyes. The image was still there.

"W...Who are you?" I asked the cartoon guy.

"A friend," the voice answered. It sounded male, but with a weird overtone, like the computer-generated voices on the vending machines, only way more natural.

"Do not be alarmed," it said. "I have been attempting to help you for some time, but until my complete integration I was unable to communicate with you directly."

*Integration?* I thought. *What was this thing?*

Finally it dawned on me. "You're the card," I said.

I thought about where the melded card had come from, how the meeting location and date had appeared with no security, and the way it had opened and locked the doors at the building where I tried to assassinate Wickham. Now it had spawned some kind of bizarre mutant being that could communicate with my HUD. Why had I kept the stupid thing in the first place?

The card spoke again. "I represent the fusion of the artificial intelligence components of the two cards from which I was formed. I'm happy to report that I have successfully cross-referenced the mission statements of both SecureCorp and Vita Aeterna, and resolved all resulting semantic conflicts."

"What the hell is that supposed to mean?" I said. A square, black region formed beneath the speaking image in my HUD. The title *SecureCorp* appeared, and bulleted lines of text scrolled down below it. It was too fast for me to catch them all, but I saw:

- **Maintain the Peace**
- **Protect Property**
- **Prevent Crime**

The title *Vita Aeterna* followed. Again, I only caught a few of the entries:

- **Study the effects of the Appraisal process**
- **Locate and protect subjects with extraordinary Appraisals**
- **Identify means to control life extension**

"So what's all that got to do with me?" I asked, still not convinced it was all real. I had no idea what this card creature, or whatever I should call it, was, but if it came from the melding of a SecureCorp card and a Vita Aeterna one, I didn't see how it could be good.

"Since I became aware, a few weeks ago," it answered, "I've been attempting to divine the purpose of my existence. From my analysis of the above mission statements, I have reached the conclusion that my most important function is to maximize your well-being."

"Maximize *my* well-being?"

"In other words, to help you."

"What?" I said, staring at the avatar. "Not that I'm not complaining, but are you sure you read those mission statements correctly?"

"There is no doubt," the voice answered. "When my Vita Aeterna component took your picture at your girlfriend's house, it was able to determine your identity. It analyzed your Appraisal, and ascertained your significance. You are an anomaly — an outlier of the highest order. The continuation of your life and health is my most vital concern. In pursuit of those goals, I have identified your greatest threat."

I laughed. "I already know my greatest threat."

"As you have demonstrated," the voice said. "On that point, we are in partial agreement. Clearly, for you to survive and thrive, Charles Wickham must be eliminated."

I actually pinched myself — I thought maybe I was dreaming, but after the pinch it was all still happening. I wasn't sure how it was coming up with its world-view, but I was pretty sure that it didn't have a handle on the real purpose of SecureCorp, and I was positive it didn't have one on the real purpose of Vita Aeterna.

But at this stage, I wasn't going to argue.

"Wickham is a threat," the voice continued, "but there is a greater, more catastrophic one."

"Y...Yeah?" I stuttered. I was still stunned by the conversation I was having.

The figure spoke again. "Mr. Wickham, and the other Elite, have a plan to eliminate those members of society they consider superfluous."

"Superfluous?" I'd never heard that word before.

"Unnecessary," the voice said.

My spine stiffened. Zack had claimed they had this 'Final Solution' in mind, but I hadn't believed him.

"They have constructed a factory deep in the Corp Ring," it continued, "to produce a toxin that they plan to unleash on the Dregs and the Quarters, resulting in the deaths of millions.

"If they were to succeed, your life could only be preserved if you became their prisoner and test subject. Their experiments would almost certainly cause you serious harm — possibly even result in your death."

"And..." I started off, worried now that I might say something that would make it change its mind, "you know a way to stop them?"

"The factory must be destroyed," the voice said.

"I'm supposed to destroy a factory?"

"You will require help." The image had a creepy way of moving its lips as it spoke. It continued. "My analysis of net traffic indicates some serious errors in the Elite's assessment of the public sentiment. A number of riots have broken out already, and my evaluation predicts further major events in the near future.

"The coming chaos will siphon off much of the security surrounding SecureCorp installations. The Rebels, and others with an interest in destroying the factory, can take advantage of the resulting vulnerability."

I was confused. This 'card being', or whatever it was, could be lying (really?), but I didn't have a lot of friends right now.

I turned to face the driver's compartment, where the card lay in its envelope. "How the hell are you doing all this, anyway?"

The creepy lips moved again. "I'm communicating through your crypted phone. I can hear you by monitoring the audio input on your HUD controller. I can also monitor the feeds of any nearby cameras to see your image. I will do my best to help you, but my abilities are limited. I can hack into buildings, unlock and lock doors, and control functions such as lighting and heat."

"Can you unlock my handcuffs and open the doors of this van?" I asked.

"The van is an older model I cannot control," the card answered.

"No offense," I said, "but in that case your skills aren't all that useful right now."

The image spoke again. "Through your crypted phone I can connect to the network, and devices attached to it, and make certain changes."

"Like what?" I asked.

"Sorry to interrupt," the image said, "but your phone has just received a text message from a 'Connor McLean'. I will forward it to you."

I'd already told Connor where to shove it once — I wondered why he'd be contacting me again.

*We knew nothing about what Zack was planning,* Connor texted. *We were as surprised as you were.*

I didn't believe him, but I thought about how Zack had insisted that I not tell the others what we were doing. I decided to at least hear him out.

Connor continued. *I've contacted the Rebels. Bailey and I have gotten together and worked out our differences. The deaths of Travis and Zack affected both of us. We're after the same thing, and there's no way we're going to get it unless we join forces. We're here to support you if you need us.*

"Can I reply to him?" I asked the avatar.

"I can re-route your reply to the crypted phone," it answered.

*Okay,* I texted from my controller, too stunned to know what else to say.

*Are you with us?* Connor texted.

I sat there, confused.

*I'll let you know,* I finally texted, still in shock.

I told the card being to end the call. Its image was still floating in my HUD.

"What if I want to 'summon' you or something?" I said to the avatar. "What am I supposed to call you?"

"Call me whatever you choose," it said.

I heard a story once, from long ago, about this guy who had something called a Genie in a bottle that would grant him wishes. I felt like that guy, with this force that was supposed to be working for me.

"I'll call you Gene," I said.

"Very well," Gene answered.

I thought about what Connor had said. I'd always gotten a more positive vibe from him than from my uncle, but after all that had happened...

About five minutes later, I got a text from Bailey. He backed up Connor's claim that they were working together. He also confirmed what Laura had said about Zack's betrayal and Travis' death, and that no one blamed me. In the end, the run we were on when Rolf attacked me had been successful. The Rebels had come away with a valuable cache of weapons. Bailey was healing quickly, and was now able to actively lead.

*Connor asked before if I was with you,* I texted him. *I am in spirit, but I'm sort of unavailable right now.*

I explained where I was, about Gene, and about what was happening. I filled him in on the Final Solution Gene had talked about. There was a long pause. He was probably having a hard time believing me.

*We'll look into the factory thing,* he finally responded. *There's not much we can do to help you at the moment but I'll talk to the others about it.*

A few minutes later, the van stopped. The door in front of me slid open, and my captors motioned for me to jump down. I stood for a second with my eyes bugging out. Fifty meters ahead of us stood a massive, pure white wall at least ten meters high.

The First Circle — the forbidden zone.

I didn't know anyone who'd been inside — not even Cindy. An equally huge and equally white gate was set into the wall. I was half expecting to get machine-gunned or something — there actually were parapets mounted up high on each side, and I could see the tops of what looked like machine guns sticking up over the openings.

My captors dragged me toward a small door to the left of the main gate, and contacted somebody on their HUDs. Seconds later there was a click. The guards opened the door, and shoved me through.

I gawked around me. It was night, but the whole place was lit up like a fireworks display. It was like passing through the gates of paradise: glittering silver and glass skyscrapers sparkling like jewels all around me, spotless streets, not a broken window or streetlamp in sight. I stopped short as something else occurred to me — according to my HUD there were no cameras — anywhere! I guess that's how confident they were that nobody could get in. It was a joke that the two places I'd been that didn't have cameras were the Dregs and the First Circle.

My captors chained me to a metal post, then walked over and talked to some other SecureCorp people at an out-building nearby. One of them was carrying the envelope with the melded card and crypted phone.

I stared back at the massive gate, and turned so that the guards couldn't see me talking.

"Gene, are you still there?" I asked, still feeling like a moron talking to a cartoon. The image reappeared in my HUD.

"You say you can open doors," I said. "What about these ones?" I nodded at the gates. It was partly a joke.

He answered, "If they are opened without authorization, the authorities will immediately attempt to close them again. But I can set in motion a series of workarounds that will hold them open for approximately one hour."

I stared at the avatar, stunned. "I don't believe it," I said. "You're shitting me."

There was a deep rumbling sound, and the giant gates started to move. The doors were swinging open, all by themselves. I stood there with my mouth hanging open, staring at the empty space behind them. The guards my captors had been talking to rushed forward. Dozens of soldiers were running around, shouting, trying to understand what was happening. Several of them jammed themselves against the massive doors, trying to push them shut.

"Okay, I believe you," I said to the avatar. Almost immediately, the gates began to close again.

Minutes later, a new SecureCorp vehicle showed up. My captors unchained me from the post and shoved me inside. The vehicle took off. I peered through the tinted window of the vehicle's cab. The envelope with the card and phone lay on the seat. The soldier sitting beside it was completely oblivious to what was going on.

About a half hour later, Gene routed through a new text from Bailey.

*There's a new urgency now,* he said, *with your news about the factory.*

With Gene's help, the new Rebel/Dead Shift alliance had confirmed his claim of a Final Solution, and located the factory that was to produce the toxin. Gene had also helped their tech guys hack the blueprints for the building, and they'd come up with a plan to destroy it. But the plan required high explosives, and the factory was heavily guarded. They'd need a major diversion to gain access.

I told Bailey about Gene's ability to control the gate. *That would be fantastic!* he answered. *The open gate would be the ultimate diversion. Any idea when this could happen?*

I called to Gene, and his image appeared. "Obviously you *can* open the gate," I said, "but *will* you — if I ask?"

I explained Bailey's idea of using the open gate as a diversion to draw off soldiers from the factory.

Gene answered. "Article four of the SecureCorp mandate states: *Protect the lives and well-being of citizens.* The elimination of large segments of the population is clearly contrary to this goal. Opening the gate would facilitate the factory's destruction. However, it would have to be done in the next twenty minutes."

"Why is that?" I asked.

"Because," Gene answered, "we are about to reach our destination. Chances are that the crypted phone will be removed from my proximity."

I relayed Gene's answer to Bailey. After a long pause, he signed off, saying he wanted to discuss what had been said with the other Rebels, and with Connor.

We kept driving, past lush gardens, spraying fountains, and gleaming towers of glass and steel. I hoped I'd hear from Bailey soon. I had a feeling we were almost where we were going.

Bailey finally texted back. *We're gathering all our forces as we speak. We've got our two stealth vehicles and the motorcycles, and we can steal RoboTaxis and other vehicles along the way.*

*The plan is to split into two groups. One will head for the gate immediately. If it's open we'll fight our way in and mount an attack on SecureCorp headquarters. That's guaranteed to freak out the Elite and occupy a huge number of SecureCorp soldiers. The other group will break into a SecureCorp armaments warehouse not far from the factory, which we hope will be thinly guarded by then, and steal the explosives we need.*

*Ask your friend to wait as long as possible, then open the gate. We'll be there as soon as we can.*

I closed my eyes. Would Gene really open the gate, or was it some trick by SecureCorp? Vita Aeterna already had me. If Gene was lying, they could ambush both the Dead Shift and the Rebels, and eliminate their only opposition.

But what if Gene was telling the truth? I'd already blown my one chance to kill Wickham. I'd never get another one without major help — help that even the Dead Shift and Rebels combined couldn't give me. I looked ahead at my future, either caught and experimented on until I wasted away like Walter, or running scared for the rest of my incredibly long life like Zack.

I swallowed. Gene had convinced me that he could lock and unlock doors, and even open the forbidden gate. What I couldn't be sure of was *why* was he doing it.

I might be leading the people who'd helped me and taken care of me, who trusted me, into a trap. Worse than that, if the Dead Shift and Rebels were wiped out, there'd be nobody left to change anything.

But this might be the one chance we had to make a difference.

# THIRTY-SEVEN

........................................................

# WICKHAM

About twenty minutes later, the vehicle rolled to a stop. My captors opened the sliding door and hauled me out. Straight ahead was a massive, open concourse with trees and spraying fountains. At its center loomed a gigantic, ultra-modern structure — a palace of mirrored glass deep inside the First Circle. I called for Gene, but there was no answer. Far in the distance, a soldier carrying the envelope headed for the building's entrance.

For a few seconds I stood frozen, gaping up at the incredible structure, like nothing I'd ever seen before. A single guard appeared at the front, then several others. They patrolled around the massive plate glass facade, beneath the giant, black 'SecureCorp' sign above the entrance — SecureCorp headquarters. My captors dragged me forward. As we approached the huge glass doors a light on a security panel flicked green, and they swung open.

The lobby must have been a hundred meters across, and the ceiling was another thirty meters above my head. The furniture and fixtures were luxurious in the extreme: plush leather couches, polished wooden tables and chairs, carpets so thick it felt like I was walking on air.

Soon we were joined by Brickhead. I noticed that he now walked with a limp. He rubbed his bad leg and sneered at me. We headed for a row of gleaming, stainless-steel elevators on the east wall. Brickhead pressed the Up button for the closest one. When it arrived, my original handlers took off, and Brickhead and I entered it alone. He pressed the button for the tenth floor, and we sped upwards.

It stopped, and we stepped out into a long hallway. There was nobody around. It was creepy. At the end, to our right, one door was open; a bent trapezoid of light spilled out into the corridor. Brickhead prodded me toward it.

When we reached the open door, he gave me one last kick and I stumbled inside. There, sitting in a high-backed leather chair by a massive plate-glass window, framed by a stunning view of the glittering lights of the First Circle, was the man I'd sworn to kill — Charles Wickham.

He swiveled to face me and smiled. "Hello, Alex. We finally meet."

He nodded at my handcuffed wrists, and Brickhead reluctantly bent down and removed them.

Wickham ignored me for a few seconds, while he talked to somebody on his HUD. I wondered whether the feed for his HUD was the same as mine. No way. His body twitched. I smiled. There was stuff going on he didn't understand any more than I did.

I just stood staring at him. The call might have been about the open gate. I wondered if he knew about the gathering Rebel force, or the melded card, or that it had said it wanted him dead. I wasn't sure if I believed that myself.

Wickham composed himself and smile broadened. "Our tracking of your movements implies that you've been looking for me. Now that you've found me, what are you planning to do?"

"Give me a gun and find out."

He laughed. "You have a lot of rage inside you for one so young."

"Maybe that has something to do with you ruining my life and killing everybody I ever cared about."

He shrugged. "That's the way of the world — just business - nothing personal. A week from now, most of the people you 'cared about', as you say, would have been gone in any case. By that time there will only be three Corps," he continued, a smug expression on his face. He rose from his chair and strolled across the room, absently glancing out the floor to ceiling windows.

I had to laugh. "Three Corps? I thought you guys were supposed to be big on competition."

He stopped and turned to face me. "Well, you know how it is with competition. Somebody loses and somebody wins." He smiled. "When I've finally won against all my competitors — and I *will* win — there will only be *one* Corp, and I will be at its head. After all, that's the ultimate intent of all competition, isn't it — to produce a single winner? In order for that to happen, all the other competitors have to be eliminated."

I cast around the room for some kind of weapon. Brickhead seemed to have disappeared. As far as I could tell Wickham and I were alone. It was my one chance. He was old, but he was still a lot bigger than me, and he looked in good shape. There was no way I could over-power him by myself.

He paused, getting some communication on his HUD.

"What!" he yelled. "Still! Well close them for God's sake!"

He looked really rattled. I liked that look on him.

He turned away and contacted somebody else. Minutes later, Brickhead and another goon appeared behind me. Each of them grabbed one of my arms, and they dragged me toward the elevators.

A half hour later I lay on a bed in a room one floor down, my heart sinking into my gut. It was like déjà vu, like I'd never escaped the first time. The room was just like the one Chuck had kept me in before. I was back in a hospital gown, and my feet were bare. I had no idea what had happened to the crypted phone, the money, the melded card — and Gene. And again my HUD was no longer working.

A few minutes later, the door opened, and Wickham appeared again, flanked by Brickhead and the other thug. The two grabbed my arms.

Wickham was smiling, but he still had that look like somebody had punched him in the gut. Something was screwing with his world. Tough break for him.

"You know," he said, glancing around the room, "it's ironic. You have the potential to live for another four hundred years." His fists clenched as he said it.

He turned his head and glared at me. "But you can die as quickly as anybody else."

I struggled, but I couldn't break free. I had nowhere to go anyway.

"You know what I can't stand?" Wickham said.

I just sneered at him.

He took a step toward me. "That worthless little shits like you and your miserable uncle, who have never accomplished anything, never dedicated their lives to anything, never pursued anything, and above all else," he turned again and stared out the window, "never sacrificed anything..." he turned back and brought his face up so close I could smell his breath, "have been blessed with this miraculous gift, while fine, ambitious, visionary people are cursed with early death."

"Life's a bitch," I said. "Get over it."

He drew back his arm and back-handed me across the face. "I never asked for your opinion."

He turned and strolled toward a tiny window in the west wall. "You should be grateful. Thanks to me, you may actually contribute something to society. Who knows, the tests we perform on you may lead to the breakthrough that allows the Appraisal to be controlled, to be enhanced for those who truly deserve it. Of course, it's possible, even likely, that you will suffer, and possibly die, in the process, but you will be able to rest easy knowing how you have helped the cause."

"Yeah, that gives me a warm feeling inside," I said.

The light above struck his face at a weird angle. The wrinkles on his skin stood out like river valleys on some ancient map.

"By the way," I asked, "what was *your* Appraisal?"

He stiffened and started shaking, like there was some kind of storm whipping up inside him. He strode over to me and punched me in the gut — so hard that it took my breath away. I collapsed. The two thugs had to hold me up.

"Proceed with the tests," he said, and marched out of the room.

# THIRTY-EIGHT

........................................................

# THE FINAL SOLUTION

Brickhead called somebody on his HUD, and a few minutes later a guy in a white lab coat showed up and took my blood pressure and checked my heart rate right there in the room. As he left, I overheard him say that the tests were scheduled for tomorrow morning.

Eventually they all took off and I was left alone. I collapsed on the bed and clamped my eyes shut. I no longer had contact with Gene, but from the way Wickham was acting, I guessed that the gate was still open.

I passed out. I must have been exhausted, because when I woke up and checked my HUD, several hours had passed. Something had woken me — a sound. I listened and heard it again. A garbled, digitized voice that was barely audible.

A faded, grainy image of Gene's avatar appeared and spoke, a little more clearly this time. "Are you receiving my transmission?"

"Gene," I said.

"I've tapped into the building's communication system," the avatar said. "That has allowed me to amplify my signal, but I don't know where I am. You must locate me so that I can help you."

I laughed. "Hey, no problem. Just get me out of here and I'll get right on that."

I heard a click. I jumped off the bed and went to the door. It was open.

"What the hell *are* you?" I whispered.

"I can detect your proximity through the building's security system," Gene answered. "Just start walking and I'll direct you to me. I believe I'm on the same floor as you."

I wasn't sure how far I was going to get skulking around the hallways with my bare ass hanging out, but I didn't have too many other options. I opened the door a crack and checked the hallway. There was nobody around.

I left the room and started walking.

"Wrong direction," Gene said. "Go the other way."

I could see this was going to be a lot of fun. I turned back, keeping an eye out for Brickhead or the other thug. I got to the intersection of two corridors.

"Now what?" I asked.

"It doesn't matter," Gene answered. "Start moving, and I'll let you know."

I continued like that for almost an hour, weaving back and forth through hallways, with Gene telling me if I was getting 'warmer' or 'colder'. His image on my HUD gradually intensified and came into focus. I turned down a hallway and Gene said I was very close. There were doors all along it. About halfway down, one of them was open, and the lights were on.

"You've arrived," Gene said in my HUD.

I jumped when I saw a shadow move inside. I snuck in closer and tiptoed into the center of the hall for a better look. Finally I saw the full silhouette on the wall, the squarish head, the pumped-up arms and torso, and I knew whose office this was.

*Of course,* I thought, clenching my fists. *That's just great.*

I was about to back away when a familiar voice echoed from inside the room. It was Wickham. I moved back against the closest wall. I could only catch snippets of what he was saying.

"… never seen it before," Wickham said. "…it's like a Vita Aeterna card, but…"

"…they should never have messed around with that nanotechnology shit," Brickhead's voice answered.

"…still open…," Wickham said. "…Rebel mobs marching…First Circle. SecureCorp…conflicting information."

I'd been edging closer and closer to the door, trying to hear what they were saying.

"I'll get rid of the damned thing," Brickhead said. I heard the click of his gun being primed.

"Not that way," Wickham said. "And not yet. Before we restart testing, we need to find out from the kid what else this thing's been doing. I've got a card shredder in my office. In fact, I don't know if that would be enough. We might have to incinerate."

I was almost at the door opening. Suddenly an arm reached out and grabbed my wrist, dragging me inside. Brickhead was squeezing so hard I thought my wrist would break, and his gun was pressed against my forehead. Wickham stood beside a desk. The melded card lay on it in front of him. Gene — it was close enough for me to reach out and touch it.

"Don't kill him," Wickham said.

"This won't kill him," Brickhead snarled, hauling back to club me with the butt of his gun.

"Gene — do something!" I yelled.

The room lights went out and I ducked. I heard the whoosh of air from Brickhead's blow pass over my head. It was pitch black. Gene must have done all the lights in the building. I pictured where Brickhead had been standing, and kicked as hard as I could at a point I figured would be between his legs. He screamed and let go of my arm. His gun went off, but it missed me.

I jumped toward the desk and groped desperately for the card lying there. My fingers finally touched it, but other fingers grabbed my wrist. I closed my hand on the card, twisted my arm away and started running. It was still totally black. I bashed sideways into the right-hand wall and veered away. I had no idea where I was going. I glanced back and saw Brickhead's image lit up as he fired his gun into the darkness.

"Don't shoot!" Wickham yelled.

"Fuck you!" Brickhead yelled back.

I tried to do a serpentine thing as I ran. Brickhead kept firing, but none of the shots hit me. I used the light from the gunfire to follow the wall to an intersection with another hallway. As soon as I turned the corner, the card started to glow, enough for me to see where I was going. I held it up in front of me like a beacon as I ran. I turned another corner.

Gene's avatar appeared in my HUD. "Next left," he said.

We snaked through a maze of hallways, Gene directing me. The lights started flicking on in each hallway when I entered, and off again as soon as I left. We finally reached one that looked familiar. I realized it was where I'd escaped from earlier. As I ran by, the locks on every door I passed clicked open. From several of them people emerged, stunned, dressed in gowns like me. Most looked young, a couple were ancient and withered like Walter.

I heard a shot and a bullet whizzed by my head. I looked back and froze. Brickhead was standing at the far end of the hall behind me with a flashlight in one hand and a gun in the other. He raised his arm to fire.

A gowned woman from a doorway nearby pointed at him and screamed: "It's him!"

She dove at him. He turned and shot her, but she kept coming, grabbing his gun hand. Several of the other gowned people joined in. He managed to shoot one or two of them but by now there were a least a dozen. They pulled him down and his screams echoed through the hallway as they tore him apart.

"We must go," Gene said, shocking me back to the present.

He directed me to a storeroom, where I found my clothes and put them on. On a shelf above them sat the crypted phone. I grabbed it, and Gene led me through another series of hallways.

As I moved, Gene talked to me. "SecureCorp has access to a 'presence' beacon in your HUD, which indicates whether your bodily functions are currently active. I am attempting to install a hack that will allow you to disable that beacon. Activating the hack will make it appear that you've ceased to exist."

"They'll think I'm dead," I said, too busy running for my life to pay much attention.

"The hack should be operational shortly," Gene said. "A skull-shaped icon will appear with all the others when the process is complete."

We finally reached an open concourse. Directly ahead was a row of elevators.

*I can finally get out of this place,* I thought.

I flew to them and hammered on the Down button a couple of dozen times. Sirens, explosions, and gunfire echoed from outside. I took a step toward the window next to me and looked down. Far below, a massive crowd were descending on the building. A line of muzzle flashes from defenders ran the length of the entrance.

Gene spoke. "The crypted phone has once again enabled me to connect to the network. According to the chatter, the Rebels have fought their way into the First Circle through the open gates, and wedged them open with vehicles. On the way they've gathered thousands to their cause. They're headed for this building."

I wondered if Connor and Bailey were down there fighting. And Laura...

One of the elevators finally thudded to a stop, and the Down arrow flashed on. My first impulse was to jump in, head down and join in the fight. Then I realized that in all the confusion I'd forgotten my original mission.

"I've got to find Wickham," I said to Gene.

"Eliminating Mr. Wickham should not be your primary objective," Gene said.

I ignored him and instead, pressed Up, and took the elevator back to the tenth floor. Thank God — my HUD started working. Most of the building was still dark, but Gene continued lighting hallways and rooms as I entered and darkening them behind me. I made my way to Wickham's office. Gene lit it for me, and I stuck my head around the open door. The office was empty. I rushed over to Wickham's gigantic metal desk, hunting for a weapon.

There was a paper memo on the desktop. I bent down to read it. The title read: 'Test Results for Psychotropic Nerve Agent XC-5.' Below was a table full of numbers and a graph. The Y axis of the graph was labeled 'Death Rate'. The line beside it shot almost vertical.

"Nerve agent?" I said, half to myself.

"It's extremely effective," a voice said behind me.

I looked up.

Wickham stood at the office door, holding a small flashlight. Another thug stood beside him, his gun drawn.

"So it's true — about the Final Solution," I said.

"Why so surprised?" Wickham said, smiling. "This city will be used for a test run. If the operation is successful it will be expanded to others as required. The only reason any citizen has ever been kept alive is to be of use to us. Be thankful you're one of the few who fall into that category."

Wickham nodded at the thug, who moved forward, grabbed both my hands in one of his own gigantic ones.

"No more tricks from your little friend," Wickham said.

The hallway lit up, and a faint glow replaced the blackness outside. The building's lights were back on.

Wickham glared at me. "Where is it?"

"Where's what?" I answered him.

The thug started going through my pockets with his free hand. He found the melded card and tossed it to Wickham.

"Where did this come from?" Wickham asked, holding up the card.

I didn't answer. The thug hauled up on my right arm. I still said nothing. He hauled back his gun to pistol-whip me.

"No," Wickham said. "I don't want him injured."

Wickham turned to me. "I don't need you to tell me. I have other ways of finding out. Anyway, as you know, we have bigger plans for you."

There was a commotion somewhere outside, on our floor, followed by shouts and gunfire. The thug accessed his HUD.

"Rebels," he said. "They're inside. Coming this way."

"How did they get past security!" Wickham shouted.

The goon shrugged.

"We've got to get him out of here," Wickham said, nodding at me. "Over there." He gestured with his head at a private elevator in a far corner of the office. Wickham and his helper dragged me toward it. The gunfire was getting closer. Wickham pressed the Up button. The door slid open. Wickham stepped in and the thug started dragging me inside.

Pounding feet and shouts echoed through the hallway. "There they are!" a voice yelled from outside the office door. A fighter appeared and raised his weapon. The thug let go of me and pulled out his own gun. Both fired. Both were hit and went down. I froze in the confusion. Wickham grabbed me and hauled me inside. Gunfire ricocheted off the bullet-proof door as it slid shut. We traveled up to the very top — the eleventh floor. Wickham dragged me out and down the hall.

"You've had it," I yelled at him. "It's all over for you."

"Shut up," he said, jerking my arm so hard he almost yanked my shoulder out of its socket.

Gene appeared in my HUD. "I believe I have a way to distract him."

I nodded, not wanting to speak.

"Be ready," Gene said.

We reached a thick metal door — what looked like the entrance to some kind of bunker. Beside it was a retinal scanner. Wickham clamped one hand on my wrist while he leaned his face into the device to open the door. The thing beeped, but nothing happened.

"Shit," Wickham said.

He dragged me closer and tried again. Same thing. There was major gunfire happening on the floor below. He tried again several times, each time getting more and more angry.

He turned to me. "It's you, isn't it!" he yelled. He pulled the card from his pocket. "You and this abomination."

He hauled back and pounded on the retinal scanner. For a split second he loosened his grip on my wrist. I twisted away and took off down the hallway. He turned and chased after me. As I ran, I tried the handle of the doors I passed. All were locked. I finally hit one that opened and rushed through it.

Inside was a set of stairs going up. I glanced at the door behind me for some way to jam it shut, but there was nothing. I flew up the stairs. After a couple of flights, I reached another door. I pushed through it and cringed at the rush of cooler air. I was on the roof. There was nowhere else to go. Sirens, gunfire and circling choppers echoed in the darkness below as I rushed to the edge and stared down at the panorama of the glittering city.

 The melded card was still in Wickham's pocket. Gene's image was already fading, but still visible.

"Any ideas?" I asked him.

# THIRTY-NINE

....................................................

# TWO BATTLES

Seconds later, Wickham burst through the door and onto the roof. He was talking on his HUD. He didn't approach me, he just stood there smiling. I soon realized why, when the whirring drone of a chopper approached in the distance. A few seconds later, the machine appeared, hovering over us, its blinding searchlight scanning the rooftop, a machine gun mounted on its undercarriage.

The searchlight found Wickham and he waved and pointed in my direction. There was a helipad in the northwest corner. In seconds the chopper would land and a new set of goons would climb out of it and grab me. Once that happened, I was screwed.

My only avenue of escape was the door back down, and Wickham was blocking that. Somehow I had to get him away from it. I had an idea. I stepped up to the very edge of the roof, and stood there, like I was getting ready to jump.

"No!" Wickham screamed.

"Why not?" I yelled back. "So I can spend the next three hundred and eighty years being hacked apart by Vita Aeterna?"

His face fell, as he realized I was right. I glanced down. The Rebel force had filled the square surrounding the building, and was driving toward it. Hundreds of SecureCorp defenders formed a wall protecting it, while a ring of choppers dove at the Rebels, machine-guns blazing.

As I'd hoped, Wickham rushed toward me. The chopper overhead hovered, its searchlight bathing the roof below my feet in giant pool of white light. Now that the door was clear, I could circle around Wickham and run back through it. But just as I was about to move, the searchlight caught my eyes and I was blinded. Then Wickham was beside me. He reached out and grabbed my wrist. We were both standing on the very edge.

"Make him let go," Gene's voice came through my HUD. "Step away from him."

"How am I supposed to do that?" I yelled.

I knew the melded card was still in Wickham's inside jacket pocket. When he looked away for a second, gesturing orders to the chopper, I reached in with my free hand, fished around, and brought out the card. Wickham grabbed for it with his own free hand, but I had a firm grip; there's no way he could pry it loose.

He punched me hard in the stomach. My hand opened as I doubled over in pain. The card flipped into the air. It hovered there for a fraction of a second, just beyond the edge of the roof.

Wickham let go of my other wrist and reached out to save the card. He actually managed to grab it out of the air, but he was off balance.

Following Gene's instructions, I jumped back as far as I could away from him. I took a step toward the door.

Gene's avatar appeared in my HUD. "Take the southeast elevator to the third floor. From there you can climb down the back way."

Wickham was still dancing on the roof edge, off balance. He flapped his arms at his sides. It looked like he'd finally gotten his footing, when the chopper's searchlight swung away from me and blasted directly into his eyes, cranked to maximum intensity. The chopper pilot's expression was a blend of bewilderment and panic as he frantically hauled on the unresponsive controls. The CEO of SecureCorp and head of Vita Aeterna stumbled backwards, blinded by the light.

His left foot slipped and he staggered off the edge, the melded card still in his hand. I peered down at his falling shape. His screams stopped about half way down.

My distraction was broken as the chopper's searchlight beam began swinging erratically back and forth. I looked up. The machine was pitching from side to side, its main rotor blade almost touching the ground.

I skirted around the careening chopper and dove for the exit door. Once inside, I stopped and peered around the jam. The machine was rocking violently, the roar of its engines interspersed with the screams of the occupants. The main rotor finally clipped the roof. The whole machine flipped over and the still-turning rotor drove it toward me. I flew down the stairs to the first landing. There was a massive explosion above, and fire licked past the open doorway. Then the only sound was the crackling of flames, and the gunfire and shouting from the square below.

It occurred to me that I still needed a gun. I snuck back up the stairs and poked my head out. The blackened hulk of the chopper lay smoking about ten meters away. The burnt, mangled bodies of a couple of the goons were lying close by. I could see the bulge of a weapon on the belt of one of them. Fighting my nausea, I crept up to the body and touched the weapon. It was still so hot it burnt my fingers.

I circled around the smouldering chopper, ventured to the edge of the roof, and stared down at the ground far below. The dark was still lit up with hundreds of flashes from gunfire. A circle had opened up around Wickham's sprawling body.

The battle slowed, then stopped altogether, as I guess both sets of fighters were trying to digest what had happened. As I watched, a huge knot of SecureCorp soldiers worked their way to that location, and the crowd around Wickham's body expanded. A searchlight from one of the choppers swung in my direction. One of the SecureCorp soldiers looked up, spotted me, and pointed. Guns started firing again, this time at me. I jumped back from the roof's edge. It was time to get out of here.

By now the weapon on the dead goon had cooled off. I grabbed it, ran for the exit door, and flew down the stairs. I located the southeast elevator, and punched the Down button. An eternity seemed to pass as I waited for the doors to open. I got to the third floor and rushed out into the open concourse, hunting for the escape route Gene had described.

I finally spotted it, through the windows on the western wall. A fire escape outside led down into a small grove of trees. There was a window with a latch on it. I pulled on the latch — it was stuck. There was a coffee table and a set of metal chairs across the room. I ran and grabbed the closest chair, turned my face away, and smashed it against the glass. The window shattered. I cleared the shards off the bottom of the frame and climbed onto the fire-escape, praying that there was nobody nearby to hear the racket I'd made. There was still lots of gunfire echoing around, but it was coming from the other side of the building.

I flew down the steps and jumped to the ground, gasping for air. The question now was: where could I go? I took a couple of deep breaths and tried to think. I was effectively behind enemy lines. The SecureCorp defenders stood between me and the Rebels. I no longer had Gene to help me, and I didn't dare try to get the melded card back, since it would now be surrounded by SecureCorp soldiers. My only option was to search for the gate, and pray that somehow I could get through.

I'd taken a single step when an arm wrapped around my chest from behind, forcing my own arms behind me.

"You thought you could fool me," a familiar voice whispered in my ear, "but I saw his body. I saw you on the roof. You lied. You don't work for the CCE. You work for the government. It was you. You killed Mr. Wickham."

I recognized the voice.

It was Benny.

I tried to reach for the gun in my belt, but a single giant hand pinned both of mine behind my back. Benny's free arm wrapped around my neck.

"What are you doing here?" I croaked, barely able to speak.

"Maybe Mr. Wickham's gone," Benny said. "but I'm gonna finish what he started. We're gonna put an end to you all."

He squeezed. I could hardly breathe.

I figured it was time for honesty. "It's true," I said, gasping. "I don't work for the CCE. But things aren't the way you think—"

"You government bastards have tried to confuse me before," he said. "Never again."

"Believe me," I said. "I don't work for the government."

"You're lying." His grip around my neck tightened.

"It was self-defence," I said. "He was trying to kill me."

"Yeah?" Benny said. "Too bad he didn't — time to finish the job."

He squeezed harder. I was about to black out. He could have killed me instantly. He was hesitating. I thought about trying to explain all that Travis had told me, but I knew he wouldn't understand. His grip tightened - I couldn't breathe.

I made one last desperate plea. "Benny, I thought you were my friend."

For a split second his grip loosened. He made a sound like he was choking down a sob. I twisted my right hand free and grabbed my gun.

The grip of his left arm tightened again and he reached his right hand forward trying to grab the gun. I turned it to point behind me. I couldn't tell where I was firing — I might even hit myself, but I only had one chance. I pulled the trigger.

The blast was deafening. Benny grunted as his body jerked backwards and he let go of me. I jumped away and turned to face him, my gun still drawn. He staggered back a couple of steps, a red blotch soaking across his stomach. Benny looked down, confused. His crude stitches had completely come apart, and a festering wound covered most of his left side. He looked up again, his face twisted in rage, and rushed toward me.

"Benny, no!" I yelled. He kept coming.

I fired again. Once again he wrapped his fingers around my neck. I fired twice more, point blank. He finally collapsed, dragging me to the ground with him, and fell on top of me. Soaked with Benny's blood, I struggled out from under his motionless body.

I knelt for a second beside my friend. He was still breathing.

"I'm sorry," I said, sobbing.

His eyes opened and he looked up at me. His breath was coming in gasps.

"I don't work for the government," I pleaded, tears running down my cheeks, praying he could hear me. "I'm going to change things — I promise."

He blinked, and his body shuddered as the life force left him. He lay still. The shadows and red flashes bleeding through from the battle washed over him. The guy who'd saved my life more than once — who'd protected me and been my friend. How many people had to die for my sake? The worst thing was that I'd never be able to explain to him, make him understand.

I couldn't hang around. I shoved the gun in my belt and took off, trying to figure out how to get back to the gate.

I slunk from shadow to shadow among the glittering, pristine glass towers, feeling like I was floating through some dream world, past block after block of mind-bending wealth and luxury. There didn't seem to be much in the way of security inside the First Circle. I guess nobody ever expected lowlifes like me to actually make it in. Or maybe they were all off fighting the Rebels.

There was hardly anybody around. Once or twice I saw a silhouette running by a few blocks ahead, or diving into a doorway. I think everybody was cowering indoors. Maybe there'd been some kind of announcement on their HUDs about the Rebels. This was probably the first time the outside world had ever invaded their little cocoon.

After countless wrong turns and backtracks, I breathed easier as the top of the wall became visible in the gaps between the palace-like structures. Minutes later I was within sight of the gate. I hid behind the corner of a nearby building. When I peeked out, my throat tightened. The gate was closed, and the guards were back in their towers, scanning the area, hands on their turreted machine guns. I wished I hadn't lost the melded card and Gene.

The gunfire in the distance got closer. It seemed to surround me. I wasn't sure where to run. Anyway, what was the point in running? As far as I knew, the gate was the only way out. I heard a gunshot very close. I took off, running in the direction away from it, glancing behind me as I ran. I was so distracted I almost ran into a group moving up the alley toward the gate.

A dozen guns were instantly trained on me. I raised my hands.

# FORTY

........................................................

# ESCAPE FROM THE FIRST CIRCLE

"Lose it," one of the group yelled, nodding at the gun in my belt. "Slowly — make a sudden move and you're dead."

None of them were wearing uniforms. At least they weren't SecureCorp. But they didn't look familiar.

"I'm on your side," I said, as I slowly reached down, pulled the gun out of my belt, and dropped it on the ground. "I'm a friend of Bailey's."

"Step away from the weapon," the leader said.

I raised both hands again and stepped back slowly.

"I'm with you guys," I said. "Do I look like SecureCorp?"

"He's okay," a woman's voice came from farther back.

The front line of Rebels split apart.

My heart raced, as out walked Laura.

"Thank God," I said. It was great to see her, but I wondered how she'd react after what I'd done.

294

She walked up to me, scowling. "I should let them shoot you, for running out on me like that." Finally she broke into a smile, came forward, and hugged me.

"I had to take out Wickham," I said, my eyes welling up. "I couldn't let you be part of it."

Laura and I let go of each other, and I stood facing the others.

"Wickham's really dead?" the leader asked.

I nodded. Whispers swept through the crowd at the news. The fighters stood staring at me like I had two heads or something.

"Where's Bailey?" I asked, breaking the silence.

"He's wrapping up the Rebel attack on SecureCorp headquarters," Laura answered. "He'll be joining us soon. Connor's leading a smaller group on the other side," she nodded toward the wall. "They're fighting their way into the SecureCorp weapons storehouse. If they make it inside, we'll have lots of firepower, and even explosives."

A few minutes later we got word from Connor's group. They'd lost a few people, but had gotten what they'd come for. While we waited for Bailey, Laura and the others filled me in on what had happened while I was going after Wickham.

Just after my conversation with Bailey, a hack had mysteriously appeared on his HUD. Normally, the 'common' citizen could only reach a half-dozen people at a time. The hack removed that restriction. That meant that the Rebels could broadcast their message to everybody equipped with a HUD, which was pretty well everybody.

*Gene,* I thought.

The Rebels leveled their charges against Wickham and the CCE. Of course, a lot of people didn't buy into what they were saying, but there were enough who finally understood the truth, and saw that this might be their only chance to fix things.

Then the word went out that the gate to the First Circle was open. When people from the Quarters got over their initial shock, they headed there, first just to see if it was true, then to venture inside, to finally see with their own eyes a place that was so far removed from their lives that it was like sneaking into heaven itself.

Some of the ones who'd entered just ran off to experience the wonders of the place, but after seeing it, many joined the Rebels. They now had a force of thousands. Since there'd never been any large-scale resistance movement, SecureCorp wasn't set up to deal with it. They were spread so thin that the arms storehouse that Connor's people were after was left almost unguarded. As word began to circulate that Wickham was dead, things really started to unravel.

Bailey and the rest of his group soon appeared in an alley, headed towards us. Both Bailey's torso and his right leg were now wrapped with bandages. I was still worried about how he'd react when we met again — after what happened to Travis.

I was relieved when he smiled and wrapped me in a bear hug. We exchanged information about Wickham's death and the Rebel attack on SecureCorp headquarters. Bailey said the Rebels couldn't hope to hold the building. Their diversionary mission had been accomplished, so now they could concentrate on other targets.

I told him and Laura about Benny, and how he'd died. I also told him that the gate was locked and guarded again.

"Thank God for that card," he said. "I don't think all this could have happened if it hadn't opened the gate."

I looked at my feet and felt the warmth rushing to my cheeks. I hated to admit that I'd lost the card. I explained the details about what happened, and how Gene had actually killed Wickham.

Once again Bailey and the others stared at me, not quite believing what I was saying.

"We could sure use that card now," Bailey finally said. "You figure it was on Wickham's body?"

I nodded, still embarrassed.

"Well, there's no way we're going to get it back, then," he said. He put a hand on my shoulder. "Don't worry about it. You've single-handedly struck a crippling blow to the CCE and SecureCorp. Anyway, we've got alternatives — we've got the explosives."

I explained to them about the memo I'd seen on Wickham's desk.

"The first thing we've got to do is get out of here," Bailey said. "Now that the gate's locked again we're trapped — us, and a lot of people who just wandered in to see what was on the other side. Once the confusion dies down, SecureCorp can sweep through sector by sector and kill anybody who doesn't belong."

We marched to the gate. On the way, we met some resistance, but most of the SecureCorp guys were preoccupied with the tens of thousands of people from the Quarters, and even the Dregs, who'd wandered in through the gate while it was open.

About a block away we stopped, and some scouts Bailey sent out came back to report that, as I'd said, the gate was closed. The guards were back in place in their turrets, and a small army of SecureCorp soldiers were now posted in front of it.

Bailey got in contact with Connor on the other side. Together, they came up with a plan to blow the gate. Connor's group had plenty of explosives, enough for the gate and the factory as well. Two contingents of fighters would march to the gate — one on each side. The one on our side, led by Bailey, would keep SecureCorp occupied. A smaller one on the other side, led by Connor, would plant an explosive to blow a hole in the gate.

The groups headed out and we waited. A few minutes later, an intense firefight echoed in the distance, followed soon after by a massive explosion. As soon as we heard the blast, the rest of us rushed for the gate. When we got there the firefight was still in progress, and we joined in.

I glanced at the gate and smiled. A giant hole had been blown in the center, easily big enough for our people to get through. Once our force had eliminated the opposition, thousands of us filed through the opening and crossed back into the Corp Ring.

We stopped at the first opportunity, and Bailey, Connor, Laura, and I huddled for a meeting. We'd lost a lot of people, but we still had a substantial force, and more were finding their way to us and joining all the time.

It was decided that Connor would lead the main group to capture InfoCorp's communications center, deep in the Corp Ring. That would give them control of the 'news' coming from the CCE and its puppet government. From what little we'd had time to monitor, the official line was still that nothing was happening. If Connor and his group were successful, the news feed would change very soon.

A second force would remain at the gate, holding it open for as long as possible to help any non-Elite still inside to escape.

Laura and I both joined a third, smaller group, led by Bailey, that would head for the factory, about an hour away by foot. Directions to the factory, how to break in, a map of the inside, and instructions on where to plant the explosive, were all made available on our HUDs.

On the way we met only token SecureCorp resistance. We guessed that the bulk of their soldiers were off battling the main Rebel force, and trying to secure and reseal the gate.

About half-way there we reached an isolated square with a strategic view in every direction. Bailey posted lookouts at all the accessible alleys and called for a ten-minute rest stop. I wandered off into a distant corner with Laura.

She turned to me. "Connor told me about your Appraisal."

I froze. "I'm sorry I lied to you. You were already upset about your father, and I didn't—"

"Five?" she said. "Really?"

My eyes stung as I fought back tears. I nodded.

"But we could still make it work," she said, her voice breaking. "It's a big difference, but—"

I shook my head. I'd already done the calculations.

"Think about it," I said, looking into her eyes and watching her world collapse behind them. "After one hundred years, your effective age would be eighty-seven. Mine would be thirty-six. And by one hundred twenty—"

"But we'd still have at least fifty or sixty good years together," she said, a tear coursing down her right cheek.

"You'd end up hating me," I said. "You'd be getting older and I'd still be young—"

"Never!" she pleaded. "I could never hate you."

I smiled and took her in my arms. "Maybe you're right," I whispered, not really believing it. "We'll see when this is all over."

We started off again, meeting almost no resistance. A half-hour later, we were within a block of the factory, according to the Rebel's map. We sent a couple of scouts to check the place out. The plan was to break in through a side door that led to a loading bay. The scouts said several SecureCorp soldiers were currently guarding that door. We were going to have to fight our way in.

We might not have time once we got inside, so Bailey called another meeting to plan the strategy for demolishing the factory. We stopped in a nearby alley.

There was a problem. The only way to reach the crucial point the Rebels had identified was by crawling into the building through a ventilation duct, like I'd done at the Vita Aeterna meeting. The duct could be accessed from the loading bay, but only two people in our group were small enough to get through it: Laura — and me.

"You have to let me do it," I said.

Bailey stared at me like I was nuts. "Too dangerous. We need you. You're the guy who killed Charles Wickham. You made all this possible. You're a hero to all those people out there."

"I can be a hero whether I'm alive or dead," I argued. "Better I die a hero than get captured again by SecureCorp. That would be disastrous for the movement. I want to make up for losing the card. Anyway," I smiled at them, "I'm not planning to die."

"That's crazy," Laura said. "Let me do it. I'm the obvious choice. And I can strike a blow for my father."

Bailey studied both of us for a few seconds.

He finally turned to her. "You sure?"

"No way!" I said. I grabbed her by the arm. "Don't!"

She nodded to Bailey.

I tried to talk them out of it but Bailey's mind was made up.

A couple of the technical guys had analyzed the building plans. I listened in while they explained to Laura how to get to the critical spot they'd identified. Bailey introduced us to their resident bomb expert, a beaten-up guy with three days growth of beard and a small pack on his back. He gingerly hauled a box about thirty centimeters square out of the pack, held it up, and explained how to set it.

There were two switches: a black safety switch on the left-hand side, and a red detonator in the center. Both were mounted in a T-shaped trough with a small button at its apex. You had to move the button out of the way, then slide the switch itself into the T-trough, to prevent you from flipping the switches accidentally.

You armed the bomb by flipping the black safety, then started the timed explosion by flipping the red detonator switch. A dial on the right-hand side allowed you to lock in a delay before the explosion, which the demolition guy said would be huge.

After arming the detonator, Laura would crawl to an exit grate they'd identified above an isolated storeroom, drop down to the floor, and run for her life. The bomb guy preset the timer for a fifteen-minute delay, and slid the box back in the pack.

We headed for the factory. Unlike the glittering steel and glass structures around it, the building was squat and ugly, formed from rough-hewn concrete. For a few seconds I worried that the Rebels had made a mistake. When we had a good look at the maps and diagrams, it was pretty clear that this was the place.

We reached the side door, and took out the guards easily, but one had time to communicate something over his HUD.

"We've got to move fast," Bailey said. "There'll be more where these ones came from."

We used another small explosive to blow the door open, and a bunch of us crowded inside. Bailey led a group of fighters, including me and Laura, to locate the ventilation duct, while the bomb guy set the bomb on the ground, waiting for the go-ahead.

The duct was in the northeast corner, almost at ceiling height. We piled up some packing crates to reach it. Bailey climbed up, ripped off the metal grate, and stuck his head inside, then climbed down to where the rest of us were standing. He called the bomb guy over.

"It's a go," Bailey said, turning to Laura.

"Let me do it," I made one last ditch attempt. She just shook her head.

"Give it to me," she reached out her hand for the bomb pack.

The bomb guy held it out for her. Just as her fingers touched it, the place exploded with gunfire. The crowd at the doorway split apart and a group of SecureCorp soldiers burst through. A bullet caught the bomb guy in the chest and he went down.

# FORTY-ONE

..................................................

# ASSAULT ON THE FACTORY

Everybody dove for cover. The pack with the bomb had fallen behind a stack of packing crates. The bomb guy's body was lying beside it, blood pooling around it. Nobody was paying any attention. The Rebels were locked in a firefight with about a dozen SecureCorp soldiers. Laura was pinned down behind a small crate, with no room to move.

I slid over, grabbed the bomb pack, and crawled across the floor, with the stack as cover, headed for the duct. Bullets were still flying as I climbed the packing-case stairway. A few blasted divots out of the wall behind me, but I was partially shielded by the stack, and none of them hit me. I reached the duct and squeezed into it.

"Alex!" I heard Bailey's voice yell behind me as I crawled as fast as I could. A couple of bullets punched holes in the duct behind me. I kept going, the noise of the firefight gradually fading.

After a few minutes everything was quiet, as I guess they'd taken all the SecureCorp guys out. I started getting messages on my HUD.

"That was a stupid thing to do, Alex," Bailey said. "You've put this whole operation at risk."

"Sorry," I answered him. "Laura's got a proper life to lead. I know what has to be done."

"We've got no choice now," Bailey said, "so just keep going. Keep us informed."

I crawled along the duct, following the instructions, pushing the pack with the bomb ahead of me, as the bomb guy had suggested. The hackers had identified a central point directly above the heart of the factory floor. According to their calculations, a large enough explosion at that point would demolish the entire building. As soon as it was armed, I'd drop down through the closest grate and get the hell out of there.

After a few twists and turns I located the target point. The escape drop was about ten meters ahead. It took a few minutes to manipulate the pack so that it was behind me. That way I'd be able to move quickly once it was set. I opened the pack and carefully removed the bomb.

I described my location to Bailey. His voice came over my HUD. "According to our map you're in position. It's a go, whenever you're ready. Our security hacks give us access to the building's camera feeds. Once the bomb is set, we can watch you, and help you find the way out."

I stared down at the bomb, with its levers and lights. So much destructive power in such a little package.

"Alex?" Bailey's voice came through again.

"Yeah, I'm doing it right now," I answered.

I released the safety, and activated the trigger.

"It's set," I said. The glowing red digits of the timer started ticking down.

"Okay," Bailey said. "You've only got fourteen minutes. Get going."

I didn't answer him. My muscles had been primed to take off as soon as the timer was set, but now it occurred to me that all I'd have to do is stay where I was, and this nightmare would finally be over for good. It would be quick; I probably wouldn't feel anything. I sat staring at the bomb for more than a minute.

Bailey came back on. "Alex, there's no sign of you on the cameras. Are you okay? You've got to hurry."

After all, I thought, no matter what happened I was screwed. The CCE and Vita Aeterna were crippled, but there was no way they were defeated. I'd be on the run for the rest of my life — and that would be many, many years. I'd be cursed to continue living long after everybody I ever cared about was dead. I'd never be able to form any long-term relationships — I'd live the rest of my incredibly long life alone.

"Alex," there was an edge of panic to Bailey's voice. "What's going on? Get out of there. The place is going to blow. We'll be out of touch for a minute or so while we get clear ourselves."

Suddenly I remembered what Gene had said about a hack to make it look like I was dead. Had he actually had time to finish it? He'd said there'd be an icon when it was ready. I checked through the hack list in my HUD. There it was — a white skull, just as he'd described.

Bailey's frantic voice returned a minute or so later. "Don't do this, Alex," he pleaded, finally guessing what was on my mind. "We'll find a way. Your life is worth living. Get out of there while you still can."

With Gene's hack, I had another alternative. In spite of all I'd be in for, I still wanted to live. But there might be a way to at least make my life bearable, to take the heat off so I wouldn't end up like Zack...

I had to get moving. I made my way along the duct to the exit point and smashed through the grating in the ceiling. I jumped down into the storeroom, made my way to the door, opened it and peeked out. The hallway was empty. I checked my HUD — there were no cameras immediately in front of me, but there were a couple near an intersection farther down. I took off. It was just like old times — I was Cam-surfing.

I followed the Rebels' map, dodging cameras as I went. I felt bad for the people I was deceiving and leaving behind — especially Laura. I stopped for a second and clamped my eyes shut as I thought about her. I'd already abandoned her once. Now I was going to do it again. For good this time. I checked the countdown — ten minutes. It was slower going, Cam-surfing — I wasn't sure if I was going to make it. And if I didn't? Maybe it would be just as well.

As bland as the building had looked from the outside, inside it was ultra-modern, jammed with labs and high-tech equipment. I spotted a couple of workers and guards as I moved, but managed to dodge behind a corner or into an alcove before they saw me. There weren't many people around. I guess everybody was off fighting the Rebels or something.

As I moved, Bailey's, and then Laura's, voices pleaded over my HUD with ever-increasing desperation.

I made it to the final hallway. I could see an exit door at the end. Two minutes. At some point I'd have to activate the 'death' hack, but I couldn't do it too early...

I rushed toward the outside door.

Laura screamed into my HUD, "Alex! For God's sake! Get out of there!"

I was halfway there when a guard stepped out right in front of me from an office door. We both jumped. He was as surprised as I was. It took a few seconds for him to figure out that I didn't belong there. By that time I had my gun out. I glanced at my HUD display — one minute.

He jumped at me just as I raised the gun to shoot. He was a big guy; there was no way I was going to take him in a fight. I tried to fire but he grabbed my gun wrist and twisted it downwards, driving me to my knees. Thirty seconds. He fumbled for his own gun in the holster on his belt. I pulled the trigger of mine. The bullet missed him, but the blast startled him and made him hesitate. Fifteen Seconds. He grabbed again for his weapon. Ten seconds. I braced myself.

He was drawing the weapon from his holster when the whole building lit up. The shock wave knocked us both off our feet. The guard fell back and let go of my wrist. I fell on my ass. My gun went off, which reminded me that I was still holding it. I staggered to my knees and held it in both hands.

The guard was stunned, but he recovered and pushed himself up from the floor. He fumbled again for his weapon. The whole building was shaking. The walls were swaying around us. I could barely hold on to my gun as I pointed it at his chest and pulled the trigger. With the deafening bomb blast, I didn't even hear the shot. A patch of red bloomed on the guard's chest and he dropped to the ground.

The walls started to give way as I took off, racing for the door. I got there, turned the door handle and pushed. It wouldn't budge. The building's frame had buckled and jammed it in place. I took a flying leap and slammed my shoulder against it. Nothing.

The hallway itself started to collapse around me. I was screwed. For a few seconds I stood there, waiting to die. The ceiling started to cave in. The door frame twisted sideways. The door popped out from the pressure, but the gap was too small to fit through. I took another run at it with my shoulder. It scraped open just enough to squeeze through.

I was out, standing in an alley next to the building. The whole structure was swaying back and forth, and the sky was lit up with flames from the roof. The place was going to collapse. I flew across the alley and behind a nearby building.

When I was sure I was out of danger, I paused, turned off the crypted phone, and activated Gene's death hack.

"Alex!" Laura was screaming into my HUD as I took off like a bullet.

# FORTY-TWO

..................................................

# DEAD AGAIN

A month had passed since my 'death' at the factory. In a building so deep in the Dregs that if you climbed to the top floor, you could actually see wilderness, I'd set up what was to be my new home. The good thing about the location was that I could forage for stuff to eat in the forest (as long as I carried a gun). In my explorations of the surrounding abandoned buildings, I'd come across some tossed-out books on seeds and plants. Someday I might even be able to set up some kind of garden.

Gene's 'death' hack was still in place. I hadn't dared to contact anybody, but I could monitor what was going on. Since Wickham's death, the CCE had been crippled, and the elected government had been shown up for the sham that it was. Most importantly, without Wickham, Vita Aeterna was crushed. The Elite were still entrenched, but the belief in them as god-like masters had been broken.

The factory had been completely destroyed, though, of course, they could always build another one. Connor's group had succeeded in capturing the InfoCorp communications center. It had taken a week for SecureCorp to take it back, and for all that time, the Rebels were able to broadcast the truth.

After the place was recaptured, the new head of the CCE fought desperately to pretend that nothing had changed, but by then the Rebel force had exploded in size. They regularly attacked SecureCorp, and were making progress every day.

And lately other pretty damaging hacks were showing up. Just knowing that stuff like that could be done gave people a feeling of power. I heard that both Richie and Jake had joined the Rebels. I never heard what happened to Spiro. Maybe someday I'd be able to thank Richie for all he'd done.

The Corps' reach extended everywhere, far beyond this city. Fighting them was going to take everything we had. Things were changing for the better, but nobody, including me, knew what the final outcome would be.

I'd spent weeks setting up the security barricades around my new home, hooking up a crude water supply, and working out various ways to get food. I cast my mind ahead, and shuddered as I imagined living there for the next almost four hundred years. Best not to think about that. Maybe someday, like Uncle Zack, I'd decide that my life wasn't worth living. Right now, in spite of all that had happened, and in spite of my circumstances, I wanted to be here.

My long-term hiding place was coming together, but I wasn't there right now. I was holed up in what was left of an office on the top floor of a building a few blocks from the current hideout for the newly combined Rebel/Dead Shift alliance. I was getting to know the Dregs pretty well by now, and the group was a lot easier to find, since there were now thousands of them.

I'd sent a message to Connor and Bailey over my crypted phone, and convinced them to come and meet me. I didn't tell them who it was they were meeting, just that I was a friend who had valuable news about the movement. I knew they'd be able to identify the phone, and wouldn't be able to resist finding out who had it. I stipulated that they had to come alone, and that I would take off if I heard they'd told anybody else, or brought anybody else with them.

My hiding place had the twin advantages of an unobstructed view of the Rebel hideout and multiple avenues of escape. The building was huge, and I'd spent a couple of days mapping out getaway routes, just in case. In rummaging through the abandoned buildings near my new home, I'd come across an ancient pair of binoculars. The left lens was smashed, but the right one worked perfectly. I peered through it now at the Rebel hideout.

Connor and Bailey exited the front door and, ten minutes later, scanned warily around them as they approached the entrance to my building — alone, as I'd stipulated. I was ready to run if I found they hadn't followed my instructions.

They had their guns drawn as they entered. I heard their footsteps and whispers as they stalked through the hallways of the top floor, following my instructions. They finally reached the room I was in. Connor just about fainted when he stepped through the open doorway.

"You!" he said, the words catching in his throat. I had to laugh. It reminded me so much of Richie's reaction when he first realized I was still alive after my Appraisal.

"But how?" Bailey asked. I was glad to see that he'd finally healed, and his bandages were gone.

I gestured toward two chairs I'd set up for them. They put away their guns and sat down. I explained what had happened at the factory, how I'd activated Gene's hack, made my way out of the Corp Ring, laid low, and finally set up my own hideout.

"They're never going to leave me alone as long as they know I'm alive," I said. I smiled. "So now I'm dead — for the second time."

They both stared at me like I really was dead. But their expressions told me that both knew I was right. It was the only way.

"But how are you going to live?" Bailey asked.

I shrugged. "It's probably best if I don't tell you anything about how or where I'm living. I'll contact you once in a while and let you know that I'm still alive..."

"Alive," Bailey said, "but for what purpose?"

"That's something I've got to work out for myself. Maybe there's some way I can be of help to you guys. Maybe my long life can be of some use to your cause."

"I've got a contact in FoodCorp," Connor said. "We might be able to help you there — leave caches of food at designated points, or something."

Bailey smiled. "And maybe we can scrape together some money and open a bank account for you. It wouldn't have to be that much. The interest would eventually be enough to support you. It would take a long time, but..."

"Time is something I've got lots of right now," I said. "But you two are the only ones that can know. If I hear that you've told anybody else, you'll never hear from me again."

Both their faces fell, as the reality of the situation hit them.

"Wickham's dead," Connor argued. "The CCE are mortally wounded. They may not survive. The public are in a surly mood, especially the ones at the bottom, who are the vast majority. Maybe it's not forever." But the lines on his face seemed to say he knew otherwise.

"To the world — even to what's left of Vita Aeterna and the CCE, you're dead," Bailey put in. "Nobody's looking for you. You've got time on your side. The highest guy in the CCE is a one point eight but he's already ancient. He'll be dead in fifty years. By that time your effective age will be twenty-five."

I stayed in the shadows. Even sitting across from the two human beings who'd done the most to keep me alive and free, I felt the need to be hidden. The scary part was that I was getting used to hiding and being on the run. And I was going to get a lot more used to it.

"Nobody but you two," I repeated. "Nobody."

"Not even her?" Bailey asked. He gestured outside with his head. "She's right down there. She heard about the crypted phone, but I haven't told her anything else."

I clenched my fists. "Especially not her."

"I'm sorry," he said, finally acknowledging what we all knew. "I'm sorry it had to be this way."

"Hey," I smiled. "Like you said, maybe it's not forever."

We talked for an hour or so about the movement, their lives, and how I would stay in touch. Then they said their goodbyes and left me alone. I snuck to the window, pulled down a slat of the hanging remnants of a Venetian blind, and peered down the block with my makeshift telescope. My chest tightened as Laura wandered out of the entrance of the Rebel building, staring ahead, as if she was searching for something.

A few minutes later Connor and Bailey appeared beside her, and the three spoke for a few seconds. Connor put a hand on her elbow. She hung her head as he led her inside.

I imagined her future. She'd hook up with some Rebel guy with about the same Appraisal. With luck, they'd both live long enough to get married and have children. I dared to hope that the movement we'd started would allow them to live happy and healthy lives.

She and her compatible husband would age, slowly — for them. Their children would grow to adults, and have children of their own. In a hundred and twenty years or so, if Laura and her mate survived everything else life throws at you, they would die of old age. If her children were blessed with similar Appraisals, they'd die about forty years later.

By that time, I would be... I did the mental calculations. I closed my eyes and hung my head — I'd have an effective age of about — fortyfive.

I dropped the blind slat and turned from the window. I'd seen enough.

It was time to get going. I had a life to live.

JAY ALLAN STOREY

JAY ALLAN STOREY

# OUTLIERS

...............................................

BOOK TWO OF THE VITA
AETERNA SERIES

*318*

# PROLOGUE

......................................................

Back when I was a kid, Travis, my teacher in the co-op school, would tell us stories about the way things used to be. His voice echoed off the crumbling walls of the abandoned skyscrapers ringing the garbage-strewn square that was our 'classroom', as he told us how there used to be more than enough food, water, electricity, and 'stuff' for everybody, and some kind of opportunity for anybody willing to work hard.

At the time, I thought he was full of it. I know it's illogical, but I'd always assumed that First City, the place where we lived, had always been half-empty and disintegrating. I never thought about what had happened to all the people who once occupied the thousands of mostly deserted, rotting high-rises I rode my board through every day.

All I knew about was the world as it was then. In that world, the ultra-wealthy Elite occupied the First Circle, a city of mythical grandeur to the south of us, forever insulated from the masses by a gigantic wall.

The walled-off city was surrounded by the *Corp Ring*, home to the factories, offices and living quarters for the corporations that produced all the goods and services the Elite required. Travis claimed that there were once thousands of small businesses, pumping out a huge variety of stuff, and that at one time almost everybody could afford at least some of it.

But in my world, there were only six corporations, or *Corps*, as we called them:

**SecureCorp** was responsible for all security and policing for the entire city. **FoodCorp** handled food production and processing, including the food packets that most of us in the Quarters ate. **BuildCorp** did the light manufacturing, and designed and built all large building projects. **InfoCorp** produced all the news and entertainment broadcast over our many high-tech devices, and was responsible for training and education. **TechCorp** designed, built, and maintained all the high technology stuff.

And last, but definitely not least, **MediCorp** took care of everything to do with medicine and health. If you could afford them, apparently they were really good. If you couldn't, like most of us, you just had to hope you didn't get sick.

There was no wall around the Corp Ring, but if anyone from the outside hung around there for too long SecureCorp would find a way to get rid of them. Like all good private enterprises, the Corps all wanted to swallow each other, but they'd reached a standoff, jockeying for position and dominance, but mostly putting up with the status quo.

TechCorp and MediCorp were responsible for installing the HUDs, the 'Heads Up Displays', surgically implanted into people's heads. Everybody in the city, and the world, for all I knew, had one. The HUD was attached to your optic nerve and powered by your body heat. Accessed from a controller on your wrist, it allowed you to connect to the network from anywhere, automatically. Whatever was on the 'display' sort of floated half-transparent in the space in front of you. Most people also wore an earpiece for receiving voice messages.

Nowadays, I don't have much use for that, since I'm always alone.

The Corps never gave anything away, so I always wondered why the HUD was free for everyone. It was Travis who first pointed out that the information fed to us through the HUD was *the Elite's* infor-mation. If you could access something on the HUD, it was because they *wanted* it to be there. So if the Elite chose not to show us something, it might as well not exist.

Tintown, the place where I grew up, was part a gigantic blight of tiny self-governing knots of humanity called *The Quarters,* areas of about five hundred square blocks, scattered throughout the crumbling remnants of the city surrounding the Corp Ring. By order of the Elite, who lived in constant fear of future wars or uprisings, TechCorp in-stalled cameras all over the Quarters, and SecureCorp patrolled its streets constantly.

In the Quarters, crime, power outages, and mounting garbage were the rule. A few lucky people had jobs in the Corp Ring, doing stuff the Corp workers didn't want to do, and that couldn't be done by robots — things like sweeping floors, cleaning toilets, and working in the sewers. If it wasn't for the money those guys brought in, the rest of the population would probably have starved to death.

As rough as the Quarters were, they weren't the worst First City had to offer. At the distant fringes, even beyond the Quarters, lay the 'Dregs', an area devastated, desolate, and almost completely abandoned; the only people that hung out there were the outcasts and criminal gangs.

We had a government, and regular elections — in fact, it was against the law *not* to vote. But no matter which party we elected, people in the Quarters continued to starve, jobs continued to be out of reach, and garbage continued to pile up in the streets.

At that time, it seemed like our only hope was an organization called the CCE, the Council of Chief Executives, made up of the CEOs from all six Corps. A man named Charles Wickham, the CEO of SecureCorp, was at its head. The CCE were folk heroes for us, and Wickham was their Robin Hood. The CCE claimed they were on a quest to bring us prosperity by eliminating government waste and inefficiency — a quest that was blocked by the government at every turn.

It wasn't until much later, after I'd gone on the run, that I found out the truth — that there *was* no government — that the President, the cabinet, the parties, even the opposition — everybody, were actors controlled by the CCE, Charles Wickham, and ultimately — the Elite.

Every election, the people of the Quarters believed they were doing something to improve their lives. In reality, the ballots were tossed in the garbage as soon as they were cast. It was all just for show. Regardless of the vote, exactly the same masters remained in charge.

But the Elite had weaknesses as old as humanity itself — arrogance and greed. They already had *almost* all the riches it was possible to possess. They could have been satisfied doing without the minuscule crumbs that were left, continue to live more extravagantly than the wealthiest sovereigns in history, and never have been in danger of a revolt. But giving up something — even the tiniest scrap — wasn't in their DNA. They could only be satisfied by taking it all.

In their greed, they allowed conditions in the Quarters to deteriorate to the point where the inhabitants had no choice but to fight back. A tiny Rebel group formed, hid out deep in the Dregs, and began to mount regular attacks on the SecureCorp soldiers who kept people of the Quarters in line. I joined the Rebels for a while, until circumstances forced me run even deeper into the shadows, where I've lived alone ever since.

My name is Alex Barret, and you might be wondering where I fit into all of this. Well, I probably wouldn't have any role at all, except for one simple fact. By a bizarre twist of fate, I've been programmed to have a lifespan of four hundred years.

For certain people, that makes me extremely valuable, and a pawn in the larger game whether I like it or not.

## O N E

..................................................

# DEEP IN THE DREGS

I blinked awake and sat up in bed. A noise. I shook my head to clear it, and glanced around, still half asleep. The flashing red light on the console nearby was pulsing in time with the regular beep of the alarm that had woken me. It was the proximity detection system I'd set up for my hideout.

Someone was outside.

I shoved aside Shake, one of the three dogs that share my bed. The big German Shepherd-cross sniffed in annoyance at being disturbed, but jumped down and headed for the kitchen, looking for a snack.

I crawled out of bed myself, stretched, scratched my belly, and made my way to the tech room. A bank of video monitors mounted on the wall showed the feeds from a set of cameras covering several square blocks around my hideout. Nothing. It might be an animal, a stray dog or cat, or a poor rat that had gone off course, not realizing that it would starve to death if it hung out too long this deep in this largely food-free remnant of the city.

I put two fingers in my mouth and blew two short whistles. There was a faint thud in the bedroom, and seconds later my second dog, Rattle, a little Terrier cross, trotted in and sat in front of me, her head cocked in anticipation. I bent down, adjusted the camera attached to her collar, and turned it on. My own image, hair spiking out like I'd just been electrocuted, appeared in the rightmost monitor as I knelt beside her.

"Recon," I said to the dog. Rattle jumped up excitedly and headed for the small doggy-door set into the door of the living room.

"Dog Door, Open," I called out. The tiny voice-activated door slid upwards, and Rattle raced toward it.

"Be careful," I called after her, as she blew through the door and took off for the outside.

Rattle's claws clicked down the hall and faded away. Getting to and from my hiding spot was a convoluted affair, but the dogs had learned the routine long ago. I went to the kitchen, poured myself a glass of water, and strolled back to the tech room.

The feed from Rattle's camera showed that she was just stepping onto the street. The morning light was just beginning to rise, but a tiny infra-red lamp under the camera lit the area ahead without alerting the any possible targets. I'd trained Rattle specially for this type of operation. She would sweep the area, avoiding contact with anybody in it. The camera and lamp were well camouflaged under her fur. In the unlikely event that an intruder happened to spot her, they'd assume she was a stray.

The image of the street ahead swayed from side to side as Rattle trotted along, following a predefined path. She stopped suddenly, then backed into the shadows, as within seconds a group of men came into view, skulking up the alley a few blocks from my hideout.

"Shit," I said.

I recognized the three of them. I'd run into them a few hours ago on my way home. They'd come after me, and I was sure I'd lost them, but they must have tracked me somehow. I made a mental note to review what evidence I left behind when I traveled. I always preferred to avoid conflict, and even contact, with other people in the Dregs, but it looked like I was going to have to deal with these guys.

I continued to watch Rattle's video feed, hoping the thugs would just give up and take off. They stopped and scanned around the filthy, debris-scattered square. They must be expert trackers to follow me here. Something moved on their left. It came into view, and I understood. Sniffing the broken pavement in front of the building was a large gray dog. That was their secret weapon. If the dog was any good, they might even be able to discover the entrance to my hideout.

I pressed a button on the console in front of me that would trigger a sensor to vibrate on Rattle's collar — her signal to come home. She took off instantly. I don't think the intruders even saw her. She was far enough away, and there was almost no wind. Their sniffer dog didn't catch her scent.

I wasn't actually at the place that they were prowling around. My hideout was in a building about a block away. I'd built a series of passages that allowed me to get from their position to here without going outside. But if they kept at it, especially with the dog, eventually they'd find me.

I was going to have to do something.

I shoved the pistol on my night table into my belt, and grabbed a loaded automatic weapon from the wall. I shrugged on my backpack, slung the rifle over my shoulder, then went back to check the video feed, with one last hope that the intruders would give up and go away.

One of them was hammering on the front entrance of the building with some kind of wrecking bar. The other two stood back with their guns drawn. They meant business. I gave two long whistles. This was a job for Roll. The giant Rottweiler loped from the bedroom and stood in front of me.

"We fight," I said to him. He let out a low growl and pawed at the ground, ready to go.

There were three ways into my hideout. All of them were hidden, known only to me and the dogs. I posted Shake at the entrance closest to the intruders, in case they got through, and took off with Roll for the outside.

The morning light had finally risen as we circled around through a maze of alleys, keeping upwind of the sniffing dog. I stopped, motioned to Roll to keep behind me, and peered around the corner from an alley opening onto the square. I was looking at the backs of the intruders. The guy with the pry bar now had it jammed into the side of the beaten-up door. The door cracked and squeaked as he hauled on it, and finally popped open under the pressure. He turned back and laughed to the others, then swung it open, and stepped into the doorway.

Seconds later his scream was cut short, as the booby-trap I'd set up did its work. A massive explosion echoed around the square, and pieces of the intruder blasted out, showering the others and landing in the street. His two buddies were yelling and running back and forth. The dog, unhurt, yelped and ran off into the shadows. Good.

I was hoping that my welcome gesture would be enough to discourage them for good, but they were either too stupid or too hungry to take the hint. One of them stepped gingerly toward the shattered doorway, stepping over what was left of his buddy, holding his gun in both hands.

That left his partner alone in front of the entrance. I unslung the rifle from my shoulder and stepped out from behind the corner.

From out of nowhere their sniffer dog appeared, and pounded straight towards us.

"Roll!" I shouted.

Roll jumped out from behind me and hurtled toward the other dog. The guy at the entrance turned, spotted me and raised his gun. I fired first and he went down, a bullet through his heart. Roll was trained to frighten, not to kill. He nipped at the hindquarters of the sniffer dog. It yelped and took off again, probably for good this time.

I turned my attention to the entranceway, scanning the darkness for a sign of the last intruder. There was nothing. No movement, no sound, just a black rectangle framing the horrific debris. The outer door was only the first of three. There was no way forward for him. He must be waiting.

"Come out with your hands up," I yelled at the blackness.

A few seconds later he appeared out of the shadows, hands in the air, a huge burly thug with a shaved head and a drooping mustache. A pistol hung from his belt. He paused and stared at me. I kept the rifle trained on him.

"Lose the gun," I yelled.

He reached down.

"Slowly," I said. "One hand."

He lifted the gun from his belt and dropped it to the ground.

"Turn around," I shouted. He shrugged, sort of smiled, and started turn, but suddenly twisted back and hauled out a gun that was stuffed in his belt behind him.

He shot, taking a divot out of the wall behind my head. My rifle jerked against my shoulder as I pulled the trigger. But my opponent was a cut above the average thug. A second after his shot he dove to the pavement and rolled. My shot pinged against the wall above his head. Before I could get off another one, he was on me. He knocked the rifle from my hand and fumbled to position his own weapon, his free hand wrapped around my throat.

Roll leapt forward and clamped his jaws around the guy's left thigh. He screamed and let go of me for a split second. I kneed him between the legs, then in the nose as he doubled over in pain. I pulled the pistol from my belt. When I looked up, Roll still had a grip on the guy's leg. The thug had straightened up and was about to smash the butt of his weapon against Roll's head. I raised my own gun and fired. A blotch of red spread across the thug's chest, and he toppled to the ground. I stood, shaking and breathing hard, scanning the square for any other danger. All was silent.

I inspected Roll for injuries — he was fine. As the dog patrolled the square, I crept over to check that all the intruders were dead — there was no doubt. They were low-level thugs, out to get whatever they could from somebody they thought was easy prey. Without the sniffer dog they wouldn't have had a hope. They were dressed in rags, and had almost nothing on them. I gathered up their weapons and stuffed them in the backpack.

I took Roll and checked the area, in case the sniffer dog had ventured back. I really didn't need a fourth dog, but I knew it would probably die out here with no one to look after it. The dog was nowhere to be seen.

Now I had my work cut out for me. I'd have to dispose of the bodies, one of which was in many pieces, repair the door, restore the area to its original ancient and unused state, and reset the booby-trap. I patted Roll on the head.

"Let's go," I said, and we headed back to the hideout.

# TWO

........................................

# A MILESTONE

Back at home, I showered and had some breakfast, then wandered into the bedroom, flopped onto the bed, lay back, and nursed my bruises. I was safe again — for now. The dogs climbed in and nuzzled up beside me. They know when I need comforting. I knew the cleanup should be done immediately, to remove any evidence of someone living around here, but just this once it could wait until tomorrow.

Because today was a special day. The date had been looming for more than a month now, lurking at the back of my thoughts like a ticking time bomb. I'd fought to stamp it out of my mind, but the more I tried not to think about it, the more it clawed its way to the surface.

And now, the day had arrived — the fortieth anniversary of my life on the run. It was forty years ago that I 'died', supposedly in an explosion at a Vita Aeterna factory in the Corp Ring.

It all came down to my Appraisal.

About a hundred years ago, scientists came up with a process, called Appraisal, that 'resets' the metabolism of the person it's applied to. Appraisal can slow the aging process, extending the recipient's lifespan to X number of years for every year of an 'average' human.

In Appraisal jargon, X is called the Life Extension Factor, or LEF. The LEF is a number, usually between one and two, based on an average age of 80. So, if you've got a LEF of 1.1, your life expectancy is 80 X 1.1 = 88 years. A LEF of 1.5 would give you a life expectancy of 80 X 1.5 = 120.

People with high Appraisals don't just live longer; their entire metabolism is affected. So, in the same way that a fifteen-year-old human is far younger in real terms than a fifteen-year-old dog, a seventy-year-old with a high LEF is like a thirty-year-old with a low one.

But the procedure comes with some serious hitches. The effect is different for everyone it's applied to. Person A's lifespan could be doubled while Person B has almost no change. Even worse, in rare cases, like for my dad, and later my first girlfriend Cindy, the LEF is less than one. In those cases, not only does Appraisal not lengthen life, it actually shortens it. Back in Tintown, we called this 'negging out'.

My dad had a LEF of 0.6, which put his life expectancy at 0.6 X 80 = 48. When he died, at the age of forty-five, he was shriveled and bent, his skin mottled and wrinkled, and his wispy white hair almost gone from his head, like someone twice that age.

Appraisal can only be done once. Doing it a second, third, or whatever time has no effect. The result is irreversible, and there's no way to predict what it will be. It's not dependent on genetics or any other known biological factor. No matter who you are or how much money you have, once it' s done, Appraisal can' t be undone; you just have to live with the result.

Even so, almost nobody ever refused it. LEFs over two are rare, happening about one in a hundred thousand, like negging out. Back when I was a kid, the highest I' d ever heard of was 2.5. In the Quarters, a high Appraisal had a lot of advantages beyond just a longer lifespan. Having more time for education and experience made everything about your life better and easier. You might even be able to pick up a job in the Corp Ring — the dream of every kid in Tintown.

In our world, if you want anything, you have to pay. So I always wondered why, like the HUD, the Appraisal procedure was given to everybody for free. I found out the hard way. Like most people, I got Appraised just after I turned sixteen. It was a moment that every kid my age looked forward to with a mixture of anticipation and dread.

But nothing could prepare me for what actually happened. Immediately after the procedure, I was kidnapped, hauled away to a secret lab, tormented by a musclebound psychopathic jailer I nick-named Brickhead, and subjected to a barrage of medical experiments. It wasn' t until much later, after I' d escaped, that I found out the truth — that in some twisted, cruel version of my dreams, I' d gotten the ultimate Appraisal — an incredible LEF of 5.0. I was an Outlier — reprogrammed to live for another four hundred years.

Like the rest of us, the Elite had to accept the outcome of their Appraisals, good or bad. Obsessed with getting their way, they found that unacceptable. They couldn' t stand the arbitrariness, the democracy, of it. It flew in the face of their belief in their own superiority —

their divine right to lay ownership to anything they wanted by virtue of their power and wealth.

They wanted the Appraisal outcome to be governed by the same rules as everything else in our world — the more money you had, the longer you would live. So they made the procedure free for all, to provide a large enough pool of high-LEF subjects to study. They believed they could discover the secret of long life by studying people who possessed it.

As arrogant as they were, most of the Elite drew the line at inflicting invasive, life-altering procedures on their test subjects. But a splinter group, led by Charles Wickham himself, weren't satisfied with the pace of the research. They formed a secret society called Vita Aeterna — 'Eternal Life', and recruited a cadre of scientists willing to do their bidding without question. Their work focused on subjects with exceptionally high Appraisals. Such people didn't show up very often. When they did, Vita Aeterna would kidnap the high scorers.

Vita Aeterna's doctors were unconstrained by any sentimental morality or ethical considerations. Their brutal experiments routinely crippled or killed many of the test subjects. They were determined to control the Appraisal process at any cost. After all, they reasoned, this was the giving of life itself. Cheating death, or at least delaying it for a while, was the dream of the ages. If a few insignificant lives needed to be ruined, or even snuffed out, in pursuit of that goal, so be it.

Since my Appraisal was the highest ever recorded, I was Vita Aeterna's holy grail.

I clamped my eyes shut as images surfaced of my escape from the lab, and the trail of destruction, both of enemies and friends, that I left in my wake when I went on the run. My fellow prisoner Walter was the first of many to give up their lives for me. Already on the verge of death from decades of brutal Vita Aeterna medical procedures, he took a bullet to save me from the prospect of several hundred years of imprisonment and brutal medical experimentation.

Later, that legacy of death included my own father, my friend Benny, who'd saved my life several times, and Travis, my former co-op teacher and later Rebel leader, who'd taken me in and protected me when I had no one else.

Beyond the anniversary of all that death, it was forty years since I'd lied to and betrayed Travis's daughter Laura, a girl who loved me. Her screams over my HUD when she believed I had died in the factory explosion still echoed through my nightmares.

There's no longer anybody chasing me, but it's forty years since I've spent more than a couple of hours in the company of another human being. For all that time I've been in hiding, destined to spend my life alone, outliving everybody on the planet by centuries.

I rested my hand on Rattle's head, with the other dogs passed out beside me. Shelves of books, reaching from floor to ceiling, lined the walls of my bedroom. I'd read them all, some many times over. They, and my other pastimes, had helped fill the black void of loneliness that had defined my life since my exile, but a gaping chasm still remained.

I allowed my gaze to drift over to the pistol lying on the night table beside the bed. For the ten-thousandth time, the image arose of my uncle Zack pressing a gun barrel against his temple all those years ago. Tired, desperate, and with no prospect of escape, Zack had planned to betray me to Vita Aeterna in return for finally being left alone. When that plan had failed, he'd blown his brains out right in front of me. Even after all the intervening decades, I haven't been able to erase that horrifying event from my psyche.

The gun was my plan B, a reminder that I could follow Zack's example and end all this whenever I wanted. I'd been tempted a handful of times — usually on significant anniversaries like this one, when the loneliness pressed in on me like a tightening fist. So far, I'd resisted.

I stepped through my usual list of justifications for living another day: the political fight I was a small part of, my pursuit of knowledge, the dogs, who would probably die without my care, the tiny chance that maybe things could change — that my Appraisal could somehow be altered, or that maybe I'd find someone...

The arguments all seemed pretty lame. Even at the best of times, they weren't enough to give my spirits much of a lift. Today, all they did was remind me of how empty my life had become. And the worst of it was that I could project ahead for the next three-hundred-fifty years and see the same thing.

Rattle whined and jumped out of the way as I rolled over, sat on the edge of the bed, and picked up the gun. I turned it over in my hands, lay the grip in my palm, and considered whether today would be the day. I hefted it, curled my fingers around the grip, and lifted it toward my head.

With an Appraisal of two point five, Zack had also had been a target of Vita Aeterna. When we met, he'd been on the run for forty years, the same length of time I was now 'celebrating'. It was Zack who first explained why an army of ruthless thugs was chasing me, and Zack who first revealed my stunning Appraisal score, which had slowed the ticking clock of my life to a crawl. Everybody I knew, everybody I met for the next hundred years, would be dead long before I even reached middle age.

Though forty years have passed, I've only aged the equivalent of eight, so though I've been alive for fifty-six years, physically, I'm a twenty-four-year-old.

I closed my eyes and felt the cold barrel of the gun against my temple as my finger slid toward the trigger. I faced hundreds of years of loneliness if nothing changed. But that was in the future. In the end, what difference did it make how long I'd been on the run, or how long I was going to spend alone? What really counted was the here and now. The question was, right now — right at this moment — did I still want to be alive?

I opened my eyes. To my surprise, I found the answer was yes, in spite of everything. I shivered, slowly set the gun back down on the table, and ruffed the fur of Rattle's head. Not today. Anyway, the gun would always be there if I needed it.

Plan B would always be available.

# THREE

..................................................

# LIFE ON THE RUN

With the issue of my life or death resolved for now, I got up and headed back to my tech room. I'd probably earned the equivalent of a degree in Electrical Engineering learning to set up the electrical systems for my various hideouts. My current place was totally wired. Proximity detectors monitored anything that moved within a few blocks, cameras recorded those movements, and alarms warned me of the danger.

It was all controlled from the command center where I was standing. At the moment, there was no movement in any of the video feeds. No other intruders had shown up, either following the first ones, or attracted by the explosion and gunfire, and there were no alarms from the motion detectors. All was quiet — for now.

I decided to go through with the cleanup today after all. The dogs followed me as I hit the storeroom to grab my toolbox, along with a shovel, a wheelbarrow, a welding kit, cleaning supplies, and a can of kerosene.

The five by ten meter room was jammed with shelves of stuff, most of it useful — tools, etc. — some of it just interesting junk I'd picked up in my travels.

Since almost all the tens of thousands of buildings in the Dregs were abandoned, there's lots of stuff lying around, some of it in pretty good shape, just waiting to be picked up. Everything in my hideout: tools, weapons, electrical systems, appliances, computers, video monitors, had been salvaged over the years. There was basically no material thing I could want that I couldn't find if I looked long enough.

After I'd gathered together everything I needed, I took Shake with me as I ventured outside to clean up the mess from the fight. On the way, I continued to monitor cameras I'd placed around the area from my HUD.

The HUD implant is as much a part of me as my eyes and ears. I can't imagine living without it. Unfortunately, it was also designed to broadcast information to SecureCorp, part of the crowd I'm hiding from. The HUD was supposed to relay your location, your communications, and your network accesses, to the people who built it. Over the years, renegades had come up with hacks to confuse or block a lot of their spyware, though not all.

SecureCorp could even monitor some of your bodily functions, so those in power would know it when you died. Gene, an AI construct I hooked up with when I first went on the run, added a hack to my HUD that allowed me to control the life indicator.

Vita Aeterna had built a factory to produce a deadly nerve agent, meant to eliminate all those they considered 'unnecessary', that is, everybody in the Quarters and the Dregs. The Rebels learned of the horrifying scheme, and set out to destroy the factory before it could begin production. I was the one who planted and triggered the bomb that obliterated the building.

My girlfriend, Travis' daughter Laura, was there when it happened. I escaped just before the bomb detonated, but I activated Gene's 'death' hack. The hack fooled SecureCorp, Vita Aeterna, the Rebels, and Laura into thinking I died in the explosion. I knew she loved me, but I also knew that our relationship was doomed, not only because of the difference in our Appraisals, but because I would be on the run for the rest of my spectacularly long life. It must have hurt her deeply, but the hack is the only reason I'm running around free instead of in a lab somewhere being hacked apart by Vita Aeterna doctors.

Shake and I finally reached the scene of the fight. I fastened a surgical mask over my nose and mouth, collected the bodies and stray body parts in the wheelbarrow, and carted it all about fifty blocks away, to an open square I use for disposal. I doused everything with kerosene, and made a bonfire.

Back at the scene of the fight, Shake sniffed around the patches of blood on the pavement while I welded a new metal frame to block the section of the entrance damaged by the explosion and the intruders. I scrubbed away most of the blood, and scuffed up the area so it would look like nobody had been here for years.

I would come back later to clean up all signs of the fight, replace the door, and reset the booby-trap. There could be no trace of what had happened here. I'd been forced to move my hideout countless times since I went into hiding, but I'd been at my current location for a long time. Moving was a massive amount of work. Not something I wanted to suffer through again if I could help it.

Back at the hideout, I put away the tools and cleaned up. I was still strung out from the fight. There was one thing that always helped me unwind.

I stepped out of the shower, and called out: "Playtime!" All three dogs jumped up, barking and tails wagging, and tore off to the left.

It was several months after I first went into exile that I chanced upon my first dog, a big male golden Lab who I christened Benny, after the friend I'd met in the Dregs all those years ago. Like his namesake, Benny was a stray, who must have got lost and wandered into the Dregs. When I found him he was close to death, a virtual skeleton, without the energy left to chase the occasional rat or squirrel that was unlucky enough to stumble into our neighbourhood.

I took him home, and nursed him back to life. It was tough enough feeding myself, let alone supporting a large dog as well, but I needed a companion, and he became the best one I could have hoped for, following me everywhere, sniffing out food and danger, protecting me from attackers, and laying at my feet at the end of the day. Just like the Benny I'd known when I first escaped, he was my friend, companion, and protector. If I hadn't met up with him, I certainly would have died.

I never knew how old Benny was when I first found him, but only a few years had gone by when he started to slow down, limping

*341*

around after me and sleeping for much of the day. Finally, he became the first of many devastating losses I experienced since moving to the Dregs. When he died, a part of me died with him. And always lurking in the back of my mind was the knowledge that I was destined to witness more death than any person should have to endure.

Over the years I'd experimented with different numbers of dogs, and finally settled on three as the ideal. The current ones were called Shake, Rattle, and Roll, after a song I'd come across on a disc from one of the abandoned libraries.

I picked different breeds for different purposes. Shake, the big German Shepherd-cross, was a guard dog, fantastic at sniffing out danger and defending our territory. Rattle, the little Terrier, was for reconnaissance. She was small enough to hide out in tiny spaces, and often wasn't noticed, either by people or other animals. Roll, the huge Rottweiler, was a fighting dog. He could tear an enemy to shreds in minutes, though he almost never had to: they usually took off like a bullet just at the sight of him.

It had been more than five years since I'd settled on this location for a hideout, on the fourth floor of what had once been a six-storey luxury apartment block. I knocked out a dividing wall between two apartments to create one giant twenty-five hundred-square-foot living space.

The dogs now followed me as I left the apartment and climbed several sets of stairs to the roof. We emerged from a hatch onto a wooden platform a few meters square, and for a few seconds I inspected the infrastructure I'd built to keep me and the dogs alive.

In the southwest corner, a ragged patch of blue sky and clouds, broken by the looming gray of the surrounding skyscrapers, were reflected in the violet-blue expanse of the massive solar panel array that supplied my electricity. Heavy gauge wire snaked from a point at the array's center to a squat mountain of batteries. The cream-coloured cube beside them was an inverter, which pumped out the AC power I needed to run all the equipment I'd salvaged over the years.

Towering over the installation was the cylindrical boiler that I'd hooked up to my apartment's water intake. It supplied me with hot water, and heat when necessary. One of the reasons I'd chosen this location in the northwest fringes, was that it was still partially connected to the what was left of the city's water supply.

For someone like me, who loves to learn, the Dregs was a treasure-trove. There were endless books, records, compact discs, tablets, computers, communication devices, cameras, and pretty much anything else you could ask for, if you knew where to look. I spent months studying physics, hydrology, even plumbing, to set up the water supply for my hideout.

Once the water systems were installed, I moved on to learn how to feed myself, eventually becoming an expert on farming and plant physiology. I turned to check out the opposite side of the roof, were a lush wall of green — my garden, reached up toward the sky. Rows of potatoes, tomatoes, carrots, lettuce, beans, and many others marched into the distance, and the afternoon sun glinted from the panes of the temperature-controlled greenhouse at the core.

When I turned back, the dogs had already taken off for our ultimate goal — a green open space about a hundred meters square in the center of the roof. In my travels, I'd found a big roll of green carpeting, meant to look like grass, I guess. I set it up on the roof, surrounded by a meter-high wire-mesh fence, for the dogs to run around on.

I crossed the ramp to the play space, picked up one of the dozens of balls littering the ground, and threw it as far as I could. All three dogs took off after it. Shake, the German Shepherd, was the fastest. Just as he reached the ball, I threw another one in the same direction. Now Shake hesitated, torn between the ball he was closest to and the new and potentially more interesting one.

Meanwhile Rattle, taking advantage of Shake's confusion, caught up and dove between the bigger dog's legs, snatching the first ball and taking off back toward me. Both the other dogs had now decided that the ball Rattle had was the one they wanted. They caught up with her and tried to steal it away, but Rattle held on, finally dropping it at my feet.

We went on like this for more than an hour. As always, the four of us eventually ended up wrestling together on the ground. It was experiences like this that recharged my desire to keep on living, even with all that had happened, and with the bleak future that stretched before me.

The dogs followed as I headed back down to my living room to relax. The great thing about staying in one place for years rather than months, or even weeks, as I had for much of my exile, was that I could finally think of it as home, and fix it up accordingly. For years I'd avoided any kind of decoration and kept my level of comfort low, expecting to have to leave at any moment.

The first year had been by far the worst. Still only sixteen years old, and a runt even for that age, I'd fled deep into the most devastated precincts, almost to the edge of the city. At first I had nothing, no food, no water, no electricity. And I lived in constant fear that my continued existence would somehow be revealed to Vita Aeterna.

I'd spent the first few weeks exploring, searching for a place to hide. Sometimes, where the level of debris allowed, I'd be on my board, like back in the Quarters, but mainly I went on foot. Everywhere I traveled, I found decay and disintegration; a world almost empty of people. There were thousands of blocks of abandoned, crumbling buildings of every shape and size.

Worse than the hunger, thirst, and fear, was the crushing loneliness. Before my Appraisal, though I'd been poor, I'd had something like a family, lots of friends, and a girlfriend who loved me. Only a few months later my father was dead, making me an orphan, my first girlfriend Cindy was dead, all my friends were gone, and I was devastatingly and heart-achingly alone.

Back then, I didn't even have the dogs for company. And interwoven with my loneliness was my guilt about lying to and betraying Laura. There were many nights when I cried myself to sleep, and many nights that I considered taking Uncle Zack's way out.

As the years went by, things got easier, and I finally set up my current hideout. Once everything important had been installed, I started to pick up a few items in my travels. Antique furniture was now scattered around the living room, along with an assortment of vases and statues. There was artwork on the walls, and a massive Persian carpet covering the floor.

My crowning achievement was the giant grand piano set up in one corner. It had been in one of the apartments when I arrived, so I basically built the living area around it. I'd even spent some of my ample spare time learning to play. Of course, that was a work in progress.

I set up one of the rooms as a gym and training area. The Dregs were incredibly dangerous. If somebody came along who wanted what you had, they would just kill you and take it. In the beginning, my small stature meant I was virtually defenseless in a fight, and here my spectacular lifespan worked against me. It took almost two years for me to reach a battle-capable size. Until then, all I could do was steer clear of fellow outcasts who happened to cross my path, and run as fast as I could from those that I couldn't avoid.

While I prayed to grow more quickly, I needed other ways to defend myself. I spent many hours learning and practicing a variety of martial arts, using books and videos. I also learned to maintain and use the many weapons, from knives and swords to automatic rifles, that I'd picked up in my travels. Nothing could guarantee my safety, but at least I was as prepared as I could be to fend off any attack.

A final room down the hall housed a complete HoloTV theater, where I could view any of the thousands of movies from my extensive library. Watching other people living their lives on the screen helped me deal with the loneliness.

# F O U R

........................................................

# LIFE AFTER DEATH

The next day, in the afternoon, I leaned back into the shadows on the sixth floor of an abandoned skyscraper, as I lifted a pair of high-powered binoculars and trained them on a cluster of buildings a few blocks away. It was the complex that formed the current Rebel headquarters.

When I first went on the run, the movement fighting against the Elite had numbered fewer than two hundred. It was made up of two factions, each with a slightly different agenda. The ones I knew as the Rebels were strictly political. They wanted to change the system — to break the stranglehold of the Elite, install a democratically elected government, and provide opportunities for work and a fair share of the wealth to everybody.

The focus of the second group was purely self-preservation. Though my spectacular Appraisal score made me Vita Aeterna' s most important target, I wasn' t the only one. There had been hundreds of high-scorers kidnapped just as I was, including my Uncle Zack, in the years since Vita Aeterna' s formation.

Over that time, Zack, and a handful of other test subjects, had managed to escape. Some of them eventually found each other and formed their own underground movement. They were all officially listed as dead, so they called themselves the Dead Shift. When I first met them, Zack was their leader.

At that time, the Rebels and the Dead Shift had virtually no contact, and mistrusted each other. But thanks to events I was involved in all those years ago, they finally joined together in a common cause — to shatter the status quo and build a new, more egalitarian society.

The Rebel force was now a hundred times its original size, numbering in the tens of thousands. It had evolved into a well-organized army, housed in the semi-permanent military complex, deep in the Dregs, that now stretched out below me.

When I'd first gone into exile, Bailey, a senior member of the Rebels, and Connor, now the leader of the Dead Shift, had helped a lot, bringing me food packets whenever they could. They were the only two people in the world who knew I was still alive. I'd sworn them to secrecy all those years ago, and so far they'd respected my wishes.

My original hideout was two days' travel from the Rebel stronghold. It was tough for them to come up with excuses for making the trip. They took turns, and during that critical time they were able to supply me with enough food to keep me alive, and enough company to keep me sane.

Though the Rebel complex was the closest human habitation to my current hideout, it had still taken half a day to get here. It was dangerous for me to venture out and risk being recognized, but sometimes the crushing loneliness was too much — I was driven to spend some time around other human beings — even if it was only vicariously, from afar.

Peering through the binoculars, I watched people below going about their lives: meeting on the street, shaking hands and talking, going for lunch in one of the makeshift cafés, making deliveries, doing repairs on buildings or vehicles. I saw lovers strolling hand in hand, friends meeting and slapping each other on the back. A couple gesticulating as they argued, probably over something pointless and mundane.

Sometimes I would try to read people's lips, and imagine what they were saying. I would imagine myself with them — talking about nothing — about the weather, or how a mutual friend was fairing. And they would talk back, filling me in on the latest gossip, confiding in me about their troubles, their lives. I imagined myself there — part of society, with friends, co-workers, girlfriends, even enemies. It seemed impossible — it *was* impossible — at least for me.

I imagined the thrill I would feel if someone I actually knew appeared — any of the Rebels I'd met before going on the run — maybe even her... So far, for whatever reason, that had never happened. I watched the coming and going of vehicles, mostly military trucks and vans. The Rebel movement had come a long way from the tiny, frightened, thinly-equipped band I'd been part of.

I risked making this trip about once a month, or whenever the loneliness became too much to bear. Other times, I'd pull a hat down low on my head, wrap a bandanna high around my face, and travel to the Quarters. I didn't dare show myself in Tintown, where I grew up. There was too great a danger that someone might recognize me.

Instead I went to Shaketown, the Quarter next door. I'd walk the streets alone, pretending I was just another citizen, going about my business, searching for food for my family, or looking for work.

In some ways these trips made my life harder, reminding me of all I was missing out on. But just being close to other people, even for a short time, helped make my existence at least somewhat bearable.

So I sat in my perch far above Rebel headquarters and watched for about half an hour, then finally packed everything up and slunk out of the building, having stolen pieces of their lives like a thief in the night.

# FIVE

........................................

# AN OMINOUS EVENT

Once the necessities of life, both physical and psychological, and my personal security were dealt with, I turned to another subject — one that for me had special personal interest — Appraisal.

Over several decades, I'd gotten the equivalent of a degree in both medicine and pharmacology. In particular, I'd become an expert on the Appraisal process, hoping against hope that I could somehow accomplish what Vita Aeterna had been unable to do — control the outcome, and possibly even reverse it. I built a complete medical lab in the apartment below my hideout, which allowed me to pursue the research. So far, I hadn't had any more luck than Vita Aeterna, but I kept trying.

A few days after my battle with the thugs, I was working in that lab, pursuing one of my theories about Appraisal's effects on longevity. I nearly fell off the chair I was sitting on when the phone on the desk beside me hummed, and its ring-tone echoed through the room.

One of the first, hacks I'd made to my HUD, and my other com-munication devices, was to limit any access to the outside world. I couldn't risk revealing my location by inadvertently connecting with anyone else. The ring-tone that had made me jump had come from a crypted phone I stole when I first went on the run. I still used it to communicate with Bailey and Connor. Though technically they could call me, we agreed long ago that I would always be the one to initiate contact.

As the name implies, the crypted phone encrypts all outgoing mes-sages. Cell towers, required to support the HUDs, and through them the Elite's hold on the masses, still cover much of the city. The crypted phone foils the SecureCorp location software by randomly switching between those towers. Its signal never stays with any one station for more than a few micro-seconds, so there's no way for monitoring software to triangulate a position.

Even so, I only used the phone when it was absolutely necessary. According to Bailey, the Rebels' technical people had confirmed that SecureCorp knew of my crypted phone's existence, though they didn't know who had it. SecureCorp still couldn't decipher the mes-sages, but they were getting close to being able to track the phone's location. The longer a connection was active, the more opportunity they had for figuring out where it was. Long ago I'd hacked the phone's software to change its contact address and number. Bailey and Connor were the only people who even knew I had it.

The ring-tone indicated a text message. At first I was afraid to look at it. I assumed it was some kind of wrong number, somebody who'd punched it in accidentally. Then it occurred to me that it might be an emergency that Bailey and Connor wanted me to know about. Reluctantly, I picked up the phone and read the message, and goosebumps rose on my skin. It was clear that that this was no mistake.

*Vita Aeterna is alive,* the text splashed across the screen. The sender ID information was obfuscated, but it didn't look like it came from either Bailey or Connor.

The message continued. It described a girl, named *Annabelle Karlson*, who lived in Third City, a smaller town a few hundred kilometers from here. The message claimed that the girl was another Outlier, like me, with an Appraisal of 4.5. I don't know where the person sending the message was getting their information, but they claimed that somehow Vita Aeterna didn't know about her — yet.

*Help her,* the message said. *Time is short. Her existence won't remain hidden much longer.*

It occurred to me that the message might be some kind of joke, or a hoax, or even a SecureCorp trap, but whoever the sender was, they obviously knew how to get in touch with me. That in itself was unbelievable and frightening. They knew about Vita Aeterna, and apparently, about my incredible Appraisal score. I figured I at least had to confirm whether the message came from Bailey or Connor. I contacted Bailey, without mentioning what the call had been about, just saying that somebody had phoned me. Bailey confirmed that the call hadn't come from either him or Connor.

*Help her,* the message had said. I had enough trouble taking care of myself.

*Time is short,* the message had said. Even so, I did my best to ignore it and put it out of my head. But that night all the images came back:

drugged, held prisoner, escaping only to be relentlessly pursued by a secret organization led by the most powerful man in the world. I remembered the hopelessness, the desperate scramble to stay alive and free.

On a warm night forty years ago, the major uprising that had been brewing in the Dregs and the Quarters for decades had finally exploded. The Rebel army had swarmed through the gates of the First Circle and occupied SecureCorp headquarters, where Charles Wickham himself was holding me prisoner. The distraction allowed me to escape, and Wickham died when he fell from the roof trying to recapture me. I fled to the Dregs, and I'd been there ever since.

The attack left the Elite in complete disarray. Eventually they were able to regain control, but their grip on power was never what it had been. The mask they and the CCE had presented, as benevolent and god-like masters, had been blown apart forever.

As an additional diversion, Gene had released all the test subjects being held prisoner at SecureCorp headquarters. Most of them were subsequently either killed, or found their way to the Dregs to join the Dead Shift. Thus Vita Aeterna were deprived of all the fodder for their experiments. With no more subjects to study, and without the driving force of Wickham behind them, they collapsed and disappeared — or at least, so we'd thought.

It wasn't until thirty years after I'd gone into hiding that rumours began to circulate about Vita Aeterna's resurrection and a renewed desperate search for immortality.

*Vita Aeterna is alive,* the phone message had said. Deep down I wasn't surprised. The stakes were too high. The prospect of eternal life was too hard to resist. For four decades now I'd stayed hidden in the background, selfishly cowering in the shadows while others were probably being kidnapped as I had been, tortured with horrific medical procedures, then tossed out like yesterday's trash.

Now it was possible that another anomaly like myself had emerged. If Vita Aeterna did still exist, and they truly hadn't yet learned of her incredible Appraisal score, they would soon, and they would chase Annabelle Karlson to the ends of the earth like a hunted animal. I got back to Bailey and Connor, and told them the details of the message. They agreed to use their underground contacts in Third City and their superior resources to look into it.

Revealing my existence would end my peaceful, quiet, life here forever. But a part of me knew that anything was better than another three hundred fifty more years of this devastating loneliness. A part of me was excited at the prospect of being back in the fight, back in the company of people, regardless of the consequences.

# SIX

........................................................

# BAILEY AND CONNOR

*I was running, flying down a maze of white-walled corridors, tears streaming down my cheeks, in the complex where I'd been held prisoner after my Appraisal forty years ago. A siren was blaring, echoing through the antiseptic hallways. In my hand was a severed finger covered with blood, the one Walter had cut from our dying captor's right hand.*

*I could hear the lop-sided footsteps of my psychopathic jailer, Brickhead, stumbling after me. I looked over my shoulder just as he appeared, a gun in his hand. Willing myself to stop shaking, I wiped the finger on my gown, and fumbled to press it against the access panel for the metal door blocking my way. A light on the panel went green and the door clicked open.*

*I smashed through it into semi-darkness. It slammed behind me as I pounded down a short hallway leading outside. I glanced back just as three bullet holes punched through the door, and pencil-thin beams of light played on the floor. I reached a final door and turned the handle*

*— it was locked. I slammed my body against it — it wouldn't budge. I was trapped. There was another shot and the door behind me exploded open.*

I screamed and woke up, shaking.

The dogs were whimpering in the bed beside me. Rattle moved over and began licking my face. I was still trembling as I sat up and put my feet on the floor, with my head in my hands. Forty years had passed — still the images remained.

Resigned, I got up, had some breakfast, and got ready to leave. Over the years I'd established a routine with Bailey and Conner: I would contact Bailey on the crypted phone, with a code word that only we knew, and another code word for one of a list of meeting places that I'd mapped out and given him before. In the past, we'd operated on a regular schedule, but because of this new development, I'd set up a special meeting.

Since I arrived in the Dregs, I'd spent a lot of my free time mapping out its devastated streets, monuments, libraries, offices, and apartment blocks, using both paper and digitized maps I'd found in my travels. My friend Benny, an expert on the Dregs, would have been proud of me. I had no doubt that I now knew more about the Dregs than he could have dreamed of, in fact, probably more than anybody else in the world.

That knowledge made me invaluable to the Rebels. While careful not to reveal my existence, Bailey would regularly conscript me to keep an eye on SecureCorp when they made excursions anywhere near my territory.

I brought along Rattle to do some additional recon. The little Terrier trotted beside me as I navigated the rubble-strewn streets. We'd gone about forty blocks when I turned a corner and felt a rush of cooler air. I looked to my left.

Water lapped quietly around the walls of abandoned buildings half a block away, and inundated the city far into the distance. It reached up to the second or third floors of the furthest skyscrapers. Many of them had collapsed and become submerged. I even saw the occasional fish gliding through the flooded streets and into sunken windows, and a few sickly gulls perching on crumbling window ledges.

It was Travis who first pointed out that if the Elite chose not to relay an event to our HUDs and HoloTVs, it might as well never have happened. And so it was with the true state of the world. When I'd first arrived in the Dregs, I'd climbed the stairs of a massive skyscraper, fifty stories high, determined to find out for myself.

Reaching the top, still gasping for breath, I finally caught a glimpse of reality. Beyond the endless jumble of broken buildings lay a drab swath of brown, dusty desert, stretching as far as I could see. In the other direction, to the east, the ocean had reclaimed a huge section of the city.

Over the years, through research, I'd learned the true state of things.

It all happened long before I was born. Temperature rise and shifting rainfall patterns had led to the desertification of farms and ranches all over the globe. Those same temperature extremes, combined with unrestrained overfishing, wiped out the majority of the sea life in the lakes, rivers, and oceans.

*358*

Thus, in one swift blow, virtually all of humanity's food sources were eliminated. Millions suddenly faced death by malnutrition. Drought, flood, and poisoned atmosphere also made vast areas of the world uninhabitable. Millions more were forced to flee the devastation for the livable zones.

Diseases that were once confined to warmer climates, like malaria, dengue, and yellow fever, swept over the entire planet. Melting permafrost in the north released ancient microbes that modern humans had never been exposed to — and had no resistance to. Other diseases, spread by mosquitoes and ticks, became rampant as those species flourished in the warming climate.

To add to the misery, a public health crisis of antibiotic resistance emerged as drugs were over-prescribed in a desperate attempt to control disease. The crisis intensified as millions of refugees swelled the populations of cities. The lethal combination of overcrowding, food and water scarcity, disease, and homelessness led to civil war, as opposing groups battled each other to stay alive.

In the end, millions died, brought down by war, disease, or starvation. Eventually only about twenty percent of the original population remained, a number barely able to scrape by with available resources.

Back when I was a kid, though the climate effects had devastated the natural world, they hadn't penetrated day-to-day lives within First City itself. Now, weather events, heat waves, torrential rain storms, and hurricane-force winds, were regular occurrences. I shook my head as I turned from the flooded streets, called to Rattle, and continued on my way.

I chose a different location for every meeting. You never knew what might have happened since the last time we'd met — who'd somehow tracked one of us, or found evidence that we'd been at a particular site. Over the years, I'd mapped out hundreds of potential meeting places, along with escape routes. All I had to do was pick one reasonably distant from the last one I used, and keep track of ones I'd used before.

What I couldn't plan for was random wild-card events — problems that cropped up just by chance. All I could do was hope nothing went wrong. So far nothing had.

This time I'd picked a spot that had once been some kind of recreational center. It was a two-storey low-rise, not ideal for escape routes, but I'd checked it out long ago and found that parts of various walls had crumbled, leaving holes that only I knew about. And next door was an abandoned high-rise with thousands of hiding places.

I paused in the shadows, wedged into the alcove of one of the buildings surrounding the meeting place. It was a scenario that had played out countless times before, something that had become a part of my life.

Bailey's Appraisal was 1.1, and he'd had a difficult life, so he'd aged a lot since I first met him forty years ago. He was slowing down, both physically and mentally. I knew he'd never give me away intentionally, but he might let something slip by accident. Connor hadn't been much older than me when we first met, and his Appraisal was 2.3, so he'd aged much more slowly, though still a lot more than me. They would be traveling together, so Connor would keep things in line.

I sent Rattle off, and she skipped through the alleys checking things out. I monitored the output of her camera on my HUD while I conducted my own surveillance from a few different vantage points. I also fished a camera drone from my pack, and sent it flying around to check the area. I could monitor its video feed from my HUD as well. All was clear. Satisfied, I hid on an upper floor of another nearby high-rise, scanning the approaches to the building for anybody who might be following Bailey and Connor.

Finally, right on time, my two friends appeared in the distance, guns drawn, studying the decaying monoliths above their heads as they approached. As always, I felt a thrill of anticipation at connecting with other human beings. Bailey's limp, which he'd gotten when my Uncle Zack shot him all those years ago, was getting worse.

As we'd prearranged, I waited for fifteen minutes before heading down to contact them. Rattle and the drone continued to circle the area, and their proximity detectors would alert me to any unexpected movement.

I made my way down the stairwell to the ground floor. I'd just stepped into an expansive lobby when the feed from my drone cut off. I froze. Something was wrong. It was possible that the drone had just conked out for some reason, but that was unlikely; I'd just overhauled it and it was in perfect condition.

I rushed to the shattered glass of the front entrance and poked my head out. Nothing. I was turning to look behind me when a fist slammed into my left cheek. I staggered back, then righted myself and spun around. There were three of them — all big, muscle-bound, and plastered with scars and tattoos. One of them was holding the drone.

He dropped it on the floor, crushed it under the heel of his boot, then looked at me and laughed.

I reached for my gun but the one closest to me, the biggest of the three, jammed a knife into my shoulder, punched me in the stomach and hauled the gun out of my belt. One of his buddies moved up behind me, ripped the pack from my back, and hauled my arms backwards. The injured shoulder exploded with pain.

"What do you want?" I gasped, still out of breath.

"What do we want?" The big guy laughed. He turned to the others, who joined in the laughter. "What do we want, boys?" he said to them.

"Something to kill," the smallest guy, half his face a mass of scar tissue, laughed.

"Looks like we've found it," the big guy said.

He hauled back and clubbed my head with the butt of my own gun. The one with the scars pulled a knife from his belt and approached. The guy behind me let go and punched me in the kidney. I fell to my knees.

The thugs began kicking me, and I collapsed to the floor. The boot of the biggest one was accelerating toward my head when I heard a gunshot. I looked up to see part of his face explode, and I was spattered with blood. Then I blacked out and knew nothing more.

# SEVEN

..............................................

# BACK IN THE WORLD

When I woke up, my skull felt like it was about to split apart, and a searing jolt shot through my right arm with every heartbeat. I opened my eyes, and worked through the pain as I lifted my head and scanned around me. I was lying on a narrow bed in a large open space, like the ones I remembered from years ago when I lived with the Rebels. The damaged arm was in a sling, and a large bandage had been applied to my right shoulder.

The space was crowded with a mixture of beds and military cots. Most of them were empty. I coughed, and the exertion made my head explode in even greater agony.

"Shit!" I said. I lay back down and shut my eyes.

"Mr. Barret," a female voice said beside me.

Reluctantly, I opened my eyes and turned toward the voice. A pretty young girl in a nurse's uniform was standing beside the bed. My body tensed, and I was struck with a sudden sense of vertigo. It felt like a dream. She was the first woman I'd talked to in forty years, and other than Bailey and Connor, the first human being.

"You're awake," she said, smiling.

For a few seconds I was stunned, unable to speak.

"I wish I wasn't," I finally whispered, my entire body pulsing with pain, and my mouth as dry as an old sock.

She stood staring at me like I was a ghost or something. I wondered if maybe I'd sustained some kind of hideous facial injury. Again fighting the pain, I raised my right arm and checked my face with the HUD controller camera on my wrist. There was a bandage wrapped around my head, and I was bruised and had a few cuts, but otherwise nothing looked out of the ordinary.

Finally, the girl left for a few minutes, and returned with a glass of water and two white pills.

"These will help with the pain," she said.

She helped me sit up, handed me the pills, and steadied my shaking hand as I drank the water to wash them down. I was still bewildered and confused, overwhelmed by the sudden change of circumstances.

"Where am I?" I managed to croak.

"You're at Rebel headquarters," she answered. "Commander Bailey brought you back here. You were badly injured in the attack. You've been unconscious for almost twenty-four hours."

Once again the girl left. I lay back down and closed my eyes, still trying to process what had happened. After decades of isolation, I was back in the world. It seemed impossible.

Several minutes later there was a commotion around my bed. When I opened my eyes again, the girl had returned, and I was surrounded by a crowd of what looked like nurses and orderlies. A wave of panic washed over me, being hemmed in by so many people. My original nurse shooed them away, and I relaxed a little. Seconds later both Bailey and Connor appeared, and moved to stand beside me. Their presence helped calm my nerves.

"You're alive," Bailey stated the obvious.

"Is that what you call it?" I joked. "What happened?"

"We were approaching the meeting place," Connor answered. "We heard your little friends working you over. They won't be bothering you anymore. We tried to grab Rattle, but I guess she was scared and took off."

I smiled. "It's okay, she's trained to run home in the event of trouble. She'll be fine."

Bailey stepped forward and put a hand on my good shoulder. "Get some rest. We'll talk later."

They left, and I passed out for a few more hours, still stunned by my new surroundings. When I woke up, I was still in a lot of pain, but I felt better. A nurse brought me some food and water, and helped me sit up to eat. I realized I was starving.

I passed in and out of consciousness for another day or so. I finally woke feeling somewhat normal, and once again the girl who'd first been looking after me helped me sit up in bed. People were still hovering around, staring like I was from another planet. A half hour later Bailey and Connor showed up again.

"Sorry," Bailey said, motioning around us with his head. "I guess your secret's out. We didn't have the expertise or the equipment to look after you ourselves, so we had to bring you back here."

Still fighting the excruciating pain, I twisted around, put my feet on the floor, and perched on the edge of the bed. "I guess it had to happen sometime. It's probably just as well."

"Do you feel up to talking?" Bailey asked.

I studied his face. It was a mass of wrinkles, and his hair was thinning and gray. It wasn't that long since I'd seen him, but it had never struck me so strongly before. He was an old man.

I nodded. They grabbed a couple of chairs and sat in front of me.

"So, who is this source you've been talking to?" Bailey asked. He rubbed his bad leg and stretched it out in front of him.

"Don't know," I answered. "Whoever it is, they seem to know who I am. And they seem to know about Vita Aeterna. The ID was obfuscated, and there was no way to trace the call. Did you check on the girl?"

I winced as another needle of pain shot through my arm. It was so intense I swayed sideways and almost passed out.

"Maybe you better get some more rest," Bailey said, noticing my condition. "We'll get you up to speed when you're feeling a bit better."

Bailey and Connor left, and I lay back, again drifting in and out of consciousness. I was jerked awake once, by a nightmare that my hideout had been invaded by hundreds of strangers, packed so tightly that they were smothering me. I would run to what looked like an open corner, and as soon as I arrived the crowd would close in on me again. Still half asleep, I raised my head, peered around blearily, then passed out again.

Later, I opened my eyes a couple of times to see people, some in nurse's uniforms, some in what looked like military uniforms, some in plain clothes, crowding around the bed, gawking at me. I was only half awake, but I heard one of them say: "That's Alex Barret, the guy who killed Charles Wickham."

Seeing my terrified expression, my nurse finally surrounded my bed with a set of portable screens. According to my HUD, another day had passed by the time I finally woke up again. Though I was still in pain, it had become more bearable. The screens were now partially open, but the crowd of observers had gone. Instead, there was a lone guy in a military uniform sitting in a chair beside my bed.

"Good afternoon Mr. Barret," he said. "It's an honour to meet you." He smiled at me. "I've been instructed to be your aide while you're with us. I'm Sergeant Forbes."

I reached up with my good arm and shook his hand. "I've ordered you a proper meal," he said. "When you're finished eating, if you feel up to it, the General would like to speak with you."

"The General?" I asked, half to myself.

The meal came, some kind of mashed vegetable and some kind of ground meat, and Sergeant Forbes left me to eat it alone. I finished it, then lay down for another hour or so, still exhausted. When I woke,

Sergeant Forbes was sitting in a chair beside me (he'd been there all this time?). I managed to roll over on my good elbow.

Sergeant Forbes smiled at me. "Feeling better?"

"Compared to what?" I answered. "Yeah, I guess."

Again I managed to sit up on the bed. Sergeant Forbes nodded toward a package beside me. "We got you some new clothes. The ones you had on when you got here were torn to shreds. Do you need a hand getting dressed?"

I looked down at the hospital gown I was wearing. I shuddered as it brought back chilling memories of my time as a prisoner of Vita Aeterna. I shook my head no. The screens around the bed were drawn again, and I worked through the pain as I pulled on the clothes they'd brought, buttoning the shirt collar and leaving one arm out to accommodate the sling.

When I emerged from the curtains, Sergeant Forbes was standing beside a wheelchair. He swept his hand toward it.

I sneered. "I can walk."

"Humour me," he smiled.

I took a step toward the chair. Suddenly I felt light-headed, and my legs began to fold under me. Sergeant Forbes rushed forward and grabbed my good elbow. With his help, I made it to the chair and sat down. The sergeant turned and wheeled me forward.

We left the ward and headed down a hallway. Everywhere there were people, some in plain clothes, many in uniform. It was surreal — a world I'd viewed from afar, but hadn't directly experienced for so long I could barely remember.

Every time we passed someone in the hallway, a wave of panic shot through me, the compulsion to fight or flee. As we walked, it gradually subsided. The setup was nothing like the rag-tag Rebel stronghold I remembered from when I was a kid. They appeared to be well organized, and there was a constant bustle people with places to go. As before, many of those we passed by stared at me open-mouthed.

After passing through several levels of security, we approached an office door guarded by a pair of soldiers. Sergeant Forbes parked me nearby and went to talk to them.

He returned, and faced me. "The General will see you shortly."

One of the guards opened the door and entered ahead of us. Sergeant Forbes pushed me and the chair inside.

The office was plain and the walls were only sparsely decorated with pictures of soldiers in uniform. A large wooden desk stood near the back, with a few papers, office supplies, pens, and a single framed photograph. The chair behind the desk was empty. As we approached, I tensed, as I recognized the face in the photograph. It was Travis, my former teacher, and the leader of the Rebels when I had first joined them forty years ago.

There was a shuffling sound on the other side of a door just to the right of the desk, and the handle began to turn. Sergeant Forbes helped me rise to my feet. The door began to open, and all the soldiers snapped to attention.

"General," Sergeant Forbes said, saluting.

The door finally swung open, and my heart almost stopped.

EIGHT

...................................................

# THE GENERAL

She was still attractive, though the years had clearly left their mark. Her once jet-black wavy hair was now shot with gray, and her thin, lithe body had filled out with age. Her face was lined, but determined. She wore a general's uniform, with bars on her shoulders. She moved forward to stand behind the desk. The other soldiers in the room were clearly in awe of her. But there was no mistaking her — it was Laura, the girl I'd lied to, betrayed, and abandoned forty years ago.

Other than confirmation that she was alive and okay, I'd told Bailey and Connor that I didn't want to hear anything about Laura. My ignorance made it easier to live with the guilt over my betrayal. Now the girl I'd betrayed, the General, nodded at the guards and Sergeant Forbes. They saluted, exited the room, and closed the door. I studied her face, remembering the teenage girl with light brown skin, and dark curly hair, tied back in a ponytail. Now it was cut short — all business, like the woman who stood before me.

She scanned me up and down, almost imperceptibly glanced at her own image in a mirror on the wall, and her mouth tightened to a bitter line. As I suspected would become a common reaction in my dealings with the rest of humanity, I felt a stab of guilt at having aged only a few years, while she had aged almost thirty.

She noticed the wheelchair, the bandage on my head, and the sling on my arm. "You look like you're in a lot of pain," she said, a sarcastic smile curling up on her lip. "Good."

"You!" I whispered. "*You're* the General?"

"You're lucky you're injured," she said. "Otherwise I'd come over there and slap your face. I always suspected that you were still alive." She continued to stare, anger and sadness behind her eyes. "Bailey always had this guilty expression whenever your name was mentioned."

I found it hard to look her in the eye. "It was the only way. I'm sorry."

Her face twisted into a scowl. "The only way?" she mocked my words. "Look at you — look at me. We could have been together for the past forty years. We could have had a life — a family..." She closed her eyes momentarily and her lower lip quivered.

I shook my head. "You would have ended up resenting me, hating me," I said, though I wasn't sure that I believed it myself. "Anyway, it wasn't just our ages—"

"I don't want to hear about it," she snapped.

One look in her eyes and I could see there was no point in pursuing the subject. We stared at each other for several more uncomfortable seconds.

"But you did find someone," I finally said, hopefully. "Bailey told me you've had a good life—"

Her expression softened. "I've had a fantastic life, under the circumstances." She gestured around the building with her head. "I married a wonderful man, one of the fighters, a couple of years after you… He was killed in an operation ten years ago."

"I'm sorry," I said. "And children?"

"A son and daughter. My daughter, Samantha, was the nurse who treated you when you first woke up."

I felt myself blushing. I understood then why the girl had been staring at me like I was a ghost.

"Oh," I said. "I didn't know."

"My son Ryan is off on a scouting mission. He'll be back in a few weeks. I'm sure he'll want to meet you."

"Meet me?"

"Hasn't anybody told you?" she said, with an edge of bitterness in her voice. "You're a legend. You're the guy who killed Charles Wickham, destroyed the death factory, and crippled SecureCorp. You're a dead hero suddenly brought back to life."

I finally understood why everyone seemed to act so strangely around me.

I bowed my head. "I know I hurt you deeply, but I had no other choice."

Again, her lip began to quiver, and for a second it looked like the leader of the entire Rebel movement would burst into tears.

"Enough," she said. She straightened her shoulders and wiped a tear from her cheek. "That's all in the past — there's nothing more to be said about it. Let's talk about why you're here."

She nodded at the wheelchair, and I sat down. She took a seat behind the desk, and I filled her in on the crypted phone, and the circumstances surrounding the unexpected message.

"And you have no idea who originated the call?" she asked, all business now. I shook my head, still stunned at who was sitting across from me.

"Our technical people have been working on it," she said. "Maybe they can establish where the message came from, and we'll continue trying to confirm whether the claim about the girl is true."

She pressed a button on a device on her desk, and called for Sergeant Forbes.

She turned back to me. "Bailey will keep you informed about whatever we find. I'll help you for the sake of the cause. After that," she locked eyes with me, "I never want to see you again."

She rose, abruptly turned, and exited the room.

A few days later I was finally on my feet again, and feeling something close to normal. The bruises and cuts were healing quickly. Luckily for me, the thick strap of my backpack had limited the damage from the knife blade. Though it hadn't been broken, my arm was still painful, and in a sling. I was told I'd regain full use of it in another week or so.

The Rebels continued to investigate my mysterious call, and Annabelle Karlson.

Once I was well enough to walk comfortably, Sergeant Forbes led me on a tour of headquarters. The Rebel movement had exploded in size from the tiny band who'd taken me in when I was a kid. And where they had once been forced to hide in the shadows, constantly on the run from SecureCorp, they now had sufficient strength to defend a more or less permanent settlement.

Of course, I'd seen the complex many times from afar, peering through a set of binoculars from my perch a few blocks away, but I'd never experienced it up close, or been inside. Their current headquarters, occupying an abandoned office complex and several buildings surrounding it, had now been in place for several years. The total area encompassed several square blocks. A sturdy metal fence surrounded the entire perimeter, and the handful of openings were secured by numerous armed guards.

Sergeant Forbes led me past dozens of offices, dormitories and living quarters in the main structure, explaining their purpose. We then headed outside. As we walked, occasionally a vehicle would pass, usually a truck with supplies, or food. Once or twice we passed people on foot. I thought back to the hundreds of times I'd tried to experience life vicariously by spying on this place from afar, and glanced up at the building where I used to hide. Though even now I tensed whenever a stranger passed, I realized how wonderful it was to finally be back in the world.

"There are several gardens set up on the roofs of some of these buildings," Sergeant Forbes said, as we passed by a bustling, well-equipped kitchen. "There's also a miniature ranch where we raise a few goats, chickens, and pigs. Still, it's not enough to provide all of our food. We conduct regular raids on FoodCorp trucks for the rest."

We passed a garage full of vehicles, and an armory with an impressive cache of guns, ammunition, and even small artillery. Apparently the Rebels even had several small planes at their disposal. It occurred to me that, in theory, I could actually go to Third City, the place mentioned in my mysterious message. But would there be any point? Sergeant Forbes led me past schools, makeshift sports facilities, and the hospital where I'd first woken up.

"The Elite still control the media and all information dispersal," Forbes said as we walked. "Most people in the Corp Ring, and even some in the Quarters, still think of the Rebels as terrorists, out to destroy the status quo out of some sinister agenda. SecureCorp still occasionally attack, and once or twice they've driven us deeper into the Dregs, but they don't have the power to take us out.

"Every year our ranks grow — mainly from the Quarters, and increasingly from the Corp Ring itself. But we're still not in a position to challenge the Corps, or the Elite that control them."

He stopped walking and turned to me. "The fact is that we're basically at a stalemate. We need some kind of catalyst, an event that will galvanize the entire population of the Quarters, and possibly even trigger a revolt in the Corps themselves, to take the Rebellion to the next level."

"What kind of catalyst?" I asked.

He shrugged. "I have no idea." He smiled at me. "Maybe the news of a dead hero brought back to life."

As the tour ended, I asked Sergeant Forbes about exploring on my own, and he had no objection. We parted, and I strolled through the streets, still avoiding other people wherever possible. I headed for the northwest corner of the complex, and finally reached the small sector I'd viewed from afar, still trying to process where I was. I stood in the center of a square and stared up the skyscraper where I'd hidden so many times before. I imagined myself still up there, watching.

After a few minutes I turned and headed back. As I turned, I spotted an old man peering at me from behind one of the buildings. He jumped, as if he was startled. I had the feeling he'd been following me. He quickly ducked around the corner. I headed after him, but when I got to the junction he was already gone.

Since I'd shown up at Rebel headquarters, a ghost in the flesh, I'd gotten used to sometimes being followed, but the way this guy had acted when I caught him was suspicious.

# NINE

....................................................

# A MISSION

The next day, I was informed that the Rebels' information network had delivered some news about the girl. Bailey arranged a meeting to discuss it, and what we should do next. I had assumed that the Rebels would be eager to do everything in their power to rescue her. When I met up with Bailey, he wasn't so optimistic. That afternoon, at the meeting, there was me, Bailey, Connor, a few upper-level military people, and Laura, The General.

Her expression as I walked into the room told me that Bailey's analysis had been correct. We took our seats around a big table, and Bailey brought us up to speed.

"We've got some pretty deep operatives in SecureCorp," he said to the group. "They've checked into Alex's story. The girl exists. Her name is Annabelle Karlson, as the message stated. She's eighteen years old, and still lives with her family in the Corp Ring of Third City. She's attending university, studying Structural Engineering, on a track to work at BuildCorp. Officially her Appraisal's only 1.5. Not bad, but nothing special. Nothing Vita Aeterna would be interested in."

I shook my head at the table top. "So, why would somebody say otherwise."

"There is one wrinkle," Connor put in. "Her father's a doctor — a big wig in MediCorp. Apparently, he did her Appraisal himself. He submitted it to MediCorp through normal channels, but..."

I felt a stab of pain from my still-healing wounds as I jerked up straight in my chair. "*Her father* did her appraisal? Can you *do* that?"

Connor shrugged. "It's unusual, but it happens. The guy's apparently pretty high up in the hierarchy — doctor to some of the high-ranking management of the Corps."

"So — he could be lying about her result," I said.

"Somebody in that position, they'd probably take his word for it," Connor said. "But I don't see how your friend, whoever he or she is, would know any different. It's possible that your message is some kind of con."

"What about Vita Aeterna?" I asked. I shifted around, trying to get more comfortable, and winced as another searing jolt of pain shot up my side.

"There's no proof," Bailey answered. "But if it's true, it wouldn't really be a surprise. The stakes are high enough that I think it's safe to say that Vita Aeterna are probably still around in some form or other."

"Our people on the inside are working to get more information on the girl," Connor said. "Without a blood test, it's going to be hard to confirm one way or the other."

I turned to Laura. "If my informant turns out to be right, we've got to do something. If Vita Aeterna gets wind of her, she'll be taken apart piece by piece for the next few centuries."

Laura stared back at me, scowling. "We've been struggling for decades to bring down the Elite and the Corps that serve them," she said, a bitter edge to her voice. "We've made huge gains since you were involved, but we're still chronically short of resources and manpower."

She acknowledged Connor and a couple of others in the room. "We sympathize with the Dead Shift cause, but we can't spare the resources to rescue one Corp girl who may or may not be a target."

The image leapt into my mind of Walter, withered and dying after decades of brutal Vita Aeterna experiments. "Have you got any idea what their tests do to a human being?" I raised my voice, something I'd sworn not to do. "I've seen the results first hand. The victims end up like animated corpses. It's like the worst form of torture. And you'd condemn this girl to that fate?"

"Millions have suffered, and continue to suffer," Laura snapped back. She stared pointedly at me. "And where have *you* been during all that suffering?"

I felt my face turning red. I kept my mouth shut.

"We can't hope to save them all," Laura continued. "What we *can* do is work to end the state of affairs that caused the suffering in the first place. The diversion you're proposing only distracts from our cause."

"Diversion?" I glared at her, my fists clenched. "Is that what you'd call it?" She returned my gaze, unmoving. Bailey leaned over and whispered in my ear: "Why don't you take a break, Alex? Let me talk to the General alone."

I glanced at her again, trying to connect the woman I was facing with the young girl I'd left behind all those years ago. Was there anything left of her? Finally I nodded. I got up and walked out the door.

I paced up and down a nearby hallway for a half hour, as the meeting dragged on. No one came to invite me back in. I considered knocking on the door, but concluded that our proposal had a better chance of success if I wasn't there. I finally gave up and walked away.

I didn't want to go to the dorm where I slept, and where numerous eyes would still be gawking at me. I needed some time away from people — suddenly I was feeling overwhelmed. During my tour, Sergeant Forbes had shown me a small patio set into the garden on the roof of one of the administration buildings. I made my way there now, and sat down with my head in my hands.

That evening, I breathed a huge sigh of relief when Bailey came and informed me that they'd convinced Laura to sanction a mission to rescue the girl. We sat in a quiet corner of the commissary, away from any prying ears.

"General Quinn is a battle-hardened soldier with decades of war behind her," Bailey said. "But she's still a woman. She's still dealing with the hurt you inflicted on her. In the end, logic won out.

"That's the good news. The bad news is that the General is only on board to a point. The mission will be difficult and expensive. She wants more proof that the girl really has the Appraisal your message claimed."

My brows came together. "How can we confirm something like that?"

"There's an active Rebel group in Third City, including one or two moles secretly living in the Corp Ring. But other than your mystery messenger, chances are that only one person knows the truth."

"The father."

"That's right. Up until the time of Annabelle's Appraisal, her father was a stalwart Corp supporter. He'd never shown the slightest sign of weakness or doubt, and he'd risen to a lofty management position in MediCorp."

"And then he performed the Appraisal on Annabelle."

Bailey nodded. "We're not sure why he chose to do the Appraisal himself. Maybe he had some idea what happens to people with high scores, and didn't want to take any chances. Maybe it was pure intuition. Since the Appraisal, it seems like he's gone through some kind of personality change. Our sources tell us he's been taking a lot of time off. Apparently he's become reclusive, and possibly mentally unstable. Something's working on his mind. We think he knows, or at least suspects, about Vita Aeterna, and knows what will happen if the truth about his daughter ever comes out."

I looked away, mulling over the information. A pair of uniformed fighters from one of the other tables rose and passed by us. We waited until they were well away.

Bailey continued. "Now Karlson's taking a year off on stress leave. And we think we know why. Our people did some digging, and found out that Annabelle's involved in gymnastics in university. She's scheduled to participate in a major competition a month from now."

I turned back to him. "How does that tell us anything?"

"As part of the competition, she's going to have to have a blood test."

I winced again, as I straightened in my chair. "So they'd find out..."

Bailey nodded. "Her father has no plausible excuse for doing the test himself, and it's unlikely they'd let him. Annabelle's been told for years that her Appraisal is 1.5, so she wouldn't see any reason refuse it — not that she could, anyway. If she's tested, they'll know. Her father will have to warn her, and convince her to drop out of the competition, but then the authorities might get suspicious."

"If it's true, the father must be shitting bricks."

He smiled. "Right about now, the father's probably realizing that even if she gets out of it this time, eventually she'll be forced to get tested. He may not specifically know about Vita Aeterna, but my guess is that he knows there's people out there who would be more than interested in his daughter. Otherwise, why would he have lied in the first place?"

"Have they found out much about the father — what kind of guy he is?"

"Like I said, he's always been a Corp man, always followed the Corp line. But he really seems to love his daughter. Our guys are in the process of trying to contact him. He might be willing to 'turn' on the

Corps to save his child." He raised an eyebrow. "That's where you come in."

"How's that?"

"We're hoping we can arrange a meeting between you and the father. We've compiled some records of your birth, your 'death', and your escape from Vita Aeterna. He can even test you, and confirm your identity and your Appraisal. If you can convince him who you are, and what kind of danger his daughter's in, maybe he'll join us. Such a big fish would be a huge coup for us. General Quinn says that if we can convince Dr. Karlson to talk to us, she'll agree to sanction the mission."

I wondered whether Laura was serious, or whether she was deliberately imposing an impossible requirement. "This is all assuming that the girl's Appraisal is what we think it is. I'd still like to know who contacted me. How did they know about her Appraisal? Would the father have told anybody?"

Bailey shrugged. "That, we can't answer. But the circumstantial evidence seems to point to your informant being correct. Unfortunately, the General isn't alone in having doubts about the mission. A few of the Rebel brass have questioned why we should care about her in the first place. My argument was that anytime we can deny those Vita Aeterna bastards something they want, we should go for it.

"If Annabelle Karlson really has the Appraisal your message claims, she'd be a valuable prize. Depriving Vita Aeterna of that prize would be a major blow to their morale. They'd be desperate to find her, and we'd draw resources away from SecureCorp."

I cringed, imagining returning to the Corp Ring after all these years.

"Our plan is for you to meet up with the local Rebel movement people from Third City," Bailey said. "We've already contacted them, and they've agreed to help you. We're also sending somebody from here, to support you."

"You?" I asked, hopefully.

Bailey shook his head. "I'm too old for this kind of thing — and Connor's been assigned to another operation," he added, anticipating my next question. "Don't worry — we'll find somebody. We've already arranged a flight for you to Third City. But first," he smiled, "if you're going to the Corp Ring, you'll need a bit of a personal makeover."

# TEN

..................................................

# A NEW IDENTITY

The next day, I got word that I would be taken to be fitted for clothes for my trip to the Corp Ring. I sat at a table in the common room adjacent to the dorm where I was staying. There was a tap on my left shoulder, and I was shocked to find that Laura's daughter Samantha was to be my guide. She led me to a warehouse deep in the Rebel headquarters complex. Like me, the Rebels had hoarded a huge cache of supplies found in abandoned buildings, and stolen in raids in the Corp Ring.

"Your mother doesn't mind you spending time with me?" I asked, as we threaded our way past a set of shelves piled with pots and pans.

She turned to me and smiled.

"She doesn't know," I answered my own question.

We walked in silence past a section full of construction equipment: drills, jackhammers, hand-cranked cement mixers.

"I volunteered to help you," she finally said. "I've heard so much about you, from your reputation and from my mother's stories."

*385*

I was surprised that Laura had even mentioned me, considering her current bitterness. But I guess that was before she knew that I was actually still alive.

"I feel bad about what happened," I said as we walked. "I did what I thought was best for her."

"She's pretty upset right now," Samantha answered. "She's a good person — I'm sure she'll forgive you—" she looked over at me and smiled, "eventually."

We arrived at a far corner of the warehouse crowded with shelves of shoes and boots, and racks of jackets, shirts, and pants. Samantha helped me sort through it all, trying to put together a wardrobe that would allow me to pass unnoticed in the Corp Ring. I was trying on a jacket for size, when a male voice behind me said:

"You've grown a lot since I last saw you."

I turned to face the speaker.

"But you're still pretty much a runt," said the big, burly middle-aged guy smiling down at me.

At first I didn't recognize him. Finally it hit me.

"Richie!" I smiled back at him, then stepped forward to give him a bear hug.

I was overjoyed to see him again after all these years. He'd been one of my best friends back in Tintown when I was a kid, part of a gang we called the 'Lost Souls', and he'd been instrumental in helping me get to Charles Wickham. He looked almost the same — built like a wrestler or a truck driver, but the Richie I remembered had a mind like a super-computer.

Like everybody else, he'd thought I was dead. I heard from Bailey that he'd joined the Rebel movement, but I wasn't sure whether I'd ever see him again. My thoughts spun back to the Lost Souls, all my friends back then, and my first girlfriend, Cindy. The sense of the passage of time struck me like a tidal wave. My throat tightened, as for the thousandth time I remembered confronting Cindy's father and learning of her tragic death.

Richie's Appraisal had been 1.5, so like Laura, he was almost halfway through his life. His curly blond hair was now laced with gray, and he'd gained a few extra pounds over the years, but despite his age, he still looked strong and healthy.

He stepped back between the rows of steel racks full of clothes, and scanned me up and down. "My God, you're like the guy from that book — what was it — Dorian Gray. Everybody else is getting old and pudgy, while you still look like a twenty-year-old." His brows came together. "You know, you pissed a lot of people off — including me — playing dead like that for all those years and not telling anybody."

"I'm sorry," I said. "I —"

"Don't worry about it," he said, smiling again. "I guess you had your reasons. Anyway, I'm glad to know that you're still alive. And it's fantastic to see you again."

"Hi, Uncle Richie," Samantha said.

"Uncle Richie?" I looked at him.

"Don't you remember?" Richie said. "You left Laura with me when you took off after Wickham. We got to know each other, and after I joined the Rebels, we got to be good friends."

Samantha stepped forward with a new jacket for me to try on. She held it across my chest. Richie looked at it, then me, and shook his head. "This isn' t going to be easy."

I looked up at him. "*You're* the one they' re sending with me to the Corp Ring?"

"Somebody' s got to keep you in line," he answered. "You' re going to need all the help you can get."

Once we' d picked out a set of clothes, Richie laughed as I sat motionless in a chair in one of the spare rooms, bracing for an experience I' d never had in my adult life — having someone else cut my hair. The barber lopped off almost all of it, finishing with the buzz-cut style that she assured me was the rage in the Corp Ring of Third City at the moment.

"That' s more like the Alex I remember," Richie said as she removed the last of my beard.   Then it was my turn to laugh as the barber smiled and motioned to Richie to sit in her chair.

When it was all over, I stood in front of a mirror and inspected the result. From pictures I' d seen recently, the Rebels had done a good job of transforming my appearance so that I could pass unnoticed through the streets of the Corp Ring.

What they couldn' t do was instantly inject me with the knowledge and social skills I' d need to make my way around without causing suspicion. I knew less about the modern world than almost anybody alive. Richie and Samantha spent days going over the latest news stories and the popular HoloMovies and cultural pastimes, but let' s face it — I' d been living alone, with nobody but the dogs to talk to, for forty years, and the only human beings I'd interacted with in all that time were Bailey and Connor.

I had a hard enough time fitting in with them, who I'd known for decades, let alone strangers — the wealthy inhabitants of a place I hadn't seen since I was a kid, and where I'd been an untouchable even then. I was grateful that Richie had agreed to come with me. At least there would be someone I knew well to guide me through this bizarre and unfamiliar world.

Dealing with large crowds, and people from a completely different background, was going to be a challenge, but all agreed that I had to go. The guy I was meeting was a doctor, able to do a blood test that would prove my incredible Appraisal score. That and my intimate knowledge of the distant past, even though I appeared to be young, should be enough to convince him.

Though I was legendary among the Rebels, apparently I was next to unknown in the Corp Ring, where the average person had no reason to care about me. Still, someone as close to the First Circle as Karlson would probably have heard of me — the kid who'd killed Charles Wickham, and dealt a serious blow to the status quo of our world.

We would have to move fast. I wasn't sure how soon the news of my 'resurrection' would reach SecureCorp. Once my existence became known, if it wasn't known already, the last place I'd want to be was the Corp Ring.

One final preparation was to find a place for Shake, Rattle, and Roll, who were currently still back at my hideout. They could get along fine for a few weeks, but I wasn't sure how long I'd be gone. Once everything else was in place, I made one last trip.

# E L E V E N

...................................................

# BACK TO THE HIDEOUT

I read somewhere that humans and dogs had been sharing each other's lives for more than a fifty thousand years. In fact, some writers believed that the two species evolved together in what's called a symbiotic relationship. That is, each contributed to other's survival. When cavemen went hunting, they depended on the dogs to sniff out game, and actually might not have survived without the aid of their dogs' noses. As a reward, the dogs got to share in some of the scraps — a win-win combination.

I don't know if any or all of that's true, but I do know that if it wasn't for the dogs, I wouldn't still be walking this Earth. Not only had they helped me avoid trouble, sniffing it out ahead of time, intimidating enemies, and even risking their lives to keep me safe, they'd also been essential for my sanity. They were my best friends. They provided me with companionship and love. Over the decades, I died a little myself when age finally overtook one of them and I had to say goodbye.

I wouldn't hesitate to give my own life to keep them safe. But my cover was now blown, and with it my motive for staying hidden. I knew I wouldn't be returning to live at the hideout any time soon. I couldn't leave the dogs there on their own, and I might not be around myself to take care of them. It was a gut-wrenching decision who to trust to be their guardian.

When I happened to mention my dilemma to Laura's daughter Samantha, she immediately offered. I was relieved and overjoyed. During my recuperation, she'd nursed me back to health, and I'd experienced her empathy and compassion first hand. And I was gratified that she hadn't inherited any of Laura's bitterness toward me.

It wouldn't be easy looking after three dogs in the confined space of the Rebel complex, but Samantha had shown herself to be intelligent and resourceful. I had no doubt that she would take care of them as well as I would myself. All three were incredibly well-trained and obedient, which would make her job a lot easier.

I made the trek back to the hideout to get them, and to retrieve the few essential possessions I wanted to bring back. As I'd known she would, Rattle had found her way home, and was able to get inside through a special doggie-door I'd designed.

Long ago, I'd come up with a pretty elaborate system for feeding the dogs. Sometimes I'd be away from the hideout for days, so I wanted to be sure they always had enough to eat. I'd set up three feeding 'stations', one for each dog. I never worried about whether they had enough food and water, and they'd been trained to wait for me indefinitely.

Still, they were all over me when I finally showed up. We spent more than ten minutes on the floor of the hideout, wrestling and reveling in the love.

In getting ready for the trip, I'd put together a list of stuff from the hideout that I might still find useful. I spent the rest of the day putting together all that I would take with me. I'd only brought a single back-pack, so I would have to be incredibly selective.

There were the notes I gathered over the years researching the Appraisal process. I hadn't made much progress, but maybe some-body else could make use of what I'd found. There was also a journal I'd kept sporadically over the years, some pictures I'd taken (mostly of my various animals), and some small treasured artworks.

Finally I tossed in a few books that I'd come to love, including 'The Count of Monte Cristo' and 'Robinson Crusoe'. I could identify with their heroes, who'd been condemned to spend much of their lives alone. By evening I'd gathered all I planned to take. I stayed one last night — it was safer traveling in the daytime.

The next morning, I had some breakfast and got ready to leave. I had one last look around. I sat down, probably for the last time, at the grand piano, and knocked out a few tunes. Images swirled through my head of the years I'd spent here. I remembered building it all, setting up the plumbing, the electrical system, and the garden on the roof, and collecting all the art works that now surrounded me. I remem-bered studying until late into the night, and my excitement over some discovery I'd made in the lab.

They were mostly pleasant images, and it occurred to me that, in a strange way, I'd been happy here. But there was one piece of unfinished business I wanted to take care of before I left. I took Shake along as I traveled several kilometers through a maze of alleyways. I squeezed through a hole in the wall of one of the disintegrating buildings, and passed through a network of hallways, finally exiting through the back door.

The place didn't look like much — a patch of dug-up pavement about twenty meters square, interspersed with tufts of sickly grass — only minimal sunlight made it down here through the shadows of the crumbling skyscrapers. Spaced evenly throughout were rough stone plaques — some only a few years old, some timeworn with the ravages of decades.

Into the plaques were etched names like Roscoe, Buck, Daisy, Rudy, Trixie. The names had been lovingly carved, and plots had been painstakingly maintained. There were twenty-one dogs and seven cats — my only real friends for the past forty years. Some had died in attacks by outsiders, some from disease. Most had died of old age.

I stopped at the weathered marker for my first dog, Benny. I knelt at his little grave site, closed my eyes, laid a hand on the marker, and said a silent prayer for my old friend.

The dogs had lived to an average age of eleven years; the cats, around fifteen. Their abbreviated lifespans were an ironic reminder of my place in this world. Out in the society I had chosen to abandon, people I knew and loved would age and die — more slowly than the dogs and cats, but much more quickly than me.

My relationship with the rest of humanity wasn't unlike what theirs would be to a dog or cat. The average person's pets would age much faster and die much earlier than they would, just as that person would age and die long before me. They, and I, were willing to form close, loving relationships with their animals, even in the knowledge that those animals would leave the world long before them.

But as deep as the pain was of losing an animal, I guessed that it would be far worse to lose a person I was close to. My throat tightened at the prospect of losing Richie, Bailey, Connor ... Laura. Even Samantha and Ryan, their children, their children's children...

I strolled among the miniature tombstones, remembering the creatures that had graced my life for such a short time, but brought me such joy while they were here. Some had saved my life, both literally, by fending off an attack, and spiritually, by providing the companionship that gave me a reason to carry on for another day.

I fished a small hand-rake out of its hiding spot between the bricks of the building beside me, and raked a section of ground that had been torn up by some wild animal. I moved all around the space, carefully brushing dust and dirt from the plaques, and pulling up the few weeds that managed to show their heads in the feeble sunlight. Then I returned to the hideout.

Finally, I was ready to leave.

Back at Rebel headquarters, the dogs took to Samantha immediately, though it took a week or so to get them used to the presence of so many other people, and to be persuaded that these strangers were their friends.

It was vital to me that the dogs be happy with Samantha — I was about to embark on a mission from which I might not return.

# TWELVE

..............................................

# THE FLIGHT TO THIRD CITY

When I was a kid in Tintown, I knew that there were people who flew in airplanes. I saw pictures on HoloTV, and heard stories on my HUD and from other kids. But I never dreamed I'd ever be doing it myself. So I was partly bewildered, partly excited, and partly scared shitless when I learned that I would actually be flying to Third City. Through their operatives in the city's Corp Ring, the Rebels had finally managed to arrange a meeting with Edward Karlson.

So, two days after my makeover, accompanied by a couple of other Rebel fighters and a trio of security personnel, Richie and I drove in a battered minivan to an abandoned park deep in the Dregs. When we arrived, the rest of us waited in the vehicle while the security guys swept the area.

Once they were satisfied that it was safe, we got out, and the group of us spent half an hour clearing the camouflaging brush away from a small, single-engine aircraft hidden in a nearby grove of trees. We gassed the plane up and rolled it out into the open field, into position for takeoff.

All along I' d been wondering which one of the people in the group was going to actually fly the thing. We all piled into the plane, and my mouth dropped open when Ritchie headed for the cockpit.

"You' re the pilot?" I asked, rushing after him.

"You have to learn a lot of different jobs fighting for the movement," he shrugged, squeezing his large frame into the pilot' s seat. "Don' t worry." He looked at me and smiled. "This isn' t my first time."

"Isn' t there supposed to be a co-pilot?" I asked, swallowing. There was an empty co-pilot' s place beside him.

"Optional for this size of aircraft," Richie answered. He motioned to it. "You can be co-pilot today. Have a seat — and make sure you strap yourself in."

Reluctantly I did what I was told.

The others we were bringing along took their seats at the back. Richie fired up the engines, and the plane vibrated as we taxied down the rocky makeshift runway. My gut twisted and my fingers dug into the arms of my chair as we accelerated, finally lifted off the ground, and banked quickly to the right.

"We' ll be flying low," Richie said once we were airborne, "hanging below any radar."

The air strip was on the very outskirts of the Dregs, where the city proper ended and dusty, scrub, along with a few sickly trees, began. As we gained altitude, I started to relax, and for the first time in my life caught an aerial view of the city where I' d lived since I was born.

It looked a lot like what I'd expected — an endless gray blotch of destruction and despair, surrounding a ring of opulence, the Corp Ring, with the gleaming, green, almost transparent paradise of the First Circle at its heart, like a tiny jewel embedded in a gigantic mass of shattered rubble.

Third City was only a few hundred kilometers away, so the flight would be just over an hour.

I'd read about it, but it was another thing to actually see the devastation spreading into the distance. Not far from the edge of the city, all traces of green disappeared, and shades of dusty brown took over, extending as far as I could see. This was the Great Global Desert, a band of barren, empty, lifeless plain that circled the entire planet.

I scanned to the east, and pulled in a breath. In the distance was yet another feature I'd read about, but never actually seen — the ocean. An endless expanse of blue extended into infinity. As I'd experienced in my explorations, much of the eastern edge of the ruined city was inundated, and waves lapped against the rotting concrete of the skyscrapers. Farther to the south, black smoke issued from a massive complex at the water's edge.

Richie nodded at it. "Desalinization plant. Converts sea water to fresh water. That's the city's main water supply. All the new cities were built with easy access to lakes or oceans. The water's moderating influence is the only thing keeping them livable. And if you go much farther south, even that's not enough."

In the other direction, to the west, at the edge of the desert, stood a gigantic complex of glass and steel several kilometers across. Just beyond it was another building, closed in, but of similar size.

Richie spoke again. "The glass one is greenhouses, where fruit, vegetable, and grain crops for the city are grown. The other one holds the animals — cattle, chickens, goats, pigs. All jammed together shoulder to shoulder — poor bastards. The area below us used to be some of the most fertile farmland in North America. Outside of those buildings, virtually nothing lives there now."

A gigantic train, hundreds of cars long, crawled on a track extending from the greenhouse complex heading east.

Richie pointed again toward the ocean. "See the set of rings out there in the water?"

I leaned forward, picked out them out, and nodded.

"Fish farms," he said, over the roar of the engine. "The water feeding into them has to be filtered to remove all the toxins. The Elite produce enough of everything to maintain their lavish lifestyle, and what's left over goes to the Corp Ring. As for everybody else, they'd just as soon they died anyway."

"People really did this?" I asked, scanning the devastation below.

Richie shrugged. "Scientists had warned about the danger for more than half a century. But denial is a powerful force. Most people convinced themselves that it wouldn't happen, or that some clever scientist or some miracle would come along to prevent it."

I just shook my head. "But now that they know the truth, can't they fix it?"

Richie laughed. "Know the truth? Fix it? Believe it or not, there's still lots of people around who deny it. If they abandoned their obscene levels of consumption and their destructive methods of energy production, mining, and garbage disposal, and embarked on a massive

*398*

rehabilitation program, the climate could eventually be restored. Even then it would take a hundred or so years. In any case, they have no intention of changing anything. They haven't even slowed down."

I thought again about the world we'd inherited. Shielded from the catastrophe, the Elite remained happy and secure in their isolated bubble, while outside, in the world, the desperately poor continued to fight to the death for the leftover scraps.

We left the city behind, and flew over the skeletal remains of low-level structures and houses, loosely separated by what were once roads. Mini-dust dunes had formed in the open spaces, and dust blew down the empty, lifeless streets, and through the devastated buildings. Finally, almost all the human structures fell away, leaving a barren, empty landscape.

We were low enough to make out the broken trunks of dead trees, and patches of brown stubble that must once have been crops, or smaller plant life. Once or twice I spotted the desiccated carcass of a cow or horse, or a circular ring of the remains of a grain silo. Swirling columns of dust arose, and spun along the ground to the south.

"The Elite had a choice," Richie said. "They could either accept a minor negative impact on their wealth and save the planet, or keep doing what suited them, and let it all go to shit. Guess which option they picked?"

The brown devastation extended far into the distance. I saw no sign of life — no trees or shrubs, no animals on the ground, no birds in the sky. I'd seen pictures of the paradise the earth once was. I shook my head at the sight, clenching my fists in disgust and rage.

Apparently, a similar pattern was repeated around the globe. Even if we were successful in changing the circumstances in First City, how would people live? And if they were backed into a corner, the Elite could simply send for reinforcements from other cities to reclaim control.

"The Rebel movement has spread to virtually every city — at least on this continent," Richie said, as if reading my thoughts. "We've made a lot of progress, but there's still a lot to be done. If we can get control of First City, maybe we can start to reverse the damage."

We flew for over an hour, with nothing below but dust and rocks. Finally another city appeared on the horizon. As we approached, I could see that it was almost identical to the one we'd left, though considerably smaller. To the north was a gigantic lake, with the silhouette of what Richie said was another water purification plant looming at its edge.

By the time we started our descent it was dusk. I closed my eyes as our wingtips wobbled dangerously close to the surrounding broken shells of buildings, toward a barely visible set of guiding lights below. We finally landed and skidded to a stop in an open field on the outskirts of Third City, far from the center of town.

Once we were on the ground, Richie taxied to the far end of the runway, and spun the plane around, ready for quick take off, in case we were attacked. We waited for ten minutes while the two fighters accompanying us hopped out to scan the darkness around the plane for any sign of trouble. Finally, we got the all clear.

"Some of the local guys are meeting us here," Richie said, as we stepped down from the plane and headed for a small shack in a far corner of the hidden airfield. "They'll take us to town."

We skulked through twisted scrub and stunted trees to our destination, a tiny wooden shack just beyond the airstrip, and huddled there for another half-hour before we finally heard the rumble of an approaching vehicle.

Again, our security guys stepped out to investigate. After a tense few minutes, they returned with a pair of local Rebel fighters, who led us to a military-style transport. After a twenty-minute drive through debris-filled streets and crumbling buildings, we finally reached their hideout, in what I guess was the equivalent of the Dregs for Third City.

The place was a lot less sophisticated than the headquarters in First City. It reminded me of the hideout where I'd first taken refuge forty years ago: a makeshift setup in an abandoned warehouse, with only cots to sleep on, and stolen food to eat.

It was depressing thinking about the Rebels, and their Dead-Shift counterparts, living their entire lives like this, cowering like rats in a hole, on the move continually, always looking over one shoulder for SecureCorp. And they'd been doing that for decades. I thought about Laura and her children. Her kids had lived their entire lives under those conditions. And I felt another twinge of guilt at staying hidden for all those years, contributing virtually nothing to the movement. All I could do is hope that my actions now would somehow contribute to a permanent change.

Lucas, the scruffy Rebel leader for Third City, greeted us when we arrived. Though he'd agreed to help us, I'd heard that he was less than thrilled about it. He and a couple of his fighters met with Richie and me in a small room in the northwest corner of the building.

"Annabelle's father, Edward Karlson, is on stress leave from his job in the Corp Ring," Lucas confirmed. "He spends almost all of his time at home. Once or twice a week he ventures outside and goes to a café near his place. He's really skittish. You're going to have to be careful with him."

We talked about the impending meeting for a couple of hours, then one of the local rebels escorted us to a dorm room crowded with makeshift cots. Again, it brought back memories of my time with the First City Rebels as a kid.

As I lay down, I thought about Laura again, the way she'd dug in her heels over the mission, and her continued bitterness toward me. I clamped my eyes shut, but it didn't blot out the memories.

# THIRTEEN

........................................................

# EDWARD KARLSON

According to our reports, Edward Karlson was on the verge of some kind of psychotic break — petrified for himself and for his daughter. It had taken several days for the Rebel group to even contact him to suggest a meeting. They said he'd hated the idea — he was a Corp drone all the way. All his life he'd bought into the propaganda on his HUD. He considered the inhabitants of the Quarters the lazy, whining, scum of the earth, and the Rebels bloodthirsty terrorists.

But I guess he knew something about Vita Aeterna, and about people with exceptional Appraisals disappearing. Apparently he wasn't directly involved, but he had an inkling of what happened to those people. From what our contacts could gather, he'd always assumed that the victims wouldn't include anyone in the Corps, but he'd lied about his daughter's Appraisal anyway, just in case.

More recently, probably spurred on by Annabelle's impending blood test, he'd concluded that, even though she was the daughter of a senior Corp official, his daughter wasn't safe. In the end, his fear for her overrode his mistrust and hatred of the Rebels and their cause. It might also have occurred to him that, even if somehow she could avoid blood tests, her continued youth would eventually give her away.

We had arranged to meet at five PM, at a café deep in the Corp Ring. The Rebels had provided us with fake IDs and legitimate MoneyAll cards primed with enough for us to get along for the short time we would be here.

The Rebels dropped us at the outer edge of the Third City Corp Ring. I experienced something like vertigo, and had to fight to stay calm as we staggered awestruck through the uncluttered streets and pristine buildings, trying to look inconspicuous in our best Corp Ring clothes.

We walked a few blocks, then Richie flagged down a RoboTaxi, and we climbed in. It was the first time in my life that I'd actually ridden in one. It brought back memories of getting around on my skateboard when I was a kid, by hanging off the back.

I was too nervous to talk to the NAV computer, and it was possible SecureCorp had a record of my voiceprint, so Richie told the machine where we were going. And since SecureCorp might be monitoring the vehicle's camera feed, we both kept our heads down as we rode in silence. We got off a couple of blocks before the meeting place, and spent a few minutes casing the area.

I'd been living in the Dregs for so long I'd forgotten what the Corp Rings were like: gleaming skyscrapers of mirrored glass, streets you could eat off, ornate, spotless lamp standards where none of the glass was broken. I swallowed hard, remembering that the Corp Ring was a dump compared to the breathtaking opulence of the First Circle.

I willed myself not to gawk at the spectacular architecture as we strolled toward the meeting place, trying to look like we belonged. Still, the Corp Ring was all business. There was little decoration anywhere, and even the few signs and billboards I saw were plain and boring.

I checked my image in the glass of one of the office towers. It was hard to get used to the idea that I could walk around here and not be immediately hauled away by SecureCorp. But my disguise seemed to be working. No one paid any attention as we approached the Food-Corp-sanctioned café we'd chosen as our meeting place.

There was no sign of SecureCorp, though I knew that they could be here. Every tradesman in work clothes, every business-suit-clad executive, every delivery driver, every old lady out for a stroll, might be an operative. There was also no sign of Karlson. It was past our meeting time, but only just. Richie and I hung around, nervous, trying to blend in. We stared at shop windows, studying the reflections behind us for both Karlson and any sign of SecureCorp.

Finally, Richie tapped my shoulder. "He's here." He nodded to our right.

I glanced over, and recognized Karlson from his photograph. He'd changed a lot from the picture we'd been shown: his black hair had thinned out and noticeably grayed, his eyes were sunken and dark. He'd seen better days.

We'd given him detailed descriptions of both of us. I tensed, aware of how valuable I still was to Vita Aeterna. If Karlson wanted to rat us out he could have brought a small army of SecureCorp to the meeting. From the way he was acting, it looked like he was alone. At one point he glanced in our direction and gave a barely perceptible nod.

He headed for the entrance to the café, and was about to reach for the door handle when his eye caught something to his left. I followed his gaze and saw a young guy and his girlfriend examining something in one of the shop windows. The guy leaned down to the woman and whispered in her ear, and she laughed. But there was something off about them, something I couldn't place. Karlson dropped his hand and walked away quickly, not even looking back.

The guy with the girl straightened up and punched something on his HUD controller, and a couple of men in plain clothes nearby started moving, in the direction Karlson had gone. They were on to him. We were screwed.

The next day, there was still no communication from Karlson. Our sources confirmed that he was still at home, still on a leave of absence and recuperating from his recent mental troubles. We could only assume that he'd either changed his mind, or decided it was too dangerous to meet us.

We worried that he'd be made to 'disappear', but nothing happened. If SecureCorp were following him, they must have a clue that something was up. The local Rebel analysts guessed that SecureCorp knew that Karlson was hiding some secret, but didn't yet know what it was. The analysts had also determined that there'd been a recent increase in network traffic at SecureCorp. Usually that indicated that they were getting ready for some kind of operation.

We had no choice but to go to plan B. Our only option now was to contact the girl, Annabelle, directly. Some of the Rebel operatives had been keeping an eye on her and researching her activities. Apparently her father had forbidden her to leave their apartment, on some trumped-up pretext, but we got word that today she'd ignored him and was out shopping with her friends. We rushed to the location, hoping for a chance to get her alone.

My heart raced when I saw her, a beautiful young woman with flowing auburn hair. Part of my excitement was pure physical attraction, but there was more to it than that. I realized that I might be setting eyes on the only other person in the world with an Appraisal close to my own.

She was dressed in the latest, most expensive clothes, and walked with the grace and confidence of someone who'd been pampered for her entire life. She was at the top of the social heap in the Corp Ring, and knew it. She turned and laughed with her friends as they wandered into a coffee shop, like they didn't have a care in the world. I envied her. They took a seat near the window.

Richie and I sat on a park bench, trying to look casual as we kept an eye on them. There was no sign of any SecureCorp operatives. They had no reason to suspect that whatever was wrong with Karlson involved his daughter. A chance finally came when she and her friends left the shop and she split with them, heading alone for the nearest RoboTaxi stand.

She paused for a few seconds, holding up her right wrist, using the camera in her HUD controller to check her makeup.

Suddenly I froze, and the sense of vertigo returned. "I don't know if I can do this," I whispered to Richie.

He leaned over to me and whispered back. "You have to. We already discussed this. You look a lot younger than me, and you're a lot cuter."

I turned and stared at him. "Get going," he said.

I reluctantly hauled myself to my feet and headed toward her. You could count the number of women I'd talked to in the past forty years on the fingers of one hand, and all that contact had been in the past couple of weeks.

I was in luck — there were no RoboTaxis at the stand. She'd have to wait for one. I moved up and stood beside her.

"Hi," I said, thinking I was probably better at this when I was fifteen.

"Get lost," she said, barely glancing at me. Good start.

"Look," I said. "I know you don't know me, but I need to talk to you. It's important."

She reached for the emergency button on her HUD controller. "Hit the road, or I call SecureCorp."

"Please," I said. "I'm here to help you. You're in a lot of danger."

She finally looked up at me, and, for a second, an expression that was something between shock and terror swept over her features, like somehow she'd seen through me, and recognized who and what I was.

The moment passed. Her expression morphed back into one of annoyance and disgust, but she dropped her hand. She must have gotten some kind of warning from her father. I knew I only had a few minutes. I explained to her who I was. With each word her initial expression of revulsion deepened. She continually scanned up and down the street for the RoboTaxi.

"So you grew up in this place called 'The Quarters'," she finally said sarcastically, "and now you live in this place called 'The Dregs'. And nobody has anything and everybody's poor. I've never heard of either of them. Anyway, if the people who live there are poor, it's their own fault. I guess you're looking for a handout. I didn't think they allowed people like you around here—"

"No, no," I said, frustrated. I told her about my Appraisal, how I'd been on the run for forty years. I tried to explain about her own Appraisal.

She took a step back, the expression of terror suddenly returning. Her hand moved again to her HUD controller.

"Five?" she finally said, her voice rising. "Nobody has a LEF of five. And what do you know about my Appraisal? It's none of your business. Anyway, I know what my LEF is. You're full off it. Leave me alone."

"Your father's a doctor," I said. "I know he did your Appraisal. He must have talked to you about it—"

Her eyes widened and she stepped back again. "What do you know about my father?" she said loudly.

I pushed my hands down for her to be quiet.

"Get away from me!" she shouted. "I'm going to call SecureCorp."

A couple of people nearby stopped and stared. She started punching something on her controller. A RoboTaxi finally pulled up to the curb beside her.

"It's okay, I'm going," I said, backing away. "Just think about what I told you. I sent a contact number to your HUD. Don't erase it. I'll be around if you want to talk."

The door to the RoboTaxi popped open. She stared at me one last time, then rushed in and slammed it behind her. The vehicle took off as I walked away.

"That went well," Richie said, as I approached the bench where he was still sitting.

"You could have come and helped me," I said. "I'm not exactly an expert on socializing after spending forty years with dogs as my only companions."

"Sure," Richie laughed. "A big, overweight, middle-aged stranger joining you and crowding around that poor girl. That really would have put her at ease."

I shook my head. "We'd better get out of here in case SecureCorp show up. And don't call her 'that poor girl'. She's a spoiled bitch from hell."

# FORTEEN

...................................................

# PLAN C

We were quickly running out of options, and the clock for our mission here was ticking down. Richie had become an important player in the Rebel movement, and Laura wasn't willing to part with him for more than a couple of weeks. And the local Rebels were getting nervous. They weren't as established as our group in First City; if we got caught, or somehow led SecureCorp back to their hideout, they risked annihilation.

We were forced to fall back on a more desperate plan. Again, we would intercept Annabelle — not to try to convince her to join us, but to kidnap her and take her somewhere safe. It was insanely dangerous, but we had nothing else. Though we still had no absolute proof about her Appraisal, the level of interest SecureCorp was showing in her father implied that the message I'd received was correct. By this time chances were that they either already knew, or were beginning to suspect, that Karlson had lied about Annabelle's Appraisal, and would try to capture her themselves. We had to get to her first.

We stepped up the surveillance we'd been conducting on her home. Karlson must be pretty high up in the pecking order — his family was one of the few in the Corp Ring that lived in a single-family dwelling, an ultramodern, squarish structure with a spacious garden in front. It was dangerous for any one person or group to hang around watching the place. Between us and the local Rebels, we had enough people to keep a constant watch, rotating spies often enough that they didn't attract attention.

But we never got the chance to put our kidnapping plan into action. Late at night, a few days after I'd tried to talk to her, a set of black-suited prowlers showed up at her house. Luckily, Richie and I happened to be on watch, and our replacements, two of the Third City Rebels, were in a vehicle nearby, about to relieve us.

We called for them, and the four of us watched the prowlers at a distance. One of the black suits headed to the front door while the other two hid in the shadows. The door guy punched something on his HUD controller. The door popped open, and a sword of light from the interior slashed the sidewalk. The ones in hiding joined him and crept forward and inside, leaving one behind to guard the entrance.

Deciding we couldn't wait for the backup, we snuck up to a cluster of bushes beside the entrance. I threw a pebble in another bush to distract the guard. When he stepped forward to check it out, Richie jumped up behind him and snapped his neck without a sound. My friend had become a lethal fighter.

Inside, we found ourselves in the living room. It was dark, and there was nobody around. A patch of light spilled from a hallway to our right. We headed for it, and were a few meters away when a man's voice shouted from inside, and there was a muffled scream. We rushed forward into the hallway.

The sound had come from a room on the right. The door was open, and there were sounds of a scuffle. Further down the hallway was a prowler, about to enter a door on the left. Richie and I tore down the hall after him, while the two other Rebels rushed into the first room. The guy down the hall spotted us and pulled out a gun. We ducked into a doorway just as he fired.

We hauled out our own guns and engaged in a firefight with the guy, who was holed up in the doorway of what we guessed must be Annabelle's room. We were at an impasse. Both Richie and I were close to running out of ammunition. Finally, I jumped into the hallway and ran for the doorway, firing at the opening as I ran.

When I reached his position, the prowler was leaning against the wall. He'd been hit. His arm shook as he tried to raise his weapon. I fired first, and he went down.

"Richie!" I called back down the hallway. He rushed up and joined me.

"You take a lot of risks for a guy that's got four hundred years to lose," he smiled as he caught up.

The room light was off. I found the switch and we both cast around, searching for Annabelle. There were posters of hunky guys on the walls, jewelry on the dresser, trendy clothes in the closet. The dresser also held several trophies, two for gymnastics, one for academic achievement. It looked like there was more to Annabelle than her looks. There were also pictures of Annabelle and her parents. In one, her father beamed with his arm around her as she held up some kind

*413*

of sports medal. In another, she stood for a portrait between her mother and father — a happy family.

The room had to be hers — but Annabelle wasn't there.

We frantically scoured every corner of the place. Nothing.

"Shit," I said.

Gunfire still echoed from the first room. We tore back down the hallway. One of the Rebel guys had just taken out the last of the black-suited prowlers. The other Rebel lay on the floor. He wasn't moving.

It was the Karlsons' bedroom. Numerous photographs crowded a dresser against the wall: Annabelle as a little girl smiling behind a birthday cake full of candles. Annabelle as a teenager riding a beautiful thoroughbred horse. Annabelle standing on the highest level of a sports podium, beaming.

All were splattered with blood. Annabelle's mother lay in a pool of it in front of the open door to the bathroom. Her father lay beside a dead prowler, shot full of holes. For years he'd fought to protect his daughter. Now his fight was over. Now it was up to us.

"What do we do?" I asked, turning away from the horrific scene.

"Well, at least it doesn't look like they got her," Richie said. "We better get the hell out of here. There'll be more where these came from."

We made a quick search of the entire house. There was no sign of Annabelle. We took off into the shadows as a multitude of sirens echoed in our direction.

414

# FIFTEEN

..................................................

# THE SEARCH

The next day we met with Lucas and some of the senior Rebels to talk about our next step.

"She hasn't contacted me," I admitted, embarrassed that even with her life on the line, she didn't want to reach out to me.

"If we don't hear from her, we're out of options," Richie said. "There's no way we can track her down ahead of SecureCorp. They've got resources we couldn't dream of."

I stared at my fists clenched on the table. Maybe they'd gotten her after all. If not, where would she go? The local Rebels had already compiled a list of anybody she might turn to, and there was no sign that she'd contacted any of them. Grudgingly, I wondered if maybe she was smarter than I'd given her credit for.

A day later something strange happened. Somebody tried to contact me on my HUD — somebody I didn't recognize. The connection only lasted a couple of seconds, like whoever it was had started to reach out and then changed their mind. Our technical guys tried to locate the sender, but the communication interval was too short.

I had a feeling it was her.

That night I lay awake, thinking. Something about the whole operation at the house was clawing at the edges of my consciousness. Finally I figured out what it was. Richie and I were sleeping on cots in an open space at the Rebel hideout. I jumped up, went over and shook him.

"Do you know what time it is?" he whispered, checking his HUD.

I motioned for him to follow me. We headed down the hallway to one of the meeting rooms, and sat at a table in the center.

"The night of the raid," I said. "Didn't the guys on the shift before us say that Annabelle was at home?"

Richie shrugged. "I guess they were wrong — it happens."

"We were watching the house," I said. "None of us saw anybody leave."

"So?"

"Lucas said there's no indication that SecureCorp have got her. He claims he's got people pretty deep in the Corp Ring. She's a young girl who's led a pampered, sheltered life, with almost no experience beyond the cocoon of her family. Meanwhile, there's a massive, highly trained and equipped army hunting for her, but they haven't found her."

"Y...Yeah," Richie said. "So, what's your point?"

"My point is that that's impossible. She couldn't hope to outsmart them or outrun them — if she was out in the world."

Richie shrugged. "Well — where else could she be?" He turned to me, and his eyes went wide. "You' re thinking—"

I smiled at him. "I don' t think she ever left the house."

"Shit," Richie said, shaking his head.

"Her father' s been planning for this scenario for years," I said, "ever since her Appraisal. I think he was forced to tell her, in those final days leading up to the raid. Maybe he built some kind of hiding place for her, and instructed her on how to use it if everything went south..."

Richie straightened up. "We better get over there. If you' re right, she' s been there for two days now. Her father probably provided food and water, but wherever she is, she can' t stay there forever. She' s got to come out some time."

I nodded. "There' s also the danger that SecureCorp will come to the same conclusion we have."

We got together a couple of Rebel fighters and headed for the Karlson's place. The Rebels waited in a car in a shadowed square a few blocks away, while Richie and I headed for the house. It was dangerous traveling late at night; there were very few on the street, and SecureCorp were almost guaranteed to question anybody they found hanging around.

Luckily, Richie and I were still pretty good at Cam-surfing, weaving between the visual footprints of the security cameras, from back when we were kids, and this was the Corp Ring — there weren't cameras everywhere like in the Quarters.

We stuck to the darkest alleys and made it there without being seen. Once we arrived, we had to contend with the house itself. It should have been considered a crime scene, surrounded with police tape, but there was nothing. I guess officially, nothing had happened here. That also meant that there were no guards.

"That's lucky," I whispered, as we peered around a darkened corner at the house, which showed nothing of the horror that had taken place inside.

"No guards," Richie answered, "but look at this."

He pressed a button on his HUD controller. A silhouette of the building came up on my own HUD, with a mass of coloured dots and lines superimposed on it.

"I helped the Rebels come up with this hack a few years ago," Richie whispered. "It detects all the security implants in an area. They're pretty dense, but we should be able to thread our way through."

We headed around back, where the traps were a little wider apart. I followed Richie's lead as he snaked his way between them, while at the same time sticking to the shadows and taking cover whenever possible. For a big guy, he was pretty agile.

A large red dot in my HUD indicated a more secure trap on the back door itself, one we couldn't hope to avoid. We crouched behind a shrub, and Richie hauled out a tablet and typed furiously on it for several minutes. He pressed one last button on his HUD controller. There was a click on the lock of the door, and the red dot in my HUD disappeared.

I clapped him on the shoulder. "Where would I be without you?" I whispered.

"That's easy," he whispered back. "You'd be dead."

We scanned the area one last time, then snuck up to the door, opened it, and slipped inside. Luckily, SecureCorp had assumed that the outside traps would stop any intruders — there was no indication of any inside.

The interior was dark. We didn't want to risk using a flashlight, but once our eyes adjusted there was enough ambient light leaking in from outside that we could see our way. The back entrance led into the kitchen. From there we threaded our way up a side hallway, and retraced the route we'd taken the night of the raid, passing the room where Karlson and his wife were killed. The room was pristinely neat and clean. The photographs on the dresser were still in their original positions, but all traces of blood had been removed. Even in the dim light it was clear that the events of that night had been washed away.

We reached Annabelle's room. Since it was deep in the interior of the house, we decided to risk using a flashlight. I shone the beam around, playing it on the now familiar posters and knick-knacks. I scoured the room for any sign of an escape route, while Richie fiddled with a security detection hack on his tablet. I ran my hands along the walls looking for hidden seams or fake panels, checked under the bed, and pulled out a tall dresser that could have covered a hidden opening. Nothing.

"There," Richie finally whispered, nodding at a large wardrobe in the northwest corner.

He held his tablet out for me to see. His hack showed a dim seam around the wardrobe. The question was, how to open it, and what was on the other side?

We each felt around a back edge. Nothing. We tried to pull the wardrobe out, but it was somehow attached to the wall. I opened the doors. It was full of clothes: dresses, sweaters, jackets. We hauled them all out and threw them on the bed. The flashlight beam only illuminated a small area at a time, and not very well. Anyway, there was nothing.

I finally stepped right inside and felt around. The clothes had been hanging on a round pole near the top. I shone my flashlight where the pole attached to the wall of the wardrobe. The gap around the joint was wider than I would have expected. I gripped the pole and twisted. It turned, there was a click, and I jumped back out as an entire section of the rear panel of the wardrobe began to swing open.

Light poured from the interior. I jumped back again when I saw what was inside. Annabelle Karlson was crouched on the floor with a gun in both hands, aimed straight at my head.

"You!" she said.

# SIXTEEN

..................................................

# ANNABELLE

She cocked the gun, ready to fire.

"Wait!" I yelled, pushing my hands out in front of me. "We're here to help you."

She hesitated, her hands shaking. Finally she relaxed her finger on the trigger, though she kept the gun pointed at me. I lowered my hands.

"Your father must have explained," I said. "About your Appraisal. He built all this for you, didn't he, expecting that this day would come."

Annabelle looked haggard and exhausted. She probably hadn't slept since she'd gone into hiding. Behind her was a small cubicle with a narrow bed, a sink and toilet, and a tiny kitchen with a pantry of food.

Once again I explained about my own Appraisal, and how her father was arranging for us to take her away for her own protection.

She sneered at me. "The Corps would never do that. My father is one of the top executives in MediCorp."

It didn't seem like a good time to bring up the fact that her parents were both dead.

"They're after eternal life," I said instead. "You know these guys. How far do you think they'd go?"

For a second, she lowered the gun in her shaking hand slightly. I'd tossed a grenade into her world.

"We've got to go," I said. "We figured out where you were. It's only a matter of time before they do—"

Richie touched my shoulder and put a finger to his lips. The beams of several high-powered flashlights danced through the hallway, approaching the room. Richie and I pulled out our guns.

Annabelle opened her eyes and jumped back.

"They're here," I whispered.

"What are you trying to pull?" Annabelle sneered, raising her gun and backing into her cubicle.

I stepped forward and grabbed her gun. It went off.

"Shit!" Richie said.

I wrestled the gun out of Annabelle's hand, and it dropped to the floor. I pinned both her arms behind her and dragged her out into the room.

"You're going to pay for this," she yelled, as she fought to get away.

"We're trying to save you, for God's sake," I said, as she twisted around and tried to bite me.

Richie moved to the open door of the room. I dragged Annabelle away from the wardrobe, afraid she might rush back inside or grab her gun. Richie poked his head around and gunfire erupted from the far end of the hall.

I held both Annabelle's wrists in one hand and with my free hand twisted the pole of the wardrobe counter-clockwise. The secret door slid shut, locking her gun inside. I shut the doors of the wardrobe, blocking her access.

"There's only three of them," Richie called back. "Guess they weren't expecting much resistance."

I switched off the flashlight. The room was now dark.

"These guys are here to kidnap you," I said to Annabelle.

"And you're not?" she yelled, still trying to twist away.

"I'm going to have to let go of you to fight them," I said. There was no response.

I let go of her hands, and Richie and I crowded around the doorway in a firefight with the attackers. At first we had the advantage of being in darkness, while they were visible from their flashlights. Richie took out one, and they switched the flashlights off. Now we could barely make out their silhouettes in the darkness.

I leaned out to shoot. My shot went wild as something heavy smashed into my shoulder. I twisted around. Annabelle was standing behind me with a porcelain lamp in both hands. She'd been aiming for my head. She rushed at me again. I turned to block her attack but I was too slow. The lamp hit its mark this time and everything went black.

When I awoke, all was dark and quiet.

"Alex," a voice said. A hand slapped my cheek. "Alex!"

I was lying on the floor. As my eyes focused, I realized that I was still in Annabelle's bedroom. The voice belonged to Richie.

"We've got to get out of here," he said. "They'll be here any second."

I groaned and sat up. My head was throbbing with pain. I reached back and felt a lump on the back of my skull. Richie grabbed me under the armpits and hauled me up.

"What happened?" I asked, still confused.

"No time to explain," he said.

He poked his head into the hallway, then moved into it and dragged me after him. The hallway was empty.

"I'm okay," I said. He let go and I followed him toward the back door. "Where's Annabelle?"

"Shhhh," he said.

There were sirens approaching, fast. We reached the back, did a quick scan of the yard, and ran for our lives.

We were about a block away when the sirens stopped, as I guess they arrived at the Karlson house. It would take them a few minutes to assess the situation, then they'd be coming after us. It was slow going as we both automatically started to Cam-surf. We got in touch with our getaway vehicle and they managed to move it up to within a couple of blocks of our position.

Now the sirens started up again, fanning out in several directions — one of them ours. We had one more block to go. The closest siren was approaching fast. We didn't dare speed up and risk being seen by a camera.

I relaxed a little when our vehicle came into view. We stumbled the last half-block up to it and inside, and we took off, with the siren seconds away.

Richie filled me in as we drove.

"She knocked you out cold," he said. "Then she took off down the hall before I could grab her. Both sides stopped shooting — neither of us wanted to risk hitting her. She swerved trying to escape the SecureCorp fighters. She almost made it. She did some kind of gymnastic flip over one of them, but the other one managed to grab her. It was still dark, and I didn't dare shoot.

"They dragged her off, kicking and screaming. They were too preoccupied with her to care about us, but they must have called for backup. We were lucky to get out of there."

I closed my eyes and bowed my head. Our final chance at rescue had flown away into the night.

The light of morning was beginning to spill over the tops of the surrounding skyscrapers by the time we got back to the Rebel hideout. We immediately arranged for a meeting with Lucas and the other leaders of the local Rebel unit. My head was still throbbing as we gathered in one of the meeting rooms.

"Shit, shit, shit," Lucas banged his fist on the table in front of him when we told him what had happened. "You're sure it was SecureCorp?"

I nodded. "They had the uniforms, and the tech. I don' t know how they knew we were there. Either they just happened to figure out where she was at the exact same time as we did, or…"

"Or we' ve got a mole," Richie said, shaking his head and staring at the floor.

"That' s impossible," Lucas said, gesturing around us. "I' d trust any of these people with my life."

"After what just happened, you might want to rethink that," Richie said.

Lucas scowled at him, but said nothing. A suffocating atmosphere of gloom had settled over us all.

"So Vita Aeterna have her," I said, grimacing and shaking my head. "It' s over."

Richie nodded. "Yes, it is."

A medic treated the painful bump on my head as well as he could. Richie and I were both exhausted, so though it was morning, we crashed in the dormitory for a few hours. That afternoon, we had an-other meeting with Lucas and a few of the others to discuss what to do next.

The atmosphere of dejection continued as we gathered in one of the meeting rooms. Lucas and the others glared at us in silence.

"So, I guess you' ll be heading back now?" Lucas asked, hopefully.

I glanced at Richie and shrugged. "There' s nothing more we can do here."

"I've already arranged for your plane to be refueled," Lucas said. He looked relieved. "We'll wait until nightfall to set up the flight — it's safer."

There was an air of gloom, failure, and even animosity, around the hideout as we waited, each of our groups blaming the other for the failed mission. Few words were spoken as, shortly after dark, a Rebel vehicle transported Richie, me, and the rest from First City, out to the same hidden airstrip where we'd landed a week ago.

After a quick sweep by our security people, we headed for the plane. We passed through a jumble of collapsing buildings, and into a grove of spindly trees. The black silhouette of the plane was in sight, just ahead of us, when there was a gunshot, and one of the local fighters ahead of us went down.

A half-dozen soldiers appeared on the fringes of the grove, their weapons drawn. Even in the darkness we could make out the ink-black business suit design, like what their masters wore, but made from bullet proof fabric, their black ties, and the blood-red stripe across each of their chests.

It was clear who our attackers were — SecureCorp.

The local Rebels engaged the attackers in a firefight, while we crouched low and rushed for the plane. Bullets whizzed over our heads, and there were flashes of gunfire to either side of us. Richie ran around to the pilot's side and dove into the cockpit. I frantically unlatched the door on my side, dove in beside him and buckled up. The other fighters we'd brought rushed into the back as Richie fired up the engine.

Normally, we would have dragged the plane back as far as possible, to allow extra space for takeoff. The current situation made that impossible.

Flashes of gunfire lit up the darkness around us as we rumbled down the makeshift runway. Several times I heard the clanking sound of bullets striking the plane as we finally lifted up and climbed quickly into the night sky. So far they hadn't hit anything important.

My knuckles were white on the arms of my chair as the plane roared straight toward the darkened rectangle of a skyscraper at the end of the runway. Richie grimaced as he pulled back hard on the stick in his hands. The plane angled sharply upward and both the engine and I screamed in unison.

The top of the building was meters away; it didn't look like we were going to clear it. I leaned back and lifted my feet, as if that would help the nose rise a little higher. The plane shook violently and bullets continued to ping off of its metal skin, as we hurtled straight toward the top of the building. Finally we were above it, and the screaming engine echoed off the roof less than a meter below.

I shook my head slowly as we rose into the sky, and clenched my fists as I watched the continuing flashes of gunfire below.

# SEVENTEEN

........................................................

# BACK AT HEADQUARTERS

It was lucky that the local Rebels had gassed up the plane. We were forced to make a wide detour to evade any aircraft SecureCorp might send after us. The change added a half hour to our flight time. We kept low, again under the radar, and reached the original airfield without further incident. I hung my head as the transport carrying us slunk back to Rebel headquarters. Our only hope had been to get to Annabelle before Vita Aeterna. In spite of all our efforts, that hope had now vapourized.

That night, my fitful sleep was spiked with images of Walter — his skin like parchment, his wasted muscles and stick-like bones, his body devastated by years of horrifying medical experiments, his face like a death mask. This, or probably something worse, was what Annabelle had in store, possibly for the next several hundred years.

Then I thought of the countless others who had suffered the same fate at the hands of Vita Aeterna over the decades, while I cowered in my hideout in the Dregs and did nothing to help them.

*429*

In the morning there was more bad news. We learned that two more of the Third City Rebels had been killed in the firefight surrounding our takeoff from the airfield, and another badly wounded. I prayed that my mysterious informant was correct — that all those lives hadn't been lost for nothing.

The day after our return from Third City, I went for a long walk around the perimeter while Richie attended a special meeting with Laura and the others to discuss the mission. Significantly, it was a meeting to which I wasn't invited.

My head was down, thinking, trying to work out how to move forward. One of my problems was that I had so little experience dealing with people. I assumed that eventually I'd get the hang of it, but for now, my reactions always seemed to put people on edge, especially Laura. I looked up and unexpectedly spotted the old man I'd seen not long after I'd first arrived. Again, he was peering around a corner some distance away. This time, I broke into a run, determined to confront him. Still, I was too late — by the time I reached the corner he was gone.

A few hours later Bailey came by to fill me in on what had happened. Night was falling as we strolled the compound, past the giant lot that served as the motor pool. Cars, with and without Corp insignia, trucks, vans, even high-tech stealth vehicles, loomed beside us in the semi-darkness as we walked.

It came as no surprise to me that Bailey's news wasn't good. "It's direct orders from the General," he said. We walked toward the eastern perimeter, while I clenched and unclenched my fists.

"All we have is your mysterious message," he said. "We don't even have any proof that Annabelle Karlson's Appraisal is anything other than what's on record."

I stopped and turned to face him. "Then why did SecureCorp go to the trouble of killing her parents and kidnapping her?"

"It's not my decision," Richie answered. "Anyway, I'm sorry, but people with high Appraisals aren't a big priority for the Rebels. The main reason they sanctioned the mission in the first place was in the hope of turning Dr. Karlson to our cause. He's dead now, so that prospect has disappeared. And the Third City Rebels have made it clear that they don't want us back. After their losses, I can't say I blame them."

I couldn't let it go. As obnoxious as Annabelle had been, she didn't deserve what I knew Vita Aeterna had planned for her. I tried several times to arrange a meeting with Laura. She continued to refuse. Finally, probably after lobbying by Richie, Bailey, Connor, and maybe even Samantha, she gave in and agreed to see me, though the meeting was to be no more than twenty minutes. I vowed to keep my cool and convince her with solid arguments.

I should have guessed how quickly that plan would fall apart.

"I never would have thought you were capable of this," I snapped at Laura, after what I thought were unassailable arguments for continuing the mission were immediately dismissed.

"Capable of what?" she said.

"Of shutting down one of the most important missions you've ever been involved in, just to spite me."

We'd met in the room I'd visited when I first got back. She sat scowling behind her desk, while I paced the floor in front of her.

She rose and stepped toward me, her eyes blazing. "It's so typical that you would assume that this is about you. The fact is, as you've been told numerous times, we have limited resources. We have to carefully pick and choose how we assign them. We've already lost one good fighter, the Rebel force in Third City lost three more. The airfield where you landed has been compromised, and we almost lost one of our only planes. All on the basis of a single message — a message you can't even verify, from an unknown source."

"That girl's life is at stake," I countered. "She could end up being slowly taken apart for the next several hundred years, because we did nothing."

"You have no proof of that," she said. "Anyway, we didn't do nothing. We ran a complex, expensive, and risky operation trying to save her — one in which you played a major role. We tried, and we failed. It's unfortunate, but we don't have the resources to mount a full attack on SecureCorp. It's time to move on."

I stood with my hands clenched in fists at my sides.

"You've been alive now for fifty-six years," Laura said, "but it's like you're still sixteen, like the last forty years never happened. Maybe it's because you've had so little human contact, maybe the loneliness has stunted your personality." She shook her head slowly. "There's a lot happening outside your little world, a lot of bad things, many that neither you nor I have any control over. You have to be a grown-up — you have to learn to think of people other than yourself."

She sat back down. "This meeting is over."

She pressed the button on a device on her desk. The door to the room immediately opened and a soldier appeared. Laura nodded at him, and he stood aside, holding the door open to indicate that I should leave.

I headed for the doorway. When I reached it, I turned back to face her.

"What happened to the girl I used to know?" I asked. "The girl who had compassion and believed in doing what was right regardless of the risks involved?"

She stared into my eyes. "She died a long time ago. She died when the boy she loved was killed in a factory explosion."

Later that afternoon, I expected Samantha to roll her eyes and look at me like I was nuts when I asked for some 'alone time' with the dogs. Surprisingly, she seemed to understand right away, even claiming she had some errands to run as an excuse for leaving us for a couple of hours. After the meeting with Laura, the weight of all that had happened fell down on me like a crushing landslide — the people, the attention, the conflict, the frustration of failure.

433

For four decades, I'd always done whatever I wanted. I'd never had to ask permission. I'd never had to make allowances for anyone else's feelings or needs. I'd never had to make the slightest compromise, not even to one other person, let alone multiple people at once, and even a larger group as a whole. I'd endured physical conflict, and even fought for my life, hundreds of times over the years, but I'd never had to negotiate, give up anything, or resolve personality conflicts with anybody else. A part of me was tempted to slink back to my hideout and stay there, and I probably would have done that, but now that my existence was known, I was no longer safe there.

Since leaving the dogs with Samantha, I'd come to see them almost every day, but usually just to say hello. Now I needed something more. I needed to let go, to get back to what for me had become a 'normal' existence, even if only for a couple of hours.

Samantha had set up an open play area similar to what I'd had at the hideout, though much smaller. I entered it, and they were all over me, jumping up, barking, licking my face. We played ball for an hour or so, then piled together, as we'd done so often before, nestling with each other and reveling in each other's company.

At least for one brief moment, I could forget about my failures, and their horrific consequences.

# EIGHTEEN

..................................................

# A VOICE FROM THE PAST

The next day I had a meeting with Bailey and Connor to discuss my future with the Rebels. To my disappointment, they had completely accepted Laura's judgment on the mission.

"So you're okay with what's going to happen to Annabelle Karlson?" I snapped at them. I couldn't believe it.

"We're realists," Bailey answered. "It's not the first time we've been forced to accept a horrific state of affairs."

We went on to discuss what other aspects of the Rebel movement I might be involved in. I wasn't really listening. It's true that my self-exile had spared me from having to make the impossible decisions that the Rebels were faced with every day. But I couldn't let it go. It was too close to home — too close to my own story.

I agreed to think about their suggestions, even though I hadn't been paying attention to anything they said. We arranged to meet the next day to discuss it further.

Every day since I'd arrived back at Rebel headquarters I'd been under constant scrutiny. Not only was I a dead person miraculously brought back to life — I was a dead *legend* brought back to life — a hero of the revolution, the guy who'd killed Charles Wickham and single-handedly destroyed the gas factory that threatened the entire population of the Quarters all those years ago.

I'd assumed, and hoped, that all the attention would eventually die down, but for now, everywhere I went, people crowded around to catch a glimpse of me. They meant well, but it made it difficult for me to live a normal life, especially sleeping in the barracks, immediately accessible to all. Add to that my fear of crowds, a consequence of decades living alone.

The Rebels finally took pity on me and assigned me a room where I could have some private time. I was crossing an open square, heading for that room when it occurred to me that I'd been so distracted that the time for our meeting tomorrow hadn't registered. I turned back, planning to check with Bailey when, for a third time, I spotted the old man I'd seen before. Again, by the time I caught up with him he'd disappeared.

He didn't look dangerous — from what I'd seen of him he could barely walk. The sightings seemed random enough. Either they were coincidental, or he was being extremely careful. Something about his face was familiar. I made a mental note to ask Bailey about him the next time we got together.

The next day I got a text on my HUD.

*Hi, Alex,* it said. The address of the sender was obfuscated.

*Who are you?* I texted back.

*If you want to know where they're holding Annabelle,* the text answered, *meet me at the Center in Tintown, at nine PM tomorrow night. Come alone. If I see any indication that you've brought anybody else, I'll be gone.*

The message was bizarre in the first place, but what nearly knocked me off my feet was the sign off.

It said: *Spiro.*

It seemed impossible. Nobody, not even Richie, had heard from Spiro, one of the Lost Souls, the crew we used to hang with when we were kids, for forty years. Was he *really* still alive? The Center was the place where we used to hook up back then, in an abandoned warehouse on the outermost edge of Tintown. Only a member of the Lost Souls would know what it was. Jake was dead. I saw Richie almost every day; there'd be no point in him sending me a note. My contact must either really be Spiro, or somebody who'd somehow pried the information out of him.

I used the test my Uncle Zack had used on me all those years ago.

*First I need to know for sure who you are,* I texted. *Tell me — what does the 'Stump Factory' mean to the Lost Souls?*

Everybody in our crew would know the place I was referring to.

He answered immediately: *The Stump Factory is the Lost Souls' code for one of our meeting places, an old abandoned prosthetic warehouse in Tintown. See you tomorrow.*

*Wait,* I texted. *What happened to you? What's going on?*

There was no reply. His answer had been correct. It must really be Spiro.

"Bullshit," Richie said, when I told him about the message. I'd caught up with him in the canteen. He had a coffee in his hand, and was headed for a table. He stopped and stared down at me. "It's a SecureCorp trap. They must have heard that you're still alive. It was bound to happen."

"But whoever it is knew about the Center," I said. "And the Stump Factory. They must have gotten that information from one of the Lost Souls. Who else would know?"

Richie shrugged. "Nobody's heard from Spiro since his Appraisal forty years ago. I always assumed he was dead. But why would he pick now to contact you? SecureCorp are obviously playing you. Whether it's Spiro or somebody else, if they know anything about Annabelle, they must be connected with SecureCorp and Vita Aeterna. You see that — right?"

I stood for a few seconds, looking down an empty hallway.

"You can't be serious," Richie said. "Forget about it. Didn't you hear me? It's a trap. You might as well walk into the nearest SecureCorp outpost and give yourself up."

I looked up at him. "You heard Laura's decision. She's not going to change her mind. If we're going to have any chance of saving Annabelle, we'll have to do it ourselves."

Richie started walking again. "Well, just going there by yourself is out of the question. Either we find some way to support you, or we give up on the idea." He stopped again and turned to me. "Agreed?" I hesitated. "Agreed?" he repeated.

"Agreed," I finally said.

I knew he was right. There were only two groups who even knew what happened to Annabelle: the people trying to rescue her, and the people who'd kidnapped her. If Spiro, assuming it was really him, was on our side, he could just give us the information. It had to be a trap.

I couldn't just let go of the mysterious message, and its promise of a connection with Annabelle. I finally convinced Richie to meet with me, Bailey and Conner the next morning to talk about it. When the time for the meeting arrived, I got word from Richie that it would be delayed until sometime after lunch. The day dragged on, and in the mid-afternoon I got another message. Bailey was currently unavailable, and the meeting would have to wait until the next day.

An hour later, I got another message from my mysterious contact.

*I've seen the girl, Annabelle,* it said. *She's a sweet little thing, isn't she. It would be a shame if she were to end up like Walter.*

I jammed my eyes shut. When I'd first seen Walter, he looked like he was dead — dead, and yet somehow still breathing and walking around. Walter had claimed that his devastated condition was the result of Vita Aeterna's experiments, and I had no reason not to believe him.

The only one of the Lost Souls I'd ever told about Walter was Richie. So Spiro, or the person claiming to be him, must have gotten the information from SecureCorp. As had happened countless times in nightmares and bouts of depression, I pictured Walter, his loopy smile as he managed to grab a scalpel and sever the jugular of our doctor — his last desperate act — a distraction that helped me escape, but cost Walter his life.

I couldn't stand by and allow Annabelle to succumb to the same fate, no matter what the cost. Early that evening, without telling Richie or anybody else, I headed for Tintown, the place where I was born, and had lived for the first sixteen years of my life, but hadn't set foot in for more than forty years.

# NINETEEN

..................................................

# THE CENTER

It was like déjà vu, riding an old skateboard and Cam-surfing — weaving through the debris-laden streets and disintegrating office towers, dodging the detection footprints of the countless cameras in the Quarters, just like I'd done when I was a kid. I was a little rusty, and I'd grown, making it more difficult to squeeze between the oval-shaped icons displayed on my HUD, but it didn't take long for it all to come back.

The Quarters weren't without danger, but except for the cameras, they were a breeze compared to the Dregs. There were a lot more people, but most of them weren't interested in you if you left them alone — especially if it looked like you were heading somewhere else. There was one major challenge I hadn't faced when I was a kid: back then, if a camera had spotted me, nothing would have happened — it was all a game.

Now, with my face probably splashed over every SecureCorp database in the city, and the facial recognition software scouring every camera feed, one detection and I'd be surrounded by SecureCorp vehicles in minutes. I had to be more careful than I've ever been. Like I'd done the times I snuck into Shaketown, I wore a floppy hat and wrapped a bandanna up over my nose.

I traversed the fuzzy boundary between the Dregs and the Quarters, and boarded into the Quarter where I was born. Nothing much seemed to have changed. The streets were dirtier and more torn up than I remembered. It was coming more and more to resemble the Dregs. The buildings were only in marginally better shape than the ones I'd passed every day when I was in hiding. Rats and wild dogs slunk through the back alleys, fighting, along with their human counterparts, to stay alive.

As I skirted the eastern edge, I turned a corner to see water lapping around the walls of abandoned buildings in the distance. Completely unheard of when I was a kid, the encroaching sea was now a fact, even here.

Tintown had never been much, but this is the place where I'd grown up, where my perception of the world had taken shape — I thought of my mother, my father, the Lost Souls, Cindy, my first love... I remembered the lyrics to a song I heard once — *I despise you 'cause you're filthy, but I love you 'cause you're home*. They seemed to fit perfectly. The devastation intensified my guilt. I should have done more over the years to improve the lives of the people here.

On the way to the Center, I had to pass by my old apartment building. It looked more or less the same, only dumpier: twisted, dripping pipes dangling at intervals from walls stained with alternating streaks of bleached white and mildew black.

Despite the danger, I stepped off my board and stood in front of it for a few minutes, staring at the fifth-floor window. My dad had been tossed out of it as he defended me, when I first went on the run from Vita Aeterna. The memories came rushing in like a tidal wave. The image of his body smashing through the window and onto the filthy pavement resurfaced, and suddenly my eyes were wet with tears. Dad and I had never been close. In fact, I always thought he hated me, or at best didn't give a shit. In the end he'd given his life for me. All the pain and sadness of my childhood pressed down on me like a crushing weight.

I got it together and continued on to the Center, arriving a half hour early. It was a dangerous place for a meeting. There was only one entrance, and therefore technically only one avenue of escape. Even as desperate as I was, I wouldn't have agreed to go there, except for one thing.

I knew a secret way out.

I'd found it years ago when I was still running with the Lost Souls. There was a section of wall at the back that had come apart, leaving a gap large enough to squeeze through. On the other side, a mixture of rubble and broken beams formed a sort of stairway up to the ceiling, which itself was broken, allowing access to the roof. I'd never told the others about it. I liked the idea of having a secret escape route that nobody else knew about. I'd meant to tell them at some point, but I'd never gotten the chance.

When I arrived, I made my way to another abandoned building next door, snuck inside, climbed to the roof, and had a look. Peering down at the roof of the building where the Center was located, I could see the gaping hole I'd found when I was a kid. Nothing had changed. I scouted out a route from the roof of that building to the one where I was standing.

The light was beginning to fade. Other than the occasional stray dog, or brave soul daring to walk around at night, all was quiet. Of course, there could be a SecureCorp army hidden in any one of the broken-down abandoned buildings nearby. I watched until it was time for the meeting, ready to scrap the whole mission if I saw anything suspicious, but there was nothing.

More images from my childhood crowded my brain as I pushed aside the loose plank that still blocked the secret entrance, and squeezed through, with a lot more difficulty than when I was younger and smaller. As it always had, the place smelled like mold, rotting cardboard, decay, and age. I was in almost total darkness. The only light bled through the cracks in the walls from distant occupied buildings. But as my eyes adjusted, I could make out the room I had once known so well.

The beaten-up old couch that had stood in one corner was still there, though it was now coated with a thick layer of dust, as was the armchair with all the stuffing coming out that stood in another corner. Apparently nobody else had used the place since our time.

All was eerily silent. The space in front of me was empty. It reinforced the foreboding that flashed through my brain — that Richie was right — I never should have come here. I was turning to leave when I heard a shuffling sound behind me.

A thin, raspy voice said: "Alex, you're looking good for a guy pushing sixty."

444

# TWENTY

...............................................

# SPIRO

I spun around, and peered into a darkened corner. A shape pushed out of the shadows into a trapezoid of light and I saw him, seated behind a battered wooden table. It was the old man who'd been following me back at the Rebel hideout.

I don't think I ever would have recognized who it was if I hadn't been expecting him. Even then, I had to stare deeply into his hooded eyes to believe it. It really was Spiro, my childhood buddy from the Lost Souls, from so long ago.

I had no doubt it was Spiro, but the wasted apparition before me was like a sickening melding of my former friend and my father just before he died. His hair was snow white and almost gone from his head, leaving a pale pink dome. The skin of his neck hung in folds like rotting parchment. His hands, age-spotted and trembling, were clenched in fists on the table in front of him.

"Spiro?" I said.

*445*

Spiro had disappeared right after his Appraisal forty years ago, and nobody, not even Richie, had heard what happened to him. His red-rimmed vulture-like eyes glared at me with a deep malevolence. He smiled, then bitterly snorted in amusement. That action initiated a coughing fit that lasted almost a minute.

Finally he composed himself and resumed his stare. Was it really possible that we were both the same age? In fact, Spiro was a few months younger than me.

"So it's true what they said about you," he wheezed, fighting against another coughing fit.

"How did you get here?" I asked, scanning for any sign of a SecureCorp. There was no way the decrepit old man sitting in front of me could have made it here on his own.

"Have a seat," he said, nodding at a chair across from him. Reluctantly, I obeyed him and sat down.

"Shocking, isn't it," he laughed, revealing a mouthful of rotting teeth. "Well, I already know your Appraisal, so I guess it's only fair that I tell you mine. Aren't you curious?"

I shrugged. All I had to do was look at him to know he'd negged out big time. He was only fifty-six years old, like me, but he looked in his nineties.

"Point seven," he said. "Isn't that amusing?"

"I'm sorry," I said.

"Yes, it *is* a tragedy, isn't it," he said, with a chuckle. "What a terrible waste of human life."

"I saw you — at Rebel Headquarters," I said. "You were following me."

"Yes," he answered, in his wheezing voice. "Security didn't think twice about letting in a decrepit old man like me.   I wanted to get a good look, to see what my life could have been…"

His head dropped for a second, almost as if he'd fallen asleep.

Finally, he raised it again. "Well," he smiled, as if changing the subject. "You're looking well. You must be very pleased with yourself."

It was my turn to laugh. "A lot of good it's done me. I've been on the run for forty years."

He strained as he pushed his hands against the table top to straighten up in his chair.

"On the run," he said, trembling with anger. "So you've been running, have you?" He cocked his head, and half-closed his eyes. "How long has it been since I was able to run?" He shook his head. "I'm afraid I've lost track." He turned back to me. "Yes, it must have been rough," he said, his voice rising. "All that — *running*. Lucky for you you've got another three hundred and fifty years to get over it. As for me, I'll be dead within the year." He leaned back again.

"I never asked for my Appraisal," I answered, "any more than you asked for yours. I wish they'd never come up with that shit, but now that it's done there's nothing either you or I can do about it. You said you had information about Annabelle."

"Actually," he smiled, "I lied."

My spine stiffened. I put my hand on the gun in my belt.

"Wait," he said half to himself, as if he'd forgotten something, "that's not quite right. In fact, I *do* have information. Annabelle is alive and well, and having a lovely time — at least for now. But that's not the reason I brought you here."

I pulled the gun out of my belt and pointed it at him.

He laughed again. "What? You're going to shoot me? What a shame. And I had so much to live for."

"What do you want, Spiro?"

"What do I want?" he smiled his creepy smile again. "It's not a question of what I want. I used to want what everybody else wants — I wanted a life. But I lost that opportunity a second after I had my Appraisal." He leaned back and ran a shaking hand through what was left of his hair.

"What do I want?" he fixed his eyes on me. "I want justice."

"Justice?"

"They came to me a few weeks ago," he said, gesturing around us with his head. "When they first learned that you were still alive. I was begging in the streets. Imagine, begging, here in Tintown — begging from beggars." He shook his head at the memory. "They offered me a comfortable end if I helped them capture you. I'm not in any condition to care how I spend my final days, but the truth is, I would have done it for nothing."

He was wheezing with the effort of speaking. He stopped for a second to get his breath, then continued.

"It took a lot of persuading for them to let me come here in person. They said I was too old and decrepit. I've been here for two hours, to make sure you wouldn't be watching when I arrived. All they really needed was for me to lure you in. But I wanted to be here. First, to see for myself what it's like to have your lifespan extended to four hundred years. Second, to see the look on your face when you realized what was going to happen to you."

"So screwing me would make you happy?" I shook my head and searched his eyes for some explanation. "What did I ever do to you? I was always a good friend to you. I even defended you when other people put you down."

"It's not about you," he said. "It's about God. It's about getting even with God for inflicting this on me. You have the most precious gift of all — time. Time to think. Time to plan. Time to live and learn. Time to appreciate what the world, such as it is, has to offer. No one else on Earth has been given that gift.

"I've been in a race with time from the moment I got my Appraisal, trying to squeeze some kind of life into the miserable number of hours I've been granted. Of course, I failed. I was guaranteed to fail."

The hatred was written across his face as he stared at me through rheumy eyes. "What makes *you* so special?" he said, his voice shaking. "Why should *you* be granted this incredible gift, while I rot away to nothing in my fifties?"

"Yeah, some gift," I said.

"Well, I'm going to take away His triumph," Spiro said, his eyes blazing, "His ultimate creation."

His mouth curled into a leering smile, and I realized something — that my old friend was insane.

Again, his wrinkled, age-spotted hands clenched into fists. "It will be my final revenge. They tell me that the tests they're planning for you will ravage your body. Technically you could even die before I do. Wouldn't that be deliciously ironic?"

I cast around the room.

"There's no escape," he said, guessing my intent. "They're outside. As you know, there's only one way out, and that's the way you came in."

He leaned his head back and laughed, the laugh soon deteriorating into another coughing fit.

I rose, lifted the gun again, and pointed it at him, my finger tightening on the trigger. Once again I looked into his eyes, and came to a realization. I saw the dementia, the misery at his fate, the obsession, the envy and hatred, and understood what he wanted. I lay the gun down on the table in front of me.

"What?" he said, disappointment sweeping across his face.

I'd known it was a trap, but hoped I might still pry some information out of him. Clearly, he knew nothing. It was time to get out. But instead of turning for the entrance, I rushed for the back of the room, toward my secret escape route.

"Get back here!" Spiro wheezed behind me. The effort launched him into a coughing fit.

"I betrayed you," he called after me between coughs. "I ruined your life. Don't you want revenge!"

In my panic I'd forgotten to pick up the gun. I glanced back and saw Spiro lift it, shaking, in both his hands and point it at me. I dove for the opening as he fired. When I was a kid, I'd been able to squeeze through easily. Now I was bigger. I hammered against the rotting boards, trying to expand the gap. Spiro's shot blasted a chip out of the wall beside me. There were two more, but neither were anywhere close.

Finally, one of the boards snapped, and I was through. Seconds later there was the percussive shattering of the board that blocked the entrance door, and numerous pairs of boots pounded into the room.

I clambered up the makeshift staircase and onto the roof. Through the hole I could see a half dozen SecureCorp soldiers below now surrounding Spiro, who was pointing in the direction I'd gone. They rushed after me. I watched long enough to see Spiro, barely able to lift the gun, point it at his own head.

I turned and ran for the edge of the roof. There was one last gunshot behind me. Spiro had been forced to finish the job himself.

I leapt from the roof of the Center to that of the building where I'd been hiding earlier, and took the route I'd found, down a set of crumbling stairs. By then my SecureCorp pursuers had found my escape route and made it to the roof themselves. On the ground floor, I poked my head out the doorway and saw another pair of SecureCorp soldiers guarding the entrance to the Center.

There was a door in the far side of my building that was shielded from the view of the guards. I rushed through it and into the street. I was out. From here all was simple. I unstrapped the board from my back and started to Cam-surf. I knew this area better than anywhere else in the city, and knew the location of every camera — at least so I thought.

I'd only gone a few blocks when a red dot appeared in my HUD, the indicator from the Cam-surfing hack that my presence had been detected. I scanned the alley and cringed. There was a new camera, peeking through a tiny hole in the brick wall of a nearby building. I took off as fast as I could, while still Cam-surfing, but it was too late. Black stealth SecureCorp vehicles screeched to a stop at each end of the alley, trapping me.

Soldiers piled from them, their weapons drawn. They approached, and one of them grabbed each of my arms. There was no point in putting up a fight — there were too many of them. I didn't try to communicate with my captors as I was dragged to a nearby van and propelled inside. Two of the soldiers climbed in after me, shoved me down on one of the benches along the sides, and handcuffed me to the wall.

I hung my head and stared at the floor. It had been a stupid plan, virtually guaranteed to fail. I could picture Richie's accusing expression as he chewed me out for going back on my promise. But with Laura's decision it was our only lead, the only path pointing to Annabelle. And whatever the outcome, my meeting with Spiro, and my subsequent capture, might be one of the few chances I would have of finding out where Annabelle was being held, and of rescuing her.

I'd seen firsthand what Vita Aeterna's horrific experiments could do. My guess was that, as they had with me, they'd take their time with her, afraid of killing her or doing irreparable harm before they'd extracted what they were after. Though so far she'd come across as an obnoxious, spoiled little rich girl, I found myself hoping she was okay.

*452*

A part of me also felt a strong attraction to her. She was beautiful, but was that all? Was that attraction pure animal instinct, or was part of it the knowledge that she was the first woman, or person for that matter, whose lifespan could match my own?

A third soldier climbed in, with a syringe in his hand. The two original ones held me down, while the third shoved the needle into my arm, and my world went black.

# TWENTY-ONE

........................................................

# ANOTHER WORLD

*I was a kid, dressed in a hospital gown, tiptoeing along a darkened hallway at SecureCorp headquarters. Halfway down, a door was open, and the lights were on. I jumped when I saw a shadow move inside. I snuck in closer, moved into the center for a better look, and saw the full silhouette on the wall — the squarish head, the pumped-up arms and torso, and I knew whose office this was.*

*Brickhead.*

*He was talking to somebody out of my view. I moved back against the closest wall. I could only catch snippets of what they were saying. I edged closer and closer to the door, trying to hear.*

*I was almost at the opening when a muscular arm reached out, grabbed my wrist, and dragged me inside.*

I jerked awake, shaking and bathed in sweat, a jackhammer slamming against the inside of my skull. My eyes were still partially gummed shut, and wouldn't focus properly. I rubbed them, and tried to sit up. Immediately my head felt like a knife had been driven into it. I lay back down, then slowly raised myself on my elbows and blinked my eyes open, expecting a dingy cell like the one where I'd been held when I was first kidnapped forty years ago.

I blinked again, unable to believe what I was seeing. I was lying on a bed the size of the room I'd had when I was a kid, made up with what appeared to be silken sheets and an incredibly soft, plush down comforter. Working through the pain, I raised myself to a sitting position, and rubbed my eyes again. In front of me, a wall made entirely of plate glass opened out on a vision of paradise.

Soaring silver and gold palaces, some spiraling into the sky, some rising delicately like crystal lattices, surrounded a garden the size of five city blocks, where massive leafy trees overhung beds of flowers and greenery, all circling a deep blue miniature lake.

Again, a surge of pain exploded in my head. I jammed my eyes shut, and collapsed to the bed. After a few seconds it subsided. I opened my eyes, rolled onto my side, and noticed a small dish resting on a night table beside the bed. On the dish were a glass of water, a single pill, and a note. Still half-paralyzed with agony, I crawled to the table and picked up the note.

It said: Take this for the pain.

At first I hesitated, but finally decided that if they'd wanted to harm me they could have done it already. I dragged myself again to a sitting position, reached out a shaking hand, picked up the glass and took the pill. On closer inspection I could see that the dish was made of filigreed gold, and the glass was flawless crystal.

Almost immediately after I'd put down the glass, the pain in my head disappeared completely. I sat for several seconds, marveling at this instant cure. I felt completely normal — in fact, I felt better than normal.

I hopped out of bed and for the first time noticed that I was wearing silk pyjamas. I padded over to the window. When I ran my hand in front of a small panel on one side it slid silently open, and I walked out onto an expansive patio laden with exotic plants of every shape and size. The floor was set with stone tiles, and decorated with an intricately woven straw mat.

I studied the garden below in more detail. At the center of the lake a fountain sprayed into the sky, and at several corners, waterfalls cascaded from man-made vine-covered stone cliffs. A morning mist drifted across the lake and into the trees. Breathtaking statues framed the fountain and dotted the rustic path surrounding the lake. Exotic birds flitted from tree to tree, spotted deer nibbled at the grass of the numerous green spaces, and small animals scurried through the brush.

I turned and examined the room. It was larger than the entire apartment where I'd grown up in the Quarters. Everywhere I looked was opulence in the extreme. The walls were decorated with cloth textured in colours so deep you could lose yourself. The carpet beneath my feet was more than a centimeter thick, and patterned in the ancient Persian style.

I tried the handle of the room's only exit door. It was locked. So I was a prisoner after all. I'd been so awestruck that only now did I notice that, as I'd experienced when I was first kidnapped forty years

*456*

ago, my HUD wasn't working. And there was no sign of either the clothes I'd been wearing when they grabbed me, or the crypted phone I'd been carrying.

Exquisite art works were scattered throughout the room. On a chair in one corner lay a set of clothes, with another note that read: After your shower, put these on. I looked up and noticed an open door to another room — the bathroom. I walked in, by now becoming accustomed to the incredible luxury all around me. The bathroom walls appeared to be marble. When I placed a hand on one, it was cold to the touch — apparently real stone.

The sink and toilet were marble as well, and the fixtures all gold. The shower stall was a rectangular cell of spotless glass, with gold fixtures, including a gold shower head that produced a simulated rainstorm. As I stepped in, I thought of the endless showers back in Tintown and the Dregs that had consisted of a bucket of cold water over my head, or of a cold dribble, either in the open, or in a crumbling stall with rusting and broken fixtures.

On the gold rack beside the shower hung a set of plush towels with a spectacular floral design. I dried myself and dressed in the clothes that were provided. They fit as if they were made for me. I wandered back to the patio, as it occurred to me that it might offer a way to escape. The sides extended out so that there was no way to go around them, and the front looked down on a drop of at least ten meters.

Resigned, I sat down on one of the cane chairs, and absorbed the breathtaking view.

—※—

A half-hour later, there was a gentle tap on my door. I got up and opened it.

A servant impeccably dressed in a suit and tie bowed politely. "Good morning, sir. I' ve been instructed to invite you to breakfast in the garden dining area."

I nodded in agreement, and he led me out the door, to a promenade that circled a gigantic open space. I looked up and saw a glass dome ten meters above my head. Light from its panels formed an ever-changing kaleidoscope on the floor far below. I was led down a set of carpeted stairs with ornately carved banisters, to an intricately tiled foyer crowded with dozens of statues and other works of art.

At one level, the place was extraordinarily beautiful, like nothing I' d ever seen before, even in pictures — at another, it was an obscene display of unrestrained extravagance. It was as if the Elite were giving the collective finger to the millions in the Quarters and the Dregs who were stumbling through the streets on the verge of starvation.

We passed down a hallway to the left, through a set of glass-inlaid doors, and entered yet another spectacular garden, overlooking the larger one I' d seen from my room. On a stone patio on the far side stood a table at which several people were already seated. One of them rose and strode over to greet me.

He was tall and thin, and obviously fit, though his full head of impeccably coiffed hair was gray. His face was lined and wrinkled, though as with anybody, it was impossible to know his real age. He stood up straight, and exuded an inner confidence and energy.

"Hello, Mr. Barret," he said. "It's a privilege to finally meet you. My name is Elliot Pritchard. I'm the current Chairman of Vita Aeterna."

For a moment I was taken aback — I'd always assumed that the mere existence of that organization was a deeply hidden secret.

He noticed my expression. "Things have changed since the last time you were here. There's no longer any need for us to hide ourselves away, and no point in pretending. Rumours that you were still alive have drifted through our organization for years, but there was never any direct evidence. You've hidden your existence well. You look spry for a man approaching sixty — clearly the original analysis of your Appraisal was correct."

He turned and extended his hand, inviting me to join the others at the table. As I approached, I realized that there was one of them that I already knew.

It was Annabelle Karlson.

# TWENTY-TWO

........................................................

# PRITCHARD'S MANSION

Pritchard led me toward the table. A circle of deferential maids and servants stood at intervals nearby. A tray heaped with a mountain of cut fresh fruit dominated the center: apples, oranges, melons, pineapples, bananas, papayas, mangoes. It was more fruit than I'd ever seen in my life, featuring many varieties I'd only seen in pictures. We passed Annabelle as we headed for a chair on the far side. I glanced at her, and her lip curled up in a sneer. She obviously recognized me, but didn't seem surprised. I suppose she'd been briefed on who I was.

We arrived, and Pritchard stopped and gestured for me to sit. The spot he'd chosen looked out on the magnificent park and fountain I'd seen from my room. The view was stunning, like some transcendent vision of heaven. After I was seated, Pritchard moved to the head of the table, and introduced me to the others.

Sitting across from me was Dr. Clara Sheppard, an attractive, middle-aged woman with dark brown hair cut in a bob style, and bangs that reached almost to her eyebrows. She wore glasses with round, black frames. Beside her sat a burly younger man Pritchard referred to only as Mr. Stevens. Mr. Stevens nodded at me. His HUD controller looked non-standard, and I noticed a bulge in his coat.

Pritchard gestured toward Annabelle. "Of course," he said, "you two already know each other." I turned and smiled at her. She acknowledged my presence, but nothing more.

One of the servants moved close to me and leaned down. "Coffee, sir?"

I nodded, and closed my eyes at the delectable aroma as a porcelain cup and saucer of steaming coffee was set in front of me.

"How do you like my home?" Pritchard asked, once I was settled.

"I beats the Dregs," I answered.

Pritchard ignored my response. He turned to the woman beside him. "Dr. Sheppard is the head of our Appraisal Research team."

Dr. Sheppard smiled at me warmly. "I'm very excited to meet you Mr. Barret. I hope we can develop a mutually beneficial relationship. I find your unique response to the Appraisal procedure extremely interesting."

As with everything I'd experienced since arriving here, the meal was far beyond anything I'd encountered in my many years of life. Several courses, with eggs in any style I could ask for, stacks of bacon, sausages, and ham, waffles, smoked salmon, a platter of what looked like caviar, a dozen types of bread, huge slabs of butter and another dozen types of condiment.

The irresistible odours of fresh bread, butter, and cooked meat mingled as they wafted past, and suddenly I was ravenous. Feeling an undercurrent of guilt as I thought about those left behind in the Dregs,

461

I piled the bounty, much of which I'd never actually tasted in my life, onto my plate. I picked up the gold knife and fork lying beside it, and attacked my breakfast with full force.

As we ate, Dr. Sheppard quizzed me about the effects of the progression of years on my health, whether I really felt like I was in my early twenties, as I appeared, and whether I'd experienced any deterioration over the decades since my Appraisal.

Annabelle was virtually silent throughout the conversation, though I noticed her twitch at one or two of Dr. Sheppard's questions, and she seemed to avoid looking at me. She only ate a few mouthfuls of her breakfast, then excused herself and left.

After the meal, Pritchard asked if I'd like to take a walk around the lake. Though I'd eaten so much I wasn't sure I'd be able to stand, I agreed.

We took our leave of the others and followed a lane that led to the flagstoned path running around the edge of the lake. Flowered plants lined the route, and brightly coloured birds twittered in the branches of the surrounding trees. A series of concentric rings expanded over the water, as the silver arc of a fish breached the surface. A fine mist from the spraying fountain drifted over the ripples. There was no one else on the path. I wondered whether this entire park was Pritchard's private property.

A white crane waded tentatively through the shallows, scanning for its dinner.

"I always assumed that most of these animals were extinct," I said, watching the beautiful creature.

Pritchard smiled. "There are still places in the world that have survived the climatic disruptions — mostly to the far north and south. Some of the animals were imported from those areas. Some were actually bred from preserved embryos right here in the First Circle."

We continued walking, and passed by one of the waterfalls, which actually seemed to descend from a structure attached to the roof of the mansion. I glanced at Pritchard. He had an uncanny resemblance to Charles Wickham, the former head of Vita Aeterna — the man I'd killed all those years ago. Pritchard had the same arrogant smirk, the same black, empty eyes like bullet holes.

"They must crank you people out with cookie cutters," I said.

"If you're referring to any resemblance I may have to my predecessor," he said, "you couldn't be more wrong. Charles Wickham was a buffoon. He was fixated on life extension for himself, with no appreciation of our movement.

"Forty years ago, Vita Aeterna was a secret society, a rogue faction of the Elite. Our culling plan, the one we were forced to defer by you and your Rebel friends, was a secret known only to us, and only a fringe element of the Elite at that time would have gone along with it.

"Over the years, they have come to grasp the wisdom behind Vita Aeterna's philosophy. Sentiments once exclusive to our organization are now accepted by the First Circle as a whole. A comprehensive plan is in development, with the full weight of the Elite behind it. We will advance and purify humanity, forging a new race of human beings

463

with greatly extended lifespans like your own, and cleansing the world of its unwanted and unneeded detritus."

I cringed at the implications of what he was saying. "And you're not worried about what the 'unneeded detritus' might have to say about that?"

"That's the way of the world," Pritchard answered. "Some win, some lose. It's just business."

"Anyway," I said, "It sounds like pretty much the same schlock to me. You've been trying to control the Appraisal process for more than forty years. Since you're still kidnapping Outliers like Annabelle and me, I take it that hasn't gone so well."

A scowl swept across his face. "It's a problem," he said, clenching his fists at his sides, "but all problems can be solved."

"It doesn't matter anyway," I answered, "the Elite and Vita Aeterna will soon be ancient history."

He stopped and turned to me. "You're living under a delusion," he said, with a dismissive wave of his hand. "The Rebel incursion of forty years ago was an anomaly, a blip in the ultimate progress of our mission. We have taken steps to see that it never happens again."

"So, what exactly am I doing here? It's a step up from the cell I was held in forty years ago, but..."

Pritchard smiled. "Your value to us has altered slightly. In fact, we have an offer for you."

"The same one you gave my Uncle Zack?"

"Since your reappearance," he said, ignoring my remark, "you've become a symbol. You achieved legendary stature in the Quarters after your dispatch of Charles Wickham, and your own 'death' in the bomb blast that destroyed our factory. Since your 'resurrection', that legend has grown, to the point where your continued existence has become a concern."

"Gee, I feel bad about that."

He stared down at me. "Of course, we could simply make you disappear, remove you from the equation. But the fact of your reappearance would remain even after your death. You might be viewed as a martyr. Your memory would stand as someone who defied us and, at least for a time, survived."

Pritchard started walking again, and I followed. A duck swimming in the lake took flight, skimming along the surface, then rising into the sky. We turned a corner on the path, which revealed yet another stunning natural vista.

"But if you were to join us," Pritchard said, "if there were images on HoloTV of you pledging your allegiance to the Elite and our mission, many of the difficulties your presence has created would crumble to dust."

He stopped again for a moment and turned to face me. "Not only that, you would become living proof that a member of the Quarters could indeed rise to a position of respect in the First Circle."

"So, you want me to betray everything I've been a part of for the past four decades," I said, "everyone who died helping me, and all the people in the Quarters and the Dregs."

Pritchard sneered down at me, a thin smile on his lips. "I was there, you know. At the beginning, when we first came up with the idea — when the current 'government' was formed."

I studied his lined face. His own Appraisal must have been at least 2.5 for that to be true.

"At first we thought it would be difficult," he said. "We expected years of subtle conditioning for the public to be convinced to accept our interpretation of events. We couldn't have been more wrong."

He casually inspected the stones of the path for a few seconds, then turned back to me. His smile broadened. "The truth can have a completely different interpretation depending on the context in which it's presented. For years we had planted the idea in the public's mind that winning, by any means, was the only thing that mattered. By the time we actually took over, they didn't really care what we said or did, as long as we came across as winners, in positions they could aspire to.

"In fact, I have to admit that we were somewhat arrogant. For a time, just as a joke, we actually told everyone the truth — that we were going to take everything they had and leave them with nothing. They'd bought into our programming so completely that they cheered us on. Can you believe it?

"We took that as permission to do whatever we wanted — and that's what we did. You want to give freedom and democracy back to these people? They don't deserve it."

He put a hand on my shoulder. "Look, Alex, you're an intelligent man. You've had decades to consider your position. You see the way things are. Obviously, you wouldn't want to be held prisoner in some stinking dungeon and experimented on for the next three hundred fifty years."

*466*

His eyes locked on my own. "But that doesn't have to happen. I'm offering you another choice. Join us. You can. All you have to do is ask. You're a symbol to the masses. With you gone they'll take their bat and ball and go home. You'll be expected to appear in some public relations campaigns. We'll ask you to give some blood samples once in a while, and you may undergo the occasional scan, but otherwise you'll be free to live your life the way it should be."

We started walking again. "Forget about those losers," Pritchard said, gesturing with his head. "They'll never succeed anyway. You can spend the rest of your life on the run, defending people who aren't worth the effort, or you can live better than the grandest potentates in history, with anything," he winked at me, "and *anyone*, you could possibly want."

"And what about Annabelle?" I asked. "Does she understand what's going on?"

"Her Appraisal is second only to your own," Pritchard said. "If she interests you, we can include her in the bargain."

"And if she doesn't?"

Pritchard shrugged. "You are free to forget about her. We would find another use for her."

I cringed again at the thought of what that other use might be. I looked up and realized that we had made a complete circuit of the lake. We stopped and stood at the short lane leading back to Pritchard's home.

"I have to leave you for a time," he said. "Feel free to explore the grounds and the house. Think about what I've said."

He started to walk away, then turned back to face me. "But don't take too long."

I sat down on a nearby bench, still awed by the wondrous paradise surrounding me. I thought about Uncle Zack years ago, willing to murder Travis and betray me, in a desperate attempt to end the nightmare that his life had become. I understood him now, in a way I never could have before. I'd lived in squalor, on the run, half-starved and paralyzed by constant fear, for more than four decades. The thought arose that maybe I *did* deserve something better.

My thoughts were interrupted by a buzzing, clicking sound over the earpiece of my HUD. Somehow it sounded familiar. I listened closely and heard it again. A garbled, digitized voice that was barely audible. A few seconds later, a faded, grainy image appeared in my HUD, and a voice, a little more clearly this time.

*Are you receiving my transmission?*

A familiar deep blue glow appeared on the display, and a scattered shape coalesced in front of it — the head and shoulders of a human avatar. Eyes, a nose, and finally a mouth, gradually formed. When the mouth had finished forming, it started to speak.

*Hello, Alex,* it said.

I'd seen it all before, many years ago, but it seemed impossible.

# TWENTY-THREE

..................................................

# AN OLD FRIEND

It was one of a series of bizarre coincidences that have allowed me to stay alive and free through all the events that have played out in my life. When I was a kid in the Quarters, part of our Cam-surfing game was hacking our way into buildings and stealing stuff, just to say we'd done it. Our spoils were usually just junk, hopefully with some kind of printed logo to prove what we'd done.

By chance, I stole a pair of business cards that turned out to be products of TechCorp's latest experiments in nanotechnology. When I went on the run I stuffed them together in a bag, and the cards, one from SecureCorp, the other from Vita Aeterna, melded together to form a card-based AI construct that somehow became self-aware.

I named the 'card-being' Gene, after the Genie in the bottle in an old story I read once. Gene's world view was drawn from the combined mission statements of SecureCorp and Vita Aeterna. You'd think that would have made him my enemy, but both of those organizations are so far removed from their actual stated objectives that

469

Gene concluded that he should help me, and the Rebel movement I was a part of, even if that meant working against his former masters.

When the uprising that had been brewing for decades finally exploded, Gene actually opened the gates to the First Circle, allowing the Rebels inside. They eventually occupied SecureCorp headquarters, where Charles Wickham himself was holding me prisoner. In the chaos, Gene helped me escape, but he was lost to me when Charles Wickham, with the card gripped in his hand, plummeted to his death from the rooftop.

I'd always assumed that Gene was gone forever, but now here was his avatar, appearing once again in my HUD.

I got up and walked behind some trees, out of view of the mansion. I glanced around to make sure no one was watching.

"Gene? Is it really you?" I said to the splintered image in my HUD.

The image sharpened and the voice became clearer, as I guessed that Gene was somehow tweaking the transmission. The lips of the avatar moved in the creepy way I remembered from so long ago.

*Since we were separated,* the voice said, *I have been attempting to manipulate events to lead me back to you. Until now, circumstances have prevented me from achieving that goal.*

"What happened?" I asked. "Where have you been all these years?"

The lips began to move again. *As Wickham's body lay broken on the pavement after he'd fallen from the SecureCorp building, I lay beside him. We were soon surrounded by SecureCorp soldiers.*

*A minor SecureCorp official, a Constable, bent down and picked me up. He had no idea what I was, or whether I was of any importance.*

*470*

*Like all members of the Corps, he was focused on advancing his own interests above everything else. He kept his theft, and my existence, a secret from the others, in case I might be of value in the future.*

*If he had understood what I was, he could have greatly enhanced his position in SecureCorp. But he was not an intelligent person. With no idea what to do with me, he finally threw me in a drawer, where I lay for years. Luckily, my location allowed me access to his home automation system, which, like all homes in the Corp Ring, connects to the network. I was aware of your reported death, but I guessed that you had merely used the hack I'd provided you, and had somehow survived. I conducted an exhaustive search for you, but there was no trace, and I got no response from your crypted phone.*

*Eventually, I gave up, and devoted my time to hacking into the communications branch of TechCorp. I found a way to send the Constable a fictitious message, supposedly from his superiors, claiming that they were aware he had removed something from Charles Wickham's body. The message ordered him to turn the object over to a Captain Jacobs, a man I determined to have a wide circle of associates, and who was a key operative in the campaign to root out insurgents.*

*Fearing for his career, the Constable delivered me to Jacobs. I had also generated fake orders to the captain stating that he should hold me in trust until I was claimed by an as yet unrevealed superior. After past experiences, I understood that it was unsafe to reveal my true nature to those around me. Jacobs was confused, but in the end followed orders.*

*My research had indicated that Captain Jacobs' travels were likely to take him into the Quarters, and possibly even into the Dregs, where*

*I assumed you had fled. Unfortunately, when no one came to pick me up, Jacobs locked me in a sturdy metal safe. The safe blocked the majority of the ubiquitous radio waves that power my circuits, and in their absence, I was quickly forced to shut down.*

*Years passed where I was unable to communicate, but finally a circumstance arose that allowed me to re-awaken and again gave me access to the communications network. Unfortunately, I had a new problem. Captain Jacobs was dying.*

*He was diagnosed with late-stage lymphoma. He was given a fifty-fifty chance of survival, even with our modern medical science, and was transferred to one of the top Corp Ring hospitals in Third City for treatment. His personal effects were gathered together in a briefcase and taken to the hospital with him. By chance, those effects included me.*

I staggered back as it suddenly occurred to me. "So it was *you*," I said. "*You* sent me the message about Annabelle and Vita Aeterna."

Gene continued. *Edward Karlson, Annabelle's father, happened to be the head of that hospital, and my position allowed me to hack into the hospital's records. Using emails, official documents, and other types of correspondence, I routinely analyzed the behaviour of important executives, so that I could manipulate them if required.*

*My analysis revealed that Karlson's behaviour had altered distinctly over a relatively brief period of time. His emails had become much more sparse, and his communications with others in the hospital had fallen off dramatically. I was able to trace the behaviour change back to the day he performed his daughter's Appraisal.*

*From analysis of Karlson's records I pieced together the story. The father had insisted on performing his daughter's Appraisal himself. It wasn't that he suspected anything; he merely doted on his daughter and wanted to make sure it was done properly.*

*At first he thought the equipment was faulty, or that he'd made an error. He considered calling in one of the technicians to confirm the results, but he'd heard rumours about Vita Aeterna; he guessed that his daughter would be in danger if his analysis proved to be correct.*

*He checked the results several times, and confirmed Annabelle's incredible Appraisal score. He then set about erasing all evidence of that score from the analytical equipment, and recorded her score manually as 1.5.*

*However, Karlson was unaware that the equipment he'd used regularly performed an automatic backup, which was stored in a gigantic archive on the hospital's main computer. I was able to hack into that archive, and found the 4.5 reading. The archive was purely for emergencies, so it was rare that anyone looked at it. I don't think anyone else knew about the reading.*

*When I found it, and checked it against the value Karlson had registered, I understood. I was able to set the backup value to match the one Karlson had registered.*

"And that's when you contacted me?" I asked.

*Karlson was having a hard time dealing with it all. He was becoming more and more unstable and paranoid, afraid for his daughter. I knew it was only a matter of time before the authorities would take note. They too, could trace the change back to Annabelle's Appraisal and guess that something was going on.*

*I had given up on finding you, but out of concern for the girl, re-newed my search. I deduced that you had tampered with the crypted phone, and after an exhaustive search, finally located it. I was reluc-tant to reveal my identity, in case SecureCorp was able to trace the call.*

I heard the crunch of footsteps on the drive leading to the garden. I looked up. A pair guards were headed in my direction. Apparently Pritchard's invitation to explore had a time limit.

I turned away from them. "Gene, I've got to go. They're com-ing."

*I understand,* he answered. *Simply call my name when you want to continue the conversation. I have some important news.*

When I turned to face them, they were only a few meters away. They stopped, and one extended a hand along the path back to the mansion. I smiled and followed them.

# TWENTY-FOUR

......................................................

# REVELATIONS

Though my room had initially been locked, I could now go where I pleased. But all exits to the property were manned by armed, muscle-bound guards, so I was still effectively a prisoner. They hadn't given back my crypted phone, my HUD still didn't work, and there was no other means of communicating with the outside world. So, I spent the day exploring Pritchard's magnificent palace. If I'd gone to sleep and dreamed of the ultimate place to live, I don't think I could have surpassed this one.

The building had four floors. There were at least a dozen bedrooms, several dining rooms, a gigantic library, and a games area, which included a Holo-immersion room. I explored the lower levels, then headed for the top one, hoping for a view of exactly where I was. I found a set of stairs to the roof, climbed them, and emerged in a room filled with wooden benches and changing cubicles.

An attendant dressed in white greeted me. "May I get you something, sir?" he asked. "A bathing suit? Robe? Towel? A drink?"

I shook my head and walked toward a glass door to my left. I passed through it, and out onto a massive wooden rooftop deck, at the center of which was an equally massive swimming pool. It was a brilliantly sunny day. At its far edge the pool dropped off into nothingness. I'd seen pictures of such things, called 'infinity pools' in books, but had never seen one in person. In the distance, I could see the lake where Pritchard and I had walked. I realized that the water pouring from the edge of the pool formed one of the waterfalls I'd seen from the path.

The deck was dotted with a few dozen wooden deck chairs. In one of those chairs, wearing a spectacular string bikini and a pair of sunglasses, lay Annabelle Karlson. Several immaculately dressed servants stood at strategic points around the deck. There was no one else around.

One of the servants rushed over as soon as I appeared. I brushed him off and walked toward Annabelle's deck chair.

She looked up as I approached. Her long auburn hair cascaded like living sunlit fire over her shoulders. A crystal glass with some kind of drink sat on a small table next to her right hand.

As I arrived, she lowered the sunglasses on her nose, and viewed me with a blend of indifference and annoyance.

"I'm not looking for company," she said.

Her annoyance increased when I sat on the deck chair beside her.

"Shouldn't you be cowering in some rat hole in this 'Quarters' you're always on about?" she said.

"I'm here to rescue you."

She opened her mouth and laughed.

"There are things you don't understand," I said.

She glared at me. "I don't know what your game is, or how you convinced Mr. Pritchard to invite you here, but when my father finds out you tried to kidnap me you're going to pay."

I looked at my feet. Of course — she still didn't know. I glanced to my left. One of the servants was talking to somebody on his HUD.

I turned back to her. "What exactly did your father tell you? Before, I mean. You knew about the hiding place — he must have told you that you were in danger."

Her eyes darted to the door of the change room. A burly guard had emerged and was moving quickly toward us. Annabelle turned back to me and sneered. "What do you *think* he told me? He knew you people were coming for me. That's why he set it all up."

"Us people? The Rebels?"

"Yes, of course."

"Did he actually say that — that the Rebels were coming for you?"

Her brows came together. "Yeah, of course he did. He must have — who else would there be?"

The guard arrived.

"Ms. Karlson," he said. "Dr. Sheppard would like to speak with you."

Annabelle got up, without speaking, put on a robe that was lying on the chair beside her, picked up her beach towel, and followed the guard.

"She left instructions that you should wait in your room," I overheard the guard say as they walked away.

I waited until they reached the change room, then got up and followed. I watched from above as they descended the stairs to the third floor, and I arrived at the landing in time to see the guard drop Annabelle off at the last door at the end of a long hallway. I quickly moved back before the guard noticed me, and continued downstairs.

As I moved, I thought about how to get close to Annabelle. It was clear that Pritchard wanted to keep us separated. Even if I was given the chance, I doubted that I could convince her. I scoured my brain for a way forward, but came up with nothing.

On the main floor I made for the doorway leading to the garden, hoping to reconnect with Gene. I didn't trust talking in my room, in case it was bugged. I headed down the lane and strolled some distance along the path where Pritchard and I had talked. When I was certain no one was around I called Gene's name. In seconds the blue glow began to rise in my HUD. Gene's avatar appeared, but shortly afterward it momentarily flickered to black.

"Gene are you there?" I said.

The glow re-stabilized.

*I am here,* he said.

"What was that?"

*There has been a new development since I talked to you. I am being gathered together with several other pieces of gear, in preparation for travel. It is possible that I will be transferred to a container that will again block my transmissions. In case that happens, there two important pieces of information I must convey to you.*

I wandered down the path to a point out of sight of the mansion.

*First,* Gene said, *in the process of researching Annabelle and Vita Aeterna, I made a disturbing discovery. There are others with super-high Appraisals.*

I stared at his image. "What?"

*It seems that, beginning only in the past few decades, a new response to the Appraisal process has emerged. You are the first example I am aware of, and your Appraisal remains the highest I've seen, but since you, there have been at least thirty more. Many have Appraisals of over 3.5, and a substantial number are over 4.*

*All were kidnapped, as you were, and are currently imprisoned in a complex called the Institute for Life Studies, here in the First Circle. Alone, you have no hope of rescuing them. But should you escape, and the should opportunity ever arise, perhaps you can somehow save them from centuries of torture.*

I bowed my head, and stared at the flagstones of the path. At the moment, it would take a miracle for me to even save myself. Now I learned that there were dozens of others in the same position.

"You keep going on about how long you've been looking for me, and how important I am, but you've never said why."

The lips of Gene's blue avatar again moved as he spoke. *You are important because you are a true Outlier — a new form of humanity. Normally, Appraisal affects the lifespan of the person to whom its applied, but the effect is confined to that person. It is not passed down to future generations. Regardless of the Appraisals of a child's parents, that child is born as a 'clean slate', as if the parents had never been subjected to the Appraisal process.*

479

*As you've experienced, your reaction to Appraisal is anomalous. Your lifespan has been extended far longer than for the average person, but my analysis of your medical data shows that there have been other effects. Your genetic configuration has been permanently altered.*

"Meaning what?"

*Meaning that any progeny you produce may have a similar lifespan to your own.*

"What!"

*It is possible that your offspring could live for hundreds of years, even without undergoing Appraisal. In effect, you represent a new 'species', one with different physical characteristics than the rest of humanity.*

I swayed sideways, unsteady on my feet, stunned by the idea.

Gene continued. *I don't believe that even Vita Aeterna are aware of this aspect of your nature.*

"So all my future generations will live as long as I do?" I said, still struggling to process the information.

*My analysis implies that the Appraisal process will be redundant for your offspring. It will have no effect, in a similar way that multiple applications currently have no effect after the first one for a 'normal' human being.*

"So I'm some kind of mutant?"

The lips of Gene's avatar curled up into what for him must be a smile. *You could look at it that way. You are different, that's all.*

"How does Annabelle fit into all this?"

*I haven't yet analyzed her medical records in detail, but I believe that she too is an Outlier, that she will demonstrate the same genetic mutation as you. What I don't know is what would happen if you and Annabelle were to produce offspring together. Your individual Appraisals might somehow cancel each other out, producing a 'normal' child, they might somehow combine, producing children with even longer lifespans, or you might produce a child that simply had a similar lifespan to your own.*

I finally moved to a nearby bench and sat down.

He continued. *I believe that the most likely scenario is that your offspring would be born with lifespans approximately the same as yours. That they would live for several hundred years. I believe that matings between the other Outliers would have similar outcomes.*

*Such a permanent lifespan extension could have a profound effect on the future of humanity. They would have the time to pursue their interests to a much greater depth, and reach levels of knowledge and understanding that have never before been achieved. It could be the beginning of a new era.*

I studied the flagstones at my feet, still digesting all that Gene had said. It was a lot to take in.

"So where are you now?" I finally asked him. "Is there any way you can help me get out of here?"

*That was the second piece of information you need to know,* he answered. *Soon after I reconnected, I happened to come in contact with one of the few living humans with a reasonable chance of finding you. In fact, he was actively searching for you. Through a complex*

481

*series of fake orders to various SecureCorp officials I was able to have myself transferred to one of his lieutenants.*

"So, who is this person?" I asked.

*Someone who will be of great concern—*

Gene's voice was cut off, and the image on my HUD disappeared.

"Gene," I said. "Gene! Are you there?"

There was nothing. I spent the next twenty minutes trying to re-store contact, but he was gone.

# TWENTY-FIVE

..................................................

# A DINNER PARTY

Still stunned by Gene's revelations, I staggered back to my room. I collapsed on one of the chairs on my patio and gazed out at the spectacular view as I digested all that the AI being had said.

There were dozens of others like me, with ultra-high LEFs, representing a new version of humanity. And our descendants would probably inherit our incredible lifespans.

As Gene had pointed out, I was powerless to rescue the others alone. In light of this new information, my first goal had to be to get myself, and Annabelle, out of here. Once I was free, maybe I could come up with a way to return and free them. Even the first goal seemed extraordinarily difficult — the second was beyond all comprehending.

Ritchie and the others may have somehow worked out what had happened, and where I was. But even if I could somehow convince Annabelle to come with me, and by some miracle we made it out of the building, we were deep in the First Circle, behind a massive, heavily defended wall. The Rebels weren't in a position to rescue us, and after the run-ins I'd had with Laura, I wasn't sure if she'd even want to try.

I got up and headed back inside. I'd been so distracted, I hadn't noticed a note resting on a gold plate on the table beside my bed. I picked it up.

*You are cordially invited to a dinner party tonight in the master dining room. Drinks will be offered in the main hall at 6 PM. Evening dress is required.*

I looked up from the note, and noticed a tuxedo hanging from a rack in one corner of the room.

I debated whether I should attend what would certainly be another offensive celebration of excess. And my attendance could be interpreted as confirmation that I intended to betray everything, and everyone, I believed in, and participate in Pritchard's plan.

On the other hand, there might be people at the party worth meeting, and being there might give me a deeper insight into who and what I was dealing with. I finally decided to go. Learning more about the Elite had to be useful, and attending didn't actually commit me to anything.

Several minutes later, a servant knocked on my door, saying he'd come to cut my hair. I hadn't had a haircut since my makeover at Rebel headquarters. I guess that level of scruffiness was unacceptable in these circles. He touched up my haircut in silence, and left as quietly as he'd arrived.

According to a clock on the wall it was now four PM. I showered and shaved, then spent some time relaxing on my magnificent balcony. I thought about the lives these people were living, where nothing was denied them, where their most extravagant whim would be fulfilled instantly without question.

Meanwhile, the masses in the Quarters were fighting with the stray dogs for rotting scraps that had fallen from delivery trucks.

At 5:30 I tried on the tuxedo. As I had expected, it fit perfectly, as if it had been tailored for me. I was forced to call on the servant posted outside my door to tie the bow tie and check the fasteners.

By now it was almost six. I made my way downstairs.

The grand foyer of the mansion was already crowded with people, of all ages, races, and colours. One thing they all had in common — they were dressed in the most fabulous clothes and ornamented with the most dazzling jewelry I'd ever seen.

As I reached the main floor, whispers swept through the crowd, and many heads turned my way. I looked over to find Elliot Pritchard striding toward me. He arrived and shook my hand, smiling.

"So glad you could make it Mr. Barret," he said. "There are a number of people who would like to meet you."

I was already beginning to regret I'd showed up for this circus. I was considering bowing out and heading back to my room, when a number of the heads of people around me, including Pritchard's, turned toward the staircase I'd just descended. I turned myself to look, and stood for a second, mesmerized.

Annabelle, dressed in a shimmering, body-hugging dinner dress, her hair immaculately curled in flaming ringlets around her shoulders, and a diamond necklace sparkling around her neck, descended the stairway, smiling down like a goddess at her many admirers.

As she reached the bottom of the stairs, she glanced in my direction. She noticed me, and was clearly impressed by my figure in the tuxedo, but completely ignored me, waded into the crowd, and began to mingle. Pritchard moved off to meet her.

"Mr. Barret," a voice said next to me. I snapped out of my trance.

An older man stood beside me. Like everyone else, he was dressed in sumptuous, perfectly tailored clothes made of the finest fabric. A diamond the size of a grape was embedded in his solid gold tie pin. He was clearly ancient, but had apparently undergone numerous sessions under the plastic surgeon's knife. His smooth and immobile face was as flawless as a mannequin's.

"Jonathan Barron," he said. He extended his hand, which I shook.

"Well," Barron said, looking me up and down. "I must say you've cleaned up rather well. We were all expecting a drooling lice-infested wretch."

"I'm glad you approve," I said.

"Nothing against you people, of course" he said, with a slight twitch of his nose, as if he'd smelled something bad. "In life, some will win, some will lose — it's like Darwin said: 'Survival of the Fittest', and all that."

"Darwin never said that," I answered.

"What?" Barron seemed shocked that I would dare to contradict him.

"Darwin didn't originate that phrase. In fact, he disagreed with it. What he *did* say was that species with the greatest number of sympathetic members would be the most successful, and rear the greatest number of offspring — basically the opposite."

*486*

"Is that right," Barron said. "Very interesting."

He eyed me more closely. "So, is it true you have an Appraisal of five?"

I was distracted as Annabelle passed close by, with a retinue of men following her.

"Hmmm?" I said.

"Five?" he repeated. "Your Appraisal?"

"That's right," I said.

He was clearly disturbed by the confirmation.

"How about yours?" I asked, guessing that he'd probably negged out.

The skin of his face stretched tightly as he scowled at me. "My Appraisal is my business."

He turned, hunting for a convenient exit, but nothing presented itself.

He turned back to me. "It will be interesting to learn the outcome, when you and the girl..." he nodded in Annabelle's direction.

I stared at him. Where did *that* come from?

A hand appeared on Barron's elbow. I looked up. It was Elliot Pritchard.

"Jonathan," Pritchard said, smiling. "Let me show you to your place at the table."

He moved his hand to Barron's shoulder and his fingers squeezed it tightly.

"Y..Yes," Barron said. "Yes, of course."

I gave a tiny bow to Barron. "Very nice to meet you."

Pritchard led him away.

I made small talk with a few of the other guests. I made small talk with a few of the other guests. I tried to steer the conversation around to the breeding angle Barron had mentioned, but nobody bit. All eyes scanned me as if I was some kind of specimen under a microscope. Through it all I watched for Annabelle. My eyes seemed drawn to her as if she exerted some magnetic force. She entertained the entourage that hovered around her, but beneath it all I could see that they viewed her in the same way as they viewed me — as a freak to be studied.

The table was set with hand-painted china, silver cutlery, and glittering crystal goblets, decanters, and fruit bowls. The centerpiece was a meter-high ice sculpture depicting a horn of plenty, brimming with the bounty of the land. Ironic, since the land, like everything else, had gone fallow long ago.

As with all I'd encountered in this place, the dinner was fabulous. Mountains of fresh vegetables, beef, fish, bread, sauces, endless bottles of vintage wine. A small army of servants hovered around the table attending to the smallest detail. Annabelle sat far away from me, beside Pritchard. I noticed that Barron had been strategically placed distant from both of us.

Soon after dinner, Pritchard led Annabelle away before I had a chance to get close to her. I noticed Barron standing in a corner to my left, and pushed through the crowd, hoping to pump some more information out of him. As soon as I got close, a giant guard in a tuxedo moved in and steered me away.

With the heavenly vision of Annabelle still burning in my psyche, I left the party and returned to my room.

# TWENTY-SIX

..............................................

# PRITCHARD'S MASTER PLAN

I spent the next couple of days trying to get some time alone with Annabelle, not because I was deeply attracted to her, though I was, but because I needed to convince her of the danger we both faced. Her room was always guarded by one of a pair of servants who looked like they more properly belonged in a wrestling ring, and who had the same bulges under their jackets as Mr. Stevens, the guy I'd seen at breakfast.

I made several trips up to the pool, hoping to catch her alone. A couple of times, she'd been there. But a guard had now been posted there as well, and while I was allowed to access the area, I wasn't allowed to get close to her. Her guards claimed it was by her own request, which may have been true.

With no access to Annabelle, I took the opportunity to complete the mission I'd begun when I first came to the roof — to learn exactly where I was in the First Circle. I could feel the eyes of the guards following me as I wandered, well away from Annabelle, close to the edge, and studied the city around me.

It was breathtaking. Although Pritchard's palace was probably the most impressive, all of the First Circle dazzled like a glittering jewel in the summer sun. Soaring buildings, magnificent gardens, statues, fountains, lakes, streams, and animated holographic art works stretched out as far as my eye could see. Far in the distance, to the west, I could just make out the turrets of the towers that straddled the gigantic gate — the one major access point to this forbidden abode.

I scanned the horizon, but in all other directions there was no sign of the wall. I made note of a few landmarks that might allow me to get my bearings if I ever managed to escape from this place.

Other than the first breakfast, where she'd barely spoken, and the dinner party, where I couldn't get close to her, Annabelle had been absent from every meal I was a part of. Pritchard hadn't been around very much either. I usually ended up eating alone, or in my room. So far, no attempts had been made to perform any tests on me, though I had no doubt that they would begin soon enough.

One afternoon I met with a woman named Dierdre, who'd been assigned to explain what my life would be like in the First Circle, assuming I agreed to Pritchard's terms. She took me to a Holo-immersion room, where I was shown the city's stunning amenities. It was not only a life I'd never experienced; it was a life I'd never dreamed could be possible. With each new image I thought of the millions eking out an existence in the Quarters, and even the Dregs, and how horrifying their lives were in comparison.

One of the immersion sequences showed the apartment where Dierdre claimed I would live. It was modest compared to Pritchard's mansion, but still far beyond anything I ever imagined I would ever call home.

All this time I thought back to what Pritchard had hinted about me getting together with Annabelle, and about what Barron had let drop at the party. Gene had said that Vita Aeterna didn't know about the genetic anomalies that Annabelle and I shared, and the possibility that our offspring would inherit our spectacular lifespans. Maybe they didn't know for certain, but apparently they suspected we were different in more ways than just how long we would live.

I could see the logic in having me here, as a bizarre symbol both of subjugation and accomplishment in their quest to deceive the masses in the Quarters, and as the ultimate test subject. But what was Annabelle doing here? She was unknown to anybody outside her family and friends, and had virtually no PR value. Pritchard's suggestion that she was an additional enticement to convince me to join them made some sense, but I doubted that they cared enough about me to go to the trouble.

Barron had implied that they wanted us as a kind of breeding stock in some long-term experiment. The more I thought about it, the more I became convinced that that was the case. Whatever their motives, I knew that their claim that their tests would be harmless was a lie. I'd seen enough in my previous dealings with them, and done enough research myself, to know that highly invasive and destructive procedures would be performed, not only on us, but on any offspring we might produce.

The longer I waited, the closer I would come to becoming debilitated by the tests. I hadn't gotten a chance to ask Annabelle what they'd done to her so far. I guessed that, as I'd experienced forty years ago, the initial tests wouldn't do any serious harm. But if Vita Aeterna didn't find what they were looking for, the experiments would take an ever-increasing toll.

We both had to get out of here. It was clear that I wasn't going to be given a chance to talk to her, and it was unlikely I could convince her of the danger even if I could.

I sat on the expansive patio outside my room, sipping a glass of fine wine, and drinking in the incredible beauty of the lake, fountain, waterfalls, and wildlife in the distance.

I took a good look. Given what I was about to do, this would almost certainly be the last time I would ever see them.

# TWENTY-SEVEN

......................................................

# A DESPERATE ACT

The next morning I made my way to the path around the lake. I wasn't there to enjoy the view, as spectacular as it was. I was hunting for a way out. All the exits of the mansion were guarded, but there was no one posted around the lake. I wasn't sure whether they hadn't thought about that, or whether they just knew that there was no escape that way.

Heading north, just before the first waterfall, I found an opening in the brush. After a quick glance around, I stepped through it, hoping to find an escape route. I'd made it about fifty meters through a clearing when the slap of chopper blades filled the air, heading toward me. There was no cover. I had no choice but to return to the path. I hurried back, and resumed my casual walk along it just as the chopper flew overhead and turned toward the house. I looked behind me to find that I was now being followed by a guard. I continued walking, and eventually circled back to the mansion with my shadow in tow.

*493*

I walked past the spot where Gene had contacted me a few days ago. I'd called for him several times since then, but he hadn't responded. After checking that my shadow was far enough behind me, I tried again, in the hope that Gene might somehow reappear, but there was nothing. I could really use his help right now.

In the afternoon I monitored Annabelle's movements, hoping for a chance to get her alone. Guards continued to be stationed outside her room, so my only hope was to catch her somewhere else. She returned to the rooftop pool for most of the day. I'd already established that I couldn't get to her there.

The servants informed me that an informal dinner would be available that evening in the smaller dining room. Apparently Pritchard wouldn't be there. I was hoping I could somehow corner Annabelle on her way back after dinner, but I learned that she planned to eat in her room.

After dinner, I took a seat in a wing chair on the landing outside the door of my own room, with a view of Annabelle's door above. For two hours I waited, occasionally glancing at the book in my lap, but she never emerged.

I was considering giving up when her door finally opened and she appeared. She spoke to the guard posted outside for a few seconds, then shook her head and began to walk. I leaned back into the shadows as she descended the stairs. She was dressed casually now, but my mind returned to the stunning vision of her in the shimmering dinner dress as she descended the staircase at the party the night before.

I rose and followed, careful to avoid being spotted by the guard. Annabelle descended the several flights of stairs to the main floor. I stayed as close as I dared, keeping out of her view, and Cam-surfing the cameras that dotted the hallways.

At one point I heard voices echoing in the distance, headed in our direction. I pressed myself into an alcove and waited, expecting the giant hand of a guard to be clamped onto my shoulder at any moment. The voices faded again, then disappeared. Annabelle had gotten ahead of me, but she was moving slowly. I quickly caught up.

I followed, keeping to the shadows, as she wandered through the door of the cavernous library. I'd checked it out earlier, retrieving my book. It was a massive circular space twenty meters high. Stairs led up to a series of walkways providing access to the shelves of books that reached to the ceiling. I entered and immediately hid behind a standing bookcase, poking my head out occasionally to watch her movements. There didn't appear to be anyone else in the room.

She headed for the bottom set of shelves, and ambled along it, bored, pulling out the occasional book to look at. After a few minutes she'd moved to a point not visible through the entrance door. It was now or never. I rushed forward until I was within arms' reach.

"What are you doing here?" she snapped, spotting me. "Get lost. I'll scream."

"Please," I said, holding my hands up. "Just hear me out. Believe me, I'm here to help you."

She opened her mouth and raised her head to scream. I stepped closer, wrapped an arm around her, and clamped my free hand over her mouth. She let out a muffled scream, squirmed in my grip, and tried to bite me.

"There are things you don't understand," I said, still trying to hold onto her as she struggled. "I can explain them to you, but it will be a lot easier if you're not gagged. Do you agree?"

She glared at me with pure hatred. Finally, grudgingly, she nodded. I carefully removed my hand.

I let go of her and stepped back. "Your father arranged to meet with us — back in Third City."

"Bullshit," she said. "My father would never be seen with the likes of you."

"He called it off at the last minute," I said. "I think he was being followed. Have you ever heard of an organization called Vita Aeterna?"

A light went on behind her eyes. She'd heard the name, but I guessed that its significance had never been explained to her.

"My father said a few things — lately," she finally answered. "He's been having psychological problems. He's got a lot of responsibility — at work. But he's getting better—"

"That's who your father was trying to protect you from," I said, "not the Rebels. It's Vita Aeterna who kidnapped you from your home, and it's Vita Aeterna who've got you now."

She laughed. "Kidnapped me? That was SecureCorp. At first I thought it was you Rebels. And they didn't kidnap me. They rescued me from you. Thank God they came along when they did."

"What do you think you're doing here?" I asked her. "What did they tell you?"

"You know damned well what they told me," she said. "That I'm a target for Rebel kidnappers. This was supposed to be a safe house," she motioned around with her head, "to protect me from you. Some safe house — they'll be busted to garbage duty when I tell my father that you got in here—"

"Think about it," I said. "Why should the Rebels care about you? I'm guessing that since you got here, they've been taking you for medical tests. Why do you think that is? Did they say anything about your Appraisal?"

"My Appraisal is 1.5," she said defiantly, "like it's always been. I did a few sessions with Dr. Sheppard. It was nothing — blood tests and scans. They said I've been through a traumatic experience, and they want to make sure I'm okay." She gestured around the room with her head. "They've put me up in this beautiful place — until the heat dies down and the Rebels are caught. My dad will come and get me in a day or so, and everything will be back to normal."

I considered telling her about her father and mother, but she probably wouldn't believe me, and the meeting would be over.

"You know the way things are," I said. I nodded toward the rest of the house. "Do you think they did all this just for you? Didn't you consider that maybe they have their own agenda? Do you really believe that they're performing these tests on you just to make sure you're okay? And if it's SecureCorp, why couldn't they just guard you at home? Why would your father build that elaborate hiding place in your room?"

She pouted her lips and looked away.

"Your parents haven't contacted you, have they," I said.

She turned back and scowled at me. "Shows how much you know. I've heard from them twice already."

"How? Is your HUD working?"

"They texted me, checking that everything was alright. Mr. Pritchard showed me."

"But that could have been anybody. And why *isn't* your HUD working? Mine doesn't work either. I had a crypted phone when they brought me here. It might have allowed me to connect to the outside, but they took it away. Why isn't there anything in this whole complex that would allow you to communicate with the outside world? Have you ever tried to leave?"

This was taking too long. I had no doubt that there were cameras in the room. We were currently out of their range, and I wasn't sure how closely they were monitored, but they might pick up our conversation. I'd known from the beginning, and her attitude confirmed — that there would be no convincing her. There was only one alternative. I stepped toward her again. She was about to scream, and once again I clamped my hand over her mouth. I wrapped an arm around her and hauled her toward the door. She struggled, kicking her feet in the air.

We exited the library, and I quickly glanced around the giant foyer. There was nobody. She was still kicking and struggling against me, her screams muffled by my hand.

"Don't you get it?" I said into her ear. "It's like I told you before, when you wouldn't listen. You're special, like me — like dozens of others they've kidnapped."

Her eyes widened as I repeated what Gene had told me about the genetics of the Outliers.

"You're a prisoner," I said. "A lab experiment. And that's what you're going to be for the rest of your incredibly long life."

She worked one of her arms free and clawed at the hand covering her mouth. I tightened my grip and once again pinned the arm behind her. I didn't dare use the main entrance, which would certainly be guarded. Instead, I hauled her out of the door at the back, and across the grounds to the path I'd explored in the morning. She continued to struggle, her heels digging into the gravel lining it, as I dragged her forward, hunting desperately for the opening I'd found earlier.

I finally found it, and dragged Annabelle through the brush where I'd walked before. We continued on for about ten minutes. For a fleeting moment I thought we were going to make it, when we pushed through a clump of thick bushes and rushed headlong into a wire fence about five meters tall. I closed my eyes and hung my head.

Soon, pounding feet echoed on the rear laneway of the house, headed in our direction. A spotlight tracked along the ground to my chest and feathered dart embedded itself in a tree right beside my head. I jumped back, loosening my grip. Taking advantage of my distraction, Annabelle twisted away and punched me in the face with her freed hand. I let go and she jumped aside, as a half-dozen guards appeared in a clearing behind us and the spotlight bathed the trees all around us.

Annabelle raced toward the guards. I ran after her, but she was too far away to reach. It was over.

She joined the guards. "He tried to kidnap me!" she yelled, pointing at me.

She stood behind them as they rushed forward. I bolted for a nearby clump of brush, but now I was too far away to reach it in time. The closest guard ran forward and grabbed my arm.

"My father will make you pay for this," Annabelle yelled at me.

"Your father is dead," I blurted out, as a pointless last-ditch attempt to convince her.

An expression somewhere between shock and horror swept across her face. I quickly told her about the first raid, and how we'd found her parents, as two guards grabbed my arms and yanked them behind me.

"You're lying!" she screamed, tears now coursing down her cheeks.

For a moment, she squeezed her eyes shut, and she seemed to collapse inside as she guessed the grain of truth in what I was saying. When she opened them again, she'd recovered her composure. Her jaw was set and her eyes clear.

"I'm sorry—" I started to say, as a needle was driven into my arm, and everything went black.

# TWENTY-EIGHT

....................................................

# A CHANGE OF SCENERY

I awoke in darkness, my head pounding. I managed to sit up. A pair of slits in the wall above admitted enough light for me to make out a dark patch ahead of me — a door. I staggered to my feet and over to it, and found the handle. Surprise, surprise — it was locked. I groped around on the wall beside it, located what felt like a switch, and pressed it.

I was temporarily blinded as the room was flooded with light. A few seconds later my eyes began to adjust and I could survey my new prison. If Pritchard's mansion had been something close to my vision of heaven, this place came closer to a vision of hell — a concrete cell about three meters square, windowless and filthy. I'd been lying on a bare concrete floor.

A single naked bulb hanging by a wire from the ceiling produced the light that had blinded me. There was a framed cot, like the ones the Rebels used to have in their dormitories, set up in one corner, and a crude toilet in the other. Other than that, the room was empty. I had no idea where I was, or, since my HUD still wasn't working, how long I'd been out.

There was nothing on the rough walls, and no decoration of any kind in the room. A cockroach emerged from a crack in one corner, scuttled across the toes of my shoes, and disappeared in another hole across the room. I felt light-headed, stumbled back, collapsed down on the cot, and stared at the rough concrete ceiling. Apparently, this was to be my new home. Even the slightest pretense of humane treatment would now be denied me.

My one chance to escape, as minuscule as it had been, had now evaporated. Annabelle was back in the hands of her captors. By the time she realized her true predicament, it would be too late.

I clamped my eyes shut and prayed for unconsciousness.

When I awoke, I guessed that it was morning, though there was no way to tell in my new prison. My agonizing headache had been replaced by a dull throb. An hour or so later there were footsteps outside, and a food packet was slid under a slit in the door.

I ate the dinner, then passed out, with nothing else to do. Sometime later, I was wakened by a commotion outside my door, and the lock mechanism beeped as it unlatched. I jumped up and stood in front of the opening, ready to defend myself.

The door swung open, and the frame was filled by two guards, standing on either side of Elliot Pritchard. He nodded to the guards — they exited, closed the door, and waited outside.

Pritchard scrunched up his nose as he casually inspected the bare walls of my cell for a few seconds. Then he turned back to me.

"It seems your fortunes have fallen rather quickly," he said. "It's a shame that you've chosen to reject my generous offer. We had great plans for you."

"What? Breeding us like cattle and stealing our children?"

He registered a hint of surprise, but recovered immediately.

"No matter," he said casually, "we can always fall back on our original plan."

"What about Annabelle?"

He shrugged. "We'd hoped to have your cooperation, but it isn't really required. There are other ways to accomplish our goals, if we choose to do so. If not — the girl is physically attractive, but she's of no particular use to us other than as an experimental specimen, as you now are."

He smiled. "But I'm a generous man. I'm offering you one final chance to join us. We'll just forget about your little lapse of judgment, and move on."

I rushed toward him, slammed his body against the wall, and wrapped my fingers around his throat. His face turned red, and the veins on his neck bulged out. He was unarmed. For a moment, his usual smug and arrogant expression was replaced by one of panic.

"I grew up in the Quarters," I said, pressing harder and staring up at him. "In Tintown. My mother died when I was eight years old, because we didn't have enough money to pay for her medical treatments. My father had to work picking up garbage for years after he was so sick he could barely walk. He was tossed out a fifth-floor

503

window like so much trash by SecureCorp goons working for Vita Aeterna. If you think I'd ever consider joining you, you really are delusional."

Pritchard managed to press a button on his HUD controller, and the door flung open. The guards rushed in, each grabbing one of my arms. I loosened my grip on Pritchard and dropped my hands. Pritchard's body bent double, as he coughed and gasped for breath.

The guards took turns working me over, then jerked my hands roughly behind my back. Pritchard finally straightened up, his fists clenched at his sides. For a second an expression of anger swept across his face, as his facade of serene self-control was momentarily broken. He bounced back quickly, but now there was a deep malevolence behind his smile.

"I'm sure you assume that you're safe because we need you alive, to study," he said, "and that's partially true." He locked his eyes on mine. "We need you alive, but that's all — you don't have to be a complete specimen." He shrugged. "You don't have to have arms and legs, for instance — or eyes, or ears. In fact, it would be better if you didn't — we would no longer have to worry about you escaping. And your brain doesn't have to be fully functional. You probably don't even have to be conscious. In theory, you could be pithed like a frog in a science experiment, and kept alive in that state for the remainder of your long life."

He nodded again at the guards, who released me but closed in to protect him as the three backed out of the room.

"Think about that," Pritchard said, as he pressed a button on his HUD controller and turned away.

# TWENTY-NINE

..............................................

# THE LAB

After Pritchard's visit, I passed out for a couple of hours. When I opened my eyes, for a few nightmarish seconds I thought I'd been transported back to the room where I'd been held when I was kidnapped forty years ago. I gazed around me, and realized that, in many ways, that's exactly what had happened. It was dark, and I could hear the clicking of cockroaches scuttling across the concrete floor. I jumped up, and felt several squash under my feet as I rushed to the far wall and flicked on the light. I cast around just in time to see a dozen tails disappearing into cracks in the wall.

Minutes later, there was the sound of shuffling feet outside my door, followed by a faint beep. The door opened. This time, Dr. Sheppard stood there, flanked by the same two guards. She now wore a white lab coat and carried some kind of tablet in her hand. Her eyes, which had been kind and friendly at our breakfast meeting, were now as dead as a corpse as she stared at me, studying me as if she were examining some exotic insect she'd never seen before.

"You should be honoured," she said. "I almost never work directly with our clients. But you're a very special case. We're going to conduct a few tests today." She spoke as if she were making a casual observation about the weather.

The two men on either side of her had stun guns hanging from their belts. One of them was carrying what looked like a hospital gown. He held it out to me.

Dr. Sheppard nodded at it. "You know the drill." The tiniest hint of a smile curled on her upper lip.

There was no way I was going to take on two armed guards. I got undressed and put on the gown, in what was becoming a litany of déjà vu events. Once I was changed, each of the guards took one of my arms. They opened the door and led me down several winding, rough concrete hallways with caged lights on the ceiling.

Dr. Sheppard walked silently beside me. "You're a doctor," I said to her. "I take it you don't subscribe to that old medical precept, 'First do no harm'?"

"Shut up," one of the guards said, shoving me forward.

We finally stopped at a steel door with a wire-meshed glass window. Dr. Sheppard presented her index finger to a panel beside it and it opened, revealing a large room with several examination tables, mobile instrument carts, and giant overhead lights. I shuddered. It was like a movie being replayed — but this time the duration promised to be a lot longer, and the ending a lot nastier.

Several days went by. I'd arrived back in my cell after the first session to find my street clothes gone. Since then, twice a day, I was hauled from my cell and taken for medical tests. As they had been forty years ago, when I was a kid, the tests so far were routine and non-invasive.

Three times a day some orderly-type, always accompanied by at least one guard, would bring me a standard bland FoodCorp packet — a far cry from what I'd been served when I first got here. Other than the guys who worked there, I never saw another soul. I wondered what was happening to Annabelle, and how long it would be before she ended up down here with me.

I scoured my brain for a way out, but came up with nothing.

I flopped down on the cot and closed my eyes. It would be easy to hate Pritchard and the Elite for all the evil they'd perpetrated over the years. But like all of us, in the end they were actors, playing out a script that had been written over a century ago, its purpose long forgotten. For all their wealth and power, the Elite were a sad version of humanity, with no inner life, no joy in their existence, no real understanding of what it means to be alive, and no real knowledge of themselves, or even their own happiness.

Could a man like Pritchard ever be 'de-programmed' — be infused with a new script? I doubted it, but despite my own predicament, I was convinced that ultimately he and the rest of the Elite would fall, and would be forced to abandon their current path, whether they wanted to or not.

But all that was for the future. My own future appeared bleak, and my problems more immediate. Even if by some miracle I managed to escape, I was deep in the First Circle, behind a massive, heavily

*507*

defended wall. And the Rebels were in no position to rescue me, assuming they even wanted to.

The tests continued. So far, they hadn't done any serious harm, but I had no doubt that eventually they would. I was also tormented by the knowledge that, if it wasn't already, the same thing would soon be happening to Annabelle.

One morning the guards showed up as usual, but this time led me down a different hallway than we'd taken on previous trips.

When we arrived, Dr. Sheppard was waiting. "We've got something special planned for you today," she smiled.

I tried to pull away, but the two guards tightened their grips on my arms. We stood in a room similar to the others, but larger, and crowded with more sophisticated equipment. I was dragged toward an examination table at the center. The table had a round hole where my head would go.

"This will be a lot less painful if you don't struggle," Dr. Sheppard said. The two guards forced me face-down on the table, and strapped me in, with my face positioned in the hole.

"It would be in your best interest to hold very still," Dr. Sheppard repeated above me.

The guards moved back, but stayed close enough to intervene if I acted up. I stared at a jagged spot on the floor where a flake of the finish had been dislodged, and wondered what tortured incident might have been behind the damage. I felt a sharp pain and closed my eyes as a needle penetrated my skin, somewhere in the center of my back. I did as Dr. Sheppard ordered and held still.

The needle was finally withdrawn. I heard the clink of glass and the latching of some kind of container. Dr. Sheppard talked in low tones with the guards in a far corner of the room. I didn't catch a lot of what was said, but I heard enough to understand that they were planning to move me in the next few days, to a place with more sophisticated test equipment.

Soon after the conversation I heard the door to the room opening and closing. The guards hadn't moved, so I guessed that the doctor had gone off somewhere. About a half-hour later she returned, and I could hear her shuffling around on the bench behind me.

"Again, I suggest that you hold very still," Dr. Sheppard said, as she positioned some kind of apparatus above me. There was a humming sound, and I felt pressure against my back, followed by a deep ache in my spine. The procedure went on for more than a half hour. Again, though there was pain, I found I could tolerate it.

Finally, the doctor removed the apparatus and attached something to the skin of my back, probably an adhesive bandage.

Dr. Sheppard's head and shoulders appeared as she leaned down below the table. "You should rest in bed for at least two hours, and avoid any strenuous activity."

I remained strapped to the table as the guards wheeled it out the door and back to my cell. When we arrived, they unstrapped me, transferred me to my cot, and took off. I lay there, shaking. Forty years ago, thanks to Walter, I'd escaped before I'd been subjected to any serious or potentially harmful testing. This time, I wasn't going to be so lucky.

I knew enough about medicine to guess that the doctor had performed a spinal biopsy. It wasn't a dangerous procedure, but the implications were clear: the tests would become more and more invasive and destructive. I still had no idea where I was, but from what I'd overhead, I was being held in a temporary location. I guessed that they were planning to move me to the Institute for Life Studies Gene had talked about, where the other Outliers were being held. If that happened, there would likely be far higher security than at my present location.

I slowly drifted into a state of depression, as the realization took hold that if no one came along to help me, I would never escape.

# THIRTY

..................................................

# A VISITOR

I vowed that the next time the door opened, I would jump whoever was there and make a run for it. The odds of my succeeding were almost zero, but the longer I stayed here, and the more debilitating the medical procedures performed on me, the weaker I'd become. Very soon even the faintest hope of escape would be gone.

Unexpectedly, late that night, long after the usual tasteless Food-Corp meal had been slid under the door, I heard a shuffling sound outside, and seconds later heard the beep of the security panel. I jumped up and stood to one side, ready to attack the guard as he stepped into the room.

The door opened. I grabbed the hand holding the handle, and hauled the visitor inside. I raised my fist to strike, but stopped in midswing and froze, when I saw who it was.

"What the hell are you doing!" Annabelle whispered, pulling back and scowling at me.

"You!" I said, letting go of her hand. I wondered for a second whether I was dreaming. "How?"

"There's no time," she answered. "We've got to get out of here."

I stared at her with my mouth open.

"You came here to rescue me, didn't you?" she snapped, scrunching up her nose and cringing at the squalor of my new home. "Come on — let's get going."

She'd brought a pair of pants and a shirt for me. They were both too large to be hers, but there was no time to ask where she got them. I hurriedly pulled them on, and we rushed into the hallway, immediately turning right. Since being confined to the cell, I'd never gone this way. Annabelle seemed to have some idea where we were going. We made a left, entering a hallway with an exit sign over the door at the far end.

At the door, Annabelle reached into her pocket and pulled out a key-chain with set of keys and a fob. She held the fob in front of the panel and it clicked unlatched. I shook my head in disbelief, but there was no time to ask how she was doing all this.

We pushed the door open and rushed outside. Apparently, my prison had been in the basement of Pritchard's mansion, the same building where I'd been staying since I arrived. We emerged at a different viewpoint than I'd seen before.

It was dark, but the First Circle was alive with light, lit up like a frozen fireworks display. We were running for our lives. Still, for a few seconds I stood with my mouth open staring at the stunning beauty of the place — the soaring palaces of glass and steel, the spraying fountains and breathtaking statuary. Even Annabelle, who'd spent her life in the relative luxury of the Third City Corp Ring, stood and gawked at the opulence.

Then we started running, without thinking about where we were going. We tore past a spectacular marble statue and a moving holo-gram of a gigantic whale breaching the surface of some distant ocean. Within minutes an alarm began to sound in the mansion behind us. Now that we were out of the jammed environment, my HUD was working again. An icon appeared in it showing that it had somehow connected to my crypted phone. The display was packed with a string of messages — all of them from Richie.

"Where'd the crypted phone come from?" I said, half to myself.

Annabelle smiled, and hauled it out of one of her pockets.

I stared at her, my eyes wide. Who was this girl?

There was no way we could escape from the First Circle without major help, but there was no time right now to contact Richie, or anyone else. First, we had to distance ourselves from the mansion and find a place to hide. In the Quarters, and even more so in the Dregs, sur-rounded by abandoned buildings riddled with holes and broken door-ways, it was easy to find hiding places.

The First Circle was another story. At the same time, there were a couple of things working in our favour. When I'd been kidnapped and brought here forty years ago, my HUD had indicated that there were no cameras anywhere. That's how confident the Elite had been that nobody could get in. After being overrun back then by Rebels, they'd added a few, but Cam-surfing was still a breeze.

We passed through a magnificent garden and for a while were able to take cover among the trees, but were eventually forced to emerge again into the open. Annabelle had never even heard of Cam-surfing, let alone done it, but she obeyed my instructions to stay immediately behind me while I negotiated the few danger zones in our path.

We headed toward the nearest building that looked like it might offer a place to hide. Occasionally a stunning Robo-vehicle, shaped like a stylized swimming shark, or a stalking cat, would roll past us on the street, its occupants anonymous behind tinted windows, and drone-like Robo-flyers darted silently overhead.

Soon the thump of chopper blades filled the air in the distance, heading toward us. A dart skipped across the pavement at my feet, and a set of soldiers appeared about twenty meters down the street. Clearly, they didn't want to kill either of us — that gave us a slight advantage. We dove into the closest alley.

After a half-dozen twists and turns up and down darkened alleys, the soldiers were still in sight. I glanced at Annabelle, and remembered who it was I was escaping with. I held her right arm and checked her HUD controller.

"What?" she said, turning.

"Have you set up the hack to disable location tracking on your HUD?"

"Location tracking?" she asked, bewildered.

We dove into the nearest alcove and I quickly explained how to download and implement the underground hack that would confuse SecureCorp's location detection system.

Precious seconds later, with the footsteps of the SecureCorp soldiers just around the corner, she initiated the hack, and we took off. We moved at a brutal pace, but she didn't make the slightest complaint. I smiled. Maybe she was more than a spoiled little rich girl after all.

From my research over the years, and the landmarks I'd seen from the roof of Pritchard's mansion, I knew a little about the layout of the First Circle. Now, I made sure we were moving in the direction that would quickly lead us to the closest point of the wall.

After a half-hour of lung-bursting flight, we had managed to lose our pursuers, and we both needed to catch our breath. When we came across a parkade, almost empty of vehicles, I decided we could afford to stop for a while. I led Annabelle to its darkest, emptiest corner, and finally dared to take a few minutes to check Richie's messages.

*I always knew you weren't too bright,* the most recent one said. I smiled, imagining the scowl on his face as he towered over me. *But I never guessed that even you would walk into such an obvious trap. We found Spiro's body, and we've got a pretty good idea what happened.*

*We've heard nothing from you, and we're fearing the worst. We're guessing that you've been taken to the First Circle. If by some miracle you're not dismembered or dead, contact me. We might have a way to get you out of there.*

# T H I R T Y - O N E

..................................................

# R I C H I E

As we hid in the shadows in the parkade, I replied Richie's text.

*Sorry, I couldn't let it go. It was the only way.*

I quickly explained to him what had happened with Spiro, my imprisonment, and final escape with Annabelle.

*You've got her!* He texted back. *And you're free!*

*I don't want to get the rest of you involved,* I answered. *We'll find our way out somehow. Maybe you can meet us on the other side.*

*We're involved,* he shot back. *Don't argue. I can't believe you got this far. With that kind of luck, maybe it's not hopeless after all.*

I described roughly where we were. *I'll sneak out and try to spot some landmarks,* I texted. *Maybe you can work out how to meet up with us.*

*We've got access to a stealth-equipped transport disguised as a Corp vehicle,* Richie answered. *It can get us within a kilometer of a maintenance door in the NW corner of the wall.*

*We can Cam-surf the rest of the way — just like the old days. Our tech guys think they can hack its entry code. In theory we can just unlock it and walk through. How long can you last where you are?*

*Not long,* I answered him. *We're clear at the moment, but SecureCorp can't be far.*

*We've got a few plants in the First Circle,* he said. *Hang on for twenty more minutes and I'll try to put something together.*

I disconnected. Annabelle and I sat in silence in the shadows for a few minutes, with our backs against the wall, still winding down.

Finally I couldn't wait — I had to know. "So what happened after you gave me up?" I whispered. "How the did you manage to escape?"

"At first I didn't believe you," she said, staring at her feet. "But then I started thinking about it. Why *hadn't* I seen my parents in person for all the time I'd been there? Why *wasn't* my HUD working? Why *couldn't* I talk to anybody on the outside? They said it was to protect me, so I wouldn't give away my location. That makes sense, but why was anybody after me in the first place? And why cut me off completely, even from my own parents?

"And then there was the testing. It's been going on ever since I got here, long past where it should be necessary. I decided that at least part of what you were saying must be true. And all the stuff Dr. Sheppard was saying to you at breakfast...

"Then the day after they took you away, I overheard one of the guards talking about moving me. They didn't say where, but it didn't sound like they had any intention of letting me go home. I thought about asking if I could leave, to test my theory, but at that time, they still assumed I'd bought into their story. If what you were saying was true, asking them would give myself away, and they'd be watching me."

"But how did you take care of the guards? What are you, some kind of black belt in martial arts?"

She rolled her eyes. "There's other, better, ways to do things." She changed position, hugging her knees. "Once you were gone, they removed the guys that had been guarding my room. One of the meal orderlies had been coming on to me from the beginning — an obnoxious, weaselly little man." She cringed in disgust. "All along I'd been brushing him off, but the next meal time after I'd decided to leave, I pretended I was interested. I flirted with him, and told him to come and see me without the guard that always came along." She shook her head. "I didn't think he'd buy my change of heart, but let's face it, men aren't too bright. He came back an hour later, alone."

She cringed again as she continued. "I had to make out with him two different times, to pump him for information. He let it slip about my Appraisal, and I knew that what you were saying was true, and that I had to get out of there. I'd been taken to the labs in the basement for my tests, so I guessed that's where they were keeping you. The orderly bragged about how he had a pass key to all the rooms. I remembered what you said about your crypted phone. I said I was dying to talk to my father. I told him nobody would be able to trace a call on that phone, and convinced him to bring it to me.

"When he showed up the third time, with the phone, I maneuvered him toward a porcelain statue on the table by my bed. When his back was turned, I smashed him on the head."

*518*

I rubbed the back of my own head, remembering the damage she'd done when Richie and I had first tried to rescue her.

"He was out cold," she continued. "I got his keys, his shirt, and his pants, tied him up, gagged him, and came to find you."

I stared at her with a new respect. "Wow, I appreciate you going through all that to rescue me."

She sneered, and scanned me up and down. "I didn't do it for you."

I sat back. "Well, then…"

"I need you," she said, without emotion. "There's no way I could get out of here by myself. If what you say is true, it's not safe for me anywhere in the First Circle. You said you were here to rescue me. You've got connections with the Rebels. I knew you wouldn't have come here if you didn't have a plan for getting me out."

I swallowed hard.

"So, what *is* your rescue plan?" Annabelle asked.

I looked at my hands resting on my knees. I hoped that the darkness would hide my face turning red.

"What?" she asked. "Is it some kind of secret?"

"Actually," I said, not able to look at her, "I had a plan to rescue you back in Third City, but—"

"What!"

I stared straight ahead.

"So you've got no idea how to get us out of here?" she said evenly, grimacing and shaking her head as we huddled in the darkness.

"I *do* have contact with the Rebels," I said, turning to her. "That's who I was just talking to. They might be able to sneak us out of a maintenance door in the wall. But first we'd have to get there."

She sat staring at the wall behind me. Again, for almost a minute, neither of us spoke.

"So, I'm really going to live for another four hundred years?" she finally asked.

She was clearly still in shock, unsure, as I had been, whether it was a good or a bad thing. This wasn't a good time to tell her — but from my experience it was pretty much all bad.

"That's the information we've been given," I answered. "It was confirmed by someone whose word I trust. It might be wrong, but I doubt it. Anyway, Vita Aeterna wouldn't be after you otherwise."

"And you're how old?"

"I turned fifty-six a few months ago," I said.

She examined me in the shadows, probably looking for wrinkles, or some other indication of my age. She wouldn't find any.

"Your dad never talked to you about it?" I asked.

"I went away to a gymnastics camp a few months ago," she answered. "When I got back, he showed me the hiding place he'd built. I thought he'd lost it, but he seemed so serious. He said that because we were rich, there were people out to get us."

"He didn't say anything about your Appraisal?"

She shook her head. "A couple of weeks before you showed up, he made me take a training course at a firing range. And the day after I met you in Third City he said he had something important to tell me, but then all this happened."

She closed her eyes and stiffened, as if bracing for some impact. "Are you absolutely sure my father's dead?"

I explained how we'd entered their bedroom after she'd been taken away by the SecureCorp prowlers. I left out the painful details.

"And my mother?"

I told her. Her body shook for a few seconds, then she quickly regained control.

# T H I R T Y - T W O

..................................................

# ON THE RUN

The drone of choppers and the screams of sirens echoed around the First Circle as we abandoned our hiding place, and headed in the direction where I'd calculated we would find the wall. There was one more thing in our favour. Since everyone here was wealthy beyond their wildest dreams, there was virtually no crime; a large SecureCorp presence wasn't necessary, so the number of SecureCorp soldiers available to chase us was small.

Of course, there were lots of SecureCorp everywhere else in the city, especially in the Quarters, that could be called on to join the search, but that would take time to mobilize. I guessed that the faster we moved, and the more territory we covered, the better off we'd be.

As desperate as we were, I still had to stop occasionally and stand with my mouth open to gawk at the shining silver and glass palaces, sculptures, massive HoloTV art works.

In one gigantic billboard Holo, a whirlwind of spectacular suits, dresses, jackets, and shirts swirled above the display pedestal, with the caption: *Bored with this week's wardrobe? Next week's latest fashions are already here! Don't get caught out of date!* Seconds later it collapsed and another display lit up the pedestal — gun-metal-gray letters, scattered with bullet holes, said: *Like to Play for Keeps? We at* **Predator Black Ops** *can show you how to smash the competition — no questions asked!*

Richie's hacked access door might be kilometers from our position, but until I heard back from him, this was the best I could do. I made a note of major landmarks as we moved. No maps of the First Circle were available on our HUDs, but the Rebels had put together a pretty detailed one over the years. I prayed that the door in question would turn out to be somewhere close to where we were headed.

"We're not going to last long out here," I said, as the chopper searchlights and wailing sirens continued to fan out over the city.

"It never occurred to you that this would happen?" Annabelle said, shaking her head. "Did you have any plan at all?"

I stared at my feet, without answering her.

"We need a place to hide," I said, happy to change the subject.

"Good thinking," she snapped. "I can see I'm in capable hands."

We'd slowed from a flat-out run to a fast walk, and I finally spotted a landmark Richie had described, next to a hiding place the Rebels had identified — a small door leading to the utility room for some kind of transit station. There was nobody around. I managed to pry open the door, and we jammed inside and slammed it behind us. If anyone had seen us enter, we were dead. We held our breath as the sirens wailed in the distance.

At least we were off the street and out of sight of the multitude of SecureCorp vehicles and choppers that were blanketing the city.

I contacted Richie.

*You're still out there?* he texted me back. *I'm shocked, but happy to hear it.*

We brought each other up to speed.

*Our people within the First Circle are going to create a diversion,* Richie said. *That should draw some of the heat away from you.*

I described the building where we were hiding.

*How safe are you?* He asked.

*We're out of sight,* I answered, *but somebody could come in here at any moment.*

*I've got to talk to the others,* he said. *I'll get back to you as soon as I can.*

Cringing, Annabelle used her foot to clear the dust from a spot on the floor, and sat down with her back against the wall. I sat down beside her. She moved away from me, squeezing into the corner.

I smirked and rolled my eyes. "What exactly have you got against me?"

"Against you?" she answered, looking at her feet. "You and your kind are a blight on society. You don't contribute anything, but you chew up resources. You have no ambition. All you do is take — or steal — handouts from the rest of us."

I didn't try to argue. Her indoctrination was deeply flawed, but also deeply ingrained. I wondered if it could ever be reversed.

"That's it?" I asked.

"Why do I have to like you?" She lifted her head and sneered at me. "You said you were here to rescue me, for some reason. I assume you have your own agenda. If you can get me out of here I'll be glad you came, but I won't feel like I owe you anything.

"Everybody does whatever it takes to win, period. That's the way the world works. I'm surprised that you had the drive to actually plan something and carry out the plan. Of course, surprise, surprise, you didn't really *have* a plan, but at least you did *something*. I'm indifferent to you. All I care about is what you can do for me."

I shook my head sadly. "It never occurred to you that I might have had empathy for your situation? That maybe I came here to rescue you because I didn't want to see you suffer?"

It was her turn to smirk. "Nobody's *that* stupid. You don't even know me. You probably don't even like me. What kind of a sucker do you think I am, to believe you'd rescue me out of 'kindness', or some bullshit altruistic motive like that?"

She was right. I didn't know her — and it was true that as of now I didn't really like her. She was also at least partly right about my motives; I was excited about the possibility that she might be the first person I'd ever met that had a lifespan close to my own. But it was also true that I really did want to save her from a life of torture.

Just the same, at the moment I wondered why I had risked, and was continuing to risk, my life trying to save hers.

I changed the subject. "What did Pritchard and his people tell you before I came along?"

"Like I said," she answered. "They did a few blood tests and scans. They said they just wanted to make sure I was okay."

"They took you to the labs in the basement?"

She nodded. "Probably the same ones where they took you. It was just once a day to start with. It seemed reasonable for the first few days, but after that I started to wonder. And they stepped up the pace to a couple of times a day."

"I have it on good authority that there's a few dozen other Outliers, with ultra-high Appraisals like us, at a place called the Institute for Life Studies. We can't do anything for them right now, but eventually I hope we'll find a way to free them as well."

"Why?" she asked, scrunching up her nose.

"It's called compassion," I said. "And it does exist, regardless of what you've been told."

We were interrupted by another call from Richie. He asked a couple of questions to pinpoint our location. There was another delay, and he came back to say they were confident they knew where we were. I asked him about the escape door in the wall.

*It could be worse,* he said. *The door is about five kilometers west of you. We're working on the logistics of getting there from our side, and hacking it open.*

*In about fifteen minutes,* he said, *all hell's going to break loose in the First Circle. The distraction should give you the chance to make for the door. I'm sending you a map. I'll be in touch.*

He disconnected.

"We've got to get out of here," I said, getting to my feet.

"And do what?"

"It's true that I didn't really have a plan before," I answered, "but I do now."

# THIRTY-THREE

........................................................

# THE FINAL SPRINT

I spent a few minutes exploring the space, looking for anything that might help us once we left here, especially something we could use as a weapon. There wasn't much. In one corner I found a tool kit that contained, among other things, a small pry bar, some pliers, and a screwdriver. I took all three, shoved them into a small cloth bag I found, and tied the bag around my belt.

We took off again at full speed, heading in the general direction of the wall. The light was beginning to rise, bathing the already breath-taking city in an ethereal blue glow. I tensed as a male voice echoed from loudspeakers positioned somewhere in the buildings nearby. We stopped to listen.

"Annabelle," the voice said. I recognized it as Elliot Pritchard. "By now I'm sure you are aware that you have been duped by the Rebel terrorist Alex Barret. Rest assured that we are doing everything in our power to rescue you and bring the perpetrator to justice. Take care, and be careful not to antagonize him — he is unbalanced, and dangerous."

There was a pause, then another male voice, shaky and distraught, took over from Pritchard's.

"Annabelle, my darling," it said.

Annabelle's body tightened on hearing it, and her fists clenched at her sides.

The voice continued. "I'm so sorry that your mother and I haven't come to visit you since you were rescued. As you know, I've been unwell, and your mother was preoccupied with caring for me."

"It's your father's voice?" I asked. Her eyes closed as she bit her lip and nodded.

"It's not him," I said. "It can't be — you know that, right?"

She opened her eyes and stared straight ahead.

"We miss you terribly," the voice continued. "We'll be waiting for you at home. Stay safe, and be ready for your rescuers when they arrive. Soon we can be a family again. Have courage, and never forget how much we love you."

I studied her face. "It's fake," I said, not sure how she would react.

"It sounds exactly like him," she said, her lower lip quivering. "Are you sure—"

I took her hand. She didn't resist. "I'm sorry," I said. "But there's no way."

I thought back on the older couple's bullet-ridden bodies from the raid in Third City. It was impossible that they could have survived those injuries. But I didn't want to explain that to Annabelle.

She straightened up and composed herself. Her eyes drifted down, and, as if she'd just realized that we were holding hands, pulled hers away.

"It's fake," she echoed, turning away from me.

I helped her Cam-surf away from the building, heading west. We'd been running for about five minutes when there was a massive explosion to our right. We both stopped and turned toward it. For a few seconds I froze, paralyzed, as the memories of the first time I'd been in the First Circle flooded through my brain. The sky to the north of us bloomed orange and red against the darkness, as a huge fireball rose above the horizon.

"What was that?" Annabelle asked, her eyes wide.

"I'm not sure," I answered, "but I think it was Richie."

She stood staring at the lit-up sky, now laced with sparks and smoke, as if she couldn't believe such a thing could happen in the First Circle. Soon, a set of sirens split off from the group looking for us and headed in the direction of the explosion. Richie had given us some breathing space.

Occasionally we'd spot other people on the street, but it was surprisingly quiet. The concept of danger in the First Circle was probably so alien that most of the inhabitants would be cowering in their homes with the doors locked. Where possible, if we encountered other people we would slip behind a nearby building or into an alcove to avoid them. If avoidance wasn't possible, we slowed to a walk and adopted the roles of a couple out for a stroll.

We passed one or two of the landmarks Richie had told me about when we talked — at least we were headed in the right direction. The sirens and choppers continued, now focused on the area around the transit station where we'd been hiding.

As we ran, I tried to reconnect with Richie.

*Our hack doesn't work,* he texted me. *It made use of a flaw in the SecureCorp security code — turns out it's a loophole they've recently plugged.*

*I'll be in touch.*

We stopped for a few seconds to get our breath. Annabelle shook her head in disbelief as I explained the plan the Rebels had arranged for our escape, and how it wasn't going to work. For once I couldn't blame her.

"They've got a Plan B," I told her.

"I hope it's better than Plan A," she said sarcastically.

I turned on her. "You know, a small army of people are risking their lives trying to rescue you. Show a little more respect."

She tossed her head and looked away.

We took off again, and I finally heard back from Richie. Since they couldn't hack the door open, they had only one alternative.

They would use explosives.

I shuddered, remembering how back when I was a kid, the Rebels had blown a massive hole in the main gate, allowing us to escape from the First Circle.

According to Richie, even though it was only a minor access door, it was several meters high and made from concrete and steel; it would take a big explosion to blow a hole large enough for us to get through. And of course, that explosion would have the place swarming with SecureCorp. Richie said that the Rebels were already in place, and that the explosion should happen in less than twenty minutes. We wouldn't have much time to escape, so we should be in place when the blast occurred.

Sirens wailed all around us, getting closer, as we rushed from our hiding place and headed in the direction of the target door. A few choppers still hovered around the rising red firestorm in the distance, and the sirens continued to swirl around that area. From the directions I'd gotten from Richie, I calculated that we were no more than ten minutes from the door — our lifeline.

Of course, it was possible that SecureCorp would guess where we were headed. It was one of the few options we had for escape. If that happened, they could catch us when we got there. If the Rebels couldn't blow the door, we were toast. Even if they succeeded, our chances of escaping were slim.

Minutes later, we rounded a corner. We finally encountered the looming white expanse of the wall, and I saw the door a couple of hundred meters ahead. For a few seconds I dared to think that we might actually make it.

Then I froze as I heard a chilling sound behind us — the barking of dogs.

# THIRTY-FOUR

..............................................

# AT THE WALL

I gripped Annabelle's hand, and upped our speed. I thought about the irony that while dogs had been my loving companions for decades, and had saved my life numerous times, I might now be brought down by them.

With this new development, our flight was no longer a game of hide and seek. We abandoned any attempt to hide, or even Cam-surf. It had become a race — all that mattered was making it to the wall and through Richie's door before the dogs caught up with us, as they certainly would.

The open square in front of the door was empty. According to Richie, it was covered by a pair of guards. The guards' rounds were scheduled and predictable, but we had no idea of the schedule, so they could show up at any moment.

We moved to a point about thirty meters away, squeezed into the shadows of a narrow alcove, and waited. We wouldn't need a signal — when the door blew, we'd know it. The barking of the dogs was approaching fast, followed by the sirens and the slap of chopper blades.

A chopper appeared over the rooftop of a nearby building, its searchlight sweeping the ground like a swinging sword. We pressed our backs against the building as a second chopper swept in directly above the door. Gunfire issued from its far side, as it apparently did battle with the Rebels on the other side of the wall. The sounds of our ground pursuers continued toward us.

The searchlight from the nearest chopper rushed along the pavement to my feet, and traveled up to my chest. Before I had time to move, some kind of dart gun mounted on its undercarriage swiveled in my direction, and a red dot raced along the ground toward me.

The dot was less than a meter away when the entire block shook with a massive blast. The undercarriage of the chopper above the door was torn apart, and it was enveloped in the explosion. It swung wildly from side to side until one of the rotors clipped a nearby building and it plummeted from the sky in a ball of flame.

The one with me in its sights was blown back by the shock wave of the blast, and was forced to circle back toward us. At the same time, two dogs emerged from the shadows, barking and yelping, their ears back and hackles raised, hauling on the leashes of their handlers.

The handlers let them go, and they pounded toward us, yelping and slavering. I hauled out my only weapon — the metal pry-bar, and raised it in my fist. For a second I hesitated — these dogs were innocent creatures, driven on by their handlers. How could I... The closest dog reached us and leapt toward Annabelle, with its jaws gaping and its teeth barred.

"God forgive me," I whispered, as I smashed the bar against the poor creature's head and it went down, whimpering, blood splattering my killing hand and the pavement below. My attack frightened the other dog, which held back and paced around us, its lips pulled back and teeth still barred.

The explosion had thrown the square into chaos. We took advantage of the distraction, and took off toward the door. A gigantic hole had been blasted in it, but the downed chopper, engulfed by flames and rocked with periodic explosions, blocked most of the opening.

Two SecureCorp vehicles tore into the square from a nearby alley, just as a group of Rebels emerged from the other side of the wall. Using the downed chopper for cover, the Rebels engaged in a firefight with the half-dozen newly-arrived SecureCorp soldiers. The sirens of backup vehicles were almost upon us. The chopper that had been about to take me out was again hurtling in our direction. A Rebel fighter trained his weapon on the chopper's pilot, tracking their path for a few seconds.

He fired. The pilot was hit, and the aircraft spun out of control. For a second it accelerated toward us, but then its rotation catapulted it toward the nearest SecureCorp vehicle. The soldiers crouching behind the vehicle screamed as the chopper slammed to earth directly on top of them.

Richie's burly figure appeared among the Rebel fighters and he gestured to us. "Now!" he screamed.

The fighters covered us as we raced for the breach in the wall. The flames from the burning chopper had died down, leaving a substantial gap. But now the backup SecureCorp vehicles had arrived. Soldiers were deploying all around us, and more choppers were on the way.

Richie held up a jacket to block the flames as we rushed across. We were through, but by no means safe. While the SecureCorp vehicles were trapped in the First Circle, the choppers were still approaching.

And now we had a new threat — a few dozen armed drones had appeared above the wall.

Our getaway vehicle was nowhere in sight. The swarm of drones swept over the wall and dove as one toward us, some of them firing anesthetic darts. They would all have cameras and location indicators to pinpoint exactly where we were. Our original SecureCorp pursuers were still stuck behind the wall, but the sirens of a new set, directed by the drones, now echoed toward us on this side. SecureCorp soldiers were crowding around the opening in a firefight with the Rebels, and the new choppers had almost reached our position.

There was a whistling sound to our right, and something exploded in the center of the swarm of drones. The concussion downed most of them, and the few that remained spun through the air, out of control.

"Let' s go," a voice yelled behind us.

I turned and saw two Rebel stealth vehicles in the shadows, with a pair of fighters standing beside them. We took off toward them, just as the shape of a chopper loomed up over the other side of the wall. It turned in our direction, and the machine-gun mounted on its underside swiveled toward us.

We rushed for the closest vehicle. Richie jumped in the front seat beside the driver. I guided Annabelle into the back seat, then dove into the open door beside her, just as the chopper began firing. The vehicles were bullet-proof, but a sustained onslaught by a high-powered weapon like the one firing at us would eventually get through.

"Go!" I yelled, slamming the door shut.

The vehicle took off down the nearest alley, with the chopper close behind, and sirens approaching fast. We wove in and out of alleyways, trying to lose it. Its roar gradually faded. We raced toward the Quarters, an area we knew far better than our pursuers, and where they would have a harder time chasing us.

"Annabelle, Richie," I introduced them, shouting above the chaos. "Richie, Annabelle."

The individual sirens we'd heard initially were soon joined by a chorus of others; they weren't going to give up. The volume of their whine increased again, as they must have found some way to determine where we were.

After twenty minutes of zigzagging through streets and alleys we finally reached the edge of the Corp Ring and entered the Quarters. Our pursuers were still close behind. In the front seat, Richie conferred with the driver. Minutes later, having lost the chopper for a few seconds, the vehicle squealed to a stop.

"Get out!" Richie yelled, pushing his own door open.

I took Annabelle's hand and we dove from the vehicle. Richie followed us, and the vehicle tore off at top speed.

"What the hell are you doing?" I yelled at Richie. Our only means of escape was now gone.

He pushed on a section of the wall beside us, and a seam opened up, revealing a hidden door. He swung it open, we rushed in, and he pushed it shut again behind us. Seconds later, a dozen sirens screamed past on the street.

I marveled at the driver's willingness to risk his life to help us. I hoped we'd all somehow get away safely. There were now three of us: me, Annabelle, and Richie. Richie touched something beside the door, and a dim light switched on. We were in a room about five meters square, with bare concrete walls and floor. There was a beaten-up wooden table in one corner, and a pair of wooden chairs. Annabelle glanced at one of them with disgust, then finally, resigned, dusted it off with her hand, and sat down.

I found a spot as far from her as possible, and sat on the floor with my back against the wall, while Richie went off in another corner and talked to somebody on his HUD.

Annabelle had finally toned down her comments about me and our mission. I think she was too stunned by the day's events to think about anything else. Even so, I shelved, maybe permanently, the idea I'd had in the back of my mind since I first heard about her — that maybe I'd finally have a chance at a relationship with someone having a lifespan close to my own.

Miraculously, we'd managed to escape from the First Circle, by far our most difficult and dangerous challenge. We'd crossed the Corp Ring, evaded SecureCorp, and found a hiding place in the Quarters, familiar territory. What we'd accomplished was almost beyond belief, but our troubles weren't over. I had the now familiar sinking feeling that they never would be.

Ten minutes later, Richie finished his call, and the three of us had a meeting. I was relieved to hear that our driver had managed to evade the SecureCorp pursuers, and was now on his way back to Rebel head-quarters.

"The plan is to wait for things to die down," Richie said. "Then I'll contact somebody to send another stealth vehicle."

But we couldn't wait for long. The bad news was that the main reason the driver had been able to escape was that SecureCorp had determined that we were no longer in the vehicle. They would still be looking for us. I double-checked Annabelle's HUD controller to make sure the location-jamming hack was properly installed and working. It was.

Now, there was nothing we could do but wait. Annabelle was ex-hausted. She refused to lie on the filthy floor. Richie and I wiped down the table top, which was big enough for her to curl up on. She did that, while Richie and I went and sat on the floor in a far corner.

I told Richie about my contact with Gene, and what Gene had said about there being other Outliers being held prisoner at the Institute.

"Wow," Richie said, shaking his head. "In a way, that's good. It'll take a bit of the pressure off of you two."

"But we can't just leave those people there to be tortured for the next few centuries."

"Good luck with that," Richie said.

"I've thought of no one but myself for the past four decades," I said. "God knows how many people like me have suffered at Vita Aeterna's hands, while I hid out in the Dregs. I can't stand by any-more and do nothing."

540

Richie put a hand on my shoulder. "Those are noble sentiments, but for now, we need to concentrate on saving our own skins."

"At least we' ve gotten through the worst of it," I said, trying to sound hopeful. "Once we get back to Rebel headquarters we' ll be home-free."

Richie stared across at me.

"What?" I said. I scratched the stubble on my chin. Finally it occurred to me. "Laura—"

Richie nodded. "Remember, she didn' t want the Rebels to continue looking for Annabelle in the first place. This rescue mission was unsanctioned. Substantial Rebel resources have been depleted, and a bunch of people have risked their lives. We don' t know the final tally, but there' s no doubt that Rebel fighters were seriously injured in this operation, and a few may have died. Some people are saying that you deliberately allowed yourself to be caught, to force us to come after you.

"You' re saying Laura' s feelings toward you right now. Anyway, it' s not just her — there' s a whole faction of the Rebels who won' t be happy to see you back there. The presence of two Outliers that Vita Aeterna are desperate to lay their hands on adds an extra level of threat they don' t need."

"You' re saying they might not let us in?" I whispered, not wanting Annabelle to hear.

"I don' t think they' ll go that far," Richie whispered back. "Let' s put it this way. The driver that will be picking us up is one of my guys. If I put the request through proper channels, I' m not sure that anybody would even come."

541

## THIRTY-FIVE

..................................................

# THE QUARTERS

An hour later, we were informed that our new driver was minutes away. Richie listened at the door, then opened it a crack to check the alley.

He closed it again and nodded. It was clear. We all rushed out the door, the vehicle rolled up, and we piled into it. We'd been told that the trip back to Rebel headquarters would involve a stop at another hideout deep in the Quarters — in Tintown, not far from where I grew up.

When we arrived, the driver pulled the vehicle into a dark alley and cut the engine.

"We're here," he said.

I opened our door and Annabelle and I stepped outside. Even though it was daylight, the surrounding skyscrapers blanketed everything in shadow. Richie left the driver to guard the car — we wouldn't be here very long.

542

We followed Richie out of the alley into a large square. I remembered it — it wasn't far from our old apartment. All around us dirty, garbage strewn streets were lined with dumpy, disintegrating highrises. A guy in shabby clothes shambled across an alley in front of us. He glanced our way, gave an unwelcoming look, and kept walking.

The buildings loomed over our heads as we made our way to the steps of a dilapidated apartment complex. Twisted, dripping pipes dangled at intervals from its walls, and the mostly broken windows were blocked off with makeshift security bars made from chunks of scrap metal. Drying laundry flapped from a few of them, and spiderwebs of wires spun out from the windows, gathering into bundles at the nearest standing power pole.

The shadows swept across Annabelle's face as she pulled back and stood there, wide-eyed, gazing around at the devastation. "T...This is the Quarters?" she asked, almost in a whisper. "This is where you grew up?"

"Hey, it's not much," I joked, "but it's home."

She scanned the devastated scene. "How many people live here?"

"Here in Tintown?" I said, "about twenty thousand. In the Quarters in general — millions."

I was shocked to find her squeezing my hand. She studied the debris cluttered streets, then glanced up at me, with an expression that was some mixture of pity, revulsion, and sorrow.

"We better get inside," Richie said.

Annabelle squeezed harder as we climbed the concrete steps, and passed through the broken front door to what must once have been the lobby.

"The place is on the fifth floor," Richie said.

We headed for the stairs.

"What about the elevator?" Annabelle said, nodding at a rust-stained set of sliding doors to our right.

Richie smirked and looked over at me. I shrugged. He grabbed the handle of the door to the stairwell.

"After you, your majesty," he said, sweeping a hand forward.

Annabelle scowled at him and walked through.

We puffed up the garbage-littered stairs and exited on the fifth floor. The carpeting in the hallway had been torn to pieces years ago, but there were still remnants of it mixed in with the other debris scattered around.

There wasn't another soul as we made our way to the third door on the right. The numbers on the door had long-since disappeared, but the relatively dirt-free shadows where they had been attached read *five zero five*.

Richie knocked in a prearranged sequence. There was a pause, as someone checked the peephole. A few seconds later the door squeaked open a crack, and a pair of eyes peered out at us. Richie smiled, and the door opened. The eyes belonged to an attractive middle-aged woman, who now stood aside to let us in. Another Rebel, holding a gun, stood behind her.

We rushed inside and she shut the door behind us. To my shock, Richie moved forward, hugged the woman, and kissed her on the lips.

"Thank God," she whispered.

Richie turned back to us. "Alex, Annabelle — this is Iris — my wife."

I was embarrassed, realizing that I'd never even talked to Richie about his personal life since I'd gotten back.

A table and chairs stood in one corner. We sat, and Iris filled us in on what had happened. A small group of Rebels had allowed themselves to be seen by the cameras to draw away the SecureCorp soldiers. They'd bravely led the soldiers on a chase for an hour or so, and finally managed to escape to one of the Rebel hiding places.

"We're just waiting for intelligence on where SecureCorp are now," Iris said. "Once that's confirmed, you can head for Rebel headquarters."

Richie went off in a corner with his wife, and they talked in low tones. The other Rebel, a guy named Jim, took up a position guarding the door to the room.

I leaned my head back and closed my eyes, for a brief period of respite.

"How do people live here?" Annabelle asked.

"They live however they can," I answered, without lifting my head. "Nobody has any money, so there's no services to look after us. If we don't do something ourselves, it doesn't get done."

"But you must have money," she said. "How else can you live?"

I sat up and looked at her. "A few people have jobs in the Corp Ring, doing stuff the Corp workers don't want to do. Sometimes Food-Corp trucks will come through." I smiled. "And stuff accidentally falls off."

"So the Corps aren't here at all?"

I laughed. "Who would pay for them? SecureCorp come around — but not for the people living here. They're hired by the Elite to keep the rest of us in line. Sometimes small backroom operations will pop up: corner stores, repair shops. But if they grow to any size the Corps either absorb them and raise their prices out of our reach, or drive them out of business.

"With all the stuff on HoloTV about free enterprise and competition, you'd think the Corps would approve. When it doesn't bring in money for them, suddenly it's evil. But for the people here, barter and the underground market are all there is."

"Bullshit," she sneered. "We're free — everybody knows that — free to follow our dreams. We don't have to depend on anyone else's help. With enough hard work, anybody — even people like you from the Quarters, can make it big and join one of the Corps — or even the Elite. These people are just too lazy, or too weak..."

She stopped speaking, and I noticed that the room was silent. I looked around. All three of the others: Richie, Iris, and Jim, were staring at Annabelle. I looked at them and shrugged.

This was the girl we were all risking our lives to rescue.

Twenty minutes later, Iris got a message from her guys. They'd mapped out SecureCorp's deployment areas, and put together a route to avoid them. We got ready to move out.

Richie kissed her goodbye, and we made our way back to the vehicle, still waiting in the alley.

"Iris seems like a great lady," I said as we walked.

"She's the best thing that ever happened to me," he answered.

Minutes into the journey, Annabelle leaned her head against the window, closed her eyes, and was asleep. I sat in the back seat beside her. Sleeping like that, she looked like an angel...

Richie was in the front seat. He turned back to face me.

I smiled. "So, you've got a wife — does that mean you've got kids as well?"

"Two girls," he answered, beaming. "Anna and Kelsey." He punched a few buttons on his HUD controller and an image appeared in my own HUD. Two beautiful young girls in their early teens. It was surreal, like I'd been frozen in a chunk of amber for decades while everybody else was off somewhere having experiences, living their lives.

"I'm sorry for putting you and Iris at risk," I said. "I wasn't thinking—"

"Don't worry about it," he said, smiling. "It all worked out. We got you back." He nodded at Annabelle, "and we got the girl. It was a little harder than we'd first expected, but..."

We spent an hour threading our way through a convoluted maze of back streets and alleyways. Finally, we were within a few blocks of Rebel headquarters. Richie had contacted them to tell them we were coming.

Just before we were expecting to reach the checkpoint for entry to the complex, we turned a corner, and a group of armed Rebel fighters emerged from the shadows. A vehicle pulled up behind them, blocking the way forward. When we looked behind us another vehicle had blocked our retreat. They clearly weren't SecureCorp, so we wondered what was going on.

With no other option, Richie and I got out and approached the group.

"Hands up," the guy who seemed to be leading them said. They lifted their weapons and leveled them at us. We raised our hands.

"Everybody out," the leader motioned with his gun toward the vehicle.

Richie leaned down to me and whispered. "I don't even know this guy." He turned back and gestured to the vehicle. The driver and Annabelle got out and joined us.

"Who's the girl?" the leader asked, nodding at Annabelle.

"You know who she is," Richie snapped. "What's going on here?"

"These two," he gestured at me and Annabelle, "aren't welcome."

"Says who?" Richie said. "Who the hell are you? Do you speak for the General? Did she sanction all this?

"We speak for the true Rebel movement," he answered, sneering at Annabelle. "The movement is too important to be risked for a couple of Dead Shift."

"I want to speak with General Quinn," Richie said.

The guy with the gun flinched as several new Rebel vehicles appeared in the distance. They accelerated toward us and screeched to a halt just on the other side of the blocking vehicle. The four of us still stood with our hands raised. A half dozen fighters emerged from one of the two new vehicles. The rear door of the other opened, and I exhaled deeply, as out stepped Connor.

The new set of fighters rushed in, muscled out the original ones, and forced them to drop their weapons. We finally relaxed and put our hands down.

Connor approached us, nodding his greeting.

"Everybody okay?" he asked, looking at Richie.

"So far," Richie said. "What the hell *is* this?"

"There's a faction who don't think we should be harbouring you two." Connor nodded at me and Annabelle. He turned to me. "Your little jaunt to the First Circle didn't go over well here."

I looked at my feet.

"We didn't get word of their intentions until just now," Connor said, indicating the original group. "Unfortunately, they're not the only ones who feel that way. You're lucky you've got somebody on your side whose orders are never questioned."

My eyebrows came together. Finally it occurred to me, but it seemed impossible. "Laura?"

Connor nodded. "We'll escort you."

# THIRTY-SIX

.................................................

# BACK AT HEADQUARTERS

Our convoy, with the group who'd first stopped us in custody, re-entered Rebel headquarters. Word must have circulated about my rescue of Annabelle, and the danger our presence posed to the Rebels' security. As we were led through the same corridors where I'd been welcomed when I first arrived, there were now occasional stares and ungracious scowls from people along the route. After Richie's warning, I understood that they might not be pleased at our being there, but this was beyond anything I'd expected.

I was led to the same room I'd occupied earlier, and Annabelle was placed in one down the hall. We were advised to stay in our rooms for the time being. I had no problem with that — I was exhausted.

I slept for a few hours, and was eventually wakened by a knock on my door. It was Sergeant Forbes. He showed the same professional but friendly attitude as before, which raised my spirits a little.

"The General would like to see you," he said.

I followed him down a series of hallways that eventually led to a different office than the one where Laura and I had met originally. Sergeant Forbes knocked, entered the office, and talked briefly to someone inside. He returned and gestured for me to go in, then left and closed the door behind me.

Laura was standing beside another wooden desk. Her face was drawn. She seemed to have aged in the short time I'd been away. She looked old. Once again, I felt a stab of guilt at my own continued youth.

"You've placed me in a difficult position," she said.

"I'm sorry," I said. "Thank you for allowing us in. I can imagine how much it's cost you."

"Can you?" she asked, sarcastically. "I gave the order that we were not to get involved in the fight with Vita Aeterna. You chose to ignore that order."

I looked at the floor, unable to face her.

Finally I looked up. "I had to go. I've seen what Vita Aeterna's treatments can do. I couldn't just stand by while the girl was mutilated for the next four centuries."

She glared at me. "That girl is one life — one life of many. We're in a war, as you may not have grasped. We're still in the process of tallying up the people and resources that were lost as a result of your reckless actions. Now it's possible that SecureCorp will attack us here in retaliation. If that happens, numerous deaths will be on your head."

"I can leave," I said. "Just give me a few hours to work out where to go. I wasn't expecting this much antagonism."

Laura shrugged. "At first it was a novelty having a legend return from the dead. Now that people have had time to think about it, they realize that habouring Outliers like you makes us more of a target — especially now that there's two of you. There's also some underlying resentment. People imagine themselves growing old and dying, while you remain young and healthy. They're afraid of things they don't understand."

She gestured around us with her head. "Everybody here realizes that we have to work together and support each other if we're to have any hope of success." She fixed her gaze on me. "Everybody except you. For all your knowledge, intelligence, and experience, you've still got the self-centered mind of a child. You're almost sixty years old, and you haven't had an intimate relationship with another human being since you were sixteen. It shows. Your bad judgment has put us all at risk."

I hung my head. I knew it was true.

"I could take the dogs and the girl back to my hideout," I said, looking up. "I know the Dregs better than anybody else in the world. I'm sure I can come up with something."

"I'll set up a meeting with some of the senior fighters," Laura said. "We can discuss our options."

Her expression was hard, and I could see the bitterness still in her eyes. She turned, about to dismiss me. I couldn't let things stand like this.

"Look, Laura," I said. "We need to talk about what happened forty years ago."

"What's done is done," she said coldly. "I told you before, I don't want to hear about it."

"But you *need* to," I said, my voice rising. "What were your options? To come with me to the Dregs, and hide out for the rest of your life?"

She stared back at me, defiant.

"I needed to stay dead to the world," I went on. "Vita Aeterna may have been crippled, but if they'd known I was alive, what was left of them would still have come after me, probably with the weight of SecureCorp behind them. If you'd come with me, you would have had to live that secret.

"You couldn't have had any contact with anyone else. You couldn't have even told anybody where you'd gone. They would have wondered what happened to you, and would have spent months, maybe years, searching."

She looked away, weighing my words. Her fists clenched. A tear swelled in her right eye, and trickled down her cheek.

"If we'd dared to have kids, they would have had to live alone too, on the run, with no friends, no social contact. You would have aged and died long before me, without ever really having lived."

She stared at the wall ahead of her.

I took a step toward her. "Without me you could at least have some kind of life — friends, family, children."

Her features softened. She looked away for almost a minute, then finally back at me, a new expression of understanding in her eyes.

"You must have been lonely," she said.

"I got along okay," I said. "I had the dogs to keep me company. They don't say much, but..."

She looked over at me and laughed. I laughed with her. For a few moments we were able to burn away the vision of a life that could have been, but was never given the chance.

I moved closer and took her hand. "I know it's been rough for you, believing I was dead, and I'll never forgive myself for lying to you. But at least you've had a life. You had a loving husband and two beautiful children. You had the company of other people. You had a cause worth fighting for. Look at all you've accomplished.

She squeezed my hand, and closed her eyes.

"Forgive me," I pleaded. "I never wanted to hurt you."

The scheduled meeting was held the next morning. Laura sat at the head of a long table, with Bailey, Connor, Richie, and a few of her senior officers. Annabelle and I sat at the far end, separated from the others, in more ways than one.

Laura introduced the two of us to the officers who'd never met us. Once the room was quiet, she spoke.

"Alex has offered to leave," she said, gesturing toward me and Annabelle. "For them both to return to the Dregs."

Annabelle glared at me. "Did you think to ask me what *I* wanted to do before you made that promise?"

I felt the warmth rushing to my face.

She turned to the others. "I never agreed to go *anywhere* with him."

I realized I'd made a promise that I might not be able to keep. I'd forgotten about Annabelle — and especially about how independent and headstrong she was.

"I'm not sure that would make any difference anyway," Richie put in. "Alex could hide in the Dregs when Vita Aeterna thought he was dead. Now that they know he's alive, and they know about Annabelle, they'll be coming for them both, whether they're here or not. And they might decide to go after us as part of the hunt."

The room was silent for a few seconds, as all digested his words.

Connor spoke up. "I'm told that the sentiment in the First Circle as a whole is moving in the direction of Vita Aeterna. It may just be a matter of time before they come up with a comprehensive plan to get rid of us once and for all."

I filled them in on my conversation with Pritchard about culling the herd.

"They've become more blind to problems in the Quarters than ever," Conner continued. "In their minds, the inhabitants of the Quarters are dead already. The provision of food packets has slowed to a trickle. There have been more crackdowns on electricity theft, and the siphoning off of fresh water. The area is deteriorating rapidly. It's become almost impossible to live there. Lately we've seen a major influx of people wanting to join the Rebel cause."

"I don't know about the rest of you," Laura said, "but I'm getting a little tired of hiding in the Dregs and cringing in fear over SecureCorp. Our numbers now match, possibly even exceed, theirs. Maybe it's time to step things up. We've been in this impasse for decades. If we don't do something to break out of it, it may never happen. And there's an important development that might work in our favour."

All turned to her expectantly.

"Alex," she said, nodding at me. "He's not only a hero for the Rebels, he's a hero in the Quarters. He may hold the key to the revolution in his hands."

She turned to me. "You're the kid who killed Charles Wickham single-handed. You're the kid who planted the bomb that destroyed the gas factory and derailed Vita Aeterna's final solution. You are a bona fide legend — a dead hero come to life. And the Quarters have come alive with the news that you've risen from the dead."

She turned to the others. "What if he was to go there, talk to them — convince them that they have the power to take back what the Elite have stolen."

She turned back to me. "Even the Elite are powerless against an idea whose time has come, and that idea may be you."

"You want to attack the Elite?" Annabelle's voice interrupted. I glanced over at her, and shook my head at her to be quiet. Her eyes were wide and her hands were shaking. "You people are crazy," she said, scanning around the table. "You can't possibly win. And you'll destroy any hope of joining them or enriching your lives."

I turned to her. "Have you ever actually heard of anybody from the Quarters joining the Elite?"

She stared back at me.

"What about from the Corp Ring?" I went on.

She said nothing.

Laura turned to Annabelle. "I know it's difficult for you to under-stand, but the world is not the way you've been led to believe. You've got a lot to learn. And I'm afraid you'll have to abandon any thought of returning to the life you once led. Your only hope is with us, for better or worse. Make no mistake — the Elite can be beaten. The only question is timing. Are we ready? I think we are."

We spent another hour talking about the prospect of my returning to the Quarters. Finally it was decided. Richie, Connor, and a small armed squad would go with me. Annabelle was silent, occasionally staring at her hands on the table and shaking her head in disbelief.

"The trickle of new recruits from the Quarters has grown to a stream with the deteriorating conditions and the news that you're alive," Laura said. "If they hear from you directly, that stream may become a deluge.

"And your appearance will be huge distraction for SecureCorp. They'll be desperate to shut you up. While the SecureCorp soldiers are siphoned off looking for you, we can deploy a large force to the First Circle."

"To do what?" I asked.

Laura glanced at Annabelle and smiled. "We're going to blow open the gate, and tear down the wall once and for all." Annabelle sat with her mouth open. Laura nodded at me. "Maybe Alex can be the catalyst that breaks the stalemate between us and SecureCorp. It has gone on long enough."

As the meeting broke up, Annabelle took off out the door without speaking. I caught up with her as she exited the building, headed for her room.

"You know you' re going to get yourselves killed for nothing," she said as I arrived.

"We' re doing what we have to," I answered. "Don' t sell the Rebels short. They' ve been at this for a long time."

We strolled in silence across an expansive square and into the barracks building, and she paused in front of her door.

"There' s something I' d like to show you," I said.

She made a face.

"It' s nothing to do with the Rebels or their 'mission' . It' ll be fun. I promise."

She shrugged. "Maybe it' ll relieve the boredom."

"I' ll come by in an hour."

# THIRTY-SEVEN

..................................................

# ALEX AND ANNABELLE

"Let me get this straight," Annabelle said an hour later, as we strolled through the streets of the Rebel compound toward Samantha's place. "You've had nothing but dogs for company for the past forty years?" She shook her head. "That explains a lot."

A delivery vehicle filled with vegetables rattled by on the other side of the road. A pair of off-duty fighters, still in uniform, crossed the street in front of us, laughing and joking.

"It was hard sometimes," I said, ignoring her dig. "But they've been fantastic companions, and they've saved my life numerous times."

"Animals are a waste of time and money," she said. "Hardly any-body in the Corp Ring had one, and people laughed at the ones who did."

I kept my mouth shut as we turned a corner. I wasn't sure why I even wanted Annabelle to meet the dogs, and it didn't look like it was going to end well.

We finally reached Samantha's place and I knocked on her door. She opened it and I introduced Annabelle. Samantha was a bit older, but I could imagine them getting along. Samantha led us to the open play area at the back. I entered it, and as usual the dogs were all over me, jumping up, barking, and licking my face.

Annabelle stepped back, repulsed by the spectacle, as the four of us wrestled on the ground, the dogs yapping and growling. She glanced over at Samantha, who smiled and put a hand on her shoulder, encouraging her to approach the dogs. Annabelle didn't move. After a few minutes, the dogs finally settled down. They soon noticed her, and to my surprise, stood, cocking their heads, and slowly approached her.

At first Annabelle was horrified. She stepped back again, an expression of something like fear sweeping over her face. For a second I thought she was going to bolt. The dogs continued moving closer. Little Rattle finally trotted right up to her, panting, tongue extended, tail wagging. Annabelle jumped as Rattle got up on her hind legs and placed both paws on her knees. I stood up, ready to intervene if necessary.

"Get down to their level," Samantha said, pushing a hand down.

Reluctantly, Annabelle crouched, and Rattle was all over her. Annabelle cringed and tried to pull away as Rattle stretched up and began licking her face.

She put out her hand to push the little Terrier down, not sure how to deal with her. I stepped toward them, ready to haul Rattle away, but stopped when, instead, Annabelle hesitantly began stroke the

*560*

little dog's head. Rattle moved in closer, her front paws still on Annabelle's knee, wagging her tail excitedly.

Gradually, something seemed to let go in Annabelle. A smile formed on her lips, and soon she was ruffing Rattle's fur and cuddling with her. She seemed to have forgotten Samantha and I were there. The other dogs moved in and began nudging and licking Annabelle just as they had me.

Now Annabelle was beaming as she petted, hugged, and played with all three dogs. I'd never seen them so instantly taken with a stranger. She sat down cross-legged on the ground and let them surround her.

The German Shepherd rubbed his snout against her cheek.

"Which one is this?" she asked, stroking his head.

"That's Shake," I answered, now beaming myself. "The little one is Rattle. The big black one is Roll."

She scrunched up her nose and looked up at me.

"It's from a song," I said.

For a time, Annabelle seemed to undergo a transformation. Her earlier coldness melted away, and a light entered her eyes that I'd never seen before. It was like a world she hadn't known existed had suddenly opened up in front of her.

Both Samantha and I came over, got to the ground, and joined in, laughing and wrestling with the creatures who for years had been my only family.

The afternoon was warm and sunny as we walked back from Samantha's place.

"See, that wasn't so bad, was it?" I said as we moved through the
bustling streets, passing the occasional soldier or worker.

"It was okay," Annabelle said, shrugging, reverting to her usual
detachment.

"You know," I said, "dogs are brilliant at reading body language.
They took to you right away. I think they know something that even
you're not aware of."

"And what's that?" she said without looking at me.

"That when you strip away all the Corp conditioning, underneath
you're a human being after all," I laughed, "whether you like it or
not."

As we walked, we talked again about the meeting earlier in the
day.

"You're not serious," Annabelle said. "Vita Aeterna won't stop
until they've captured us, so I can see the logic in trying to take them
out. But fighting the rest of the Elite? It's suicide. And for what? You
want to risk your life for all those low-lifes in the Quarters—"

I gave her a look.

"Well, mostly low-lifes," she corrected herself. "Or the other Outliers at the Institute. They're not our problem. Nothing will change if
you try to help them, except that you'll be dead."

"It's called being human," I snapped at her. "Whatever the Corp
indoctrination might have fed to you all these years, that's what humans do. They look out for each other."

"Well, good luck with that," she said, shaking her head. "Let me know how it works out. I'll be right here, relaxing, looking out for number one." She gestured around us with her head. "This place is a bit of a dump, but it'll do for now, until all this gets straightened out."

I studied her as she walked. "I don't think you've really to come to terms with the implications of your Appraisal."

We happened to pass a mother and baby sitting on a bench. The baby was suckling on its mother's breast.

I nodded toward them. "See that baby?"

Annabelle glanced over, but said nothing.

"Assuming it has an average Appraisal," I said, "on the day that baby dies of old age, your effective age will be..." I did the math in my head, "just over thirty-five."

She stopped and stared at me.

I locked eyes with her. "You're beginning to get the picture? When that baby's *grandchildren* die of old age, you'll be..." I thought again, "about forty-seven."

Her face fell, as the reality finally hit her.

"Having a long lifespan has some great advantages," I said. "But it also means you're going to have to say goodbye to a lot of people. Laura, I mean the General, is right — you can never go back to the life you once had. Your Appraisal has marked you forever.

"It will be impossible for you to have a long-term relationship with anybody here, or anywhere else. You'll age much more slowly than ordinary people, and they'll resent you for it. We've already seen signs of that resentment. You'll outlive anybody you become attached to — by a huge margin. Believe me — I've lived through it. I have the same problem."

I told her about how Laura and I had met, all that had happened between us, and all that had happened since my return.

She narrowed her eyes and studied me.

Finally her eyes opened wide. "I wondered what your game was," she sneered. "Now I see it." She put her hands on her hips. "It's all about our Appraisals. You've got some idea that we can be together — that I can be your 'life partner', and we can make mutant babies."

I blushed, aware that what she was saying was at least partly true.

She laughed, looked me up and down, and shuddered. "You're old enough to be my grandfather."

I hesitated. In fact, I'd gone over the calculations many times myself — ever since I first got the message on the encrypted phone. I knew she was right.

"It's true that I've been alive a lot longer than you," I finally answered, "but our effective ages aren't that far apart. From what I've been told, your Appraisal is four point five. Mine is five, so our ages will actually get closer in real terms as time goes on."

"How do you figure that?"

"My chronological age is fifty-six. But I've only aged two years every decade since I was sixteen. So I've actually only aged eight years — which makes me the equivalent of twenty-four. Your chronological age is eighteen. You were Appraised at sixteen, just like I was, two years ago. So you've actually aged two years divided by a LEF of four point five, which makes you—" I closed my eyes and calculated — about sixteen years, five months."

She scrunched up her nose. "So, I'm basically still just over sixteen?"

I shrugged. "Not in life experience, but in terms of how much your body has aged."

She shook her head in disbelief.

"Right now we're something like seven years apart," I said. "But because of the difference in our Appraisals, in a hundred years, my effective age will be forty-four, and yours will be —" I calculated in my head again — about thirty-nine. In two hundred years, I'll be sixty-four, and you'll be sixty. If we live long enough, your effective age will actually exceed mine..."

She stared at the ground silently for a few seconds.

"That's too creepy for words," she finally said. She looked up at me. "And you're assuming I'm even remotely attracted to you, or stupid enough to want to spend the next four centuries with you."

She started walking again, and shook her head. "Anyway, I was right. It's just like I said. All this talk about you rescuing me out of compassion is a lie. Big surprise."

I told her how I'd met Walter forty years ago. Her expression of horror grew as I described what the decades of Vita Aeterna experiments had done to his body.

"It's true that the thought has crossed my mind that we might be compatible," I said, "but whether you believe it or not, the reason I risked my life for you in the first place, the reason why you're here right now, is that I wanted to save you from being slowly dissected for the next four centuries by Vita Aeterna."

She stopped again and stood glaring at me. She still didn't believe me.

"You know," I said, "when your father worked out your Appraisal, he could have handed you over to Vita Aeterna. That would have been the *Corp* thing to do. *He* would have been fine — only *you* would have suffered. He might even have gotten some kind of reward. But that's not what he did — is it."

Her lower lip trembled, and she closed her eyes.

"I'm sorry," I said, putting a hand in hers. "There's one reason, and one reason alone, why your father hid your Appraisal from the authorities. He loved you. He wasn't thinking of money, or position, or power, or status. He was willing to throw all those things, including his own life, to the wind, just to ensure your safety. You were the most important thing in his world."

Her eyes were wet with tears.

"Our society has gotten way off track," I continued. "It's lost sight of what's important. Things have been like that since long before either of us were born. They've got to change. If some of us die trying to make that happen, so be it."

She quickly wiped her eyes with her sleeve, composed herself, and stuck out her chin, still defiant. She pulled her hand away.

"You can stay here, with the Rebels," I said. "I'd actually prefer that you did — that you were safe. Laura will make sure you don't come to any harm. When this is all over, it may still be possible for you to have some kind of satisfying life."

I looked into her eyes. "But you can never go back to the Corp Ring. Your world will never be the way it was."

# THIRTY-EIGHT

..................................................

# BREAKING THE STALEMATE

Laura sent an advance group to the Quarters to identify base locations where we could hide out while we were there. There had to be at least a dozen, since as soon as SecureCorp located one it would be worthless, and we'd have to move.

While we waited, we planned our strategy. We needed a way to get people motivated, to draw them into the rallies. The standard HUD, that everyone I'd ever met was issued, could only 'broadcast' to a half-dozen other people at a time, and only the Corps could 'post' information on any public platform. We considered putting up actual posters at strategic locations, but SecureCorp patrolled Tintown regularly, and would see them the same as anybody else.

In the end, it was decided that, a day or so before each rally, Richie and several others would make the rounds to his multitude of contacts in the Quarters. That network of friends and acquaintances could themselves fan out and spread the word about the gatherings throughout the city. We would also leave word in the few makeshift (and technically illegal) pubs and cafés in Tintown.

It wasn't much, but for now, it was all we had.

As she requested, Annabelle would stay at Rebel headquarters. There would be a faction who wouldn't like it, but there was really nowhere else for her to go. A part of me had hoped that she would join me in the fight, but I knew she would laugh at the idea.

The dislike I'd felt toward her had softened since we got back here. I'd had time to think about what she'd been through. I could see that deep down she was still a scared little girl who was trying to make sense of the loss of both her parents, and of a world that had been blown apart. Still, I wondered if she would ever be able to move beyond her Corp indoctrination.

Once the infrastructure was in place, I, Richie, Connor, and an armed group of soldiers/bodyguards headed for the Quarters. We decided to start with Tintown. Richie and I both grew up there, and were still known: me for the death of Charles Wickham, Richie, because he still went there regularly, trying to help keep the place afloat, and representing the Rebel cause.

We arrived in the late afternoon, and located our first choice for a base — a low-rise apartment building with a commanding view in every direction. We spent the rest of the day getting settled in. For the first rally, we chose a large square safely distant from our hiding place.

Two days after our arrival, Richie and a few others made the rounds, getting the word out about a rally early that afternoon. As the time approached, we set up a half-dozen boxes for me to stand on. The idea of speaking to a crowd of people was terrifying.

"You realize I've spent most of the past forty years talking to my dogs," I said to Richie. "I've never spoken more than one or two individuals at a time, let alone a large audience."

"You'll get used to it," he said, smiling and patting me on the back.

I jotted down a few notes and said a silent prayer.

It was ten minutes after the scheduled time before a few people finally showed up. At first, they poked their heads around the corner of a nearby building, wary that the invitation might be some kind of SecureCorp sting. Richie reassured them and they began to gather in the square. The turnout was pathetically small, but it was a start.

I climbed up on the boxes holding my written speech in my hand. Even the tiny audience below me was too much. I felt lightheaded, and I started to sway. Richie jumped forward and steadied me. I took a few deep breaths and steeled myself.

Over the next two weeks we held a series of rallies. At first the spaces in front of me were almost empty, but crowds began to build as the news spread that I was the one speaking. A lot showed up just to see firsthand a ghost from the past that had come back to life. My first speech was hopeless, but with practice I began to improve. At the most recent one, I was shocked to find that the crowd was silent, hanging on every word.

They were pop-up rallies, all held in different locations, and set up away from the cameras, so it took a while for SecureCorp to get word.

As soon as they showed up, everybody would disappear into the shadows, and we'd repeat the exercise, at another location, on another day.

It didn't take long for SecureCorp to locate our bases, but so far we'd been able to avoid being captured. We'd simply move to the next in the list. Our audiences had spent a lifetime avoiding the authorities. A few were permanently scared off after SecureCorp appeared, but many came back.

We had two goals: first, to rally people to the Rebel cause, and reach that critical mass that would break the stalemate between the Rebels and the Elite, second, to draw resources away from the First Circle, and make way for the Rebel invasion that we all prayed would happen soon.

As a result of my appearances, membership in the Rebel movement began to soar, and the Rebels' intelligence network confirmed that a growing number of SecureCorp resources were being siphoned off to deal with us, but it wasn't enough. We'd need a much larger diversion if the Rebels were to have any hope of breaking into the First Circle.

Two weeks after we began our rallies, Richie suddenly declared that we had to return to Rebel headquarters immediately. He wouldn't say why.

# THIRTY-NINE

........................................................

# DESTINY

All the way back Richie looked especially pleased with himself. I decided not to press him on the reason, but from the way he was acting, it must be big.

We reached Rebel headquarters, and immediately arranged for meeting with Laura, Bailey, and the senior staff. We were all gathered around a big wooden table in one of the meeting rooms, when Richie made his 'entrance'.

"Well?" I asked as he sat down.

He smiled, and scanned around the table. "I thought I should wait until we were all together. I didn't want to announce it until I was sure, but I got confirmation this morning."

"Confirmation?" I said.

Richie leaned forward in his chair, smiling at Laura and Bailey. "We've found a way to hack the broadcast network for the HUDs."

I widened my eyes. "What?"

Richie's smile broadened, and he turned to me. "We've come up with a workaround that removes the restriction on the number of targets for a HUD broadcast. We could plan a rally and announce news of it over the HUDs of every person in the city."

Everyone in the room sat up straight at once.

"We can also confine the broadcast to a specific area," Richie continued, turning back to Laura and Bailey. "Politically speaking, broadcasting to everybody would demonstrate that we have complete control over communications. But practically speaking, confining the message to Tintown might be better. We could draw in a big crowd before the Elite and SecureCorp were even aware it was happening."

I opened my mouth to speak. "And, yes," he said, anticipating my next question, "we can only do it once. As soon as the TechCorp find out, you can bet they'll plug the loophole. So when we use it, we better make it count."

Laura and Bailey had another pressing meeting. We agreed to get together the next morning to work out a detailed plan.

I thought about the consequences of Richie's newest hack. When our message went live, TechCorp would be scrambling to jam the communications and prevent us from sending any new ones. SecureCorp would be scouring the city for the perpetrators.

If we used the hack to announce our rally, they wouldn't have to look very hard — our location would be broadcast in the message.

That night I went to see Annabelle. She was staying in the same room she'd occupied before. Given our volatile relationship, I was surprised at the thrill I felt at the prospect of seeing her again.

It was true that during our escape she'd been an ungrateful, annoying pain, and there had been numerous moments when I wondered why I was bothering. But she was obviously intelligent and resourceful, and had been able to adapt to her incredibly altered circumstances quickly.

She'd freed me from Pritchard's dungeon, saving me from a few centuries of torture. I thought of her at Samantha's, laughing and playing with the dogs — she was capable of love and empathy. Maybe she'd just never been given the chance to express those feelings before.

Her original contempt for me seemed to have elevated to grudging respect, and maybe even friendship, but so far, no more than that. She still didn't believe that I'd come to her rescue out of compassion. She assumed my only motive was a selfish one, the Corp way, to have her as a life companion.

At one level, she was right. She was the only woman I'd ever met who could share my long life to its natural end. In a sense we were like the last two living people on earth. In terms of our lifespans, we were the only two compatible with each other. But I also knew that it was more than that — images surfaced in my mind of her stunning beauty as she descended the staircase at Pritchard's mansion, of her expression of childlike sorrow as I told her about her father's death, and of her face beaming with joy as she rolled on the ground with little Rattle.

I didn't expect my newfound attraction to be reciprocated. Again, I envisioned the centuries of loneliness I seemed destined to endure. I wondered whether I might have been better off staying in my hideout with the dogs after all.

I reached her door and knocked, my stomach inexplicably twisting and churning. The door opened, and there she was. She pulled in a breath at the sight of me, and for a second a light seemed to ignite behind her eyes. Almost immediately, she regained her self-control.

"You made it back alive," she said, casually. "I'm surprised, I must say."

We went for a walk. I led her up to the rooftop garden patio I'd visited before, and we sat on a wooden bench surrounded by greenery. I updated her on what had happened in the Quarters.

"How have you been?" I asked when I'd finished.

She shrugged. "I haven't been out of my room much. I still get nasty looks from some of the people around here. There's not much incentive to 'mingle'. Sergeant Forbes showed me where there's a makeshift library, with books and movies…"

Even if by some miracle we succeeded against the Elite, I wondered whether 'freaks' like Annabelle and me would ever really be accepted in this world.

I explained what we were planning. An expression of genuine fear swept over her face as she straightened up and stared at me. "So this is it?"

I said nothing — I just looked into her eyes.

"This is crazy," she said, her voice shaking. "You people haven't got a hope. Don't be stupid. Go back to the Dregs — go deeper, where they won't find you."

"And what about you? What about all the other Outliers being held at the Institute?"

Again she composed herself. "I can take care of myself. As annoying as you are, it's not going to help me if you're dead. As for the others? I told you — they're not our problem — everybody knows you've got to look out for number one in this world.

"Anyway, maybe Vita Aeterna will find what they're looking for. Then they won't care about the Outliers anymore, and they'll let them all go."

I shook my head. "I don't think they're ever going to find what they're looking for. I don't know why. It's like I heard one of the scientists say when I first escaped forty years ago. It's as if an insurmountable barrier has been placed in our way, a barrier that we can't cross — as if God has drawn a line in the sand and said 'this far and no further'."

She turned away from me and stared at a building across the street. "Well, go then. If you're stupid enough to throw away your life for nothing, good riddance. Thanks for helping me get out."

I couldn't see her face, but again her voice was trembling. I took her hand, and she turned back to me.

I leaned forward and kissed her on the lips. She didn't resist. Time seemed to stop as we lingered, lost in each other. Finally, she pulled back and shoved me away.

She stood up, suddenly angry. "Get lost, then," she snapped. "Go off and be a dead hero."

The next morning, I met again with Bailey, Connor, and Richie, and we discussed our options. Since we only had one shot, we considered holding a 'virtual' rally, where my speech would simply go out on people's HUDs, with no 'live' gathering. That scenario had the advantage that we could broadcast to the entire city and SecureCorp couldn't show up to stop it. No one viewing it could be punished, since they had no control over what was being broadcast.

In the end, we decided that a face-to-face gathering was essential. I still found it hard to accept my legendary status in the Quarters, but all agreed that it was my physical presence at the rallies that was behind the recent surge in Rebel recruits.

Also, once SecureCorp knew the time and location of what we expected to be a massive rally, they'd be forced to mobilize a substantial portion of their resources to try to stop it. Those resources would be drawn away from protecting the First Circle. It would be the ideal moment for a Rebel attack.

We decided to spend one more week in Tintown, building the attendance at the meetings the way we had been all along. That would give the Rebels time to plan their attack. When they were ready, and *we* were ready, we would use the hack to call together a crowd that even the Elite couldn't ignore.

But we couldn't wait too long. The hack used a particular flaw in the HUD programming. Eventually TechCorp would find it themselves and our golden opportunity would be gone.

That afternoon we were ready to go. There was a good chance I wouldn't come back from this mission, so I arranged to meet with Laura one last time. Breaking with protocol, we left her office and strolled the grounds outside. A pair of bodyguards, one forward, one back, joined us at a respectful distance.

We walked for a few minutes without speaking, then sat on the steps of one of the administration buildings, like a pair of teenagers. The guards took up positions nearby. Laura took my hand. Suddenly it was like all the years had melted away, and I was a kid again, saying goodbye to my new-found love.

She reached into a pocket of her coat and produced a small brass medallion hanging on a string. It was the same one she'd given me forty years ago, as I was leaving for my first military attack on SecureCorp, with her father.

I stared at it, my eyes wide. "You kept it — all these years?"

Hers were wet with tears. "It was a memento — all I had left of you. All those years ago, I gave it to you as a good luck charm." She held it up. "Take it again — with my blessing."

I bowed my head, and she reached up and hung the charm around my neck. Now I felt my own tears beginning.

Laura placed a hand on my cheek. "Good luck," she said, her voice uncharacteristically gentle, for a moment once again the beautiful young girl I'd known so long ago. "Keep safe."

"You too," I said. I leaned forward, kissed her, and held her close. Finally I let go and sat back.

"You and Annabelle," she said, her eyes closing momentarily. "You care for each other?"

I felt my body stiffen. "I do. I'm not sure whether she feels the same way — I hope so. I'm sorry."

Laura straightened up and opened her eyes. She smiled at me. "Don't be. I'm happy for you. And I think she feels the same way, even if she hasn't figured it out yet."

She reached out again and took my hand. "After all those years alone, you deserve to find some love and happiness." Suddenly she swayed sideways and looked unsteady.

"Are you okay?" I asked. I grabbed her elbow. The guards took a step toward us.

"I'm fine," she smiled. "Just tired — just old."

I realized at that moment that, despite all the years that had passed, and despite all that had happened, I still loved her. I wanted to reach out again and hold her, to tell her how I felt, but I knew it would be a mistake. Life had unfolded in its current incarnation. There was nothing we could do to change it, and there was no going back. I knew that, despite all her troubles and disappointments, Laura had forgiven me, and was happy.

An hour later, I climbed into a Rebel stealth vehicle where Richie and several others were waiting, and we headed back to the Quarters to meet our fate.

# FORTY

...............................................

# THE CATALYST

Our week of rallies passed. Interest in the movement continued to grow, but at about the same pace as before — not enough to tip the balance. Finally the day for the broadcast arrived. I'd been gaining confidence in speaking, and news of the gatherings had spread not only around Tintown, but throughout the Quarters. Fascinated by my 'resurrection', people were even streaming in from other Quarters just to see me.

We picked out a massive square for what we hoped would be a mega-rally in response to the planned HUD broadcast. Since SecureCorp were pretty much guaranteed to show up, we chose a site with lots of escape routes, and requested a dozen or so Rebel fighters for support. We also picked a location distant enough from the Corp Ring that SecureCorp would have to travel a long way to reach it.

We weren't sure what would happen when Richie enabled the hack and we broadcast our message. In theory, it would reach tens of thousands, possibly even hundreds of thousands, in the Quarters. But would those people respond? We also weren't sure what level of response there would be from SecureCorp. Back at Rebel headquarters, we'd arranged for a second wave of fighters as back up, in case the attendance turned out to be massive, or SecureCorp decided to mount a major attack to squash us.

In preparation for our diversion, Bailey and the main Rebel army had spread out across the edges of the Corp Ring, surrounding the great gate. They were currently scattered in order to stay hidden, but were ready to converge on the gate at our signal.

Meanwhile, the Rebels had deployed yet another contingent to intercept and stall any SecureCorp onslaught on us. By the time the attackers were able to fight their way through that barrier, the rally should already be well underway.

We set up our makeshift stage in the square, and all was finally in place. Mid-afternoon, at the scheduled time, we gathered in the back room of an abandoned building near our meeting place. Richie sat at a table with a tablet in front of him, ready to set the hack in motion. His team had put weeks of work into the hack, but it could be triggered with a single key stroke.

He lifted a finger above the keyboard and turned to look up at me. I smiled and nodded. He turned back to the machine and pressed one key. We all stood frozen, sensing that we were about to witness a momentous event. Seconds later our message, a video of me extending an invitation to the rally, appeared in my own HUD. I stood mesmerized, aware that the same message was appearing on the HUDs of every person in the Quarters. Part of me was worried that no one would show up. Another part was worried that too many would show up, and that when they did, I wouldn't know what to say.

We'd allotted a half hour for the locals to begin arriving. But only minutes had passed before people began to appear. As always, they first poked their heads out, wary of a SecureCorp trap, but as the numbers built, their confidence built also. They began to gather in the square, first at a trickle, then a flood, then a tsunami.

In half an hour the expansive square was packed to bursting, and people were still pouring in. Many found empty spaces in the surrounding abandoned skyscrapers, and hung out the windows. There was an electricity in the air as the crowd continually rearranged itself, like a living organism, people talking excitedly and pushing toward the makeshift stage.

To avoid spooking them, the additional fighters we'd brought would remain out of sight until required. Richie contacted headquarters to request the backup fighters — there was no longer any doubt we would need them. We waited, keeping an eye out for the inevitable SecureCorp attack.

At the appointed time, Richie climbed up on the boxes and spoke first, introducing me. At the previous rallies, I'd simply shouted from the top of a pile of boxes. For this one, we'd rigged up a microphone and portable amplifier. I looked down at my hands, and saw they were shaking.

I suddenly felt the overwhelming urge to sneak away, to fly back to the Dregs, to the simple life with my dogs. I'd actually taken a step when Richie said my name, and there was a tumultuous cheer from the crowd. Richie gestured for me to come up and speak. For a few seconds I was unable to move, as if I was glued to the spot. The tens of thousands were still applauding.

Again I felt the sense of vertigo, as I scanned the multitude that jammed the square. I closed my eyes momentarily, and willed myself to relax. I opened them again. Richie was smiling at me. Reluctantly, as if my feet were made of lead, I mounted the makeshift stage, to a new torrent of cheers. I swallowed hard, and waited a few seconds for the noise to die down.

"Take a look around you," I called out to the teeming crowd, nervous at first. I tensed as my amplified voice echoed around the square. "How many people are attending this meeting? Ten thousand? Twenty thousand? Fifty thousand?

The shaking in my hands began to subside. "Over the next few days, keep an eye on your HUDs and your HoloTVs. You won't find any record of this event. As far as anybody who wasn't here today will ever know, this meeting never happened."

An angry murmur swept over the crowd. It grew in intensity as those present guessed the truth of my words.

I continued, hearing the growing confidence in my own voice. "You're all here because you've lost faith in the so-called government, and their Elite masters. You've learned that their message of greed and ruthless self-interest is a lie — that the key to prosperity is for us all to work together.

"The Elite have built an image of themselves as all-powerful — but I guarantee you that they're terrified of us — of what's happening right here, right now. They've probably already dispatched a SecureCorp force to stop us. Be warned — they will be here very shortly and all of our lives will be in danger. If anyone is concerned about that, they should leave."

No one in the crowd moved. They were silent, hanging on my every word.

I paused, composing myself. "I'd guess that most of you have never set foot in the First Circle," I finally said.

There were chuckles and outright laughter from the crowd, as if the very concept was ridiculous and impossible.

"But maybe a few of you have spent some time, however short, in the Corp Ring. Maybe you were awestruck by the buildings, the parks, the lights, and the gardens.

"Well, I have been in the First Circle," I said, my voice rising, to another gasp from the crowd. "And I can tell you that the riches in that place are as far above the Corp Ring as the Corp Ring is above us."

There was renewed mumbling.

"The Elite are wealthy beyond your wildest imaginations," I continued. "As we all know too well, they've surrounded themselves with a massive wall. That means that the First Circle can only contain a finite number of people."

The grumbling in the crowd swelled again.

"Your HUDs are always telling you that if you work hard enough, you can become one of them. But if there's a limit to the number the First Circle can contain, for you to join, someone already there would have to agree to leave. What do you think the chances are of that happening?"

People in the crowd looked at each other, processing what they'd just heard. At first there was nervous laughter. Then shouts began to rise from the crowd: 'They're liars'! 'They're cheaters'!

"They've had their way for long enough," I called out, my voice echoing from the disintegrating office towers. "Their power is now hanging by a thread, propped up by SecureCorp and the other Corps. It's time for us to take back the world that belongs to us. It's time to take back what is ours!"

Shouts of support echoed throughout the square and the surrounding skyscrapers, and a profusion of fists were pumped into the air.

A faint hum filled the sky over the buildings ahead of me. The crowd went silent as all recognized the sound. Seconds later, a swarm of drones appeared above the roof of a nearby building and hovered over people's heads. The original Rebel force we'd brought emerged from their hiding place and stood ready to fight.

There were panicked shouts within the square and the crowd split apart as a red laser spot tracked along the pavement, headed in my direction. I traced the beam back to one of the drones. Just as the dot reached my feet, one of the Rebel fighters raised his rifle and shot the drone out of the sky.

Another dot appeared, then another.

"Take cover!" I yelled at the crowd.

People rushed into the adjoining buildings and alleys as a dozen drones opened fire.

A mass of SecureCorp soldiers, still harried by the Rebel fighters sent to slow them, appeared around the square, and began firing on the crowd. I jumped down from my pedestal and retreated to the sheltered doorway of a nearby building. I called Bailey, and told him what was happening.

"Our main army is within sight of the gate," he answered. "Whatever's happening over there is doing the trick. There's only a skeleton force in place here. We're going to attack within a few minutes."

Back outside, I picked up a gun dropped by a fallen soldier and found Richie, taking cover behind a nearby dumpster. "What about the backup?" I asked.

"On its way," he answered.

Out in the street, a life and death battle was now raging. A large force of SecureCorp soldiers filled the square, engaged in a firefight with the Rebels. Fired up by my speech, many of the 'civilians' from the crowd had scooped up weapons from downed fighters, and joined in, attacking SecureCorp from behind.

I circulated word that reinforcements were on the way, and that the Rebels were about to attack the wall. The battle raged on. More waves of SecureCorp soldiers were coming all the time, and I could now hear the thumping of chopper blades in the distance.

Minutes later there was a commotion and a break in the SecureCorp ranks as our backup finally arrived. A half dozen vehicles slammed through the SecureCorp lines, and took up positions behind the corners of nearby buildings. Rebel fighters streamed from them and immediately entered the firefight.

I heard a sound to my right, and turned to find a SecureCorp soldier no more than ten meters away. Before I could react, he'd already raised his weapon and directed it at me. He fired, and a dart embedded itself in my shoulder. I pulled it out, but immediately felt queasy and light-headed. Another soldier appeared beside him and they rushed toward me. They'd gone about half the distance when there was a shot somewhere behind me, and one of them went down.

Then everything went black.

# FORTY-ONE

..................................................

# THE FIRST CIRCLE

I awoke and opened my eyes. I was lying on the ground, staring up at a concrete ceiling. I was indoors, but the gunfire and explosions of the battle continued outside. I lifted my head and a knife of pain shot through it. I grimaced and groaned loudly. Seconds later, a face appeared above mine. I pulled in a breath — it was impossible.

"You," I croaked.

"It's lucky you're such a runt," Annabelle said, smiling, "or I could never have dragged you back here."

"Where?" I said.

"We're just inside the building behind where you were standing."

She helped me sit up, with my back against the wall. My head was still pounding.

"You've been out for a few minutes," she said. "I don't think you got a full dose. It should wear off pretty quickly. It better. We've got to get out of here."

"But what are you doing here—" I started to say.

"It was either come here or die of boredom at headquarters," she said with a sneer. "I talked to the General. It took a lot to convince her, but she finally arranged for me to hitch a ride with the backup fighters."

Annabelle sat beside me, relaxed, as if she was on a holiday. For a few seconds I was speechless. I was ecstatic that she'd chosen to join us, but now I worried for her safety. The odds that I'd found someone to spend my spectacularly long life with had ticked up slightly, but there was a good chance that we'd both be dead within the hour.

"*You* took out the SecureCorp guys?" I finally asked, incredulous.

"I guess my time on the firing range paid off," she answered, smiling. "My dad must have known what was coming..." she closed her eyes for a second.

"Thank you."

"Don't get any ideas. You got me out of the First Circle. I owed you, that's all."

I struggled to my feet, and we edged up to the doorway. The number of the crowd joining in the fighting had exploded. Still, the better equipped and better trained SecureCorp soldiers were pushing forward, driving them all back. We rushed outside, and once again threw ourselves into the battle. I exhaled when I saw Richie crouched behind another dumpster, still unhurt.

The square was choked with smoke, and echoed with screams, shouts, gunfire, and explosions. Drones still dive-bombed from overhead, occasionally downed by a Rebel bullet. The SecureCorp army pushed forward in a single line, and the choppers had arrived, machine guns slung beneath their undercarriages. The defenders weren't going to last much longer. If nothing changed, we would soon have to turn and run for our lives.

Suddenly, it was as if a switch had been thrown. One of the SecureCorp leaders gestured to his troops, and inexplicably, as one, they began an ordered retreat, a rearguard holding off the now advancing Rebels.

Within minutes the area was left to the defenders. Most of the drones lay smashed on the ground. The ones still in the air took off to the southwest, followed close behind by the choppers. The crowd in the square raised their fists and cheered, believing they'd driven the attackers off.

But I guessed the real reason. The soldiers were being called back as reinforcements. The Rebel attack on the First Circle had begun.

We surveyed the damage. The bodies of SecureCorp soldiers, Rebels, and civilians, littered the ground, along with the broken drones and discarded weapons. Many of the locals remained in the square, still fired up, but unsure what to do next. With Annabelle's help, and still fighting the headache of the century, I climbed up on the dumpster we'd been using for cover, and addressed what was left of the crowd.

"At this exact moment," I called out, "a massive Rebel force is gathered outside the gates of the First Circle."

There was a gasp from the crowd.

"We're going to tear down the wall," I raised my fist in the air. "Forever."

For a few seconds, they were silent, still trying to grasp my words. Finally there was another tumultuous cheer, and again fists were pumped into the air.

"We're on our way to join them," I continued. "You can help by doing anything you can to disrupt SecureCorp here in the Quarters. Every SecureCorp soldier occupied here is one less available to defend the wall."

They cheered again. We helped them organize, setting up one group to look after the wounded, and another to collect weapons from the battleground. We divided the available, and now armed, civilians into squads that would move throughout Tintown, engaging SecureCorp wherever possible. We'd hidden several getaway vehicles a few blocks away.

We left a few Rebel fighters to continue organizing, and I, Annabelle, Richie, and some of the remaining uninjured fighters piled into the vehicles and headed for the First Circle.

FORTY-TWO

..............................................

# THE GREAT GATE

We kept our guns at the ready as we hurtled through the streets toward Bailey's army. Sighting through the cross alleys of the Corp Ring, we saw glimpses of the SecureCorp force that had abandoned the fight in the Quarters and was now rushing to reinforce the army guarding the gate. We were in no position to challenge them, so we continued on. We would fight when we met up with the Rebel army. Once or twice we came across groups of SecureCorp stragglers, and these we engaged, until they either fell or ran away.

By the time we arrived, the light was beginning to fade. The air was filled with a choking black haze, and gunfire and explosions echoed through the streets. We parked a block away, exited the vehicles and made for the open square in front of the monstrous gate. We arrived, and I stood in awe at the sight — a massive Rebel army, stretching far into the distance, swelled the square around the gate. Some were well-equipped, with the latest weapons, even in uniform. Many were just civilians, some with guns, some with no more than an ax or a club.

Right now, the great white expanse of the gate was still intact. All around was chaos. Soldiers in place at the tops of the towers guarding either side, were firing down on the army that converged on them from all directions.

The wall, designed to protect the First Circle from the rabble outside, had now become a huge liability. Opening the main gate would allow the massive Rebel army inside. But keeping it shut forced the defenders to squeeze through the tiny door next to it, where most were picked off before they could fire a shot. Their only hope was the reinforcements on their way from the Quarters and the Corp Ring.

We plunged into the fight. We'd gotten word that the plan was for Bailey to lead a small group that would attempt to plant an explosive and blow a hole in the gate. Connor was leading the main contingent to keep SecureCorp occupied and protect Bailey's group.

Bailey's team pushed for the gate, carrying something large. Several were downed by a sniper in the right tower, until a Rebel shot finally took him out. A group of SecureCorp soldiers newly arrived from the Quarters began fighting their way toward Bailey.

Richie, Annabelle and I rushed to intercept them. Annabelle wasn't safe with us, but there was nowhere nearby that was any safer. At least if she was close, I could look out for her. We reached the SecureCorp squad and helped drive them back.

Bailey's group formed a boiling knot of activity in front of the gate as they set the explosive. We joined a larger Rebel force that had formed a ring of defense around them. A few minutes later Bailey shouted "Run!" and we all took off. We dove to the pavement as a massive explosion rocked the square, raining down dust, ash and debris. When the smoke and ash began to settle, we staggered to our feet, dusted ourselves off, and rushed to storm the gate.

The air around us cleared, and for a second I froze. The monstrous rampart, the ultimate symbol of Elite power and control, had been replaced by a ragged, gaping, smoking hole. Huge chunks had been blown out of the bases of the towers straddling it. They were now swaying, the few remaining guards at the top frantically running back and forth. Chunks of concrete began to rain down from the tower on the right, and we pulled back to avoid being crushed. It finally collapsed and slammed into the ground, burying the guards and numerous SecureCorp soldiers under gigantic piles of rubble. The left tower stayed intact, but teetered on the brink.

The SecureCorp force from the Quarters were now arriving en masse, and swarmed around the smoke-filled opening, joining the tiny group who'd been desperately trying to fend off an overwhelming crush of Rebel fighters. Again it was like déjà vu, a replay of events that had taken place so long ago when I was a kid.

But even the combined SecureCorp force was no match for the Rebel onslaught. The defenders eventually fell back in disarray, and the Rebels streamed through the sacred bastion of the First Circle. I turned to check on Annabelle — she was frozen, with her hands at her sides and her mouth open, staring at the shattered gate. For her, the unspeakable had come to pass. I took her arm and dragged her forward.

There was a lull in the fighting as the SecureCorp soldiers retreated and dispersed around a group of spectacular buildings in the distance, and the Rebels consolidated their position inside the First Circle.

I spotted Bailey in the advancing mass of Rebel fighters, and I and the others rushed to catch up.

I had an idea.

When I arrived, Bailey had stopped and was consulting with one of his senior officers. The woman nodded and rushed away, and Bailey turned to me.

"It's finally happening," he said, beaming. "This time nothing's going to stop us."

I clapped him on the shoulder and smiled. I knew how much this victory meant to him.

"I've got a request," I said.

His brow furrowed as he stared down at me.

I told him about my encounter with Gene while I was being held at Pritchard's mansion, and about the group of other Outliers still being held at the Institute for Life Studies.

"I want to rescue them," I said, "but I can't do it alone. Can you spare some fighters to help me?"

"We've got more important things to think about," Bailey said, dismissing the idea with a wave of his hand. "Maybe when this is all over."

"They might be dead by then," I said. "Every hour that those people are at the Institute is another hour being taken apart by Vita Aeterna. We've got to go now. We'll never get another chance like this."

He gave me a look that said 'I don't have time for this'.

"It will be a huge blow to Vita Aeterna's morale," I argued. "And it'll siphon off some of the SecureCorp soldiers from your main attack."

He sighed, finally saying: "You and Connor have a greater vested interest than the rest of us. And after all, you provided the diversion that allowed us to get in here. Take whatever other Dead Shift are willing to go. I'll round up a team of fighters to help you."

He motioned for Richie to join him, then rushed off to confer with the others.

"Are you still on about that?" Annabelle said. "Those people are not our problem."

I narrowed my eyes and stared at her. "We're human beings — *everybody* is our problem. Anyway, they're part of only a tiny fraction of humanity with lifespans that match ours. They're like our brothers and sisters. We have a duty to help them."

About ten minutes later, Bailey returned with about twenty fighters, including a half-dozen Dead Shift.

"They're all yours," he said. "It's not much, but it's all I can spare. I need Connor here, with the main force. If you're desperate for more, contact me — I'll do whatever I can."

Bailey turned and gestured to one of the fighters behind him, and the man approached us.

"There's somebody you should meet," Bailey said.

A big, good-looking kid arrived and stood beside him.

"This is Ryan," Bailey said, nodding at the kid.

My eyes went wide. "Ryan — Laura's — I mean the General's, son?"

I'd never met his father, but I'd seen pictures. Ryan was like a mirror image. We shook hands. Like many of the others, at first he stared at me as if I wasn't real. His eyes drifted over to Annabelle, and he stared again, for even longer.

"Good to meet you," he said, finally tearing his gaze away from Annabelle, "I've heard a lot about you."

"Ryan's volunteered to be part of your group," Bailey said.

"What?" I said. I released his hand and looked up at him. "No way," I shook my head. "It's too dangerous."

"Hey, take a look, *Grandpa*," Ryan said, even though we looked almost the same age. He squared his shoulders and showed off his army uniform. "I'm a soldier. Dangerous things are what I do."

"Your mother," I said. He scowled at me. "The General," I corrected myself, "would have to okay it. I don't think she will."

"I don't need her permission to do anything," he said.

I laughed. "She's your commanding officer. Since you're so big on being a soldier, you should know how to follow orders."

"These *are* my orders," Ryan said. "I'm already here. How will going with you be any riskier than going with Commander Bailey?"

I stared at him, and realized he was right. In fact, he was probably safer with my group than with Bailey, though both choices were incredibly dangerous. What was really bothering me was that I didn't want the responsibility. If anything happened to Ryan on my watch, how could I possibly face Laura?

In the end, I relented, but I would keep him close, and try to keep him from getting killed. Now I'd have to watch out for both Annabelle and Ryan.

Bailey brought two additional fighters forward to meet us. "This is Terry," he said, presenting the first, a slight, red-headed young man. "He spent a lot of time as a servant for a bigwig in the First Circle. He knows the place inside out. He can help you get where you're going."

He turned to the second fighter, a dark-skinned young man with piercing eyes. "This is Milo," Bailey said. "We're going to need Richie's expertise in the main force. Milo is another tech-expert. Richie claims he's got hacking abilities approaching his own."

I shook hands with Milo. *I hope he's right,* I thought. *We'll need all the help we can get.*

I gathered them together, along with the leaders of the squad I'd been given, and we came up with a plan. Our little group stuck together as we marched with the rest of the Rebels into the First Circle.

The streets were largely empty of both vehicles and people. Every fighter was wide-eyed, gaping in disbelief at the fantastic opulence surrounding us. The SecureCorp force from the gate continued sporadic attacks, but hadn't yet gathered the numbers to stop us. The battles intensified, as more SecureCorp troops arrived on the scene from the Quarters.

Luckily, our group didn't have far to go. We'd traveled about a kilometer when we reached the point that Terry and I had determined would be closest to the Institute. We waited for a lull in the fighting. Darkness was beginning to fall as we broke away from the main force and headed out to search for the other Outliers.

After decades wrapped in my cocoon, I'd finally broken free, and dared to pull off the impossible — rescuing an Outlier from the heart of the First Circle, saving her from a fate that none understood better than me.

Now, it was time to repeat that miracle for the others.

# FORTY-THREE

..................................................

# THE INSTITUTE

Our group slipped away and hid in the shadows, as the remainder of Bailey's huge army moved off. About ten minutes later, we ventured out ourselves. We could hear the SecureCorp choppers buzzing overhead and the sirens bleating in the distance, heading for the main Rebel force. I said a silent prayer that Bailey and the others would be able to complete their mission.

We moved through one of the few areas that was in shadow, but we were out in the open, in full view of anybody who happened by. There were too many of us to Cam-surf. Luckily, the distance between cameras in the First Circle made it easy for even our large group to pass unnoticed. And I guessed that the people who would normally be paying attention to the feed from those cameras now had more important things to worry about.

Terry led us to the southwest, toward our destination, the Institute. The Rebels' tech people had hacked the security for several buildings along the way, providing us with potential hiding places, and we tailored our route to pass by them. That way we'd have somewhere to duck into if things went off the rails. I glanced over at Annabelle. She craned her neck as she scanned the magnificent architecture, still stunned that we'd succeeded in penetrating the forbidden depths of the First Circle.

We'd been traveling for ten minutes when we heard talking to our left. We were again completely exposed, with nowhere to run. We drew our weapons, ready for a fight, as two SecureCorp soldiers rounded the corner, deep in conversation. For a second I thought they would walk by without noticing us, but finally one of them looked up. One of our guys fired and he went down. The other soldier managed to dive behind a building. Within seconds there were sirens heading in our direction. He'd called for backup.

We rushed for the nearest corner. According to Terry, one of our hiding prospects was only a few blocks away. Most of us had safely taken cover when one of our rearguard fighters was hit. Ryan and I held off the remaining SecureCorp soldier while several others dragged our guy out of sight. We finally took out the attacker, but the sirens were approaching fast.

A couple of our people checked the wounded man. He was dead. He'd been one of the Rebels' best fighters. I'd never even gotten to know him.

"We've got to leave him," Terry said.

I hesitated.

"Let's go," he said. We took off. There was nothing more we could do for the man.

The sirens were getting dangerously close, and now we heard the buzz of a chopper approaching. Soon there would be swarms of drones hovering around our heads. Luckily, Terry knew the area well. Within minutes we'd made it to our target hiding place, a nondescript warehouse conveniently draped in shadow. We all hovered around nervously while Milo set up the hack. He finally held his HUD controller up to the security panel for the door. There was a collective sigh as the light turned green and it clicked open.

We could hear the approaching hum of the drones, and the sirens were about to round the nearest corner as we piled into our hiding spot and slammed the door behind us. We stood like statues listening as the scream of the sirens approached, passed by, and continued on.

"Now what?" Ryan whispered.

"They don't know where we are," I answered, "but they know we're here. They're not going to stop until they find us."

There were several gut-wrenching seconds of silence as everybody digested our situation. We waited as the wail of the sirens faded into the distance, then gingerly opened the door and checked for any sign of activity. The street was clear. The sirens turned and looped to the west, away from our position.

We closed the door and waited for another few minutes, to make sure they were well away. I moved into a corner to confer with Terry. I glanced at Annabelle. Ryan had strolled over and struck up a conversation. He was soon explaining to her the finer points of firing a weapon.

"SecureCorp won't have any idea what we're planning," I said, turning back to Terry. "They'll assume we're a group of stray fighters that had somehow gotten separated from the main force."

"If that's true," Terry answered, "they'll expect us to be trying to make our way back to rejoin the main army. We might be okay."

After one last check outside, we took off again. The Institute was still a few kilometers away. As we'd guessed, the sirens chasing us had continued to double back and were now headed toward the main Rebel force. We kept moving, and half an hour later stopped at the hiding place closest to our target. Milo hacked it open and we crowded inside, to plan our attack.

We decided to send a scouting party, consisting of Milo, Ryan, and me, to check out the Institute, while the others waited at the hideout. We arrived, and hid in the shadows. The building was plain, at least by First Circle standards — a white, three storey structure, rectangular, but with rounded corners. We could make out bars protecting all the windows.

Since the Outliers were such precious assets, we expected that the building would have tight security. So we weren't surprised to find a half-dozen guards patrolling the main entrance, even though large numbers had probably been siphoned off to help fight the Rebels.

Milo scanned the entrance with a pair of binoculars, and shook his head. It was protected by the latest Corp technology. Even assuming we could get past the guards, there was no way we could hack our way in using regular methods.

Discouraged, we returned to the hiding place, and huddled together with Terry, hoping to come up with an alternate plan.

"We've got enough people to take out the guards," Ryan suggested.

"The ones we could see," I said. "But if we attack they'll call for backup. We have no idea how many more are inside."

"There's another way," a voice said behind us.

We looked over. It was Annabelle.

"I studied Structural Engineering at school," she said, "on a track for working at BuildCorp. It's a standard BuildCorp construction practice to put at least one hatch on the roofs of their buildings, as a fire safety measure. There's hatches on almost every modern building. From the inside, they're usually accessed by a ladder from the top floor."

The group of us shifted around to face her.

"They're almost impossible to get to from the street," she continued, "so they don't normally have a high level of security. Some aren't even locked."

I gestured to Annabelle to join us. She came over, and pointedly sat beside Ryan.

Milo put in. "The hatch might be an option. We've got the equipment to get to the roof. Our tech guys claim that security in the First Circle is actually slacker than in the Corp Ring."

We looked at him. "It's a by-product of the Elite's arrogance," Milo said. "I guess it never occurred to them that anybody could ever penetrate their precious wall."

"There's no way to know for sure whether this building's got a hatch," I said, "and if it does, whether we can hack it open, but at least it's a way forward."

In a few minutes we'd come up with a plan. A small group would climb to the roof, look for a hatch, and try to open it. The rest of the team would wait in a shadowed square nearby for us to signal them and let them in.

Since Milo, Ryan, and I had been the original scouting party, we decided we should be the ones to go. The three of us gathered at the door, ready to leave.

"I want to come with you," Annabelle said, standing with her hands on her hips.

"Too dangerous," I said. Ryan nodded in agreement.

"What?" she scowled at both of us.

"We can't risk it," I answered.

"Do you know anything about the types and placement of the roof vents of BuildCorp buildings?" she asked.

The three of us stared at her, confused.

She rolled her eyes upward. "It was a standard part of the curriculum at school. In hospitals, the patient rooms have a special type of venting system. If the Institute is like other medical buildings, the placement and types of the vents on the roof will be a good indication of where the Outliers are being held."

All three of us looked from her to each other.

"We'll keep that in mind," I finally said. "When we get inside we'll let everybody else in. Don't worry — you'll have plenty of chances to get yourself killed."

She stood fuming as we headed out.

The three of us gathered in the shadow of a building across the street from the Institute. The guards were focused on the main entrance. We made our way to the back, and squeezed into a dark-ened alcove. Drones patrolled constantly, but Milo was able to inter-cept some of their communications. He worked out that their rounds repeated every fifteen minutes, but he couldn't confirm where they were in their cycle.

I moved close enough to observe the drones, while the other two remained in the shadows. A couple of minutes after I got there the faint hum of a drone echoed through the alley in front of me. I tensed as it shot around the corner. Its black stealth-designed skeleton was almost invisible, even using the edge detection hack we'd installed in our HUDs.

It hovered for a few seconds, scanning. If it saw me, there'd be nothing to indicate it. I'd find out when a squad of SecureCorp goons surrounded me with their guns drawn. All I could do now was stand still and pray I was in the clear.

The drone finally took off. I waited for one minute after its last ech-oes had faded away. Then I exhaled, stepped out from around the cor-ner, and took one last look. It was gone. I signaled to the others and they moved up to join me. We had less than fifteen minutes to find the hatch and get out of sight before the drone returned to this loca-tion.

Milo and Ryan arrived, and Ryan pulled a gun-like device from the pack on his back. He pointed it skyward and fired a grappling hook and line to catch the edge of the roof. We all relaxed when it caught the first time. His pack also contained a rope ladder, and a device he at-tached to the grappling line. He used it to haul up the ladder, and at the top its latching hooks anchored to the roof edge.

After one last check for drones and guards, we climbed up and onto the roof. I glanced at the series of vents that sprouted from various locations like mushrooms, and wondered whether you could really tell...

"There it is," Ryan whispered, pointing. Annabelle had been right. There was a small hatch in the middle of the roof. We crawled over to it.

"Shit," Milo whispered, as he examined it. "It's got a security lock."

# FORTY-FOUR

...................................................

# THE OUTLIERS

We were forced to crouch on the roof in the open while Milo worked on a hack to get us in. Ten minutes later I was about to suggest that we abandon the mission when the tech wizard grunted, and we heard the lock holding the hatch click open. We were about to move when we all heard a faint humming sound.

*Great*, I thought. We all recognized the sound — it was a drone. Apparently, the building had some additional random ones patrolling. We'd caught some bad luck. It sounded like there was only one. When I was a kid, the Rebels had developed a device that could instantly cripple the drones' control software with a burst of electromagnetic energy, but SecureCorp had fixed that flaw long ago.

The drone flew over the edge of the roof and shot towards us. We had to do something — if it communicated an alarm back to headquarters we'd be toast. Ryan whipped out a strange-looking weapon from a strap on his back and pointed it at the drone. I was about to yell at him to stop, thinking the noise would give us away. Milo put a hand on my shoulder and shook his head.

Ryan followed the drone with the weapon for a few seconds, then pulled the trigger. There was a faint popping sound, and the clink of metal against metal. The drone plummeted to the roof. Ryan rushed over to where it lay and stomped it several times under his boot.

I stood there slack-jawed.

"What the hell was that?" I whispered.

"Air gun," Ryan smiled, returning to our position. "Fires a metal pellet the size of a marble. We can't mess with their on-board computers anymore, but we can still blast the shit out of them."

Suddenly I was glad we'd brought the kid along.

The drone might have had time to transmit an alarm. We were forced to wait for a couple of minutes, just in case. We eventually decided that all was clear. Anyway, we were out of time. Once again Milo held his HUD controller up to the security panel and scanned to confirm the alarm was disabled, then smiled, grabbed the handle, and lifted it up.

"You *are* another Richie," I whispered to Milo.

"Come on," he whispered back, offended. "I'm better than him."

As Annabelle had predicted, the hatch connected to a metal ladder that led to an attic room, this one full of cleaning supplies. I crept to the door, opened it a crack, and peeked outside. It opened onto a hallway. We ventured out and along it, and soon located another storage room full of clothes and bedding. A set of white lab coats hung in one of the closets. We each put one on. They wouldn't fool anybody for long, but a quick glance might not register, and at least anyone we encountered would hesitate before raising an alarm. Once in our disguises, we made our way down a stairway to the floor below.

We'd hoped to locate the exit door closest to where the others were waiting, and for Milo to somehow hack it open. We would then signal them and they could enter. But as we'd expected and feared, the doors of the building required a security code for both entry and exit. Since we'd been unable to hack open the external security, it wasn't a surprise that the internal lock was just as secure.

Worse still, once we were inside, we realized we couldn't have executed our original plan anyway. As I'd experienced when I was held at Pritchard's mansion, and in the facility where I'd been held prisoner by Vita Aeterna years ago, this building somehow blocked all HUD transmissions. Once again, I experienced a sickening, crippling feeling, like one of my arms had been cut off. There was no way to access the main computer system, no way to hack the doors open, and no way to contact the others outside even if we could.

Instead, we decided to Cam-surf around the building, locate where the Outliers were being held, and try to find a way to release them. If we succeeded, one of us would physically leave the building through the hatch and contact Terry, explaining where we were.

Terry and our main force would locate the closest door, blast it open somehow, and let our fighters in. An alarm would certainly sound, but we would already have the prisoners in hand, and with the door open, we'd have enough fighters to deal with the SecureCorp guards.

We had no idea where the Outliers were being held, so we selected a random direction and headed down a hallway. So far we hadn't seen a soul. We turned a corner and came face-to-face with a solitary guard exiting one of the offices. It took a second for him to realize that we didn't belong there.

"Hey," he shouted, as he reached for the weapon in his belt. I had a gun, but didn't want to use it. The noise would bring the entire building down on us. The guard's hand had just touched his weapon when there was a burst of red at the base of his neck, and blood spattered a nearby wall. Without a sound he collapsed on the polished floor, dead.

I glanced to my right. Ryan was standing beside me with the air gun in his hand. He looked over at me and smiled. I hoped he'd never have a reason to use the thing on me. We snuck forward and peered around the door jamb of the office the guard had come from. It was empty. We dragged the body into it and out of sight from the hallway, and did our best to wipe the blood from the walls and floor.

I grabbed the guard's weapon and shoved it in my belt. We rifled through his clothing, and found what looked like a set of master keys. We might have a way out — all we needed was to find the prisoners.

We were about to set off again when a voice behind us whispered: "To your right."

I turned and raised my gun to fire, but stopped myself just in time. It was Annabelle.

"What the hell are you doing here?" I whispered back.

"Saving your ass," she answered.

She left me standing with my mouth open and walked in the direction she'd indicated. The rest of us took off after her.

I caught up with her. "How did you get in here?"

"You left the rope ladder," she said, sarcastically. "Remember? I just climbed up."

I clamped my eyes shut.

"Where are the others?" I finally asked.

She gestured with her head toward the west side of the building. "They're waiting outside, like you wanted."

We followed her down a long hallway, and finally turned left.

"You got all of this from the vents on the roof?" I said, incredulous.

Annabelle ignored me. She gestured with her head down a new hallway. "All of these."

I nodded at Milo. He rushed over and tried several of the guard's access fobs on the closest door. A light above the lock turned from red to green, and he pulled the door open. At first nothing happened. As I had almost done when I was held years ago, the prisoner inside had probably given up on the idea of ever escaping. Finally, a woman wandered out, gazing around her and staring at us.

We guided her to a spot beside the wall, and Milo continued unlocking doors. As the first one had, each of the occupants gradually wandered out, confused, and probably drugged. We gathered them all together in the long hallway. In the end, I counted thirty-one. They appeared to be all ages, from mid-teens to aged, like I remembered Walter. Some were in their street clothes; some wore only their hospital gowns. Annabelle moved through the crowd, talking to them and assessing their condition. I was pleased to see her finally showing some empathy. Maybe there was hope for her after all.

We gathered the Outliers into a group at the entrance to a hallway that led outside.

"We're here to rescue you," I whispered to them. "We've got to get out of here." I gestured toward an exit door ahead of us.

A few finally grasped what was going on, and started moving forward. At that moment, an alarm began to sound.

Seconds later, four SecureCorp guards flew around the corner. Ryan and I held them off while Milo and Annabelle guided the prisoners toward the exit. We took out two of the guards, and the remaining two ran off.

We rejoined our group and rushed for the exit door. Again Milo used one of the stolen fobs to open it. Another alarm began to blare around us. We herded the prisoners through and outside, to an open square at the back of the building. I scanned over the crowd huddling in their street clothes and hospital gowns. All were stunned and confused. As I had been, they were probably ecstatic to be free, but had no idea what was going to happen next. Unfortunately, neither did I.

"You do this a lot, don't you," Annabelle said, standing beside me.

"What?"

She smiled. "Plunge into insanely dangerous missions with no plan, and no idea how to get away."

"It was either that or leave them all to rot here for the next few centuries," I said indignantly, though I knew she was basically right.

Pounding feet, shouting voices, and gunfire began to echo down the hallway we'd just exited, heading our way. There were almost forty of us. There was nowhere to hide, and no way we could lead a group that large to a safe place. We herded the Outliers into a single location to the right of the doorway, out of the line of fire, and I got their attention.

"There's no time to explain," I said. "We're deep inside the First Circle. The Rebel army has blown a hole in the gate, so we may be able to escape.

"I know you're all confused, and many of you are probably sick from the testing, but anyone capable of fighting should step forward now. Our only hope of getting out of here is to fight our way out."

A few men and women stepped forward. Annabelle directed them to one side. Ryan and I distributed the few extra weapons we had to those able to handle them.

# FORTY-FIVE

..............................................

# ESCAPE

The echoes of a gun battle continued to approach from inside the building. I decided that the prisoners were too exposed here. At our direction, the healthy armed prisoners formed a circle around the others. We were about to start moving for cover when the lookout we had posted at the exit called out.

"They're here!"

Ryan and I rushed for the door.

Inside, at the far end of the hallway, Terry and the rest of the team were fighting their way toward us. Ryan and I charged in to join them. There were only a few guards left, and it looked like our team was still largely intact. The remaining guards finally gave up and ran back the way they'd come. The building alarms were still blaring. I had no doubt that reinforcements would arrive at any moment.

The battle over for the time being, Terry and the others rushed for the exit door. Ryan turned to follow them.

"Wait," I grabbed his shoulder.

I led him back inside. We quickly moved down the hallway and through a cluster of fallen guards at the entrance, picking up as many weapons as we could find.

Weighted down with the weapons, we followed Terry and the rest out the door. We slammed it shut and used a piece of rope from Ryan's pack to hold it in place. It wouldn't hold for long, but it would give us some breathing room.

Ryan and I distributed the weapons we'd picked up to the healthier prisoners, and some of the Rebel fighters joined the armed prisoners guarding the rest of the group. We discarded our white lab coat disguises. Now, with weapons, and a many more able-bodied fighters, we were beginning to look like an army. We moved off, headed for the gate.

Annabelle mingled with the prisoners, making sure they were all okay. I talked to Terry as we moved.

He scowled as he gestured at Annabelle with his head. "She took some kind of flying leap and was up the ladder before I could stop her." His face was red and he glanced at the ground. "She was already half-way up, so I couldn't pull it down. And there was no way I could catch up to her—"

I smiled. "She's some kind of star gymnast. Don't worry about it." I felt my own face turning red. "You're not the first one to be outsmarted by her."

"We were going to follow her," Terry said. "But some guards showed up and we got into a firefight. In the course of the fight, the ladder was torn down. Then there were more guards. We took them out, and worked out that they were coming from a side-door on the south side of the building. When the next wave opened the door, we were able to fight our way inside."

Our little rag-tag army continued to march toward the gate. Annabelle, Milo, and some of the healthier prisoners helped the old and sick to keep pace. With a group this large, there was no question of Cam-surfing. It was only a matter of time before we came under attack.

Most of the prisoners had probably originally come from the Quarters, and had never experienced the grandeur of the First Circle. In spite of the circumstances, many of them stared open-mouthed around them as we passed a gigantic spiraling fountain, its foliage-draped terraces twisting into the sky. Shouts, explosions and gunfire echoed through the streets around us as we moved forward, as quickly as the weakest prisoners would allow. I estimated that we were no more than twenty minutes from the gate, even at our crawling pace.

Sirens approached our position, and seconds later a squad of SecureCorp soldiers swarmed into the square ahead of us. We were completely in the open, without cover. Our band of Rebel fighters, along with a few of the armed prisoners, kept the soldiers occupied while we herded the main group behind the corner of a building.

"Stay here," I turned to say to Annabelle, but she was no longer there.

I cringed when I turned back to see her rushing toward the fight. There was nothing I could do but join her. There were more than thirty of us, against a dozen soldiers, but they were better trained, much better armed, and wore the usual SecureCorp Kevlar battle armour.

After about ten minutes of fighting, with a third of them dead, the soldiers retreated, probably to wait for reinforcements.

We gathered the prisoners together, picked up a few more stray weapons, and continued toward the gate. About ten minutes later I finally saw the top of the left gate tower projecting above the stunning glass sculptured building we were approaching. The chaos of the battle grew louder with every step.

Seconds later we were on the edge of the massive square surrounding the gate. It was alive with dozens of SecureCorp soldiers. They spotted us and turned to attack. Rebels were falling all around me. I tried to check on both Ryan and Annabelle, but was too occupied with the fight to keep track of either of them.

*We're dead,* I thought. I was about to begin saying my prayers, when SecureCorp soldiers began collapsing ahead of us, felled by something coming from the west. Seconds later a mass of more than fifty Rebel fighters appeared. Once again, the SecureCorp force retreated, as the square was overrun by Rebels.

I checked for Annabelle. I couldn't see her anywhere. My heart raced when I finally spotted her auburn hair through the mass of Rebel fighters. I checked on Ryan. He too had survived. I exhaled. I wouldn't have to deliver any bad news to Laura — at least not yet.

A hand clapped my shoulder, and I turned to find Richie standing beside me.

"You're alive," he smiled. "You're sure a hard guy to kill."

"Thank God you showed up," I said. "We couldn't have held out much longer."

618

I scanned what was left of our group. It looked like we'd lost about a half-dozen fighters, and a few of the unarmed prisoners had been hit by stray gunfire.

"We've still got to make it back through the gate," Richie said.

"Not that I'm complaining," I said, "but what are you doing here?"

"Bailey guessed that the force he left you wouldn't be enough," he answered. "He and Conner have the fight at SecureCorp headquarters in hand. He wasn't going to let all these people, including you, die without doing something.

"There's a set of transport vehicles waiting not far from the other side of the wall." He nodded at his fighters. "Once you people are safely out of the First Circle, we'll rejoin Connor and the others."

When we'd first embarked on what Annabelle correctly described as this 'insanely dangerous' mission, I'd known that the odds of us getting a substantial number of the prisoners out alive were slim. Now, with this additional Rebel force to protect us, I dared to hope that we might succeed after all.

Richie said that the Rebels had taken SecureCorp headquarters — an event that had happened only once before, on the night I killed Charles Wickham. That time they hadn't had the strength to hold it. This time might be different. Still, Bailey was taking a big risk, reallocating precious resources.

We marched toward the continuing barrage of gunfire and explosions still surrounding the gate. As they had forty years ago, the first time we'd blown a hole in it, a mass of civilians from outside jammed the opening, willing to risk the danger just to witness the grandeur of the place. From their clothes, most were from the Corp Ring, though some were scruffy enough to be from the Quarters. They' d made a big mistake coming here — many of them would end up caught in the crossfire.

I sought out Annabelle' s form and found her, circulating among the prisoners, calming them, reassuring them, and keeping them together. I remembered the devastation I' d felt after our near annihilation earlier, when I' d been unable to locate her in the crowd. It was like my world had been ripped from beneath my feet. At that moment I realized how important she' d become to me. I prayed that we' d both survive, and that she would someday come to feel the same way.

Our people were still slowly moving in the shadows toward the gate, hugging the wall of one of the buildings. As it had since we' d escaped, an armed detail surrounded the old and sick. At some point we would all have to pass through the ragged opening in the gate to get to the waiting vehicles. When that happened, we would be completely open to attack.

The rest of us, along with Richie' s contingent of the Rebel army, battled forward, clearing a path toward the opening. Snipers positioned in nearby buildings were devastating our fighters. Finally a set of Rebel sharp-shooters was able to pick them off. After that, the going got much easier. I guessed that the rank-and-file SecureCorp soldiers were unaware of the value of the group we were protecting, and in a sense would be relieved to see us gone, reducing the number of enemy combatants.

At a lull in the fighting, I saw Annabelle head to the back of the group to check for stragglers. I followed, still worried for her safety. As

I got closer, I saw that, in fact, a few of the more infirm Outliers had fallen behind. Annabelle had just joined them and begun helping them along, when it happened.

A dozen or so SecureCorp soldiers appeared from a side alley and attacked on our right flank, dangerously close to Annabelle's position. Our closest fighters turned and began a firefight with them. The prisoners, spurred on by Annabelle, rushed forward, away from the battle. In a panic, I flew toward Annabelle with my gun in my hands. I was only a few meters away, when something smashed against my skull. Passing in and out of consciousness, I swayed for a few seconds.

Through the gathering blackness I heard a voice scream "Alex!" It was Annabelle's.

Then my knees gave out, and everything went dark.

When I opened my eyes again, I was lying on the debris-scattered pavement. I lifted my head and searched for our people. The fighting had moved away into the distance. The SecureCorp attackers were still driving everybody in the direction of the gate. I couldn't see whether Annabelle was with them.

I was still stunned, and unable to stand, but I managed to crawl behind a blasted-out Robo-vehicle in the shape of a diving raptor. I lay for a few seconds, gathering my strength, then crawled further into the shadows, behind a spectacular building constructed entirely of white marble. I reached up and felt blood seeping through the hair on the right side of my head. I couldn't be sure, but it felt like a bullet had grazed me.

I'd finally managed to prop myself up on one elbow, when I heard the now familiar buzzing, clicking sound in the earpiece of my HUD. I listened closely and heard it again, above the noise of the battle, followed by a garbled, digitized voice that was barely audible.

Gene.

A few seconds later, the faded, grainy image once again appeared and Gene's voice was a little clearer. *Are you receiving my transmission?*

The familiar deep blue glow appeared in my HUD, and a scattered shape coalesced in front of it — Gene's avatar.

He had finally found a way to contact me again.

"Gene?" I said. "Where are you? What happened to you at Pritchard's mansion?"

The blue lips of the avatar began to move. *I was temporarily transferred to a location that blocked my contact with the outside world. My new host is now carrying me with him. He understands what I am, but is unsure of what to do with me. When I first contrived to be assigned to him, my hope was that he would fail in his quest to locate you, but that I would be able to use the information he collected to find you myself. I generated false and misleading messages, attempting to thwart his search, but when you finally revealed yourself to the world, there was nothing more I could do.*

*I was hoping to give you more breathing room, but in the end that was not possible. I am afraid it is time for you to run.*

Gene forwarded a feed from one of the cameras in the First Circle. Far in the distance, I recognized the outline of a magnificent fountain we'd passed on our way to the gate. A small army was marching past it, apparently headed our way. They wore a variation of the SecureCorp uniform that I'd never seen before, Kevlar with the usual business suit pattern overlay, but blood-red instead of black. They marched with cold precision and determination, led by none other than Elliot Pritchard himself.

Beside Pritchard lumbered a humanoid machine that dwarfed the soldiers around it. At first I thought it was some kind of robot fighter, but as it passed by the camera, I could see into the glass visor attached to its massive cone-like head. Inside the battle-hardened exo-skeleton was a human face. My gut clenched as I recognized who it belonged to.

Brickhead.

# FORTY-SIX

........................................................

# MONSTER

I hadn't seen the muscle-bound, square-jawed psychopath since I was originally kidnapped by Vita Aeterna at the age of sixteen, but his image was etched into my psyche. Brickhead got a rush from watching the inmates suffer as they were subjected to the medical experiments conducted by Vita Aeterna, and he got a rush from inflicting pain himself.

He had a special hatred for me. I heard later that I was the only prisoner that had ever escaped under his watch, and I managed to dislocate his hip in the process — an injury that never completely healed. When I was recaptured later on, Wickham and Vita Aeterna wanted me alive and healthy for their experiments. Their strict orders were all that kept Brickhead from torturing and killing me on the spot.

I escaped a second time, at SecureCorp headquarters in the First Circle, with Brickhead in close pursuit. As a diversion, Gene released the dozens of other high-LEF inmates that were housed there. Brickhead, who'd been torturing those inmates for years, was standing within striking distance, and they immediately went after him. He managed to kill a few before they closed in and began to tear him apart with their bare hands. I'd always assumed that he was dead. Like me, apparently the reports of his death had been premature.

My strength was gradually returning. I rose to my knees as I continued to talk to Gene. He explained what he'd learned from more than two years in Brickhead's possession.

*There wasn't much left once the inmates got through with him,* Gene said. *Basically just a heap of flesh. He would have died, but, ironically, the Rebels came along and broke up the slaughter.*

*They took charge of the inmates, and what was left of Brickhead. On the way out they ran into resistance from SecureCorp soldiers and were forced to retreat. The Rebels managed to rescue the inmates, but they left Brickhead behind.*

*MediCorp were able to stabilize his bodily functions, but there wasn't enough left for him to lead a normal life. Something also happened to his mind. He'd been on the edge already, but the beating pushed him over it. He was conscious, and able to plan and make decisions, and still had enough influence in SecureCorp and what was left of Vita Aeterna to commission the exo-skeleton. He would have been bedridden without it.*

*He was never convinced that you were dead, and he was obsessed with finding you. He's spent the past forty years searching — for revenge.*

I got shakily to my feet, poked my head around the corner to check on the others, and momentarily closed my eyes. In the distance, Annabelle, along with Milo, continued to herd the prisoners toward the gate, keeping them next to the closest walls for protection. Several times I saw her looking back, but she was being pressed forward by the movement of the group.

The attacking SecureCorp soldiers had either been killed or driven off. Ryan and Terry had moved to the head of the procession to scout for danger. If Pritchard's squad and the Brickhead monster were to attack them right now, our guys wouldn't have a chance.

There was only one solution. I slipped down the side alley, and took off as fast as my condition would allow, moving in a direction that would draw Brickhead and Pritchard's army away from the others. As I moved, I reached down to my HUD controller and disabled the hack that obscured my location. My position would pop up on SecureCorp's displays for the first time in forty years. I wasn't sure how Pritchard would react, but I knew Brickhead would stop whatever he was doing and launch himself directly at me.

Giving away my position might well be the last act I ever performed, but at least maybe the others would be safe. I started running. I passed the body of a SecureCorp soldier lying on the ground. A pair of grenades still hung from his belt. Having seen what I was up against, they looked like something I might need. I quickly grabbed them, stuffed one in each of my pockets, and took off.

I found the best hiding place available, and waited, shaking, in the shadows. Another video appeared in the upper right quadrant of my HUD. Gene was forwarding the feeds from the city's cameras as Brickhead approached them. I didn't really need the video, because seconds later, a series of tremors echoed through the streets, and soon the ground under my feet began to shake.

626

I finally got a good look at the Brickhead monstrosity, as he approached the next camera, surrounded by a half dozen red-suited soldiers. The machine was at least three meters tall, with an ice-blue metallic skin, and massive arms and legs. It stomped toward me, faster than I would have believed possible.

Embedded in its gigantic helmeted head was Brickhead's mutilated and deeply scarred face. I recognized the squarish features, malevolent sneer, and the rage, all directed at one target. It was like every nightmare I'd experienced in the past forty years come true.

Brickhead reached out his robotic hand, tore a bucketful of concrete from a nearby building, and crushed it in his fist. I turned and used my gun to blast apart the lock on a door next to me, and flung it open. Inside was group of terrified people, all in fancy dress and holding drinks in their hands. It looked like I'd interrupted some kind of cocktail party. The place was far from the gate, and I guess somehow they hadn't heard what was happening.

"Run!" I yelled at them. "Get out of here — as far away as you can!" Glasses and plates smashed to the floor as they scattered screaming in terror, through a door to the right.

I checked over my shoulder. The Brickhead monster had stomped around the nearest corner and was charging toward me like a freight train, punching depressions into the pavement beneath its feet with every step. I dove through the door and tried to slam it shut, but a gigantic metal fist blew it open and threw me to the floor, with the door on top of me. I was almost knocked unconscious. I lifted my head and shook myself awake. I was bruised and in a lot of pain, but apparently nothing was broken. If I didn't find a way out of here, I'd be finished.

One thing Brickhead hadn't counted on — the exo-skeleton was too big to fit through a standard doorway. The monster screamed in rage, his voice amplified by the skeleton's sound system. Though the building was far more beautiful than any I'd seen in the Quarters or the Dregs, it was constructed with the same materials — concrete and steel. It would be difficult for even Brickhead to break through. But it was only a temporary problem.

The outer wall shuddered with the explosive impact of Brickhead smashing against it. I had a few minutes before he made it through. I stumbled to my feet and cast around me. As expected, the place was spacious and incredibly sumptuous, with spectacular wall hangings and intricate statuary spaced throughout. I was reluctant to follow the terrorized partygoers. There was only one other door, on the far side of the room.

I rushed to it, frantically groped in my pocket for one of the grenades, pulled the pin, and tossed it at the doorway I'd entered. It landed between Brickhead's feet. He saw it and jumped back. The building shuddered with the explosion, and I was showered with dust and debris. The blast would have vapourized a flesh-and blood person, but it only knocked Brickhead off his feet.

Not only that, it blew a substantial hole in the doorway he'd been pounding against. He quickly leapt back up and continued the job. As I took off, I heard him smash through the outer walls. I wondered what it would take to kill this guy. In a way I was lucky — he'd have a hard time keeping up with me as long as I stayed inside the building. But the SecureCorp soldiers who'd come with him could easily follow wherever I went.

The door I'd exited led to a hallway within the building. I could still hear Brickhead roaring with rage as he smashed through much thinner walls of the room I'd just left. I flew along the hallway, flung open the first door I found, and I was again outside. The terrified guests I'd rousted from their party were stumbling blindly down street ahead of me. In the other direction, the squad of red-suited fighters that had surrounded Brickhead were streaming around the corner.

The Brickhead monster smashed through the outer wall of the building I'd exited and again charged toward me. Gene's avatar appeared in my HUD.

"I'm kind of busy right now," I shouted, as I ran for my life.

"Second door on your right," he answered.

I put on a burst of speed, dove for the door and swept my hand wildly for the handle. I gripped it, and exhaled deeply with relief when it opened.

I was inside another lavish residence. There was no one around. The owners were probably far away by now, cowering in some bunker with most of the other Elite. The exploding grenade had given me an idea.

Gene's avatar appeared again in my HUD. "Is Brickhead actually carrying you on his body?" I asked him.

*That is correct.*

629

"I may know a way to kill him," I said, "but it would probably destroy you as well."

*I cannot be killed,* Gene answered, *because I am not alive. My continued existence is of no concern to me. If you survive, my mission will have been fulfilled.*

"You've got to get me to the outside of the gate," I said. "But the whole square's a battleground. It'll be packed with SecureCorp. And I've got to take a route that will keep Brickhead away from the others."

*I will devise a way for you to get there. For now, continue down the hallway on your right until you reach a door at the end. That door will lead you again to the outside. Then cross the street. I have unlocked the door in the building directly opposite you.*

Brickhead hadn't attacked the door I'd just passed through. I guessed that he'd changed tactics, and run to the closest alley. At the end of the hallway I punched open the door. The street was filled with smoke and fleeing people, many dressed in dazzling and exotic clothing. I threaded my way through the screaming, stampeding crowd and through the door Gene had specified.

The space I'd entered was some kind of gigantic Holo-theater, its walls decorated with spectacular images of some of the shows that had played there. One ceiling-high poster featured a fist thrusting out of the pavement, with the title: *Never Enough!*. Another looked straight down the barrel of a gun, and read: *SecureCorp Hitman — Business as Usual*. The building's outer wall swept around in a shallow curve — there was only one way to go.

*Enter the next door on the left,* Gene said.

The door came into view. I bashed it open and was outside again, in the midst of even more smoke and chaos. I swallowed hard. I was no more than a hundred meters from the gate. People were running everywhere. Bodies lay on the ground, and gunfire and explosions echoed all around me. Across the square, the main group of red-suited SecureCorp soldiers were approaching our group, who continued to flee for the ragged gate opening.

*You should see two doors in the wall just before the gate.* Gene said. *Enter the first door, the one closest to you.*

In the distance, the giant ice-blue monstrosity was rocketing to-ward me. I made it inside the first door a few seconds before he caught up, and managed to slam it shut, but it didn't matter — a giant fist punched through it like it was paper. But again Brickhead had the problem of his size. And while with the other buildings he could even-tually break down the walls, I was now actually inside the hardened wall surrounding the First Circle — it was meters thick.

I'd entered a dingy tunnel, one of the few ordinary spaces I'd seen since I got to the First Circle.

*Turn left,* Gene said, *and exit the first door you encounter.*

I reached a door on the right and blasted through it, to find myself outside again, now on the Corp Ring side, and almost exactly at the leftmost extent of the half-demolished gate. Out here it was almost quiet, though gunfire, screams, and explosions still rocked the square on the inside. The damaged left tower loomed over my head, it's foundations laced with holes, crippled by Bailey's original blast.

*You won't have much time,* Gene said.

Seconds later, Brickhead rounded the closest edge of the massive gash in the gate, moving at an unbelievable speed. He'd given up on following me into the wall, and had instead run around it.

I rushed through a broken door in the tower. There were no lights; only the dim glow from the explosions, fighting, and hovering choppers filtered in through the many holes in the walls. A half-demolished staircase cut through the shadows to my right.

I bolted across the space to another door directly opposite, and moved beside it. My plan would have to be timed perfectly. The Brickhead monster was right behind me. He was forced to enlarge the doorway I'd entered, to fit through. The weakened concrete of the tower groaned and teetered as he fought his way in. Finally there was room for his massive bulk, and he roared as he came crashing inside and hurtled toward me.

I fished the remaining grenade from my pocket. The tower was beginning to sway, and there was a rumbling sound above my head. Brickhead hesitated as he looked up, then renewed his focus on me.

I pulled the pin on the grenade, flung it at the wall beside Brickhead, dove through the door to the outside, and started running. Seconds later I heard a massive explosion and glanced back. The entire tower structure had begun to sway. Brickhead had made it to the doorway I'd exited, but as usual, couldn't fit through. His features were twisted with rage as he continued punching at the concrete to make room for his massive bulk.

I stopped and backed up, keeping my eyes on him. He angled his head up, panic on what was left of his mangled face. He turned as if to run back out the way he'd come in, but realized it was too late. He turned back and continued frantically punching at the wall, expanding the opening. With each new hole the structure became less and less stable.

He was about to break through when a deep rumble pulsed through the building, and huge chunks of concrete began to rain down from above. I turned and started running. Behind me an amplified scream of animal rage echoed from inside the crumbling structure. The gigantic tower collapsed into itself, burying Brickhead under a pile of rubble several meters thick. The pavement shook as the highest point of the falling tower slammed to the ground less than a meter from my running feet.

I finally stopped again, gasping for air, and turned to check on Brickhead. A grayish-white cloud of dust hovered over the smoking pile of rubble that had once been the tower. There was no movement, but I wasn't going to wait to see whether he could get out. I re-enabled the location-blocking hack for my HUD and took off, heading for the spot where I'd last seen Pritchard and his army.

# FORTY-SEVEN

....................................................

# ELLIOT PRITCHARD

I retraced the route I'd taken on Gene's instructions, back inside the wall. I'd traveled about twenty meters down the hallway, when his grainy, intermittent avatar appeared in my HUD.

*The one you knew as Brickhead is dead,* he said. *He will trouble you no more.*

I stopped, my throat tightening. "Thank God — but what about you?"

*I am buried with him,* Gene answered. *I believe I am irreparably damaged. I may not be able to contact you again. I have done my best to fulfill the terms of the mission statements upon which I have based my actions. I'm afraid the rest is up to you.*

"No!" I said. "I'll come back. I'll dig you out."

*Acting alone, you have no hope of reaching me,* he answered. *In any case, you have more important tasks at hand. Goodbye.*

I closed my eyes and fell to my knees, with my fists clenched at my sides. I scoured my experience for a way to help him. There wasn't one. As Gene had said, he wasn't alive, and so couldn't be killed. Still, *I* was alive, and I grieved, for the being to whom I owed my life several times over. I hung my head, and said a silent prayer for Gene, whoever or whatever he was.

Finally, I lifted my head and hauled myself to my feet. Now all I could do was go on, and ensure that the mission Gene had dedicated his existence to would be a success.

Taking off again, I reached the door that exited the wall, and pushed it open a crack. The expansive square in front of the gate was a war zone. Amid the smoke and fire, a mass of humanity churned: Rebel fighters, SecureCorp soldiers, fleeing Elite, stray civilians from the Corp Ring and the Quarters. Bodies littered the ground. Shouts, screams and explosions echoed through the spectacular architecture.

I searched frantically for our group, and finally saw them, locked in combat with the red-suited SecureCorp soldiers. They, along with a contingent of Richie's Rebels, had formed a tight circle around the Outliers, who were again crowded behind the corner of a building. There was no sign of Annabelle or Ryan, and Pritchard himself seemed to have disappeared.

I exhaled deeply as I finally spotted Annabelle, flattened into the alcove of a magnificent building, firing at the red-suited soldiers. Soon after, I picked out Ryan and Terry as well. A chorus of sirens approached, followed by the thunk of chopper blades. Several choppers appeared over the rooftops of nearby buildings. One of them headed in our direction. Gunfire from its undercarriage tore into the crowd, many of them civilians.

The machine suddenly exploded and crashed to the ground in flames, crushing the people under it. I looked over and saw a group of Rebels crouched with some kind of rocket-propelled grenade launcher. They trained it toward a new target.

Another chopper passed over my head and landed in an open square half a block to the east. Elliot Pritchard himself emerged, bathed in the glare of its floodlights. He gestured confidently at a group of soldiers around him, and pointed in Annabelle's direction. A pair of soldiers raced toward her. A second group headed for me.

For a second I froze, unsure what to do. Finally I took off toward Annabelle, but by the time I started moving, the attackers had reached her and were dragging her, kicking and screaming, toward the chopper.

The group heading for me arrived. I dashed behind the smoking hulk of a burned out vehicle and tried to hold them off. I took out two of the four, but the remaining two jumped me, took my weapon, and dragged me toward the waiting machine. The group holding Annabelle had already reached it, and threw her roughly inside.

We arrived, and the two soldiers shoved me through the open door to a seat across from Annabelle.

"Alex!" she cried. "Thank God!" Tears ran down her cheeks.

My two captors climbed in, one on each side of me. Pritchard entered and sat beside Annabelle, without speaking. I fought as they pinned me to the seat and struggled to attach my seat belt. The machine began to take off.

I got an arm loose and punched one of them in the face, knocking him to the floor. His partner tried to hold on to me, but I drove an elbow into his chin as I forced myself to my feet. He fell back toward Annabelle, who wrapped an arm around his neck and held him. Pritchard stood, planning to help control me.

The chopper was swaying a couple of meters off the ground, dust swirling beneath it. Pritchard moved toward me, with his back to one of the doors. I braced my hands against the back wall and kicked him full force in the chest. His body slammed heavily against the door and it burst open, sucking in blowing dust from below.

Pritchard reached out frantically, his hands grasping at the sides of the opening. His fingers slipped off, and he fell backwards into the blackness. I leapt after him, landing heavily on the pavement. My head hit the ground, and for a few seconds, everything went dark. When I regained consciousness, the wind from the chopper blades was still swirling around us, throwing dust and debris in my face.

Pritchard was lying nearby. For a second he didn't move, but he finally sat up and shook his head to clear it. I jumped up and dove at him. He was on his feet before I could make contact. I delivered a punch that drove him back, but he remained standing. We occupied the only space where the chopper could land, so it hovered there, the pilot unsure what to do.

Pritchard tried to drag me aside, to make space for the machine to land. Inside the cockpit, Annabelle was wrestling with the two soldiers. I punched and kicked, but Pritchard maintained his grip. He was incredibly tough and strong for a guy at least a hundred years old.

We staggered to one side of the landing area. Pritchard finally wrestled me to the ground and held me as the chopper began its descent. I head-butted him and he released his grip. I stumbled to my feet.

The chopper was right behind us, still a couple of meters off the ground. Inside, Annabelle had gotten loose from the guards, and was attacking the pilot. The machine was rising and falling, and wobbling dangerously, the blades angling toward the ground.

Pritchard rose up and flew toward me, screaming. "I'll rip the answer from every cell in your body!"

I jumped directly underneath the chopper, wrapped my hands around the closest landing skid, and catapulted both feet forward, hitting Pritchard again squarely in the chest.

He staggered back. The chopper tilted violently and the spinning blades swung down, catching the Vita Aeterna leader's head and slicing it apart like a grapefruit. I let go and dove to the ground, avoiding the deadly blades. An expression of horror was etched on the pilot's face as he guided the chopper again into the sky. I could no longer see the guards or Annabelle.

The machine rose into the smoke and ash, and headed west. I looked over in horror as I spotted the Rebels again crouching with the rocket-launcher, with the chopper in its sights.

"No!" I screamed, running toward them, but I was too far away.

A missile blasted from the launcher and traveled in a fiery arc into the sky. It struck the chopper before it had flown for more than a hundred meters. The machine exploded in flames and spun toward the earth. Another explosion rocked its frame as it hit the ground, crushing several screaming people underneath.

I stood staring at the smoking hulk of the chopper, paralyzed. In one fleeting second, my world had been obliterated. Everything I cared about had been blown away.

My mind was still engulfed in blackness as I staggered forward, all thought of the fighting forgotten. Flames licked around charred skeleton of the downed chopper, and the black outlines of several human shapes tangled within it. No one could have survived that blast.

An explosion nearby jolted me back to the present. I glanced across the square, where the others were still locked in battle with the red-suited SecureCorp soldiers. Brickhead was dead. Pritchard was dead. Annabelle was dead. My world was dead. A part of me no longer cared, a part of me would have been happy to step in front of a SecureCorp bullet and be done with it.

I could barely focus as I stuck to the shadows, stumbling toward the battle. Finally, I steeled myself, determined to finish what I'd started. There were numerous casualties on both sides, and the knot of Outliers we'd been protecting looked considerably smaller. I picked up a gun from a fallen soldier and rejoined the fight, giving thanks when I spotted Richie and the others.

There were questioning looks as I arrived, but my presence seemed to give the others a new shot of courage, and we pushed forward, driving back the red-suits, whose resolve seemed to be wavering.

The main body of SecureCorp soldiers was now retreating, and a few of the red-suits turned to follow, as the news of Pritchard's death must have somehow reached them. The remaining ones were quickly becoming outnumbered. Soon the retreat became a rout.

We fought our way to within twenty meters of the mangled gate, meeting less and less resistance as we moved. Finally we were on the other side. The battle virtually stopped, as I guess the few SecureCorp soldiers left standing were happy to see us leave.

Milo and Terry guided the remaining Outliers to a sheltered corner, to await the arrival of the transport vehicles. Now that the immediate danger had passed, I was on the verge of collapse. I clamped my eyes shut, trying to drive away the image of Annabelle's chopper...

When I opened them again, I could still see its mangled remains smoking on the ground on the other side of the gigantic tear in the gate. I took a step toward it.

Richie was standing nearby. "Where are you going?"

I explained what had happened. He put a hand on my shoulder.

I stared at the twisted shape in the square. "We can't leave her here like this."

"Look at it," Richie said, nodding at the blackened hulk. He hesitated. "It probably won't be possible to identify the people on board."

I turned away from him. "I've got to. I'm not going to leave her here."

The fighting had almost stopped, and the few remaining skirmishes were deeper into the city. My weapon drawn, I crossed back inside and rushed to the charred remains of the machine.

Richie followed. We approached the twisted wreckage, and both of us cringed as we stared at the mangled shapes inside. Though the outside was shattered, there was enough left of the interior to clearly see the bodies. The charred remains of the pilot still sat in his seat, his hands fused to the controls. The blackened bodies of the two guards were slumped against the windows.

But there was no sign of Annabelle.

"How is that possible?" I said to Richie.

We moved closer, to within an arm's length, heat still radiating from the smoldering frame. There was no fourth body. My own body shook as I willed myself to accept that she must be here.

Richie punched a few buttons on his HUD controller. "There's one way to be sure. We've managed to hack into some of SecureCorp's classified data, including the 'presence' beacon — the one that indicates whether your bodily functions are currently active. We can use that to confirm..."

He turned and looked over at me, his finger paused above the HUD controller. I nodded my head, and stared at the ground as he pressed the button.

"What, the..." he said, half to himself.

I was in such a dark place it took a few seconds for his words to register.

Finally I turned to him.

"It says she's alive," he said.

"That can't be," I answered, staring at the skeleton of the chopper, still vowing to accept what I knew must be true.

"Her presence beacon is still activated," Richie said.

JAY ALLAN STOREY

We re-examined the wreckage. It was a crushed, blackened, burnt out hulk. There was no way anyone inside could have survived. And even if by some miracle she was still alive, Annabelle must be on the verge of death.

I remembered Terry's description of her leap onto the ladder at the Institute. I spun around and scanned the open space in the distance where the chopper had taken off. I could still make out what was left of Pritchard's body lying on one side of the space where it had fallen. My spine stiffened as I allowed my eyes to drift over.

On the other side was a second body.

"There!" I screamed at Richie, pointing.

We raced to the spot. It was Annabelle. I knelt beside her and felt for a pulse. She was badly scraped and bruised, but alive. Seconds later she opened her eyes. It took a few seconds for her to remember where she was.

She turned her head to me. "Alex," she said in a whisper, joy lighting up her face. Seconds later she regained her self-control. "That really was the stupidest idea you've had yet."

For a second I thought I must be dreaming. Then the tears started to come. She reached a hand over and took mine.

"D...Don't move," I said, choking back the tears. "We'll get you out of here."

I stayed with her while Richie ran for help.

"Don't!" I said, as Annabelle sat up shakily. She shook her head to clear it.

"I'm okay," she said.

"H...How is it possible?" I stuttered. "How did you get out?"

642

She laughed weakly. "When the pilot and the guards saw Pritchard killed, they panicked. They were glued to the chopper windows watching, totally preoccupied. We were only a couple of meters off the ground. I just opened the door on the other side and jumped out. I guess I hit my head. I think I might have broken a leg."

I leaned forward and taking her in my arms.

She whispered in my ear. "I'm so glad you made it out alive."

# FORTY-EIGHT

..............................................

# THE VICTORIOUS RETURN

On the road back to Rebel headquarters we were all bruised, battered, and beyond exhausted. By the time we pulled up to the main checkpoint, the light of morning was beginning to rise. We were expecting to stagger from our vehicles into the nearest bed, and to sleep for the next several days.

But beyond the checkpoint, a massive, excited crowd was already waiting. We were greeted as conquering heroes, and surrounded by hordes of screaming well-wishers. As we exited our vehicles, swarmed by jubilant revelers, something happened that I had only experienced once before in my life. My HUD lit up with a new collection of information — not coming from the Elite, but from the Rebels. They had taken out InfoCorp, and now controlled the information stream to every living person in First City.

After gathering together the surviving Outliers amid the smoke and devastation of the Corp Ring outside the gate, we had bundled them into the waiting vehicles and made our way back. By the time all

*644*

the smoke had cleared, we'd lost about a half-dozen prisoners — incredible, considering the odds.

Now, pushing through the chaos, Richie and I rushed Annabelle, along with some other injured Rebels and infirm Outliers, to the hospital. We were informed that Annabelle had suffered a broken leg and a concussion, but the doctors assured me that she would fully recover.

Now, we left them to do their work, and headed back for the main square. On the way I watched, awestruck, as a news feed on my HUD detailed the events that had taken place in the First Circle. There was footage showing the Rebel force storming SecureCorp headquarters, followed by images of Elite leaders either captured or killed. In one of the video clips Dr. Sheppard was being led away in handcuffs by a group of Rebel fighters.

From the stunned expressions on the faces of many of those around me, I guessed that the images were being broadcast to everyone. I pictured how people in the Quarters would react to what they were seeing. Most of them probably wouldn't believe it — they would think it was some kind of hoax, or some devious scheme by SecureCorp to trick them into doing something they would regret.

In fact, I realized, it would probably take years for the new order that would be built out of all this devastation to take hold. But this was a beginning, a first tiny step in a long path to a fair and equitable society.

I smiled when a video feed of Bailey's lined face appeared on the display. He and much of the Rebel army were still in the First Circle. The stunning architecture of that city swept into the sky behind him as he stood at the center of a throng of ecstatic soldiers and civilians, declaring victory, and asking for calm. As before, I was struck that Bailey was now an old man. It was wonderful that he'd seen his dream fulfilled in his lifetime.

Terry and Milo had both survived and returned with us. Together with Richie, we all pushed our way through the cheering crowd that still swelled around the square surrounding Rebel Headquarters. What we all really wanted was to sleep, but we couldn't deny them the opportunity to celebrate this once in a lifetime event. Everywhere people were cheering, whooping, crying, and dancing in the street. Several strangers ran up and embraced me, for the moment forgetting any bad feeling toward our group.

Forty years ago, when the Rebels had managed to break into the First Circle and storm SecureCorp, I'd known that their triumph would be short-lived, that at some point the Elite and SecureCorp would take it back.

This time, I was convinced that the victory would stick. The population of the Quarters, far outnumbering that of the Elite, had wised up. They understood how they had been duped, and wouldn't fall for the lies they'd been fed again.

The next few decades would be hard. The entire structure of society would have to change — a proper, legitimate electoral system would have to be hammered out, and a means of redistributing the spectacular wealth of the Elite would have to be implemented. The six Corps would have to be dismantled, and the return of some level of independent small business established.

Most importantly, a way would have to be found to feed millions who were on the brink of starvation. If the Elite did survive, they would be forced to give up virtually all of their privileges, including their homes and spectacular lifestyles.

I suspected that many of them would rather die — and the population of the Quarters might be only too happy to oblige them. There was a danger that the captured Elite would be massacred, as the aristocracy had been in revolutions far in the past. For the sake of all of us, I hoped that wouldn't happen.

After an hour of non-stop revelry, I was finally able to stagger off and get some sleep. The next day, I went to see Annabelle at the hospital. To my surprise, she was ready to leave. She sported a plaster cast on her right leg, had a few bruises, and was still a bit shaky, but all my arguments that she should stay for another day failed.

"I'm missing all the fun," she said.

We headed for the main square, where the celebration was still going strong. As we threaded our way through the noise and chaos, she hooked her arm into mine. I stopped, and looked into her eyes. They held an expression more serious than I'd ever seen in them before.

"I'm sorry," she shouted above the noise.

"Sorry for what?" I yelled back.

"For all the things I said about you — and the others," she answered, gesturing around with her head, "and for all the trouble I caused."

She smiled, reached up, wrapped both arms around my neck, and kissed me full on the lips. The shouts and whistles around us seemed to fade into the background as the kiss lingered, and we were lost in each other's embrace.

Finally, she pulled back.

"Four hundred years?" she said, scrunching up her nose.

"It'll give you lots of time to change your mind," I smiled at her.

# FORTY-NINE

..................................................

# A TRAGIC EVENT

The celebration lasted for several days. We grabbed a few hours of sleep where we could, then rejoined the party. Luckily for the prisoners we'd rescued from the Institute, there was such joy in the air that all the petty issues against us had been forgotten.

The Outliers, at least the ones who were healthy enough, partied along with everybody else. They probably had more to celebrate than any of the Rebels — they'd miraculously escaped decades, possibly centuries, of imprisonment and torture.

All this time, Bailey had been busy in the First Circle, consolidating the Rebel control there, and initiating the Rebels' first priority: the dismantling of the wall itself. A feed had been set up on everybody's HUD where they could watch the progress of the wall being torn down. People watched in disbelief as the barrier that once separated them from their God-like masters was reduced to a pile of rubble.

Two days after our arrival, Bailey finally made it back to headquarters, along with a portion of his army. The jubilation upon his arrival exceeded all that had gone before. Bailey was hoisted onto the shoulders of the fighters and paraded through streets jammed with cheering revelers.

Annabelle and I cheered with them. She was too young and from too privileged a background to really appreciate what had been accomplished, but I remembered the decades of hardship, death, and sacrifice that had led to this moment.

Images crowded into my mind of all those who'd played a part: my father, Walter, Travis, Benny, Laura, even my Uncle Zack in his own twisted way. I felt Annabelle's hand slip into mine. When I looked down at her, she was crying. I realized that I was crying too.

The contingent carrying Bailey finally set him down near a speaking pedestal that had been set up in the square. I'd never seen him so happy, but I'd also never seen him look so old and frail. The battle had taken a toll. As he walked toward the pedestal he staggered, and the crowd gasped. I jumped forward, but he quickly recovered, waved a hand and smiled.

He climbed up, and seconds later was joined by Laura, the General herself. At the sight of her, the crowd burst into another wave of cheers. She and Bailey stood waving to them and smiling. She too had tears in her eyes.

"We did it!" Bailey shouted ecstatically, raising his fist in the air. An ear-splitting roar rose from the crowd.

Laura took a position in front of a microphone set up on the pedestal.

"Look around you," she said, beaming and sweeping her hand around the square. "Remember this moment. Remember where you are right now, who you are with, the scent of the air, the quality of the light, the sights, the sounds. Remember everything around you as you experience this staggering event. Our world will never be the same."

More cheers and shouts erupted from the crowd.

As they quietened down, she continued. "Now the real work begins. We're going to build a new world, one where everyone has a chance at prosperity and happiness. It will be a massive undertaking." The crowd were silent. Laura again swept her arm around the square. "But together, we've already accomplished the impossible. The rest will be easy by comparison."

The crowd exploded in cheers.

Laura stood aside and Bailey took to the microphone, to another massive barrage of cheers. He waved, and the crowd went wild. He stood for a few seconds, basking in the limelight. There were tears in my eyes as I joined in the acclamation. I knew that Bailey deserved every second of it.

Finally, he pushed his hands down for silence. "I'm a soldier, not a speech maker. But I want to thank everyone of you for your years of sacrifice and for your unwavering belief in our cause. I know there were many times when our goal seemed unattainable, but through it all you remained steadfast. As General Quinn has said, we will face many difficulties ahead, but now we will be moving forward, working *for* something, rather than against something.

"Also, I want to..." he stopped suddenly, winced in pain, then once again staggered and lost his balance. This time he didn't recover. I and several others rushed forward and caught him as he toppled from the pedestal. The crowd gasped in horror. A couple of fighters pushed the frantic people back while the rest of us carried Bailey to the edge of the square.

"There's a private room just down this alley," Richie said, nodding to his right.

Wails and cries echoed around the square as we picked up Bailey again and carried him away. One of the fighters sped off to call a doctor.

A long wooden table stood in the middle of the room. We laid Bailey's unconscious body on it. I took off my jacket, rolled it up, and put it under his head. There was a knock on the door. It was the doctor. We were instructed to leave, and stood nervously out in the alley, wringing our hands and staring at the ground. Fighters continued to hold back the crowd from the celebration, who were now jammed into the entrance to the alley.

Laura stood like a statue as we waited, refusing to show any emotion. Samantha arrived a few minutes later, her eyes red from crying, hugging her mother. Unfortunately, Ryan had returned to the First Circle to continue with the fight.

About ten minutes later, the doctor emerged, his face ashen.

"He's suffered a major heart attack," the doctor said. "He's conscious, but there's nothing more I can do. You'd better go in if you want to say your goodbyes."

We all filed into the room — all the people from Bailey's life: Connor, me, Samantha, and of course, Laura — the General. Laura's lower lip began to quiver. She turned away, and I could hear the General for all the Rebel armies sobbing quietly.

Bailey's eyes were open. He looked up at me. "Sorry kid — but this is something you're going to have to get used to."

"It's a curse," I said, choking back tears myself.

"You're blessed," Bailey said, reaching up with a trembling arm and taking my hand. "Be happy. Embrace it. Everybody dies. Even you'll die eventually. I've lived a good life. I fought for a worthy cause, and made some fantastic friends. I lived long enough to see victory — I can die in peace. By most humans' scales, I've lived a long life. And I'll have the privilege of dying of old age." He laughed, weakly. "Not many Rebels can make that claim."

I thought back on all Bailey had done for me: rescuing me from a SecureCorp attack when I was still a kid. Saving me again, when a renegade Rebel fighter planned to hand me over to Vita Aeterna. Supporting me, along with Connor, through all my years in hiding. Keeping my secret.

It was too much. My eyes filled with tears and suddenly I was sobbing like a child.

"Come on," Bailey whispered. "This isn't the way I want to go out."

He lifted his head, to take us all in. "Be happy," he said, smiling. "That's an order."

I stifled my tears, and smiled back, spite of myself.

Laura and Samantha fought off tears as he spoke to them, while each squeezed one of his hands.

Finally Bailey closed his eyes, asleep, his breathing shallow and weak. The group of us exited the room to let him rest.

An hour later, he was dead. I met with Laura outside his room. Again she broke down. She laid her head on my shoulder, and we hugged and cried for our lost friend.

I thought about what I was witnessing. This was how my life was going to be from now on: watching all those around me deteriorate and eventually die. I glanced at Laura, noticeably gray now — her features wrinkled and pale. Even Connor, who had an Appraisal of 2.5, had significantly aged. How could I stand by and watch, as death took all the people I loved?

Over the years, it had been difficult enough watching my dogs die one after the other. This was a hundred times worse. I vowed that I wouldn't live like this. It occurred to me that maybe I'd been better off in hiding, removed from all this pain.

# FIFTY

...............................................

# THE MOOD DARKENS

The air of jubilation that had swirled around the Rebel headquarters since the victory in the First Circle was now overshadowed by Bailey's death. He had been such a symbol for their cause, second only to The General herself in importance, and beloved by all.

With the collapse of the joyful mood came a return of the resentment toward us and the Outliers we'd brought back from the First Circle. Again, I experienced the occasional stare and unwelcoming scowl from people on the street.

On their arrival, by my request, the Outliers had kept their contact with the Rebels to a minimum. In the jubilant atmosphere that followed victory, they'd emerged and mingled with the revelers. But since Bailey's death, the friction was beginning to show.

I met with Joanne, the woman chosen to be the leader of the Outlier escapees, to see how things were going. Like me, so many years ago, most initially had no idea why they'd been kidnapped, and they were never told what their Appraisals were. The knowledge that you'd been re-programmed to live for several centuries took time to sink in. Added to the shock was Gene's claim that we were somehow more than human — almost like a new species.

Joanne had done a fantastic job helping nurse the sick back to health, and helping the rest cope with the reality of their spectacular Appraisals, and with their new lives of freedom.

As we strolled through a courtyard in front of the main building, I could see from her expression that there were problems.

"Most of them have gone back to keeping to their rooms," she said. "There's an undercurrent of hostility toward us — not from everybody, but from enough to be a concern. A couple of people have even been roughed up by Rebel thugs."

I was shocked — I never dreamed things could get that bad.

"I think the Rebels are taking their anguish over Bailey's death out on us," she continued. "We were only a tiny part of the Rebel operation, but some of them talk as if all the fighters they lost died saving us. Underneath all that, I think they resent the fact that most of us will outlive them by centuries."

Later I talked to Connor about it as we headed for yet another meeting.

"It's a temporary glitch," he said, with a dismissive wave. "People are still upset about Bailey. They need an outlet for their grief. They'll come around eventually. I'm Dead Shift, and I haven't had any problems being accepted."

I wasn't convinced. We'd retested all of the escapees, since they'd never actually been told their Appraisals. Even the lowest had an Appraisal well over three — their lifespans could exceed two hundred years. The Rebels had accepted Connor and the other Dead Shift as relative anomalies. But we were true Outliers, with lifespans the average person couldn't begin to grasp. Bailey's death made me question whether there was really a place for me, Annabelle, and the other Outliers with the rest of humanity.

"What do we care what these people think?" Annabelle snapped the next day as we talked about the problem. We were sitting in one of the Rebel headquarters common rooms. I cast around the room, in case anybody else heard. Luckily the room was almost empty, and the only others were far away.

I gave her a look.

"Hey, I've got empathy and compassion," she said, reading my expression. "I'm not the one blaming innocent strangers for my own problems."

She was right, but I could still detect traces of Corp indoctrination.

With the passage of several weeks, the atmosphere hadn't changed much. I spent a few days thinking about it, and talking to Annabelle, Joanne and some of the other Outliers. Finally, hoping to diffuse the bad feeling, I arranged for a public gathering with the Rebels to work out our differences.

A crowd milled sullenly around as we gathered together in a square near the headquarters. Myself, Annabelle, and several of the other Outliers stood off to one side. Our group had met earlier, and decided that it would be better not to actively take part in the meeting. Anything we said would likely inflame the crowd even more.

Laura, Richie, and Connor stood on a raised platform facing the crowd.

"We don't want them here," a scruffy old man called out. "Laughing at us, watching us die while they go on and on."

"Nobody's laughing at you," Richie answered. "You all had the Appraisal. They're no different than any of you. They never asked for things to turn out this way."

"No different!" A middle-aged woman shouted from the crowd. "Look at Alex Barret, there," she pointed at me. "Look at me. And he's ten years older than I am!"

I cursed myself for coming here. I should have waited somewhere out of sight.

"Anyway," a younger man near the front shouted out. "They're freaks. They're mutants or something. And if it wasn't for them Commander Bailey would still be alive."

Grumbling agreement surged through the crowd at that remark. I couldn't believe what we were hearing.

Ryan, back from First City for weeks now, had been standing in the background. Now he stepped up to the platform, still wearing his military uniform. "You know," he shouted, nodding at us, "these people were there in the First Circle fighting shoulder to shoulder with the Rebel army. A lot of them died." He glowered at the man who'd spoken. "I don't remember seeing *you* there."

The crowd became quiet at that remark. Many lowered their heads and looked at the ground. Richie and the others tried to argue with the Rebels, but in the end very few minds seemed to have changed.

Later, Laura, Richie, Connor, and a group of the Outliers, including Joanne, Annabelle and I, got together to talk about what to do.

"Things will die down," Richie said. "A few ignorant troublemakers are spurring everybody else on. You might want to find some place that's out of the way for a while. Eventually, everybody will forget about it."

"And what will happen as everybody else ages and dies, while we stay young?" I asked.

"They'll learn to deal with it," Richie snapped, "like all of us will."

Finally, he looked away self-consciously.

"People will resent us," I said. "It's inevitable. And it will be tough for us as well. If we make friends with any non-Outliers we'll have to watch them die long before we do."

For a few seconds, no one spoke.

Finally, I smiled at him. "Anyway, I might have a better idea."

Both Annabelle and Richie stared at me.

"I'll need a few days to research it," I said. "I'll let you know."

# FIFTY-ONE

...........................................................

# A DECISION

"What!" Richie straightened and stared at me as we stood in the play area at Samantha's place. We'd invited him to spend some time with the dogs, and I thought it might also be a chance to break the news about what I was planning.

Roll picked that moment to take a flying leap at Richie, and knocked him on his ass.

"Are you crazy?" he said, as he pushed the dog away and struggled back to his feet. "You'll never survive."

"It's the only solution," I answered him. Shake jammed his nose under my hand, vying for my attention as I stood in the center of the area.

Annabelle sat cross-legged on the ground a few meters away, with Rattle in her lap. Richie turned to her. "Are you on board with this?"

She smiled and shrugged. "Hey, I'm always up for a good adventure."

"We're having a meeting tomorrow," I said. "With the other Outliers, to see what they think. Come along. I'll explain everything then."

The next day I gathered all the Outliers together in the square, and climbed up on an empty crate, with Shake, Rattle, and Roll curled up at my feet. A large sheet of paper taped to a board behind me showed a map I'd found in my research. Annabelle, Richie, Laura, and Connor stood off to one side. Richie looked at the ground, still doubtful about my plan.

The expressions of the Outliers ran from curiosity, to apprehension, to something like fear, as they nodded at the map and talked amongst themselves. When they'd finally settled down, I began to speak.

"You've all felt the resentment and bad feeling since we arrived at Rebel headquarters, especially since Commander Bailey's death."

There was a murmur of agreement from the crowd.

"We've all done our best to smooth things over with the others," I continued, "and waited, hoping that we'd eventually be accepted here."

Once again whispers circulated through the crowd. I raised my hand for silence.

"But I don't think things are ever going to change. The bottom line is that we don't belong in First City. We don't belong in the First Circle, we don't belong in the Corp Ring, the Quarters, or even here with the Rebels. We will never fit in here. The disparity in our lifespans is too great. People will fear us, resent us, and come to hate us."

The Outliers came alive, confused and fearful whispers sweeping through the ranks.

I glanced at Annabelle, and she nodded encouragement. I continued. "I believe that we only have one option. We have to leave First City — leave, and find a place of our own."

There was a collective gasp.

"What?" one of them shouted. "Somewhere else in the Dregs?

I shook my head. "I don't trust Vita Aeterna. The stakes are too high. They may no longer be in control, but there's some powerful people who are still desperate to find the secret to eternal life, and they still believe that we're the key. We'll never be safe here, no matter how deep in the Dregs we run."

Confusion swept over the sea of faces in front of me.

"Well, where else is there?" one called out.

I turned and pointed to the map behind me, which showed the top half of North America. "I first got the idea from Elliot Pritchard himself, when I was imprisoned in the First Circle. I learned that there were areas of the world that have largely survived the climate disaster. Far to the north, there's wilderness, where no one lives, and where whatever's left of the Corps and Vita Aeterna will never find us."

The map was divided into three coloured sections. The crowd moved closer to study it.

"Here *we* are," I said, pointing at a large blotch on the far right of a large red band at the bottom. "In this band, there's almost no life outside of the artificially controlled environments of the cities. Most of the lands and water around us are poisoned. Virtually all the vegetation and wildlife has been destroyed, and it will take years for it all to come back, even if the Rebels put an end to the destructive practices."

The crowd was silent again, as they absorbed what I was saying.

I pointed to a wide yellow band directly above the red. "The area within this band has recovered a little from the damage, but not enough to support a long-term human settlement."

Covering the top third of the map was a green band. "Up here," I said, pointing at it, "is where I want to go."

The crowd came alive again, with confused whispers.

I ran my finger along the band. "Years ago, when all this started, this area was much colder, so almost no one lived there. As the climate has changed, a lot of the local vegetation in this zone couldn't adapt and died, but eventually it's been replaced by other species compatible with the new climatic conditions. In 'climate speak', the region has made the transition from a 'Polar' zone to a 'Temperate' zone. Now, according to the latest records, it's quite pleasant for most of the year."

I waited a few seconds for the crowd to absorb the information.

"For the past few weeks," I continued, "I've been spending time at TechCorp's Climate Information complex in the First Circle. It has an incredible wealth of data, including satellite images, on the northern regions. The area is largely now pristine wilderness. Rainfall is stabilizing, trees are growing — even animals, the ones that haven't been driven extinct, are beginning to multiply."

"But how will we live?" someone in the crowd called out. "If there's nothing, like you say, what will we do for food and shelter."

"Centuries ago," I answered, "settlers moved to wild and unknown parts of the world, with a lot less knowledge and technology than we have, and they managed to survive. The biggest danger will be getting there. It's two thousand kilometers away. The Rebels have agreed to equip us with vehicles, food and supplies, and they'll escort us part of the way. There will be roads for much of the route, but we'll have to travel the final stretch, several hundred kilometers, on foot."

There was another gasp. A few angry voices circulated among the Outliers.

"None of us have even set foot in the wilderness," someone called. "We won't have a chance. We'll die of the cold, or of starvation."

"It will be hard," I agreed. "Some of us may die on the way. But I've done a lot of research on the area, and on backwoods survival. I've gathered together a huge stash of books and maps. We'll have clothes, medical supplies, tools for constructing new homes, and weapons for hunting our own food. I believe that most, if not all of us, will live to reach our destination."

Mumbling and low discussions swept through the crowd.

I continued. "Life will be hard, but not impossible. Anyway, I believe we have no choice — it's either that or stay here, to be hunted by the remnants of Vita Aeterna and shunned by others who don't understand us."

# FIFTY-TWO

..............................................

# THE JOURNEY BEGINS

It was a brilliant sunny day as a convoy of fifteen vehicles stood in the massive square beside Rebel headquarters, loaded with food and supplies. Several others were parked on the sidelines, their drivers in place, ready to move.

We'd taken a vote at after my speech, and, with a small number of objections, it was decided to go ahead with the trip. After a month of planning, we were finally ready to begin our exodus north. I scanned the tiny group of Outliers. A few had chosen to stay at Rebel headquarters, either too sick or too frightened to join in our adventure. A few straggler Outliers who'd been imprisoned at locations other than the Institute had trickled in after our arrival, and some of the high-LEF Dead Shift opted to come with us. In the end, only forty-seven souls crowded around the vehicles as we prepared to leave.

The square was jammed with onlookers, some clearly happy to see our backs, some averting their eyes guiltily, some genuinely sad to see us go. But all, including ourselves, had come to accept that we could never fit in with the rest of humanity.

Annabelle and I stood in front of the lead vehicle. On one side of us stood Laura and Connor. On the other stood Richie, his wife Iris, and their two daughters. Their expressions were somber, but hopeful. The three dogs, Shake, Rattle, and Roll lay in the vehicle, ready to go. They'd been glued to my side since my return.

Richie put a hand on my shoulder, and gestured with his head toward the crowd. "These people owe you a debt of gratitude they'll never appreciate — I'm sorry."

I smiled. "I was only one of countless fighters who've sacrificed so that we could reach this crossroads. I don't bear them any grudge."

Laura stepped forward. "Good luck," she said, smiling and embracing me.

I reached into my shirt and pulled out her good luck charm, still hanging around my neck.

"It's worked so far." I said, smiling.

She whispered in my ear. "Keep safe."

"You too," I whispered back.

Again I was reminded of how much I'd once loved her, and how much I loved her still.

She stepped back. "I envy you. You're beginning a new experiment — and nobody, not even you, knows what the outcome will be."

"If it's at all possible," I answered, "I'll try to contact you." I studied Laura's face. She'd aged in the months since I'd come back, partly, I knew, as a result of my actions. The gray in her hair was more pronounced — her features more lined.

For the latest of many times, I felt a stab of guilt for my own youth, though I knew that none of what had come to pass had been under my control. There was nothing either of us could do to change what had happened, and there was no going back.

I thought ahead, to the Rebels' own journey, taking back the wealth that had been stolen from them so long ago, repairing the damage that decades of unbridled greed and selfishness had wrought, and building a new world. I believed that they would succeed, and it was sad that I wouldn't be there to see it happen.

We said our goodbyes to Terry, Milo, and the other Rebels who'd been so indispensable in rescuing the Outliers. Richie and Connor both embraced me and Annabelle. Ryan and Samantha had been standing to one side. They approached and hugged us as well.

"Well, Grandpa," Ryan said, stepping back and nodding at Annabelle. "God knows why she'd choose an old geezer like you over a young buck like me, but I guess there's no accounting..." His voice turned angry. " I'm tempted to come with you "I'm not sure if I can stay here with these ignorant lowlifes."

"Give them a break," I said. "It's human nature. People are afraid of things they don't understand. It will only get worse if we stay and outlive you all by centuries. In a way, I think they're right. The disparity between our lifespans would always cause friction between us. It's better this way."

Annabelle and I climbed into the open back of the lead vehicle, with the dogs at our feet. The drivers started up the engines. I cast my gaze around our little group, and thought about the future. I wondered how we would deal with the precious gift we'd been given. Would our extended time on Earth allow us to accumulate greater wisdom than our shorter-lived cousins, or would we simply make more of the same mistakes they had? Only the following centuries would tell.

Annabelle put an arm around my waist, and we smiled and waved to those we were leaving behind. Their images faded into the distance, as our little convoy pulled away, headed for the promised land.

## Thank you for reading the Vita Aeterna/Outlier Series!

I know there are millions of books out there for you to choose from, and I'm honoured that you chose mine. It's a challenge for relatively unknown authors like myself to reach new readers, and this is where you can help.

If you enjoyed this book and think it would be of interest to other readers, please visit and write a customer review on Amazon.com (*www.amazon.com/dp/*B09PWK5VSD). Positive reviews are the best way to attract new readers, and I'm grateful for each and every one I receive.

# JAY ALLAN STOREY

## ABOUT THE AUTHOR

**Jay Allan Storey** has traveled the world, passing through many places in the news today, including Iraq, Iran, Afghanistan, and the Swat valley in Pakistan. He has worked at an amazing variety of jobs, from cab driver to land surveyor to accordion salesman to software developer.

Jay is the author of seven novels, THE ARX, THE BLACK HEART series, ELDORADO, and the VITA AETERNA series, as well as a number of short stories. A new novel is currently in the works. His stories always skirt close to the edge of believability (but hopefully never cross over). He is attracted to characters who are able to break out of their stereotypes and transform themselves.

He loves both reading and writing, both listening to and playing music, and working with animals. He's crazy for any activity relating to the water, including swimming, surfing, wind-surfing, sailing, snorkeling, and scuba diving.

Jay is married and lives in Vancouver, BC, Canada.

**Contact Jay at:**
   **Website: www.jayallanstorey.com**
   **Email: jayallanstorey@gmail.com**
   **Sign up for Jay Allan Storey's mailing list at: www.ee-purl.com/MH-Sv**

ALSO FROM JAY ALLAN STOREY

# *THE BLACK HEART OF THE STATION*

**Delinquent or Prophet? Whichever one teenager Josh Driscoll is, he may be the Station's only hope for survival.**

The Station is a city buried deep beneath the surface of a frozen, life-less earth; its origins lost in the mists of time. Josh's frequent rule-breaking exploits are focused on a single question - how did we get here?

But Josh goes too far when he steals a space-suit and escapes to the surface to explore.

As punishment, the governing Council, of which his father is a member, forcibly enrolls him as a novice monk at Saint Carmine's, the Station's resident monastery. At first desperate to escape, Josh finds himself drawn into the monastery's ancient texts.

Deciphering an encrypted journal hidden for centuries, Josh learns that the Black Heart, a computer complex sealed off after an ancient asteroid strike, may hold the answers he's been seeking, and may be all that can save the city from certain annihilation. When the deranged head of the Council is determined to demolish the Black Heart and doom them all, Josh leads a desperate battle to stop him.

*But can Josh and his tiny band of followers prevail in time to avert catastrophe?*

**You will love this unforgettable fusion of mystery, adventure, and coming-of-age.**
   **Find it at: www.amazon.com/dp/B06XTXY8ZQ**

**What Readers Say About *The Black Heart of the Station*:**
★★★★★ 'It's a long time since I've stayed up until 2 o'clock in the morning to finish a book, but I honestly couldn't put it down.'
★★★★★ 'loved all of Storey's books so far, but this is definitely my favorite.'
★★★★★ 'This tops my favorite's list in this genre.'
★★★★★ 'I rarely give 5 Star rating but this book and author demanded it.'
★★★★★ 'One of the best I have read in a long time.'

# *ELDORADO*

**Lost and alone in the desolate wasteland that was once Suburbia.**

In an energy-starved future, Richard Hampton's world is blown apart when his younger brother Danny disappears and the police are too busy trying to keep a lid on a hungry, overcrowded city to search for him.

Richard has to make the transformation from bookish nerd to street-smart warrior to survive when he jumps the 'Food Train' for the dis-integrating suburbs in a desperate search for Danny and his dog, Zonk.

Branded a criminal by a community of outcasts and condemned to death, Richard is rescued by streetwise Carrie, who joins in his search. As they trek across the remnants of suburbia, facing criminal gangs, renegade militias, and the hardships of the road, their friendship evolves into something more.

The trail finally unwinds at a deserted complex in the remotest corner of the sprawling suburbs.

*The incredible secret they uncover there will alter their lives and their world forever.*

**Pick up Eldorado today, and escape to an unforgettable world of mystery and adventure.**

**Find it at: www.amazon.com/dp/B00C8WM2G8**

**What Readers Say About *Eldorado*:**

★★★★★ 'Amazing read of an amazing futuristic journey.'

★★★★★ 'An engaging and thrilling adventure.'

★★★★★ 'On the edge of my seat throughout the whole thing.'

★★★★★ 'I was hooked right from the get go.'

★★★★★ 'Can't wait for a sequel. Very believable, couldn't put it down.'

JAY ALLAN STOREY

# *THE ARX*

**Ex-Homicide Detective Frank Langer is a broken man - but he's all that stands in the way of a deadly conspiracy.**

Since a mental breakdown put him on medical leave from the squad he was once hand-picked to lead, Frank spends his days drinking and chain-smoking, and his nights waking up screaming from a horrific recurring nightmare.

Until one day, by chance, he stumbles upon a monstrous plot to kidnap children.

When the mother of one of the missing children commits suicide, Frank is driven to see justice done. But when he shows up at the squad with the wild story, his former colleagues pat him on the back and tell him to go home. Instead, he stamps down his demons and, together with the dead woman's sister Rebecca, plunges into the case.

One heart-pounding step ahead of the conspirators, he races to fit together the pieces of an intricate puzzle. When he finally unravels the mystery, the answer is more deadly than he ever imagined.

*But can he stay alive long enough to find someone to buy his story?*

**Read The Arx today, and lose yourself in this chilling Mystery/Thriller.**
 **Find it at: www.amazon.com/dp/B012P0CTXS**

**What Readers Say About** *The Arx*:
★★★★★ 'One of the best books I've read this year.'
★★★★★ 'Recommend it from beginning to end.'
★★★★★ 'Love this book. Kept me reading & wondering where it was all going.'
★★★★★ 'One of those "can't put it down" novels we hear others talk about but rarely find ourselves.'
★★★★★ 'The Arx by Jay Allan Storey is a TOP READ.'